André Brink

rumors of rain

Also by André Brink

The Ambassador
Looking on Darkness
An Instant in the Wind
A Dry White Season
A Chain of Voices
The Wall of the Plague
States of Emergency
An Act of Terror
The First Life of Adamastor
On the Contrary
Imaginings of Sand
Devil's Valley
The Rights of Desire
The Other Side of Silence

Mapmakers (essays)
A Land Apart (A South African Reader), with
J. M. Coetzee
Reinventing a Continent (essays)

André Brink
rumors of rain

SOURCEBOOKS LANDMARK™
AN IMPRINT OF SOURCEBOOKS, INC.®
NAPERVILLE, ILLINOIS

Published by Sourcebooks Landmark, an imprint of Sourcebooks, Inc.
P.O. Box 4410, Naperville, Illinois 60567-4410
(630) 961-3900
Fax: (630) 961-2168
www.sourcebooks.com

First published in Great Britain by W. H. Allen & Company Ltd. 1978

First published in the United States of America by William Morrow and Company, Inc. 1978

Library of Congress Cataloging-in-Publication Data

Brink, André Philippus.
  [Rumours of rain]
  Rumors of rain / André Brink.
    p. cm.
  Originally published as: Rumours of rain.
   ISBN-13: 978-1-4022-1110-2 (pbk. : alk. paper)
   ISBN-10: 1-4022-1110-4 (pbk. : alk. paper) 1. Businesspeople—South Africa—Fiction.
2. Afrikaners—Fiction. I. Title.

PR9369.3.B7R8 2008
823—dc22

2007040703

Printed and bound in the United States of America.
CH 10 9 8 7 6 5 4 3 2 1

this land asking for water is given blood
this land which carries the fire within it
—*Breyten Breytenbach*

Memo

GNATS. A WHOLE SWARM OF GNATS plastered on the wind-screen and the wipers out of order. This, senseless as it may seem, is the first image to present itself whenever I try to recall that weekend. And it is just not good enough any longer. Let me put it this way: it is time I cleared up the ambiguities about exactly what happened in the course of those few days, from Friday to Monday. A curious thing to admit, since I was fully alive to what was happening all the time. Yet I've always felt that something must have escaped me, a submarine something—the way one sometimes wakes up knowing one has had a dream of tremendous importance, if only one can grope back towards it, rowing upstream against the sluggish water; but in the end the dream remains beyond one's grasp.

I have simply not had the time for exploring it. If one is occupied, for twelve to fifteen hours a day, with meetings and memorandums, consultations, options, decisions, timetables and travels, time for a "private life" or for re-examining the past becomes a luxury and memories almost obscene. Now, suddenly and quite unforeseen, I find myself with nine days in London, an existence in transit between the conference of the United Nations Association, from which our delegation was forced to withdraw this morning, and my next negotiations in Tokyo not due until Thursday week.

I truly cannot remember when last I had this experience. It came so unexpectedly that I'm quite overwhelmed. Whenever during the past ten years or so I allowed myself a break of a week or a fortnight, I was accompanied by the rest of the family—Elise and Louis and Ilse —either to the sea or to the farm. Even so I usually returned earlier on my own to catch up with work. During that particular weekend, too, Louis was with me. Admittedly there were the occasional "lost" days or weekends, but then prearranged and with a fixed goal, with Bea. Once, two years ago, we had a full week in Mozambique, the last time before Lourenço Marques became Maputo. The sandy road to the south, the violent and vulgar purple of bougainvillaea, tatty gardens and scraggy fowls, emaciated Blacks waving and grinning in the dust, and at sunset the red and yellow bungalows of Ponta do Ouro. I remember our curious isolation, deprived of radio and newspapers, and the company of Portuguese soldiers in their dilapidated khaki trucks, accompanied by the small crippled Black boy they had with them as a mascot; and at night, when the day's dull accumulated heat drove us from the bungalow, we slept on the beach, resigned to attacks by mosquitoes, sand-fleas and God knows what other heathen pests.

But this time it is different. I am utterly and irredeemably alone. Without any planning or prearrangement I am left with these nine days on my hands. In a way it is quite terrifying; at the same time I feel dazed by the almost sensual luxury of the experience. Here I am with no one to consider and nothing to account for. No dead to bury, no arrangements to make, no guilt to explain or exorcise. Just left completely to myself. Nobody even knows in which hotel I'm staying.

Of course I could have returned to Johannesburg with the rest of the mission earlier this evening as I would have done without hesitation a year ago. But that would have meant two extra flights within a week and something inside me resents the thought. Weariness? Apathy? Middle-aged inertia? Perhaps, sooner or later, one inevitably reaches this stage of simply feeling either unwilling or unable to go on before clearing up whatever lies behind in order to catch up with oneself. And now this coincidence has suddenly made it possible to indulge myself. It may in fact be more of a need than a luxury. It is difficult to explain this cornered feeling. I have to write myself out of it. It is reputed to be a form of therapy.

Is it only a retrospective illusion or was there indeed something unreal about that weekend? Even something apocalyptic, although I hesitate to use the word? In my more romantic days, when I still seriously thought of writing as a career, I might have described it as "the last weekend before the end of the familiar world," or some equally melodramatic phrase. But I have shed my romanticism long ago and even my sense of humor is, according to Bea, no more than the positive side of my cynicism.

What was at stake was the future of the farm. As simple as that. But it involved more than a piece of land. If I may try to define it at this early stage I believe one may call it a sense of loss. (So much can come to an end simultaneously even though one fails to recognize it as an end at the time.) I can specify a fourfold loss. A father, a son, a woman, a friend. Perhaps even these are no more than tokens, symptoms.

But I must try not to presume, however difficult I find it, conditioned as I am by half a lifetime devoted to figures, statistics, programs and prognoses, all the projects of Free Enterprise. I must try to come to grips with a larger and clearer landscape beyond the diversity of facts. Yet without the sentimental self-exposure fashionable in certain circles, since my Calvinist heritage frowns on such a striptease of the soul.

Exclusively for myself, I must take stock of what I have accumulated and see what happens. An intellectual exercise, like chess. (My "photographic memory" has so often amazed people and influenced business deals.) Let us call it a form of mental massage relaxing the knotted muscles, soothing the nerve ends and finally, with precise timing, effecting the so-called "complete relief" which makes a new start possible, without any aftereffects.

✧ ✧ ✧ ✧

The Thai girl (that is if she really comes from Thailand: they all lie without batting an eyelid; but she was unmistakably Oriental, quite attractive in fact) left three-quarters of an hour ago with a discreet click of the door. (DO NOT DISTURB.) I didn't even hear her soft feet on the thick blue-grey hotel carpet, and remained with closed eyes, lying completely relaxed, the small white towel covering what Ma would call my "parts." (How would a masseuse remember a client? Only by the size and shape of his prick? Or would she observe more keenly? "Middle-aged gentleman, stocky but 'distinguished' as the phrase goes, dark hair graying at the temples, thick-rimmed glasses on a 'Roman' nose, rather flabby round the waist...?" One forfeits a lot with the removal of one's clothes.)

More often than not with these girls one runs into a wall of transparent lies: they pretend to be "secretaries" or "shop assistants" or even "students" eager to earn a few extra quid as part-time masseuses. The Orientals tend to be both more honest and more thorough, as well as more sympathetic, which is why I generally insist on them. And tonight's Thai girl—I neglected to ask her name—had the manner of a real professional. I dislike conversation while a girl is working on me (what is there, after all, to talk about?), but some seem to regard it as part of their duties to keep the client talking. Not this one. While I was first lying on my stomach, then on my back, she quietly and calmly and thoroughly went her way, leading deftly up to the moment when, "accidentally" brushing against my erection, the final service could be agreed on with a mere smile, a nod, and a confirmation of the tariff involved. Without any hesitation she went to the bathroom where I could hear water running; a couple of minutes later she returned naked, looking even more frail than she had in her clothes. A delicate bird of a girl with thin wrists, narrow hips, neatly trimmed pubic triangle, and the small barely swollen breasts one would expect of a fourteen-year-old, with a tiny crucifix on a golden chain between them. Lazily I lay caressing her nipples, watching them stiffen as she demurely went about her own duties, her fringe covering her eyes.

Call it the luxury of the perfect pasha, the arrogance of the supreme male chauvinist; or simply the easiest way out for a man with a "heart complaint." (I've never had sex since that afternoon with Bea.) Yet I am inclined to see much more in this total surrender to a woman who demands from you no more than an arranged fee and who, outside the serene hour she has shared with you (nice romantic phrase this), has no further claims on you at all. It is one of very few situations which leave one completely free because no responsibility is imposed on either of the persons involved. You are not required to prove anything or attempt anything; you need neither anticipate anything nor interpret anything; you need not go to any trouble to find out more about her past or her state of mind: all that is, in fact, precluded and irrelevant. She offers no threat to your status or your integrity or your self-sufficiency, since she in turn neither expects nor demands anything from you. She is entirely at your disposal, and provided you pay her fee she is prepared to do anything and everything you require of her.

If I ask her name she will most likely give a false one. If I ask her about herself she will undoubtedly answer with a lie, just as I would if she were to inquire about me. And yet there is in our situation an honesty more profound than that of biographical detail. There is nothing equivocal about the nature of our contract or the implications of our association; supply and demand are in perfect balance. Consequently treachery or betrayal is inconceivable and the very possibility of disappointment excluded.

This does not suggest that we despise one another. On the contrary, I feel I can assert that in our mutual exposure and reticence we respect each other. I have often had the impression of getting closer to a woman in an hour of such contact than in the course of a lengthy affair. For in any close relationship there are so many other elements involving and distracting and distorting one; you are never really left intact; inevitably the situation imposes responsibilities and inhibits liberty. Which doesn't mean that I am trying to deny or diminish someone like Bea in any way. Perhaps I should rather admit, however unlikely or incriminating it may seem, that I still do not understand her. And of all the factors involved in that weekend she remains one of the most inexplicable and ungraspable.

In my wallet I carry photographs—here they are—of Elise and Ilse, my wife and daughter (in discussions with Latins this has occasionally clinched a contract); yet it is Bea I can recall most immediately. Bea in a loose sweater and denim skirt, with boots or sandals; her short black hair and narrow face with high cheekbones, her large eyes smoldering behind the dark glasses with which she habitually masked her myopia; straight nose, wide mouth, strong chin; hands with long fingers and closely bitten nails. Not "beautiful," I should imagine, in conventional terms (I once served on the panel of judges in a Miss South Africa contest), but with an intensity and, well, a strangeness which became more fascinating the longer one looked at her.

Passionate Bea. In different circumstances she might have led a Simbionese army; she might have inspired crowds on barricades or thrown bombs in Belfast—if only she'd found a cause in which to believe implicitly. But quite simply too intelligent to accept anything so absolutely as to plunge headlong into it. Angry, rebellious, uncompromising, and—I suppose—lost.

Was that why I couldn't refrain from trying to "protect" her? A totally misplaced urge, of course. Because deep inside her she was quite independent: "For heaven's sake stop trying to annex me. You Afrikaners are all imperialists by nature. Always want to be the boss, even in love."

You Afrikaners. How often did she use that expression? Sometimes irritably, sometimes off-hand or mocking: provocation came natural to her. Yet it has occurred to me that actually she may have envied me the certainty of that despised definition. For what could she call herself? True, she had the same green passport as I (with what hideous photograph inside!). But her mother had been Italian, her father allegedly a German officer who had arrived in Perugia at a crucial moment and soon moved on again; after the war the family left to join some distant cousins in the States; and by the time Bea was seven and her mother already dead, she emigrated to South Africa with a Hungarian stepfather. The only constant element of her youth was her Catholicism. Until, with the fierce determination characteristic of her, she broke away from that as well. "One has got to stand on one's own feet. I don't need any crutches. And I want to look the world squarely in the face." Even though she constantly wore those sunglasses.

This fear of crutches or blindness or dependence on others, anything that could be construed as an easy way out, determined much of our relationship. Sex, for instance, played a relatively minor part whereas in all my other fleeting liaisons through the years it was the only *raison d'etre.* I've often wondered: if there had been more sex between us, would the relationship have foundered like all the others? In which case I would have been freed from her. The sexual bond was there, but kept very much in the background. Not through any wish of mine: but Bea had a will and hang-ups of her own. And yet I've never known a more passionate woman, on the few occasions when she really let herself go. Actually I suspect that what inhibited her was basically the very fear of knowing *how* passionate, in fact, she was. Perhaps she was afraid of being swept away by her feelings and consequently by any other person involved in them. She was determined to remain in control.

Except for those few times. Our first night—the evening of the roaring party in Aunt Rienie's small apartment choked by nearly a hundred guests, the drinking and perspiration and noise, chairs splintering and bottles breaking, and the frail old lady in the middle of the floor, oblivious of it all, reading Blake, with tears running down her rouged and powdered cheeks; and much later, the rustling of the wind in the leaves of the plane trees in front of the open window, and the obtrusive awareness of Bernard sleeping next door.

And then, of course, the afternoon we met for lunch at the hole. We'd often arranged to meet at Dullabh's Corner from where we'd go to the small curry place in the block, or to a discreet restaurant in Hillbrow, or somewhere out of town. I can no longer remember how it first became "our place": the choice may have been influenced by the din and color of an otherwise rather squalid district, since Bea always responded to that sort of robust street life. (Remember Diagonal Street.) Then there was a break of a month or so, nothing unusual. I was off to New York, returning via Brazil; other business came up—and when I finally turned up at Dullabh's Corner that afternoon there was nothing but an enormous hole where the buildings had been. It took some time to connect it with newspaper reports about Indian shopkeepers removed by the government to another group area, angry demonstrations and resistance, and forcible eviction (nothing serious: only a couple of injured and some children bitten by police dogs).

I can't recall any strong feelings one way or the other in myself—one does grow immune—but Bea was very upset. There was something quite surprising about the violence of her reaction, which I found hard to reconcile with the woman I thought I knew. (But of course I shouldn't forget about the war. She'd been only three years old when she left for the States with her mother, but who can tell what remains submerged in the mind of a child? And there must have been many bombardments in Italy at the time.)

When I arrived at Dullabh's Corner there was no sign of her yet. As a result of the demolition there was more than enough parking space, so I got out to peer through a slit in the corrugated iron fence at bulldozers and cranes and men in orange helmets at work among the heaps of rubble. The sort of activity which had fascinated me since childhood. And it was only when Bea grabbed me by the arm that I discovered her presence.

She said something like: "Oh here you are. I was afraid I wouldn't find you."

And I: "But I said I'd come, didn't I?" I tried to kiss her but she turned her cheek.

Obviously I can no longer recall our dialogue in detail, only the general drift. (Perhaps I should use the opportunity to practice for my novel! At least I can try.)

She said, "I thought perhaps you'd driven right past." And when I shook my head she went on: "That's what happened to me. It was several blocks before I suddenly realized.... So I turned back, and once again I drove past, looking for Dullabh's building. How can they do a thing like this?"

"Didn't you see the papers?"

"Yes, but I never realized. It used to be *our* place, Martin!"

I couldn't help smiling. "You didn't expect them to first ask our permission, did you?"

"You know very well what I mean." Through her dark glasses I could see the darker burning of her eyes. "It's as if they've taken something away from us." And after a moment, almost resentfully: "We've got little enough as it is."

"We're still the same, aren't we?"

"Are we? Can we even be sure of that?" She turned her head as if to look at the excavation, then looked away. "I know we don't come here very often. Once every few weeks or so. And then we go off again. But still: Dullabh's Corner—I suppose it's ridiculous of me, but this place has always been here, always exactly the same, an ugly old landmark, comforting, reassuring. I used to think: one day you and I will be gone, but some things will remain and keep something of us alive in a way. Dullabh's Corner will remember us. And now it's just a hole."

"I suppose one has to learn to live with holes," I said, deliberately trying to sound light-hearted. "Intimations of mortality."

Strange I should have said that. (Did I really? Or am I making it up?) In the light of what happened later the same afternoon, when mortality suddenly became very real.

To continue with the dialogue:

"Please let's go," she said. "I don't ever want to come back here. I'll go with you in your car."

"What about yours?"

"I left it over there." She motioned. "I'll fetch it later, it's not important. At the moment I feel too shaky."

"Aren't we going to the curry place?"

"No, let's get out of town. As far away as possible."

In the car she lit a cigarette and sat smoking in silence. Traffic was bad and it took a long time to reach the M1.

"Strange," she said after a while, more subdued, "the way one keeps on trying to find things to hold on to. Proof of the passing moments. One never learns that a mirror can't hold an image. Stupid, isn't it?"

"Does the mirror on the wall really matter? Provided you yourself know who you are."

"Are you really so sure about it?"

"I think so."

"I don't." With a wan smile she blew out smoke. "It's part of your illusion. Part of your arrogance. That's what drives me up the wall about you. And perhaps that's why I love you."

"At least I'm not such a merry mixture as you are!"

"No," she said, staring at me through her dark glasses. "But you're an Afrikaner. And that may be worse."

❖ ❖ ❖ ❖

"We are Afrikaners and that identity we shall never renounce. We shall not be dictated to by anyone. Even if the rest of the world, like Gadarene swine, prefer to plunge into the abyss of permissivity caused by lack of identity we shall remain steadfast." In the freely paraphrased words of Minister Calitz at the press conference following our withdrawal from the conference this morning.

We had some problems with His Excellency. Things may have turned out differently if he'd attended last night's reception for delegates, which still offered an occasion for last-minute lobbying. But at the cocktail party in the Embassy preceding the reception his over-enthusiastic consumption of KWV brandy, in spite of our frantic efforts, forced his early withdrawal to his hotel. (From where, it was reported, he later slipped out to Raymond's Revue Bar *et al.*)

I should briefly explain our mission. The British United Nations Association organized the conference on economic development in the Third World, with an emphasis on the exploitation of mineral resources. The Afrikaans Institute of Commerce regarded it as an excellent opportunity for pushing South Africa's leading role in this field; at the same time it could be used to negotiate a few mineral export contracts and attract new investment capital. As chairman of the Mining Chamber of the AIC I gave my wholehearted support to the project and also initiated arrangements to negotiate with a number of major importers in Stockholm, etc. But the moment Calitz learned of the conference he indicated in a very unsubtle way that he would be "available" to accompany the mission—with the praiseworthy objective of political bargaining under the cloak of a commercial enterprise. So it was only natural for the president of the AIC to invite His Excellency to take over the leadership of the mission.

These developments were only publicized upon our departure from Johannesburg, causing immediate repercussions in London and elsewhere: accusations of our trying to turn a meeting of economists into an international political forum etc., the sort of argument to which a British Labour government proves particularly vulnerable. From that moment the further course of events was clearly predictable. Calitz had no credentials for the conference but obviously assumed that our Embassy would arrange everything for him. When this proved impossible and he was refused admission, our entire mission had to withdraw in a show of loyalty. The sort of incident provoked regularly by people like Calitz at a stage when, God knows, we bloody well can't afford it.

What else could one have expected of the man? When he became Minister his only claim to fame was a Hitler moustache, which had shrunk with the years until it resembled nothing so much as a blotch of silver snot on his upper lip. It must be conceded, I suppose, that he did his best to serve the interests of the South African economy by acquiring directorships in various companies, as well as a wine farm in the Western Province, a sheep farm in the Free State, a hunting farm in the South-West, and a strategic block of land in the Eastern Cape. At one stage he also owned a hotel and a holiday resort in Transkei, but those he soon sold, at three times the original price, to the South African government who promptly transferred it, at twenty percent of the amount, as a gesture of goodwill to two prominent members of the Transkei Cabinet.

After Calitz had left on his Soho exploits last night a few of us delegates met with the Ambassador to compose a diplomatically worded statement to be issued in the event of our forced withdrawal from today's conference. And when the foreseeable happened I handed the document to His Excellency. Perhaps it would have been better for someone else to have done so, as there isn't much love lost between Calitz and myself (see later, when the Eastern Cape affair is discussed: for on the practical level that was the motivation for the entire "apocalyptic" weekend I am concerned with). Deliberately ignoring our cautious formulation and obviously playing to the gallery at home, he called a press conference "to make it clear to these bastards once and for all that we won't be trodden on."

I had to swallow my annoyance, knowing better than to clash with a man like him in public. I'll get even with him in good time, just as I got even with him that weekend. But I must admit that his performance thwarted me personally. The paper I was to have read at the conference (*The Strategic Value of South Africa's Mineral Resources to the West*) was aimed at the sort of reaction, abroad as well as at home, which would have aided me in becoming president of the AIC within about two years. For twenty years, ever since Elise and I returned from my studies overseas, I've been planning my career like a game of chess. Legal adviser; PRO for the mining house. And when the moment came to take the plunge and become an entrepreneur in my own right (the details are of no concern), I was ready for it. The rest was simple logic: buying out small worked-out mines which had become unprofitable for the large companies; prospecting and buying options until I could field my own team of geologists; shares; moving in at the right moment with takeovers and consortiums; property deals: all the time, thanks to my contacts in the Cabinet and elsewhere, staying just one step ahead of the others. The constant careful maneuvering within the AIC, based on the calculation that the Afrikaner was still a newcomer to mining, which meant that competition was less fierce than in other areas of industry. So I chose that as my field of action, attending AGMs to be "seen," supporting key figures, seconding proposals, later introducing my own motions, and getting elected to the executive. Like a general planning his strategies. Until I have now reached the top, with my headquarters on the eleventh and twelfth floors of the premises in Main Street. My own building (one of my shrewdest coups in a takeover). My personal domain. The spacious office, modernized with carpets and perspex and potted plants, watched over by my eagle-eyed secretary (fortyish and efficient: ever since the episode with Marlene I prefer a middle-aged lady in this position), and the rest of my staff within immediate reach. Public officer, chief accountant, personnel manager, consultant geologist, consultant engineer; and the juniors, ranging from draughtsmen to typists (these are both young and attractive, and eagerly at the disposal of the boss). None of this came to me by chance. Nothing has happened through fate or fortune. Everything has been planned and worked for. And this London conference had been intended to give me another indispensable push, now temporarily undone through Calitz's criminal bungling. (And I am not his only victim: the country as a whole will suffer the results.)

Still, in public one remains "loyal." We Afrikaners have our own way of doing things. And in the eyes of the world our delegation stood by our leader. Immediately after the press conference all the other members of the mission returned to South Africa with His Excellency.

I moved to this hotel. Not that I had much against the first one in "fashionable Mayfair," except perhaps that, at twenty-five pounds a day (plus VAT) they did not even offer a cup of morning tea without charge (only the cockroaches were free). But with what in my early romantic period I would have called a "blinding clarity" I just knew the time had come for me to be alone and incognito until I must fly to Tokyo.

In a curious state of elation about this sudden freedom I cabled my secretary not to expect any news from me until after Tokyo; next I phoned my wife to tell her that I was off to the Lake District for a week. She was less resigned than I'd expected.

"Why don't you rather come home, Martin?"

"It's too close to the office. You know very well they won't leave me in peace."

"We can go away together for a few days." There was an unexpected fervent note in her voice. "It's such a long time since we last—"

"Do be reasonable, Elise. I've got to be in Tokyo before the end of next week."

"If you catch the plane tonight you'll be home tomorrow morning."

"I just can't face another trip. I'm tired. And I'm not getting any younger."

"Nonsense, Martin. You're forty-five. That's nothing."

"You know what the doctors said."

"As if you've ever paid any attention to doctors. Or to anyone else for that matter."

"That's an unkind cut."

"I'm sorry, I didn't mean it like that. It's just, well, that I'm also getting uptight and smothered here."

I could guess what she really meant to say. "Having problems with Ma again?"

"What else did you expect? I know she doesn't mean it. But she insists on taking everything out of my hands and I can't stand it. I still think it was a terrible mistake to bring her back from the farm. She's much too independent to live with other people."

"We discussed all that long ago, Elise."

"Did we? You said what you thought and that was that." A short pause. "Don't let us go through all that again on the telephone, Martin. It's no use. I'm just upset because I thought you'd—"

"How's Ilse?" I interrupted.

"Cavorting in the pool with her friends. Refusing to listen to anyone. She knows you'll take her side when you come back."

For a moment I hesitated before asking: "No news of Louis, I suppose?"

"Of course not." Her voice was strained. "I wonder whether we'll ever hear from him again. Unless something—But you're wasting your money now, you'd better ring off." More quietly she added: "Do look after yourself, Martin."

"Of course. Goodbye."

Strangely discontent I sat looking at the receiver, trying to imagine Elise at home as she put down the phone (but where would she be? Bedroom or study?), following her through the house. The clear placid stone surrounding one with its reassuring coolness in these summer months; subtly heated in winter. The woolly flokatis in the bedrooms, terracotta and ceramic tiles elsewhere; the few antiques Elise had skillfully harmonized with large and comfortable modern module pieces. A few of her pots on shelves or in alcoves; her roughly woven mohair curtains covering the windows. On the walls, paintings by South African artists, including two early Pierneefs and a Wenning; also a Picasso litho and the Klee drawing I picked up in Cologne. Slasto surrounding the fireplace, built-in bookshelves on either side.

Outside, the "flowing lines" characteristic of most of my brother Theo's designs, functional and satisfying in their Mediterranean echoes. The garden with its lawns and terraces, shrubs, trees (strelitzia, proteas, wistaria on the pergola, three precious cycads smuggled from the farm on the back of Dad's truck, years ago, before the cancer and the funeral, when we still had the farm; before that fatal weekend). The tennis court behind the poplar row, the aquamarine curves of the swimming pool where Ilse and her friends were splashing at this moment.

The curiously unsettling incident of her last birthday, her fifteenth, when she and a dozen other girls were fooling around the pool in their tiny tangas (Ma: "It's just two milk doilies and a cookie cloth they're wearing these days"), as I lay in my deck chair with one eye on the newspaper and the other on those pert provocative nymphs. I suddenly glanced up to catch Louis watching them just as eagerly. (That was before Angola; before everything.) For a moment our eyes met. He blushed, and smiled to cover his embarrassment. And for the first time I realized what it meant to have a son of eighteen sharing my stealthy fervent interest in those budding bodies. But instead of feeling solidarity, I found the discovery had stirred something like guilt inside me, even resentment, as if it had revealed something much too secret of myself to him.

There was an even less wholesome sequel to the episode. While Louis and I remained in our chairs, he with his Coke and I with my beer, both pretending to be unaware of each other and those smooth girl-women, I noticed a movement behind some shrubs on the far side of the pool and saw the Black gardener. He too was peering at the scene, his spade forgotten in the ground. We'd only hired him the week before after his predecessor had left without warning. Had I known him better I might have been willing to give him another chance but these days one cannot take any risks, not with a teenage girl about the house. So I had to fire him. In any event I paid him two months' notice, so he really had nothing to complain about.

It wasn't easy to find a replacement. They're asking such exorbitant wages, yet they're reluctant to offer anything in return. Years ago one could still rely on convict labor, which was how we managed to get the garden laid out in the first place. A team of twelve once a week really works wonders. It was the same when I was a child, except then we only had them once a month: in that arid region of Griqualand West there was no point in any fancy gardening. Fourteen inches of rain a year, if it was a good year. Three inches more often than not. And when it stayed away everything just shriveled up and only dust and stones and thorn-trees remained. Our team of convicts used to eat their lunch in the sparse shade of such a thorn-tree, taking a long time over their mealie porridge and their thick slices of brown bread. Often, when the guard was not looking, they asked Theo or me to smuggle them cigarettes from Dad's box of *C to C*. There was one who used to ask for methylated spirits. He would up-end the bottle in his mouth and gulp it all down, just like that. Took away all his fear, he said. With that stuff down his throat they could try anything, he didn't care a fuck. The language he used. Then came the day he tried to run away. Whoever thought a convict would try to escape in that little village with its dusty streets and pepper trees, surrounded by an infinity of barren plains? But he did, true as God. And just as he was climbing the fence the guard emerged from the outdoor lavatory, buckling his belt. I was standing in the back door with a slice of bread and golden syrup; Theo was still spreading his in the kitchen. The convict looked round and began to run, followed by the guard. Consternation in the backyard. Ma's red and black fowls jumping up from where they'd been lying with spread wings under a broombush, their yellow eyelids half-closed. The guard was much too corpulent to catch up with the convict. So he shot him. The meths drinker dropped down in the dust, kicking like a sheep with its throat cut. The guard waddled towards him, tearing his khaki uniform as he scrambled through the fence, and started kicking him where he lay with his back broken, kicking and kicking until, unable to take any more, I fled into the kitchen. There was a commotion of people and voices. The Black Maria came. Through the kitchen window I saw them pick him up, hurling him into the back of the van like a bag of potatoes, a ragged little bundle of blood and dust. When I turned round all I saw was the cluster of black flies on the slither of flypaper hanging from the bulb.

"Why did the man kick him like that, Dad?" I asked the next day. "He couldn't run any more."

"One can't take chances with a kaffir, my boy." His kind, vulnerable eyes looked at me through his spectacles. "He was a criminal and he tried to escape. If you go back in our history...." That was his stock defense and solution to everything. *If you go back in our history.* It was his subject, after all; he was one of the few people I've ever known to be completely happy in their work. Very few outsiders could understand how on earth a man could take pleasure in teaching the same dreary span of history year after year. Most of the other kids at school found him boring; the only thing that kept them working was their fear of the cane with which he tried to impress his authority on boys and girls alike—something I never managed to reconcile with a person as meek as he was. Personally I drew a measure of inspiration from him, but whether this was due to the history he taught or to a quality in himself I don't know. In a sense he always remained remote from us, with an absence in his eyes as if he was staring right past us to those distant battles and great men who seemed to suggest some sense or stature of life to him: all those causes and consequences of war, the achievements of ancient civilizations, which appeared so much more ordered and understandable at a distance than the confusion surrounding oneself. History to him was as clear in line and meaning as the shape of a fish; whereas the present appeared wild and aimless and absurd. At the same time, through an interest in history, it seemed possible occasionally to break through to him and grasp something of his silences and his absence, lending sudden and startling meaning to the word "Dad."

To him, I think, history became a metaphor for everything he couldn't understand about the world around him. And the day he was forced to abandon his career and take over the family farm something began to wither inside him. He went on reading as much as before; every week loads of books were carted from the town library to the small outbuilding on the farm which he'd converted into a study, and whatever was unobtainable there he ordered from elsewhere. But there was no longer anything he could do with it, no one he could convey his knowledge to; and it was beginning to press heavily on him. In the end cancer sent him to his grave. But to my mind that was mere coincidence. If it hadn't been cancer it would have assumed some other form. The real cause of his death was the farm itself, that fertile valley in the Eastern Cape with its aloes and its pale-blue plumbago, its dark thickets and blood-red earth. Amazing how immediate it all returns to me here at such a distance.

"Our" farm. No longer, of course. All I have now is the well-kept suburban garden protected by the six-feet-high stone walls topped by broken glass, and the double wrought-iron gates with the spikes on top. Guarded by our dogs, our two magnificent Alsatians, as gentle as lambs with the children but wild wolves to any stranger. Ma can't stand them. Quite understandably, of course, because she still misses her three unruly farm dogs. The Alsatians would have torn them limb from limb, so all I could do when she came to live with us was to have them put down. It was in their own best interest, after all.

Thinking back now, in this luxury hotel with its plush and velvet, blue-grey and gold, its Victorian prints on the walls and—I swear to God—Sir Joshua's *Age of Innocence* above my bed, it appears to me, however distant in this setting, that all my life I've been surrounded by violence. Not in the way any of my quite long line of pioneer forefathers experienced it, leaving their *velskoen* tracks through history—the uprising of Graaff Reinet, Border Wars, Great Trek, Boer War, Rebellion, or the *Ossewa-Brandwag* underground movement of the Second World War. Without exception they were themselves the agents, the doers, and often the victims: men who landed in the Dark Hole of the Castle, who were killed by the spears of Kaffirs or the bullets of Englishmen, or who found their farms raided and their houses burnt, so that every time they had to start again from scratch (which, somehow or other, with the Bible on their hearts, they managed to do). My experience is different. I am surrounded by violence, yet untouched by it myself. Unlike my ancestors on their *via dolorosa* as Dad liked to call it, I realize only too well that I have always gone scot-free. (With the exception of that one afternoon with Bea.)

It is a strange thought, in view of some of the things which have taken place before my eyes. I have often wondered, not without cynicism, whether perhaps I have a "gift" for this, acting almost as a catalyst for violence which breaks out all around me yet leaves me unscarred.

Would that convict have run away and got himself killed if I hadn't been standing there in the back door eating my bread and golden syrup? A preposterous thought, admittedly—if it had been an isolated incident. But it wasn't. I can recall at random: Theo and I playing a Tarzan game in the pepper tree; after jumping from a high branch I dare him to follow me, which he does, breaking his leg. A group of boys playing in the river which skirts the village. One of them is scared to dive from the top of a willow. "Come on, don't be a sissy!" I shout at him. So he dives into the muddy water and doesn't come up again. His head has struck a submerged log. We manage to haul him out and his life is saved, but he remains paralyzed from the waist down. The most gruesome and at the same time the most comic episode: in my third year at university I was standing beside the road, just outside Bellville, hitchhiking to Cape Town, when a lorry came past, loaded with building rubble, a couple of sheets of corrugated iron protruding on one side. A motorcycle swerved out to pass from behind but the poor bastard probably never noticed the iron sheets. And when I became aware of what had happened, a headless man came whizzing past me on his cycle, a red fountain of blood spouting from his neck.

There was Greta, my varsity girlfriend, riding past me on her bicycle just a week after we'd broken off. As she sat up and turned round to call to me, the bicycle swerved and struck a tractor pulling a trailer piled high with boxes of purple grapes.

Charl Kamfer, brilliant lecturer (History of Art), witty and cynical and homosexual. The night I phoned him on a sudden impulse to ask whether I could come round; the house blazing with light when I arrived, all the doors and windows wide open; and his naked body lying on its back on the carpet in the lounge, wrists cut, and a neat blue circle painted round his navel.

At Park Station, the woman jumping in front of the train a moment after she'd asked me the time.

After the mine riots, the bits and pieces of human bodies washed from the road with fire hoses, the way one would clean gnats from a windscreen; like rain trying to wash out the scars of drought (but something always remains).

And I suppose I should add the murder on the farm, that weekend. And perhaps, if one thinks of it, even Bernard; even Bea. Or am I going too far?

In a sense that whole weekend had been conceived and born in violence. Perhaps it was the first presentiment of an apocalypse. I'd better write it down: it makes a good situation for a novel.

I hadn't slept much the previous night. Normally I would have set out by six in the morning for it's nearly five hundred miles to the farm. But I had to go to the Supreme Court in Pretoria first. In the early stages of the trial it had still been possible not to go, but in the end —except when the riots at Westonaria forced me to stay away—I felt a compulsion to attend every session. Only the conclusion still lay ahead, that Friday. I'd told Elise that there was some work I first had to finish off, as I somehow found it impossible to discuss anything about the trial with her. With Louis I'd arranged that I would meet him at the parking lot in Pretoria. For some reason he'd gone there several days before. I hadn't even tried to question him about it, having got used to his stay-offishness ever since his return from Angola in February. The very fact that he'd agreed to accompany me to the farm had been surprising enough. I would have preferred to go on my own. But I'd promised Elise to be careful. "In my condition." Also, I suppose I had a parental duty.

Everything looked wild and strange so early in the morning. It might have been another continent, a different planet. It was long before sunrise and very cold; here and there something suddenly appeared through the thick fog: a building, traffic lights, a row of scraggy trees. The Ben Schoeman highway, a wide barren lane in the mist without any glimpse of the yellow highveld landscape; only, from time to time, the dull flare of headlights approaching in the opposite lane and disappearing soundlessly. The turn-off at the Monument (remembering the day with Bea!); the buildings of the University of South Africa like the hull of a vast ark stranded on a hill. Followed by the luring presence of the city. Traffic lights at empty crossings, caught in a senseless routine of green, yellow, red; green yellow, red. Trucks. Putco buses belching out hundreds of black shapes; moments of noise and movement, then the thick silence of the fog again. Early cafes where boxes and stuff were being carried in or out; shutters and railings removed from doors and windows. The hiss and clatter of milk carts. Sudden whiffs of fish-and-chips; shreds of newspaper fluttering in the gutters.

I parked my car on the empty lot in Vermeulen Street. Recognizing me, the caretaker approached, a shapeless bundle in his army overcoat, offering a flamboyant salute before he gave me my yellow ticket. I set off in the direction of Church Square and the Supreme Court, my feet stung with cold, my face burning. On the way I stopped to buy the papers from a sullen man huddled beside a black drum of glowing coals. Without a word he immediately resumed blowing on his clenched hands. His eyes appeared bloodshot and feverish. Last night's *skokiaan*. Following the small white puffs of my breath in the cold, I walked on. There was still time for coffee at a cafe counter, served by a Greek with dirty fingernails.

There were a few others in the cafe: a hobo with a stubbly face; a gaunt fellow absurdly out of place in black evening suit and bow-tie; three laborers in blue overalls, clutching food-tins; a Black who sent the Greek into a rage when he offered a note to pay for a loaf.

"Where you think I get change for two rand, bladdy fool?"

"I know you got change in that till."

The Greek came from behind the counter, coarse hair showing like a coir mat through the gaps of missing buttons on his cardigan and check shirt.

"You look for trouble, hey?"

"I want my bread."

"Go get the right money first. Now fuck off."

His client refused to budge. The Greek came nearer. But as he tried to grab the Black he was thrown off balance and sent stumbling against the counter, knocking a glass jar to the floor and scattering the multicolored sweets all over the place. He swung round, to find the Black crouched in front of him, knife in hand.

The workmen in overalls all moved at the same time, as if it had been arranged long before. One pinned the Greek's arms behind his back as the others went for the Black. There was a brief, violent struggle during which the glass front of the counter was kicked in; then, in a swift twisting movement, their victim broke loose and fled. The Greek and his clients all stormed out, but it was too late to catch up with him.

"I phone the police," said the Greek, panting like a man suffering from his heart.

"Leave it, man," said one of the men in overalls. "If you don't watch out they'll come and arrest you. A White man's word isn't worth anything any more."

The Greek started dialing—wrong numbers, most likely, for he was too angry to notice the holes into which he was poking his blunt fingers. "You all see it," he said over his shoulder. "You witness for me."

"I'm off," I announced, counting out my coffee money in the cracked saucer beside the till. There were more than enough other witnesses. After all, it wasn't all that serious. And I don't like getting involved in that sort of thing.

The incident did cast a certain gloom over the day. And it was deepened by the last few hours in court.

Bernard, thinner and paler than I'd ever seen him (without any obvious reason I remembered his sinewy, brown back in the canoe ahead of me in the raging white torrent); but he seemed imperturbable and composed all right. There was a church-like atmosphere in court, a hushed sense of awe, when finally the judge began to speak. No other sound at all, except for the ballpoint pens of the journalists scratching on their pads, a doorframe creaking when a security policeman leaning against it shifted his weight without moving his eyes from the crowd.

And then the shock of the Black spectators rising to their feet and breaking into song the moment after the sentence had been pronounced. *Nkosi sikelel´ iAfrika.* Interrupted by the judge's hammer and the orderlies shouting: "Clear the court! Clear the court!" And the police jumping over the balustrade.

I didn't go down to say goodbye to him. Perhaps they wouldn't have allowed me to, anyway. And what was there to say? Still it kept on worrying me. Perhaps I should have made the effort. But with *Nkosi sikelel´* in my ears I really was much too upset to face him, even though it would probably have been for the last time.

On my way back through the streets, now overflowing with impatient traffic and pedestrians, I found it hard to concentrate. Time and again I bumped into people. Once I even sent a woman's parcels flying over the pavement, so that I had to bend down and pick them up while she kept on asking: "Can't you look where you're going, hey?" So I didn't immediately realize what was happening when I was stopped by a crowd blocking the entrance to the parking lot. Only when I discovered that it was impossible to get through did I become conscious of horns blowing, a police car braying, people shouting.

Nine or ten stories up a building in the process of construction a Black man was sitting on a narrow ledge, his legs dangling over the edge. All the windows were crammed with people leaning out to watch him; below, in the parking lot, a crowd was jostling round a small circle cordoned off by constables standing arm to arm.

"What's he doing up there?" I asked a man next to me.

"Been up there since eleven, they say he wants to jump."

From a window overlooking the ledge a police officer was trying to talk to the Black man. It was too far away to make out what he was saying. The Black pulled up his legs, tautening his whole body, obviously preparing to jump.

The crowd on the pavement and among the cars in the parking lot suddenly started shouting:

"Jump! Come on, jump!"

I could see him hesitate, balancing himself on the very edge. Turning his head. Even at that distance I could see the terrified whites of his eyes, like an animal's.

"Jump, man! Jump! Come on, jump!"

He was trembling on his narrow ledge. For a moment he leaned back, resting his head against the concrete wall. Perhaps he was dizzy.

Above him, the officer was once again talking to him. He showed no sign of hearing a word.

"Jump!" roared the crowd. It sounded like a rugby match. "Come on! Now! Now! Now!"

Up there the man moved again, shuffling a foot or so closer to the corner of the building. Below him the crowd opened up a new circle for him. He pushed one foot over the edge like a man testing the water with his toes before diving in to swim. A few women's voices screamed ecstatically. He pulled back his leg.

"Jump!" thundered the crowd.

He was crouching on his haunches now. The ledge was so narrow that his toes protruded over the edge. He was barefoot, his shoes standing a few yards farther along the ledge.

He leaned forward. I couldn't make out whether his eyes were shut or open.

A new roar went up from the crowd. And then he jumped, right into them. It was some time before they realized that it was all over.

Then it slowly grew quiet, so quiet one could hear a fruit vendor a block away shouting: "Bananas! Bananas!"

I began to push through the crowd. Only when he took my arm I looked up and saw him.

"Louis! How did you get here?" But of course, we'd arranged to meet here.

"Did you see what happened?" he asked.

"Yes. I'd just arrived here when he—"

I looked into his eyes in search of—what? That day beside the pool when we'd caught each other watching the girls I'd discovered something defiant in his strangeness. He was no longer a boy, the son I'd fathered, but a stranger I couldn't handle because he was too much like myself; a rival. Since that day months and droughts and deaths had come between us. Now, suddenly, startlingly, we were once again involved in the same thing, branded by the knowledge of what we'd shared. With a surge of vehemence I no longer expected from myself I wished he hadn't been there and seen what he had. (Ridiculous: after all, he'd lived through a war.) Or if he had, I should have wished him not to have seen it with me. Perhaps, with a touch of old-fashioned and unreasonable sentimentality, I would have preferred one of us to remain innocent, unblemished by our presence in that crowd.

"Let's go," I snapped without looking at him, as if it was his fault. "We have a hell of a long drive ahead."

Innocence. It was something many people associated with Bernard. It's difficult to formulate, but I suppose what it comes down to is that, in spite of his incisive intellect and all his sophistication, Bernard primarily struck one like, well, a sort of elemental force, something as natural and basic as wind or water. (Is this a regression to the terminology of my

Early Romantic Period? My writing seems inexorably to drive me back to that. All right, then. Whatever wants to get out must be said even if it tends to carry me away from time to time. It is a normal risk, I presume, when one takes to the typewriter.)

In his grey suit and blue tie he could be the polished man of the world, comfortably at home among the diplomats; in his legal robes, in spite of his shock of unruly blonde hair, he showed a dignity reminiscent of the courts of a bygone world, like the Florence of the Medici. Even then he retained the air of the "noble savage." And it became even more obvious when he was relaxing or taking part in sport: on the tennis court or in the swimming pool, on that canoe trip which decided so much between us—one of the boys; *the* boy.

On women he seemed to have an electrifying effect. Even Bea admitted: "I don't know what it is, but when he looks at one it's as if your stomach contracts and your legs go all watery." Bernard could pick and choose. And he did, too. Not that he ever gave the irritating impression of being a professional chaser, a Don Juan in search of security in one bed after another. He didn't boast about it either. But invariably, in discussing this girl or that, it would transpire that he's already, as it were, "taken stock" of her. His innate courtesy must have been some sort of a passport to his success in this field. But above all, Bernard had the rare ability of intimating to all the people he came across, male and female alike, that he was deeply interested in them, that they were important to him, that they were in fact sharing a special adventure with him.

And then there was the curious impression—perhaps this is what I've really been trying to say all along—that he'd never outgrown his boyhood. I don't mean that he was childish in any sense. Only that he carried with him the suggestion of the directness, the simplicity, the "barefootedness" of a boy. Even in middle-age he remained something of the *enfant terrible*. I'm sure he really meant it when he said, as he often did: "All I ask of life is that I won't ever grow too old to kick a sacred cow in the balls." Then he would add with his radiant impish smile: "Because if one doesn't do it sacred cows have a tendency to shit on your head."

It was meant as a very special gesture when, nineteen years ago, I invited Bernard to be Louis's godfather. Since my first year as an LL.B. student, when he'd been my lecturer in Roman Dutch Law, Bernard had been my "hero." It was he who encouraged me to write once he discovered that I had some talent in that direction. And it was to him, rather than to lecturers of literature like John Pienaar that I took my first romantic efforts for comment. He could be as devastating as he was sympathetic. Once he even flushed a short story of mine down the toilet and when upon learning of it I stared at him in horror he merely shrugged: "It *was* a load of crap, don't you agree?" he asked. His attitude was that one either did something well or not at all. I was still learning my trade; but provided I was serious enough about it I would get my novel written sooner or later.

I never have. The nearest I came to it, apart from a pile of short stories, was in the stacks of notebooks I filled after returning from our canoe trip. In that adventure I recognized something tremendous I tried to define. But something eluded me. After typing thirty-odd pages I tore it all up and started again. This time I reached fifty pages before I got tired of it all and gave up. Instead, I became a business-man. (And now, suddenly.)

I'm still not sure that I can interpret that canoe venture. It happened so long ago and one grows so far away from one's previous selves. If it hadn't been for these nine days and the opportunity, or the urge, to sort things out and organize them and exorcise them once and for all, I would never have returned to the episode. But ever since the weekend on the farm things have become more complicated, less obvious, more elusive. I've already said that, haven't I? (It's very late; even the caressing hands of the Thai girl have faded into memory.)

31

Even in my years at university we'd been talking about such a trip, but it never materialized. Then he left to join the Cape Bar while I went overseas after completing my LL.B. Neither of us proved a good correspondent. During the first year I continued to send him more or less "literary" letters (keeping carbon copies for "one day"); later it was reduced to cards or telegrams at Christmas or birthdays.

But a few months after my return from England he arrived at our flat in Johannesburg without any warning. Through the years these sudden appearances became characteristic of him, usually when he had accepted briefs for the Transvaal Supreme Court. The remarkable thing was that every time he arrived we found we could carry on effortlessly from where we'd left off the previous time. The only lasting friendship of my life.

Elise and I had just settled down when he arrived that first time and it wasn't easy to persuade her. She was pregnant with our first child, the one she lost a year before Louis was born, and she felt a need to have me with her. What Bernard proposed was rather outrageous in the circumstances. I'll try to reconstruct the conversation:

"That canoe thing we always used to talk about—are you still interested?"

"Of course," I said, more from habit than true conviction. "We really must do it one day."

"Not 'one day.' I've come to fetch you. You're taking a fortnight's holiday and we're off to Aliwal tomorrow."

"You must be off your rocker."

"Right, so I'm off my rocker. What about you? Or have you become too respectable?"

"No, I haven't. But one can't go off just like that."

"Why not? It's the only way to get something done. You make up your mind and you do it. Once you start weighing it all up and trying to be reasonable, it's useless."

"I'll have to talk to Elise."

"I want to know what *you* think."

"If it depended on me...."

"Right, then it's settled. We're going."

"But, Bernard...."

"Wait." He shook his blonde hair from his forehead, his eyes mocking and grave at the same time. "Listen to me, Martin. Next year I'll be thirty. You're turning into a thoroughly domesticated animal. Soon it'll be too late for both of us. It's now or never."

I knew he was right. We talked until the small hours; and then I had to confront Elise. She was so upset she didn't even come out to say goodbye when we left the next afternoon. I nearly turned back. (What stopped me?)

If I had to rationalize it now, so long after the event, I'd say that neither Bernard nor I had ever experienced anything truly extraordinary before. Admittedly, he had the faculty of turning anything into adventure, but seen objectively his life had been as predictable and unexciting as my own. Neither of us had lived through a war. To us the Second World War had been restricted to radio news and the talk of grown-ups: "Germany," "the Russians," "Churchill," "a bomb"; and flags in the streets on V-day (I even got a hiding when I came home, for having been seen in public waving a Union Jack). Everything had been reduced to rumors instead of reality. And perhaps one does have a deep-seated need, even if it were for only once in one's life, to pit one's own nothingness, one's whole existence, against something of true magnitude. Other men, other generations, seemed to be precipitated willy-nilly into such events. But our knowledge was second-hand; we had to actively set out in search of reality. In the notebooks I filled at the time I think I interpreted the whole affair as a quest for heroism, the need to discover for oneself something great and awe-inspiring. Today I tend to regard the opposite as much more important: not our attempts at heroism, not the ecstasy of greatness, but a shattering experience of our own insignificance.

33

There was one stretch of rapids, about four days downstream from Aliwal, where within a matter of a hundred yards the river changed from a wide slow expanse into a narrow gorge between sheer red cliffs, a wild mass of water churning among black ridges, the white foam flying. We could hear the low booming of the river from far away but were too inexperienced to know what it meant. The first we saw of it was when, coming round the last bend, we found ourselves right inside the preliminary rapids. I knew immediately it was no adventure any longer but a matter of life and death. It was impossible to think coherently. All thoughts were suspended as we sped into that narrow funnel. Fear? Obviously. At the same time it was a sort of death ecstasy. There was nothing heroic about it at all. On the contrary. It seemed so bloody foolish and unnecessary to head for those white waters. There was still time to steer our canoes to the bank and carry them overland to the end of the rapids, but neither of us gave it a thought. I don't know about Bernard, but I almost wanted an accident to happen so that people could say: "How on earth could they have been so stupid?"

After about fifty yards there was a hairpin bend in the gorge. Bernard was right in front of me. All of a sudden I saw his canoe hurled forward as if it had been flung by a giant hand. The staggering waves rose seven, eight feet high. Then he disappeared in the muddy orange mess round the bend. And I think this will be the image of Bernard I'll take with me to my grave, long after the scene in the courtroom has vanished: his tense, straight, bare back and wet blonde hair, and the movement of his shoulder muscles as he flailed his oar to keep his balance.

The moment he disappeared I knew my turn had come.

I was hurtled headlong into the rapids. I couldn't see through the spray, and in the thundering of the waters it was impossible to hear a thing. Beyond the bend the current spewed us into a pool where every-thing was rotating dizzily among cliffs so high that the sun couldn't reach all the way down. Something shrieked—a fishing eagle, I thought afterwards—the eerie sound piercing one's ears like a splinter.

Bernard was still there, in front of me, his canoe spinning madly before he managed to get it under control again. A few yards ahead of him was a log, a huge willow torn, roots and all, from some distant bank. Both of us were watching it as it slowly turned and rolled inward towards the heart of the whirlpool where it went under. It didn't come up again.

I shouted at him; he called back. Frantically we tried to row in a futile, ridiculous effort to counter the suction of the undercurrent. In that cauldron we were less than two bobbing walnut shells. Incredibly, inexplicably, we skirted the fatal inner circle and were hurled right out of it, drifting downstream again into a new wide stretch of placid water. After a long time we steered to the bank and dragged the canoes out on the grass, kicked off our wet bathing costumes and lay down on the ground, shivering in the sun. Neither said anything. Later we made a fire to roast some sausages, and sat down to eat. Even then we found it impossible to talk about what had happened. The only way we could articulate was to sit there and chew our sausages.

And now I'm caught here, in this blue and golden room, with a lifetime trapped in a whirlpool, faced with the narrow gorge of a single weekend in which everything was at stake. I'm still not sure how I'm going to handle it. All I know is that I have no choice.

What I really want to know is this: Why can't you let me be, Bernard Franken? I didn't have anything to do with it, did I? No one can hold me responsible for what happened, damn it.

Charlie Mofokeng: "Of course I hold you responsible. You and every other White in the country."

"Now you're being unreasonable, Charlie. I inherited this situation exactly as you did. Neither of us can be blamed for what our forefathers did."

"That's not what I'm blaming you for. What gets me is that history didn't teach you anything at all."

"My history provided me with the means to survive in this land!"

"That's what you think. All your history taught you was to mistrust others. You never learned to share anything or to live with others. If things got difficult you loaded your wagon and trekked away. Otherwise you took aim over the Bible and killed whatever came your way. Out in the open you formed a laager. And when you wanted more land you took it. With or without the pretext of a 'contract.'"

Such fierce prejudice was characteristic of Charlie Mofokeng. I never took him altogether seriously—just as he, I believe, never took me without a pinch of salt. Between the two of us this type of argument became a form of intellectual exercise. Bright chap. What some people would call, either with appreciation or with suspicion, a "clever Kaffir." B.Comm. at Fort Hare; then another degree at Cambridge. A diminutive person, small of frame and delicate of bone structure, chronically lean and hungry; not humpbacked or anything like that, yet with something crooked about him, something off-center, like a small tree stunted by frost and never able to grow quite straight again. Wearing glasses much too large for him; and on his face a perennial smile like an open wound.

Charlie and I might have become close friends had we met abroad; as, years ago, I'd known Welcome Nyaluza. That friendship had been made possible not only by the lack of social pressure but mainly by a spontaneous urge attracting us like iron filings in a magnetic field. We had in common a dislike of the English (now shared by Charlie). But it went further than that. If once again I may romanticize a bit, I'd say that in the cold northern hemisphere we managed to preserve, for and through each other, the warm reality of our southern world. So far away from home we were not only bound by the land we shared but also strangely freed from it. Inside us, like chromosomes, lay the memories of acrid shrubs in the Karoo, coarse heather in the mountains, bleeding sunsets and nights filled with stars, of orchards and vineyards and wind-blown mealie-lands, of rocks covered by the lichen of a thousand years, the steel and concrete of modern cities and the dust of villages, of blue lamps in front of police stations and the carefree tunes of pennywhistles, of guinea-fowl clicking in the early morning grass or the delicate tracks of the sandpiper, the smell of buchu and veld fires: together we missed it and recalled it, talking about it for hours on end, often at night as we sat on a curb drinking cartons of milk from a slot-machine.

Something of all this, I suppose, was transferred to Charlie. It is difficult to find a logical explanation for it. Perhaps his deep bass reminded me of Welcome's voice; perhaps it happened simply because he was the only Black man I could more or less claim friendship with. Not that we ever really opened up completely to each other. For obvious reasons. We got along quite well at work. Sometimes there was occasion for discussion or heated arguments or banter. There was, of course, the visit to Soweto. And from time to time I invited him to a business lunch with foreign visitors. But we kept our distance.

Still, we got along. I think I can claim that as an Afrikaner I know my Black man. To a large extent we have the same history, the same rural background; in the course of a few centuries we've had the opportunity of getting exposed to the land itself, unlike the English who arrived much later merely to administrate and control; and both of us, however urbanized we may have become, are conditioned by the same tribal consciousness. In a way we respect one another. That's how I generally try to explain it to foreigners.

Which of the large British-oriented mining houses in the country would have appointed a Black like Charlie in such a responsible position at the time I did it? (Admittedly, it was Bernard who'd brought him to me and twisted my arm: "I don't care what your conservative associates may have to say about it, you're going to create a job for Charlie Mofokeng. And I'm not talking about a messenger or something. I want to see him in a key liaison position between you White bosses on Olympus and the diggers of your holes down below. Before you get buried in your own holes.") I did it because Bernard's demand fitted in with my own views. I'm not in favor of Black trade unions. At this stage they've simply not developed far enough to handle such sophisticated forms of Western organization. A matter of evolution. First of all they must learn to grasp the relationship between effort and reward. They need training and experience. In our economic system they've first got to become consumers in order to increase production. That, as I see it, is the only logical starting point for the proper exploitation of human resources in the country. And that is why I immediately realized the possibilities of a post for Charlie. A link in the chain; a step in the right direction.

It soon proved successful, too. Through eighteen months of increasing industrial tension in the land my own complex of companies continued to develop surely and peacefully. That is, until May this year.

The events are so well known from the papers that there is no need for me to review them extensively: in any case, what I am concerned with here is a more private and personal inquiry, in which public events are important only inasmuch as they influenced or determined a subjective reaction. (I'm beginning to sound more and more like a writer.)

There was the wage unrest, settled very soon in most of my concerns but persisting at the Westonaria mine. I'd had this sort of trouble before, usually in the form of a conflict between migrant laborers and local shebeen keepers. Theoretically, these laborers come to the mines to earn money which they can take back home. Their concern is to buy wives or something; mine is the development of the economy by directing capital towards the homelands. But what happens as a matter of fact? The laborers spend all their money on liquor and whores, compromising the basic economics of the situation. For that reason I stipulated that in the future half the earnings of the migrants would be sent directly to the recruiting offices in the homelands where they could collect it after their return. An administrative fee of a few cents on the rand had to be imposed, which meant that in the end the laborers received fractionally less cash than before, but in view of the fact that in the past the money had been wasted anyway I couldn't understand why such a trifle should have upset them so out of all proportion.

Agitators, most likely. It happens all the time. Otherwise the mine manager at Westonaria had bungled the affair. I know from painful experience how much patience and circumlocution is required to negotiate with Blacks; it is quite likely that the Westonaria manager acted too hastily. And when the signs became ominous in early June I decided to take matters in hand myself. I drove to Westonaria, taking Charlie with me.

It was deadly quiet when we got out of the car. One of those colorless, naked Transvaal winter days when the world is so silent that in a breath of wind you can hear each brittle blade of grass stirring separately. We were welcomed by the mine manager and his White staff, their faces drawn and tired as if they hadn't slept for a long time. Beyond the corrugated iron offices the mine's two or three hundred laborers stood waiting in a sullen mass. There was a low murmur as we appeared with a megaphone on the dusty patch between them and the buildings; like a swarm of bees in an ant heap.

In long-winded repetitions studded with every image I could think of I explained the whole matter of the new wage system to them and asked Charlie to translate. It took over an hour to convey to them that even with the loss of a few cents from their total wages they would still be left with more cash to spend at home. Only when I was quite sure that they accepted the situation did I adopt a sterner tone, knowing that Blacks despise hesitation and mildness. The language they respond to is that of strictness and authority, a hard but just hand.

They derive it from their tribal tradition which is not all that different from our own Old Testament background.

"Now I won't stand any further trouble," I said, or words to that effect. "Our output is beginning to be affected and that cannot be tolerated. In the end you are the ones who suffer most. Those of you who do not report for work in the morning will be sent home straight away."

Once again I asked Charlie to translate. For a few seconds he stood with bowed head before he started talking very rapidly, going on for at least fifteen minutes. Thanks to our farm in the Eastern Cape I know some Xhosa but I couldn't follow Charlie's Sotho or whatever it was he spoke. Not that it worried me, for by that time I knew Charlie to be a born negotiator. He appeared to handle their barrage of questions with consummate skill. And when finally he handed the megaphone back to me he was applauded with a thundering: "*Siya vuma!*"

After a cup of tea with the mine manager I returned to the pale grey Mercedes, where Charlie sat waiting at the wheel.

"Well," I said, "it just shows you, doesn't it?"

"Yes." He waited until we'd passed through the gates in the high fence surrounding the mine area and reached the Johannesburg–Potchefstroom main road. Then he said casually: "The real trouble is only starting."

"What do you mean?"

"I couldn't tell them what you said."

"What!"

"I thought you'd prefer to get out from there in one piece."

"But how dare you...."

"You don't know how angry those men really are."

"It doesn't matter."

"It does!" He'd never spoken in such a tone to me before but I managed to restrain myself. "Listen," he said, "it's bad enough for those who work in Johannesburg. They're also locked up in compounds like

a lot of animals in a bloody zoo. But at least they can get out from time
to time to do some shopping, or even to dance for your White tourists
on the mine dumps on Sundays. But this lot–Jesus, man, here they're
kept behind barbed wire with nothing but dust and dry grass as far as
you can see. They want liquor, they want women. They need *something*."

"So what did you tell them?"

He flashed his smile at me, exposing the pink of his gums. Behind
his thick lenses his eyes looked like a chameleon's. "Don't ask me," he
said. "You know the saying: 'When you return to the fire, don't talk
about the nest you found, for the birds will take away their young.'"

He stopped at a yield sign, allowing a pantechnicon to pass before
turning smoothly into the left lane.

"What did you tell them, Charlie?" I insisted.

"I told them you knew how dissatisfied they were. You knew they
had every right to feel upset and you're going to fix it for them. But
first you've got to discuss it with the big-heads in Johburg. They said
it was O.K. But they must have your answer before the weekend,
otherwise they're not coming back to work."

"My God, Charlie!"

"Most of them had sticks with them," he said quietly. "Some had
bicycle chains or crowbars concealed under their coats."

I was prepared to waive the administration fee, provided they
stepped up production and put an immediate end to all demonstrations. After all, I couldn't allow them to blackmail me.

The announcement was phoned to the mine manager at
Westonaria. That was on the Thursday. On Friday morning the
strike began. The small number, less than ten percent, who were
prepared to go on working were intimidated by the majority; two had
to be taken to hospital with serious injuries.

On Saturday the violence spread. From all over the Reef police
reinforcements were moved to Westonaria. Even before they'd
been mobilized the mining offices went up in flames. Fortunately

the manager succeeded in getting out just in time. Then all the different tribal groups turned against each other. Xhosas, Zulus, Tswanas, Sothos. It happens invariably. And it wasn't until Sunday that the police could risk it into the compound to start clearing up the mess.

On Monday I sent Charlie to Westonaria to take stock of the situation, and the next morning I went myself. The police (about a hundred of them, equipped with automatic rifles, and stationed some distance from the gates) were very reluctant to let me through but I insisted.

"It won't be the first time I've had to deal with a rowdy mob," I told them.

But I did feel rather ill at ease when I stopped at the gates and blew the horn. In the distance a few men in blue uniforms were spraying the tarred ground surrounding the burnt-out offices. Just stay calm, I decided. Whatever you feel, don't let them notice you're anxious. It's just like confronting a strange dog: if you look him in the eyes and convince him you're not scared, he'll respect you.

It was Charlie who came to the gates. But he was followed at a short distance by the whole horde-—a vanguard of ten or twenty, with a solid phalanx in the background. They were no longer wearing their overcoats: in spite of the June cold they were all naked or half-naked. Most shocking of all was the sight of Charlie in this savage guise.

I leaned out of the window. "Open up, Charlie. I want to talk to them."

"No!" he shouted back.

Behind him the vanguard was drawing a few steps closer.

Without switching off the engine, I got out to demonstrate that I was quite alone and unarmed, and unafraid.

Once more there was that subdued humming as of bees.

"They don't want you here," Charlie said.

"Do you expect me to turn tail like a coward? What will happen to my authority?"

"They shit on your authority as it is."

Again I became aware of his eyes behind the thick glasses: now more bloodshot and swollen than before. Had he been up all night? Or had he drunk some unspeakable concoction with the mob?

"Open the gate, Charlie!" I ordered.

He pushed it open, but just wide enough for himself to slip through. Behind the fence the crowd was pressing closer.

He caught me unawares. Half turning round to them he shouted something, raising a clenched fist. The next moment he stooped to pick up a brick. Looking at me squarely, his grin frozen into a grimace, he hurled the brick through my windscreen. A shout went up among the crowd. Far behind me I could hear the police cars starting up.

I didn't wait a moment longer. Jumping back into the Mercedes I broke out a section of the shattered windscreen and drove off, revving the engine. A cloud of dust obscured the compound gates.

"What the hell did you think you were doing?" I asked furiously when, exhausted and disheveled, Charlie turned up in my office the next day. "You were acting like a bloody savage."

For once there was no sign of a smile on his face. "What did you expect me to do?" he asked. "If I hadn't scared you off they'd have torn you to pieces. And me too."

"Were you really only play-acting, Charlie?" My throat felt tight.

"I'm resigning," he said. "I can't go on like this. I've become a sellout, working with you the way I've been doing."

"You're exhausted, that's all. How can you be a sellout by trying to restore some peace and order?"

"And turning against my own people?"

"You can only turn against them if you think in terms of mono-lithic groups."

"Who taught us to think in terms of groups?"

"Be reasonable, Charlie."

"I'm sick and tired of being reasonable."

"Do you really identify with a mob like that?" I asked. "You?"

With his ancient chameleon eyes he peered at me as if, over a great distance, he found it difficult to see me. My God, I thought, the man really is at the end of his tether.

"Will you help me?" he asked. His voice sounded like dry grass scraping on rock. "I think most of their violence is spent by now. Perhaps we can get them to cooperate if you and I had a go at it together."

"Of course we can. I've got to go away for the weekend, but I'll be back by Monday night."

"It would be safer to try and settle this first."

"It's impossible, Charlie. I must go to the Eastern Cape. No choice. It's urgent. After all, you said they're all right now."

"Well, if you really can't make it." He smiled from habit, quite mirthlessly. "But it's a pity. A great pity."

✧ ✧ ✧ ✧

Strange how much resistance I had to overcome to get to the farm that weekend, as if all sorts of people and events were trying to restrain me. Charlie. Bea, most fervently of them all. But even Elise who, after twenty years of married life, should have been used to my comings and goings.

"I can't see why you should go there for a weekend, Martin. If you took a proper holiday for a couple of weeks, all right, then the children and I can go with you. But this is pointless."

"It's impossible to take more time off now."

"But it's too far for a weekend. In your condition."

"For God's sake stop talking about my 'condition' as if I were pregnant or something."

"But it's barely three months since you—"

"So what? I'm not going to stay an invalid for the rest of my life." I had a brainwave: "And I want to take Louis with me."

She was surprised. "Louis?"

"It's high time he and I had a proper chat. He's been hanging round since February now, refusing to go to university or do anything constructive. And it's no use confronting him with it, as you know. He just closes up like a clam. But if he goes with me, maybe we can have a proper man-to-man talk."

"Do you promise?"

"Of course."

She sat watching me intently for a while. We were still at table, the reading lamp burning in the corner. Ilse had excused herself earlier on to prepare for her exams. Louis was—somewhere. He hadn't come home for supper. And so we were alone, Elise and I. Which was unusual, since more often than not I work late at the office and come home to something warmed up in the oven; otherwise we'd have a party or a reception or something. But that afternoon I'd driven straight home from Westonaria, too upset by what had happened there to go back to work, and in no mood for arguments.

In that silence I was forced to look at her, to take cognizance of her. Perhaps it was the side lighting which caused me to discover for the first time that she was also getting older, looking her real age, forty-two. Here and there a grey line in the dark-blonde hair tied loosely in a chignon. An old shapeless sweater round her shoulders, although the central heating made it unnecessary; but she'd been wearing it in the garden and neglected to take it off when she came in. Her eyes were still the same intense blue of so many years ago, that Sunday afternoon on Bernard's farm. The same blue, but not the same expression. Again a matter of *Songs of Innocence—Songs of Experience?* No *song* at all, in fact. I believe that was what really struck me that evening. Previously I'd wondered, sometimes, which of the extremes in her would finally take over: the cleric's daughter who, back in the early fifties when such things had been much less conceivable than now, had dived naked into a dam with me, or the one who, on our wedding night, had said: "Let's first pray to ask the Lord's blessing on us"? But that evening, in our strange isolation on opposite ends of the yellow-wood table, such memories appeared unreal if not irrelevant. In cruel sincerity I had to acknowledge that Elise was still a person with strong convictions, except that she no longer knew of what she was convinced; she was still strong, only she had no idea of what was threatening her; she would still go her way unswervingly, but she couldn't tell where it was leading her.

After the long silence her question was, I suppose, inevitable: "But *why* are you going down to the farm? Surely not just for Louis's sake."

"No. I've got to talk to Ma."

She sat in silence, waiting for more, watching me.

"She can't stay there all on her own," I continued. "She's getting too old for that sort of life."

"But you know how often we've tried to talk her out of it. She won't leave her graves."

"Things are changing. It's getting dangerous. You realize the farm is on the very edge of the Ciskei."

"It's always been there."

"But the Blacks are getting restless. I'm just not happy about her down there. We've got to sell the farm so that she can come and live with us."

Another long silence before she asked, deadpan: "How much are you getting for the farm?"

"That's not important. The point is—"

"Of course it's important. I know you'll never sell the farm unless you get very good money for it."

"I keep telling you I'm concerned about Ma."

"Martin." The lines beside her mouth deepened slightly. "You think you can gloss everything over with words. All your life you've been able to have things your way because you've got the gift of the gab." Absently she started toying with a heavy silver knife, but without taking her eyes off me. "Well? What's the price?"

"Two hundred and fifty thousand."

"The farm isn't worth one quarter of that!"

"That's what I've been offered."

"And for that you're prepared—" A pause. "You can't do it, Martin. Not the farm." For the first time she raised her voice; and she put down the knife.

"It's all settled. I've just got to discuss it with Ma."

The doorbell rang. Annoyed, Elise looked up, but I felt relieved.

It was Neels Jansen, our church elder. Not on any official business, just one of his periodic "look-ins." The man had a special sixth sense which unfailingly informed him whenever I needed peace and quiet so that he could come and disturb it. A huge bulky ox of a man, looking more like a butcher than anything else, with a kind but sallow face and close-cropped hair. Not the sort of person whom I'd normally count among my friends, but from the first day he'd arrived at my house (accompanied by the *dominee* in the service of the Lord) he seemed to take a liking to me. That had been late one afternoon while I was working on the filter pump of the swimming pool. I'd been struggling with it for over an hour when I looked up to find Neels standing behind me in a black suit much too small for him, his tight white collar digging into the lower section of his many chins.

"Give it to me, man," he said. "You're stripping that screw." With obvious relief he removed his jacket and waistcoat and took over the spanner; and for the next half hour I looked on, fascinated, while his large soft hands took apart the entire pump and refitted the parts. When he switched it on with immediate positive effect he uttered a loud guffaw, at the same time bringing down his butcher's paw between my shoulder blades with such violence that I was left gasping for breath while he put on his formal gear again to lead me home to the patiently waiting *dominee*.

I'm not by any means a regular churchgoer. Three or four times a year I am prepared to make the sacrifice and I'm not ashamed to admit that it is mainly because it is good for business to be seen in such circles. (Prosperous congregation; all we still need is a wine list for Holy Communion.) But Elise goes regularly, often twice on Sunday, mainly as a result of the conditioning of her childhood as a *dominee's* daughter, but also because she regards it as a good example to the children, especially Ilse.

After that first visit Neels Jansen returned at more or less regular intervals, usually to check that the filter pump was still working, that the pH and chloride levels of the pool were in order and that all other mechanical installations on my property were functioning as they should. His two main interests in life (roughly for identical reasons) were cars and women. But he also seemed concerned about my salvation ("A man's soul is like a car engine, it needs a regular overhaul").

He turned out to be not a butcher after all but a member of the Security Police; a major, in fact. As he gradually took over the maintenance of all my machinery he also started conveying juicy tidbits from the "inner circles," generally punctuated with an enigmatic wink before any point was reached. And in the course of time I developed a soft spot for him, the way one learns to grow fond of a large, clumsy mongrel.

This was the *deus ex machina* which interrupted our bitter inquisition that Tuesday evening. Elise soon excused herself and went to make coffee (unnecessarily, since both servants were still washing up in the kitchen), while Neels Jansen flopped down in an armchair with a large brandy he'd poured himself. As usual when not on an "official" visit he was wearing his red tracksuit. It soon became clear what had brought him: I'd missed Communion the previous Sunday.

But he tried to be "tactful" about it by approaching it along as circuitous a route as possible; so I tried to ease his discomfort by asking him about his right hand, swathed in plaster of Paris from fingertips to beyond his wrist.

"Oh, this?" he snorted, tasting his brandy. "Broke it on a bloody kaffir."

"What?" I couldn't make out whether he was serious. "You're joking."

"No, genuine."

"Did you hurt him?"

"Hurt him? He's gone, man. Zap, one time."

"But then you're in serious trouble, Neels!"

"*Ag*, no," he said cryptically. "Don't you worry. We got it all squared." He crossed one massive leg over the other, revealing, between the bottom of his track pants and the edge of his canvas shoes, a length of hairy shank. "Now forget about it, man. I tell you it's nothing. What I want to talk to you about is why you didn't come to Communion last Sunday."

That night, when Elise was already sleeping soundly in her own bed, I lit a forbidden cigarette, wondering: Shouldn't one do something about the matter? But after reflection I knew it was out of the question. What Neels Jansen did or had done was no concern of mine. One couldn't get involved in that sort of thing. I had a job to think of. I stubbed out the cigarette. I felt relieved that Elise hadn't said anything more about the weekend.

✧ ✧ ✧ ✧

I'm not sure that I am altogether happy about this whimsical way of writing down whatever comes to mind. But I have to explore the terrain first: I must allow myself to discover the full extent of the area involved before I try to get down to that weekend as such. As an entrepreneur I owe much of my success to the thoroughness of my investigation before embarking on a new project, as well as to my perseverance in not abandoning anything once I've taken it up. I owe it to myself to proceed with this undertaking too.

It is necessary to say something about my convictions so that there can be no misunderstanding whatsoever. I am an Afrikaner. I'm a Nationalist. I've never had any reason to be ashamed of it. On the contrary.

My political memory goes back to May, 1948 when I was seventeen years old, and in Matric. I sat up all night with my parents in front of the radio, the upright old-fashioned Atwater Kent with its cut-out curls and leaves covering the speaker. There were several friends and neighbors with us, all listening to the election results and consuming vast quantities of coffee. When the Standerton result was announced and Jan Smuts lost his seat we all jumped up and down shouting and embracing and stumbling over chairs; and the old carpenter, Oom Hennie, got so excited and jumped so high that he fell right through the worm-eaten floorboards and had to be dragged out by the jubilant crowd. A few days later the whole family was piled into Pa's old blue '42 Mercury to drive the seventy-odd miles of dusty corrugated road to Kimberley where the train of the new Prime Minister, Dr. Malan, was due to stop on its triumphal journey to Pretoria. For four hours we stood waiting in the blazing sun as the crowd grew larger and larger. All streets and open places near the station were filled with vehicles of every description, from the latest American cars to the horse-drawn carriages and donkey carts of farmers who'd driven for innumerable miles, many of them right through the night, in order to be present when the Doctor arrived. The train, when it came, more than an hour late, didn't stop for long: barely ten minutes. A mayor weighed down by his glittering chain, and a few other dignitaries escorted the Doctor to the small high platform where the stationmaster usually stood to catch the passing drivers' messages. Dr. Malan said something—God knows what, I don't think anybody heard or cared. It was enough to see him there. All the men had taken off their hats, pressing them against their chests; and the women stood up from the food baskets on which they'd been sitting. In my young mind there was only one comparable image: the entry of Jesus into Jerusalem. And looking at some of those old patriarchs with their great beards and their faces stained with tears and tobacco juice, one could well imagine them saying: Lord, now lettest thy servant depart in peace, according to thy word; for mine eyes have seen thy salvation.

On our way back home, Pa said: "Well, children, from this day we Afrikaners needn't go about with hanging heads any more. Now we're boss in our own country."

Of course, 1948 belongs to a remote past and much of that exuberant energy has been dissipated. We live in a harder and more urgent world. One can't remain standing forever bareheaded in a blazing sun on a station platform. But we're still here, a quarter of a century later: here where we first arrived three hundred years ago. And we've come to stay. I'm not pretending that all that happens around us is good or right; there is much need for change. But to surrender everything to Black hands is to exchange the wind for the whirlwind. Look at the rest of Africa. Look at the world, "free" or otherwise.

My convictions are based on the belief that revolutions, although they change political power, make no difference to the basic lot of people. There will always be those who have and others who have not. And the solution doesn't lie in sharing your cake equally among all. It sounds good in theory, but if you are conditioned by practical experience as I am, a different picture emerges. People want to compete: it is a basic urge. And as they differ in their capabilities and basic equipment they cannot expect the same reward in the end. The only answer is to make your cake bigger so that each contender can get a bigger share, without expecting all shares to be equal.

How can you add to your cake? Through education and encouragement; by offering a higher reward for more effort you can increase production and reap more profits. And once the Black man has learned to handle this economic system I won't have any objection to his political advancement either.

So much of the greatly overrated "political consciousness" among Blacks these days is no more than the product of manipulation by Whites. (How can the Black man be expected to suddenly master sophisticated concepts if in all the centuries of his evolution in Africa he failed to even discover the wheel on his own?) The real priority is a combination of strong discipline and as much education as the Black is able to absorb in his development from one stage to the next.

It is not a matter of clinging to power. What is really at stake is the maintenance of values. The peace and prosperity Southern Africa has been enjoying for so long (in contrast with the chaos on the rest of the continent where White patronage was withdrawn with disgusting promptness) must be ascribed to the fact that the Boer conquered the land with a gun in one hand and the Bible in the other. Both are indispensable. By spreading the Gospel values are preserved (democracy, individual achievement, our whole Western Protestant ethic). And we cannot give up the gun before the other man has accepted our values. I must be very emphatic on this point. It concerns our specific set of values and no other. One need only look at Mozambique where an attempt was made to impose another system, to fully appreciate the difference.

I always tend to get carried away when I start on this topic (I've addressed so many *Rapportryer* and other meetings on the subject), but I do regard it as the crux of the matter. That is why my economic philosophy, in all my mining enterprises, is aimed at directing a flow of capital towards the homelands, where the roots lie. That is the place where any raising of living standards should start. Which, in turn, is the only logical way to influence the birthrate: the man at the bottom of the ladder has got to multiply rabbit-wise, it's his only security; as soon as he achieves more economic stability his birthrate drops.

For these reasons I must reject Bernard's views out of hand. I know many liberals: it springs from the nature of my work. I even admire some of them. (I'm not referring to those dwellers of Houghton and similar suburbs who are rich enough to allow themselves the luxury of nice liberal gestures while treating their servants worse than any Afrikaner civil servant would.) But to my mind these people are involved in a wholly futile crusade. They are trying to wage a moral war in a world determined by other, economic, forces. And all their efforts can lead to, is a spate of new victims and martyrs. Utterly irrelevant victims, like Bernard, on the periphery of the realities of today.

So I can't take seriously the accusation of some of my liberal friends that I'm living off the fat of the land. Whatever I possess, I've earned. It is a just reward I'm entitled to in terms of my economic contract with the land: that I'm allowed to take from it what I can; and that, in return, the capital I've earned with my know-how and hard work be used to stimulate the economic development of the underprivileged to the point where they can assume greater responsibility for themselves. In this way the country at large benefits from it.

My people and I have come a long way to where we are—I'll come back to this in due course—and we shall continue to fight for our right to be here, if it is necessary. We know only too well what it means to be powerless and exploited and oppressed in our own country. It's time we started reaping the fruit of our labor. And I am prepared to make any reasonable change or concession to ensure that I retain what I've acquired with so much effort.

This is no mere abstraction. I experience it daily. Sometimes it gives me an almost voluptuous feeling to take off my shoes and walk barefoot on the incredibly thick pile of the carpet in my hotel room. Or to phone down for a light snack at one or two in the morning. Or to contact an agency to send round a masseuse. For however much, through the years, I've grown accustomed to these luxuries, nothing can ever obliterate the memories of being a bare-foot boy limping to school on cracked footsoles on the frosted earth in winter, or stepping in chicken shit in summer, or breaking my shins in the erosion ditch among the pepper trees. When I nurse my glass of whisky, I remember Granny's homemade lemon juice on the farm, or opening my mouth to the warm jet of milk straight from the cow's udder, or making clay oxen to pull our toy cars fashioned out of sardine cans. I remember ash-cakes and golden syrup, or collecting eggs, or baking a sheep's head in an antheap; ghost stories, and wanking off behind the shed to see who could shoot the farthest; and Grandpa's booming voice reading *And have not charity* at evening prayers, and swimming bare-arsed in the dam on the farm together with all the other Black and White boys of the neighborhood.

It was in that very dam I came closer to death than I'd ever been in my life until earlier this year: when, one Sunday afternoon, I went in too far trying to retrieve a boat of tin and planks—the others had warned me not to, but I'd paid no attention—and suddenly began to sink into the soft clay, unable to pull loose. I started shouting for help. The others took fright and ran off. By the time the mud was up to my hips I was getting hysterical. And then one boy came back into the water to help me, a Black piccanin, I believe his name was Mpilo but we used to call him *Pieletjie*, which means *Prick*, because at the age of twelve or thirteen he already had a penis which, even in its flaccid state, dangled down halfway to his knees. He grabbed hold of me. We nearly went down together into that slimy mud. But in the end he managed to pull me out and I rewarded him with a shilling (although he really wanted my new pocket knife). All these memories are intimately mine and I can't deny them. Without them I would not have been me. Even in my dreams they return to me.

✧ ✧ ✧ ✧

It had been planned as "our" weekend. What we really needed was another week like the one in the red bungalow at Ponta do Ouro, but we were both too busy to break away. (In addition to her work at the University she was helping out, as on some previous occasions, with Afrikaans lessons in a Soweto school.) In the circumstances even a brief weekend suggested paradise. Then it became imperative for me to go to the farm before His Excellency, Minister Calitz, could sabotage the deal; so I had to phone her to cancel our plans.

"Is it because of the riots at Westonaria?" she asked.

"No. I've got to go to the farm."

"Your mother ill?"

"No. It's on business."

There followed a long pause before she said: "I see."

"I'll tell you all about it later."

She didn't reply.

"I'll be back by Monday night. So I can see you on Tuesday."

"All right."

"Why do you sound so negative?"

"I'm not negative. I'm used to taking second place. That's my 'role', isn't it?"

"Please, Bea."

"I'm sorry. I didn't mean to—I suppose if you've really got to go there's nothing else to be said."

She was in her flat in the dilapidated old block in Berea, sheltered from the narrow uphill street by a row of jacarandas. She would be standing by the window. I could almost visualize her, with her back turned to me. The inclination of her neck, the narrow shoulders and hips, long legs; barefoot, most likely. In those familiar surroundings her eyes would not need the protection of the sunglasses. The "woman of thirty," with all the experience of winters and summers; all the superfluities of adolescence and spring stripped away; no need for

55

deviation or illusion, unashamed about the sincerity of either desire or disgust. Essentially naked, exposed to light and pain, no longer prepared to betray others or fool herself. Yet it is remarkable how vulnerable a woman like that can also be. Not the vulnerability of youth or virginity, but exposed more uncompromisingly to loss; no longer bending, but prepared to splinter or to break. Every scar bare and hard and clear. (*Look: I am prepared to suffer, I am suffering, I don't mind. What else is there? For I'm alive, I am delivered to life. Yet I'm at no one's ready disposal.*)

"I'm terribly sorry, Bea," I insisted. "You know how much I've been looking forward to this weekend. But we can always do it later. Next week. Any time. We're not bound to anything."

"Of course." Her voice sounded flat and tired. And I could imagine the stubborn line of her shoulders against the window: *Why don't you ring off, for God's sake? Don't try to be "kind" or "considerate" to me.*

"Please, Bea, you must believe me."

"I told you it didn't matter."

"But I can hear you're upset." I moved the telephone to my right hand. "Tell me what's the matter."

A short silence, as if she first had to draw her breath. "There's something I must discuss with you. But not on the telephone."

"I'll see you on Tuesday."

"I know. It's just—It seemed rather urgent, but I suppose it can wait. Anything can wait."

"Look after yourself. It's only a few days."

Suddenly, abandoning her restraint, she asked: "Martin, is it really quite impossible to postpone this farm business just for one week? I *must* see you."

"But I told you."

"Oh well, if it's out of the question." Adding in a smothered tone, as if she didn't mean me to hear it: "Oh, God."

"Goodbye, Bea. See you Tuesday."

She rang off.

One remembers every word of such a conversation. Because it was our last.

There's this dam with a water lily in the center growing all the time. I want to wade in to pick it for Bea who stands waiting on the other side. But the moment I touch the stem, my feet are caught in quicksand. Out of the corner of my eye I can see a black shadow hovering on the edge. It must be Mpilo, but he looks like Charlie. "Help me!" I scream. "Help me, I'm sinking!" But he stands there with his arms crossed, watching me sink into the muddy water until I drown. Of course, it's only a dream.

Friday

1

A WHOLE SWARM OF GNATS plastered on the windscreen. I'm
starting there again, because for some reason or other it
remains important to me. In itself there was nothing unusual
about it: it often happens on a long trip, especially before the rains.
Suddenly that cloud of whirring wings and their greasy, greenish,
yellowish smudge on the windscreen, speckled with blood. And when
I switched on the wipers and pressed the button for the windscreen
washer nothing happened. That was the real reason for my dismay.
One simply does not expect it of a 350-SE. I know some people
have questionable motives for acquiring a Mercedes, but I chose
it because I was prepared to pay a lot of money for this form of
security, this promise of technical perfection, this aesthetic satisfaction. Now, unexpectedly, a minor mechanism like the wipers
refused to function, casting doubt on everything I normally took for
granted on a journey. If the wipers wouldn't work, anything else
might fail me. (Even the pistol in the cubbyhole, which accompanied
me on all my trips. Suppose one day I needed it?) That wasn't what
I'd paid for. Moreover, it reminded me all too ominously of the
afternoon, three months before, with Bea: the day we'd met at the
hole and gone to my apartment; the day the body, another of those
mechanisms one relies on without questioning, had proved its fal-
libility. And now those gnats, on the dreary stretch of road after

Theunissen. Who'd predicted that if man were to disappear from the earth the insects would take over?

It was very likely that the defect had been caused by the garage who'd replaced the windscreen shattered at Westonaria, a memory I would have preferred not to recall. Like others. But having started I must now go on.

To forget and get away from it all: in the confusion of the preceding days that had become the overriding motivation of the weekend, for which I yearned like a farmer for rain in a time of drought. (And it was a time of drought. All the way we traveled the land was reduced to dust and bareness and dry winter grass.) I'd sent a telegram to Ma, announcing my arrival on Friday night, but without giving any details, the matter being much too delicate to discuss on the telephone, especially a party line like hers. I had to see her personally to persuade her of the necessity of the sale. That was the essential reason for the whole excursion, and without it nothing else could have happened. Still, whenever during that last week I'd thought about it my main consideration had not been the sale but simply the opportunity to escape from the tensions accumulating around me: Louis, Bea, the unrest at the mines, Bernard's trial. He is the first I must deal with so that I can finally be free from him.

I'd hoped to escape from the courtroom, but I took it with me all the way. The paneling behind the bench under the high canopy, the red leather upholstery of the seats, the long tables protected by ornamental rails, the threadbare brown carpet and the grey curtains on the side walls, the two yellow skylights in the ceiling, the three-bladed fan suspended from a rod which swayed precariously when it was operated, the large chandelier with floral shades covering the dusty bulbs. (There had been an identical lampshade in my room when I'd been a child. I can remember the sound it made when I knocked against it, the night I struggled upright in a daze to grope for water; and the doctor ran into the room, then stopped to turn back to my parents and announced: "You can relax now, he's pulled through.") And Bernard in the dock, taking a full day to recite his prepared statement. I took away a copy in my briefcase. For some reason I've never got round to re-reading it or destroying it and I still have it with me as I'm writing this. It lies on the fake Queen Anne table beside me.

When a man is on trial for his political beliefs and actions, two courses are open to him. He can either confess to his transgressions and plead for mercy or he can justify his beliefs and explain why he acted as he did. Were I to ask forgiveness today I would betray my cause and my convictions, for I believe that what I did was right.

I accept the general rule that for the protection of a society laws should be obeyed. But when laws themselves become immoral and require the citizen to take part in an organized system of oppression—if only by his silence or his apathy—then I believe a higher duty arises. This compels one to refuse to recognize such laws. My conscience does not permit me to afford them even such recognition as a plea of guilty would imply. Hence, though I shall be convicted by this Court, I cannot plead guilty. Neither will I offer mitigating circumstances or ask for clemency when the moment arrives. This I do in the firm belief that the future, and history itself, will vindicate me.

I should have liked to deny or undo his words, that Friday in the car on my way to the farm; preferably, if only for a weekend, I wanted to forget about him entirely. But how could I, when Louis was there beside me? With him, I was really taking everything else with me. From time to time I glanced at him sideways, but he was staring fixedly through the messy windscreen, although he must have been aware of my eyes on him. A profile like my own, almost disarmingly similar; only much younger, of course. (That in itself was unsettling.) And consequently more stubborn, more arrogant. Above all, reserved, secretive and strange, just as he had been when, a couple of hours before, we'd met in the crowd surrounding the suicide.

Nineteen. At that age one would have expected him to be like his contemporaries, all emotion and eagerness, bravado inspired by the first fumbling discoveries of rampant sexuality, and stirrings of vulnerability, susceptible to the spell of the moon or the shape of a girl's ear; all storm and stress. But Louis was different. In his eyes was something very old and disconcerting. Weariness? Disillusionment? Cynicism? At nineteen! It was more than that. One had the uncomfortable impression that there was nothing which could either shock or please him any more. As if he'd arrived beyond the territory to which I could offer him a map. And it was presumptuous, if not absurd, to expect that in the course of a single weekend I could diminish the distance between us.

I didn't want to stop because of the gnats; through the smear one could still see enough of the road and it wasn't dark yet, barely five o'clock. I don't like interrupting a journey; I never did, not even when the children were small and wanted me to stop at the most impossible times and places. When I'm driving I want to continue until I reach the other end, finding something inwardly satisfying about the very momentum of motion. It's like a swinging bucket of water: only by going on can one keep everything under control. Once one's rhythm is disturbed one's very mastery of the situation is in jeopardy.

"I think we can manage for the moment, don't you?" I asked Louis. "One can still see, even though it's through a glass darkly."

He stared ahead without giving the slightest sign that he'd heard.

2

I T HAD, IN FACT, gone wrong from the start. We were thirty miles from Johannesburg when I discovered that I'd taken the wrong road. I'd meant to travel on the customary, faster route via Vereeniging and Parys; now we were on our way to Potchefstroom, the road I'd driven several times that week to the mine at Westonaria. It wasn't so much the reminder of the riot that annoyed me as the discovery that I'd made a mistake. As with the gnats, later, it made me feel, momentarily, that I wasn't in complete control; as if something had taken its course against my will.

In the long run it couldn't make much difference, except, of course, that it would have eliminated the gnats. But I hated the idea of changing my routine. That in itself was more annoying than the mere fact of an extra fifteen or thirty minutes' driving. Time wasn't all that important, especially since we'd set out earlier than I had anticipated. We'd stopped at *Uncle Charlie's* outside Johannesburg for a quick snack.

"You order," I told Louis, in a deliberate effort to mollify him. "Whatever you wish."

"I don't know what you like."

My fake enthusiasm waned, but I insisted: "Anything you want."

Shrugging, he turned down his window to order: a hamburger and Coke for himself, tea and a toasted cheese-and-tomato sandwich for me. Perhaps I'd hoped, secretly, that he would order the same for him and me; something boyish and outrageous like a double-malt or a cream soda float or a parfait. He probably didn't even know that I couldn't stand cooked tomato; but in order not to insult or disappoint him I finished my sandwich. I'm not sure that I achieved anything through it, still I wanted to do all I could to create at least the illusion of comradeship.

What is the "natural" relationship between father and son: friendship, rivalry, antagonism? Or doesn't there exist such a "natural" relationship? Perhaps the problem lies in one's very effort to determine what the relationship "ought" to be. It might be easier to approach the situation like any other, in which two strangers are introduced and either find their way to each other or don't. But the circumstances surrounding a family suggest the presence of other factors, of something "natural," integrally part of it from the outset. Then something happens quite by chance—an accident, a death, a touch of fortune, a war in Angola—and suddenly you discover that you know nothing of one another at all; there is no secret bond, no instinctive alliance. In different circumstances both would be free to go their separate ways. But because of the family setup you feel the need to "do something about it." Denying our private liberty in the process, if I may borrow Bernard's terminology.

Between Bernard and me there had still existed a choice: we were free to become friends, or not; to get to know each other, or not. Or was that, too, an illusion? For many years, in answer to the question: *Who is the person you know best?* I would have said, without a moment's hesitation: *Bernard Franken.* And yet I had to discover and acknowledge, time and again in the course of his trial, that I really knew nothing of that man in the dock; that he was a total stranger to me. And I actually blamed him for that. It felt as if he'd betrayed me by changing into someone other than the man I'd known.

Why am I always confronted by the strangeness of others: Elise, Louis, Bea, Charlie, Bernard? Without the break of these nine days in London I would have been able to contain it, as before. But having started this exploration I am forced also to take the trouble of asking: What is the reason or the cause of it all? Trouble, indeed. At my age, after the sort of shock I had, one becomes increasingly aware of the trouble involved in so many things; and one tries to eliminate it where possible. But of course it was futile even to hope for it now.

After his sensational arrest in the last week of February the newspapers began a systematic buildup of the story, carefully fed from "informed sources." And by the time the trial opened in Pretoria in the middle of May the rumors had acquired a tone of hysteria.

During the past few years it had often happened in similar trials that after the extravagant expectations kindled by the press beforehand the actual court proceedings proved something of an anticlimax. But not in Bernard's case. The charge sheet in itself was more than impressive: a list of twenty-three indictments under the Terrorism Act and the Suppression of Communism Act, referring to a countrywide organization aimed at urban terrorism, sabotage and even political assassination; the recruiting and training of guerrillas abroad; the distribution of inflammatory pamphlets; the stockpiling of grenades and other arms, etc.—the whole book. In addition, there were rumors of accomplices who would be brought to court later (that is, apart from those who had already been caught and sentenced three years earlier).

A long row of witnesses played their predictable role in spinning out the case against Bernard: security men, including a few who had been planted in the organization; recruits and accomplices who'd elected to give evidence for the State; and several prisoners who'd been convicted earlier and had to be brought from jail for the occasion, two of them even from Robben Island. (And all of this against the background of sensation caused by suicide and attempted suicide in detention.) The clear intention was to prove that far from being a mere cog in a vast machine Bernard had been the mastermind and instigator of it all. That, at least, corresponded to the image I'd had of him.

"Aren't you going to Pretoria for the trial?" Elise asked as soon as a date had been announced.

"Why should I? I've got too much work to catch up with."

"But you were such close friends."

"You were as close to him as I was," I said. "Why don't *you* go?"

She avoided my eyes. "I only thought it might mean something to him if he saw you there."

"It's out of the question. In my position."

She didn't broach the subject again and as far as I was concerned that was the end of the matter. But, of course, it proved to be more difficult than I'd thought. There were newspapers, radio bulletins, TV: wherever one went there were reports or rumors of the trial.

Still, in the beginning I managed to satisfy myself with the radio reports, which were the most concise of all. I steered clear of all conversations in which Bernard was mentioned. Only to Charlie, who insisted on discussing the case, did I speak my mind: "I can't understand it at all," I said. "Bernard is the last person who should have felt the need to do a thing like that."

"What do you mean, 'need'?"

"Haven't you noticed? The only people who ever get involved in such matters are ones with private hangups. They play around with politics and violence for the simple reason that they're trying to solve personal problems. But surely that doesn't apply to Bernard. He had everything a man could wish for. Friends, women, money, travels, success in his career, recognition, fame, the lot. I fail to understand how a man in his position could willingly give up everything to go and fight for the sake of others."

Charlie blinked behind his thick glasses. Was he mocking me?

"There's one thing you forgot, Martin."

"What's that?"

"Morality."

"What morality?"

"A matter of conscience. I'm just as bad a believer as you are. But on Bernard's farm, where he and I grew up, the *oubaas*"—I'm sure he said that deliberately—"the *oubaas* loved to read us the text about gaining the world and losing your soul. Don't you think that's where you should go and look for your explanation?"

"Nonsense. Bernard will be the first to disagree with you."

"If you really knew him so well, why did you say you couldn't understand him at all?"

"Now you're splitting hairs."

But I had no peace of mind. I wanted to stay away from the court, I wanted to keep out of the whole thing, but something drove me back to it. I began to buy more and more newspapers, covering the whole political spectrum; and those I'd missed at first I dug up in the public library. I accused myself of going "soft." I blamed Bernard for undermining my resistance. There were days when I actually hated him for it: it must have been the first time in years I'd felt so strongly about anything. But in the long run I couldn't stay away any more. On the Friday of the third week I drove to Pretoria very early in the morning; but then I wasted so much time wandering through the streets that I was too late to find a seat in court. Much to my relief, really. It made it easier to stay away on the Monday and Tuesday. And the unrest at Westonaria gave me more than enough reason not to go to Pretoria again. But in the end I couldn't resist it; and on the last few days of the trial I was there. The conclusion of the State's case. The sensation when Bernard, conducting his own defense, announced that he would neither call witnesses nor give evidence himself. The argument. His own long statement from the dock. And, on that final Friday morning, the verdict; Bernard's refusal to plead in mitigation; and the sentence.

Now, driving on through the drought-stricken land, all I knew was that I was moving farther and farther away from Johannesburg and Pretoria, from Church Square and the massive statue of Paul Kruger and the Supreme Court.

In the city one didn't notice the drought so much. There were water restrictions, but secretly, in the evenings, we continued to water the garden. (Why not? I could afford whatever fine might be imposed.) That was all there was to it. But as soon as one reached the open veld on the road to Potchefstroom, and especially after Westonaria, it became oppressive. Once we'd crossed the Vaal River it got even worse. There had been no rains since the spring; some areas hadn't had a drop in two years. Even in good winters the Free State appears bleak, but this time it was devastating. The tough white grass had given up, leaving the earth bare in large patches, dark red like dried blood on a carcass. No sign of life. Not even flies. Only, just after Theunissen, that plague of gnats from nowhere; the wipers refusing to move; and the two of us staring through the dirty glass.

3

WE WERE FORCED TO STOP AT BRANDFORT to have the windscreen washed after all. Once again it was not so much the loss of time which irritated me as the disruption of a rhythm and a pattern. It frustrated my planning, because I'd hoped to reach Reddersburg to fill up with petrol before the service stations closed at six. With this delay we had to fill the two large plastic containers in the boot; an unnecessary risk I usually tried to avoid. Fortunately there was nothing wrong with the airconditioning of the Mercedes so that we needn't be bothered by fumes.

It was cold when we got out at the garage. The sun was still a short distance above the bare stony hills in the colorless sky; but the cold air cut one to the bone. On these plains there was no shelter. The village was an untidy assortment of square houses on bare plots surrounded by tumbledown fences; corrugated iron tanks in backyards, some of them corroded with rust; outdoor lavatories and fowl-runs; here and there a few pigeons, puffed and windblown on a rooftop. On the *koppie* behind the village, the unsightly red-and-white skeleton of an FM tower. Normally one whizzed past on the main road circling the village. But now it seemed as if the departure from routine forced me to take stock of—what? The scene remained irrelevant and incoherent. Here, in the luxury of my London hotel, the memory seems even more pointless and out of place.

At the corner of the garage, in a spot of sunshine sheltered from the icy wind, stood a group of Black youths, huddled close together for warmth, talking in earsplitting voices, while two younger ones were scavenging for food in a refuse bin. An African woman came past, a paraffin tin balanced on her head; by the time she was two blocks away she was still conversing with the youngsters at the garage, shouting at the top of her voice.

Across the street, on the dusty pavement in front of a dilapidated white gate, a little girl was skipping, on her face a frown of concentration as she went on monotonously, without the slightest variation in her step; while leaning against a verandah pole on the stoop of a house diagonally opposite, an old man stood watching her, his pipe lifeless in his mouth. He, too, was "taking stock"—of what? Bernard once told me of his grandfather in the North-West who'd sat on his stoop one morning watching a neighbor girl skipping, causing her dress to fly up at every jump. Apparently she wasn't wearing any panties. Grandpa Bernard sat there, gripping his stick more and more tightly until the knuckles showed white through the skin. When he couldn't take it any longer he called his wife out to the stoop:

"Woman, will you chase that child with her bare cunt out of my sight before she gives me a stroke?"

"Why don't you look away?" she asked.

Whereupon Grandpa Bernard uttered his immortal word: "It's no damn use. That thing's like lightning. You see it without looking."

Today I find myself wondering: Did I, too, see what I was trying not to look at that weekend?

Returning from the toilet, Louis thrust his hands back into his jeans pockets.

"Cold, eh?" I said.

"What time will we get to the farm?"

I looked at my watch. "About eleven. Are you tired?"

"This is chicken-feed," he said, sneering. "That day we pushed on past Sa da Bandeira—"

"You know, you haven't really told me anything about your whole trip to Angola yet."

"What is there to tell? You blokes here won't understand it."

I felt insulted by "you blokes here," but tried not to show my annoyance. It was no use antagonizing him so soon. But already I felt the whole attempt was going to be futile.

The garage boy was still struggling with the mess caused by the gnats. Holding a watering can in one hand he aimed a thin jet of water on the windscreen while wiping furiously with a bundle of newsprint in the other.

"How are you getting on?"

"It's sticky, Baas." He grinned briefly.

Men in blue uniforms washing bits of human bodies from the tar. Charlie had told me what it had looked like immediately after the riots. Bodies hacked to pieces with pangas. Tongues torn out and eye holes gaping. The pulped faces smeared with excrement. Just as well they kept this sort of violence hidden behind the barbed wire of compounds. In a civilized community it would be unbearable.

Right in the beginning, after Bernard had first brought him to me, I'd said to Charlie: "For God's sake, man, why did you come back to South Africa? Over in England you had all you could wish for. Even a university post. Why didn't you stay there?"

He smiled with bare gums. "You also went overseas, didn't you? Would *you* have preferred to stay there?"

"No, of course not. But—"

"Well?"

On a certain level I can accept it. But it remains an emotional reaction with nothing logical about it. And although I know one is tempted to react emotionally to Africa, I find it hard to credit Charlie with such an unreasonable decision.

Still, there was the day in Gibraltar, on our honeymoon. We were standing on the rock looking out across the sea to the blue of the African coastline against the even paler blue of the sky. Not once in all the time I'd been away had I missed it as much as at that moment.

In the end I took Elise by the hand, saying: "Let's go." We had to reach Malaga before nightfall. As we turned to go, we noticed the Black man behind us, also staring across the strait. And with sudden unashamed pride, like a child announcing his birthday to a total stranger, he said: "That's my land over there."

"Morocco?"

"No, Africa. My home is farther to the south, Nigeria."

"We're from Africa, too."

"It's not good to be away from it."

That was the full extent of our conversation. But through it, for the first time in my life, I really became aware of Africa: that continent linking me to so many generations of men, past *homo sapiens*, millions of years back to *homo habilis:* my land and that stranger's.

Perhaps I shouldn't be too harsh in my judgment of the mine mob. How could they have been expected to cope with a life behind barbed wire, in single quarters, in a compound—after the huts and mealie lands and hills of Transkei or Lesotho, women working in the lands, gourds of sour milk, *dagga* pipes, circumcision, dancing, goats and cattle?

I myself hadn't known how to operate a lift before going to university. If Bernard or I had suddenly been uprooted from the villages of our youth, what would have become of us? It was difficult enough for us as it was.

Consequently I have a duty to explain to the Court the views I hold, how I came to espouse them, and why, in the course of time, I felt compelled to act as I did.

At the outset I must emphasize that I was born from a family who had proved their loyalty to the Afrikaner cause through their share in the Anglo-Boer War, the Rebellion of 1914 and even the underground activities of the Ossewa-Brandwag during the Second World War. Until about my twenty-fifth year I was a Nationalist by conviction. Like many young Afrikaners of my generation I grew up on a farm. Like them, I was lonely in many respects, having no brothers, only four sisters, all of them much older than myself. In the southern Free State where we lived the farms were large and far apart. Except for the neighboring children who attended the farm school with me, my only constant companions were the Black children of our farm. There was one especially whom I still regard as a dear friend. (Or perhaps I should say that after many years we rediscovered our friendship.) Unfortunately I cannot refer to him by name here as the mere mention of it may create problems for him. For years we were, when I was not at school, always in each other's company. We roamed the farm together, we hunted meerkats and hares, raided birds' nests, modeled clay oxen and swam together; often I ate putu porridge with his family, from an iron pot in front of their red-clay hut. And never can I remember that the color of our skins affected our fun or our quarrels or our close friendship in any way. I don't think we were even aware of the fact that one of us was Black, the other White. Only later, when in my twelfth year I was sent away to boarding school in town, did I...

In my final year at university Bernard took me home with him for the Easter vacation. I have good reason to remember that fortnight! We went to the Free State by train, reviving memories from my earliest childhood: the smell of the green leather upholstery; the rattling on the door whenever the conductor or the waiter came on their rounds; lowering the narrow table over the tin wash basin to have a meal: slices of mutton, eggs, tomatoes, biltong, brown bread; the Jeyes' Fluid in the toilet. Upon our departure Bernard had a stomach problem and at the very last minute he had to run off to the station toilet. I was scared he'd miss the train. When he reappeared in the nick of time, I couldn't understand why he was grinning so broadly.

"What's so funny?" I asked as I gave him a hand to board the moving train.

"Just had the most expensive shit of my life," he said.

It appeared that he'd been in such a hurry entering the toilet that there hadn't been any time for looking round; only after he'd finished did he discover the total absence of paper. The only solution was his check book. And being Bernard, he first wrote out three checks for one thousand pounds each before using them.

The stomach complaint was referred to again on the journey, in the course of an argument on religion (which had just begun to become problematic to me). When he grew tired of it, Bernard stretched himself out on the upper bunk and said, smiling: "Even when it comes to religion you mustn't forget what Sartre said about thinking and experiencing things *in situation*. I mean, one's concept of the hereafter is influenced to a large extent by the condition of one's stomach. If I had too many prickly pears, or if I'm forced to suddenly start writing out checks like this morning, I lose much of my certainty about what may happen after death."

At three or four o'clock in the morning we were bundled out of our compartment by the conductor who'd promised to wake us in time and then overslept himself. Before we properly knew what had hit us, we were standing on a dark platform in our pajamas, clutching the suitcases the old man was heaving through the window, his bald head glaring through sparse but tousled grey hair (he hadn't even had time to put on his cap). While I was still trying to stack the luggage, the whistle blew and the train pulled off into the night.

It wasn't even a proper station, just a siding in the veld. A patch of tarred platform; a narrow red-brick building with a row of empty fire buckets on the side; a small waiting room with two brown benches and an old-fashioned black stove; a *Ladies* and *Gents* to the left, under a pepper tree; and on the other side of the tracks a corrugated iron structure for Blacks.

There was nobody to meet us, not even a station foreman. A postbag flung from the train was lying limply at the far end of the platform. Close by stood a row of milk cans, probably awaiting the arrival of a goods train.

We dressed in the waiting room—not without some hilarity when we found that one of Bernard's shoes had remained on the train. Giving the foul-smelling toilets a wide berth to have a pee under the pepper tree, we went round the station building and installed ourselves on the front step.

There is something incredibly serene about such a night. (I'm beginning to discover why writers are seduced by scenes like this.) We'd shed the last lingering drowsiness of sleep; we were out of reach of the toilet's fishy stench; the rumbling of the train had died down in the distance. It was very quiet, except for an occasional rustling of wind in the frayed branches of the tree; cocks crowing sporadically; a dog barking. The stars appeared incredibly large, as if they were so low one could pluck them from the sky. The village, Bernard had said, was at least two miles away, hidden by a row of hills. There wasn't the slightest hint of a light to be seen. Nothing at all.

We didn't speak. After a long time—perhaps it was only fifteen minutes or so, but it felt much longer—a light appeared in the distance; after a while a spluttering, chattering sound could be heard.

"Must be Pa coming to fetch us," said Bernard.

An ancient upright Austin stopped beside us and the engine was left running as the driver got out. A tall, impressive old man, much older than I'd expected, possibly seventy, with a wild mane of grey hair, a pipe clenched between his strong teeth, a face covered with a cobweb of wrinkles caused by worry and laughter, and two amazingly youthful eyes which appeared to be staring right through one.

"Well!" he said after he'd examined me in silence for some time. "Where were you hatched?"

"This is Martin Mynhardt, Pa," said Bernard. "I wrote you all about him."

"You only said you were bringing a friend home for the vac. And with you one never knows whether that means male or female." Turning his eyes back on me: "Looks all right to me, but one can't be sure these days. Anyway, hop in, let's go."

Gnashing the gears he pulled away at great speed. Most of the way he drove on the wrong side of the road (thank God it was too early for traffic), while he carried on an interminable inquisition at the top of his voice, to make himself heard above the noise of the car.

"What you doing for a life?"

"I'm in my final LL.B. year, Uncle Ben."

"Hm. Another law man. Another farm down the drain."

"I don't understand."

"You all going off to the cities looking for money and fun and tail, leaving the farms to the Devil."

"I'm not just leaving the farm," interrupted Bernard. "Sis and her husband are going to take over, aren't they?"

"What's the use?" He spat through his open window, spraying me on the back seat. "Nothing wrong with that husband she's married, but he isn't a Franken."

I soon discovered that the old man really felt very proud of his rebel son; and, much to Bernard's annoyance, his mother couldn't stop talking about his achievements at school and university, proudly showing me, in spite of his angry protestations, all the framed diplomas which she'd hung on her bedroom wall.

The cocks were crowing more persistently when we reached the farm and drove recklessly round the house accompanied by a pack of yapping dogs and just missing a broken-down old wagon in the backyard. The gauze door slammed like a gunshot as a tiny old lady emerged from the kitchen carrying a gas lamp in one hand. She kissed her husband; then Bernard picked her up in his arms as if she were a little girl.

"Not in front of people, Bernard!" she protested, embarrassed and panting.

"It's not people, Mum, it's only Martin."

"Hello, Martin. We've been waiting a long time to meet the boy Bernard keeps on writing about. Come in, you must be thirsty. Coffee is waiting."

Coffee and rusks at the scrubbed table in the kitchen, in front of the black stove which, even at that ungodly hour, was already blazing like a furnace, while three or four Black women moved about soundlessly on their bare feet, like cats, stoking the fire and scrubbing and topping up the water pail. The old man wanted us to go out with him straight away, but Bernard's mother objected. Frail and mild as she appeared, I soon discovered that she ruled her household, including her husband, with an iron hand. In the unfamiliar night, where I still felt lost ever since I'd been bundled out of the train, she led us through the back door to the outbuilding where Bernard's room had been prepared for us. Strange how vividly it all comes back to me now. The two iron bedsteads covered with crocheted spreads; the porcelain pitcher and basin on a washing table behind the door; the soap dish decorated with violets; the smooth dung floor cool under one's feet; flypaper against the doorframe. The walls were covered with model airplanes and a few cars skillfully fashioned out of wire; there was a collection of stones and skulls on a long shelf (birds and hares, a monkey, sheep, a horse): the room of the boy Bernard, obviously untouched through the years. A cool night breeze blew through the room from the gauzed window to the wide-open door; on the threshold a fat farm dog flopped down and, sighing deeply, went to sleep; outside, shattering the silence, the cocks were crowing.

That is what I remember most readily: the way in which, in front of my very eyes, Bernard changed into a boy again. The brilliant lecturer, the persuasive orator, the nimble dancer, the irresistible ladies' man: all of that was suddenly, disarmingly, reduced to dutiful son: *Yes, Pa, yes, Mum. All right, Pa. I agree, Pa.*

Especially during the Easter weekend I continued to be amazed and even startled by it. At university I'd become accustomed to see him as the relentless opponent of Christianity, the Church and everything smacking of tradition: he had been the one, in fact, to first sow the seeds of doubt in me. But back on the farm he submitted obediently to the routine of his parents: morning prayers, evening prayers—reading from his father's Dutch Bible, singing, kneeling at the *riempie* chairs until one's knees were aching—saying grace at mealtime: he regularly took his turn, praying like a clergyman. Over the weekend we attended each one of a seemingly endless series of church services. We drove in to town on the Thursday afternoon (still on the wrong side of the road: but the inhabitants of the district all seemed to be used to it, giving the old man a wide berth as soon as they saw him coming—even if it meant driving through the veld). Early that morning a foreman had been sent in with a trailer loaded with produce for the Co-op, taking with him a small army of servants to air and clean up the family's town house for the occasion; and by the time we arrived in the afternoon, everything was ready. Most of the servants were transported back to the farm by the foreman, leaving only two to look after us. The next day the church took over. Morning service on Good Friday. Two preparatory services on Saturday. Morning and evening on Sunday (missing only the children's service in the afternoon). That left us with Monday morning's exuberant sports meeting on the square before, saturated by religion, we returned to the farm. And Bernard took it all without a hint of protest or embarrassment. In fact, when I glanced at him in church from time to time, he sat there with as pious an expression as any deacon.

To me the weekend was the beginning of something quite different. I first noticed the girl on Sunday morning, and immediately scolded myself for not having been more observant during the services on the previous days. Tall, darkish blonde, her head held erect in an attitude both of independence and defiance. And as I sat gazing at her she looked back without flinching, such a cool and calculating stare that I dropped my hymn book; when I looked up after retrieving it her clear, steady eyes were still watching me, now, I thought, in irony. In the maddeningly slow motion of the throng following the service I lost her; and I felt so disappointed that I even snapped at Bernard when he innocently spoke to me. When I saw her again, at the sports meeting the next morning, I was overjoyed. Instead of the sober costume and gloves and wide-brimmed white hat she'd worn to church, she was barefoot now, in a summery dress. Seated on the log rigged up for the pillow fights she dislodged one opponent after the other with swift and deadly accurate blows, and her laughter could be heard to where I stood. Before I had time to react, Bernard had left my side and turned up beside her. The next moment he straddled the log opposite her. And in a second he sent her tumbling to the ground in a cloud of dust, her dress whirling, revealing for the briefest of moments her long, bare, tanned legs.

I could have expected it of Bernard. In games or courting he was as fast on the draw as any bloody cowboy from the West. And I knew immediately that, with him around, I stood no chance. But for once I was mistaken. He wasn't interested in this blonde girl—at least, not in the way I'd feared.

Just after he'd unseated her from the log he brought her up to me, her face still smudged with dust, a few strands of hair clinging wetly to her cheeks and temples.

"This is Martin," he said. "Elise."

"I saw you in church yesterday," I said.

"I remember, you dropped your hymn book. I was looking at Bernard when I saw you."

Bernard. Of course. Same old story. While in my state of elation the previous day I'd thought—

I tried to cover up by explaining limply: "I never expected a girl like you in a backwater like this."

"I thought you'd have met her in Stellenbosch," said Bernard.

"What are you doing in Stellenbosch?" I asked her, in surprise.

"Training College. I'm not as lucky as you are."

She'd wanted to go to university, I learned, but her father— none other than the vicar who'd dominated our weekend!—had objected: Stellenbosch was too far away and much too dangerous for an innocent young girl. When she insisted, he grudgingly relented, but on the condition that she only went to college, not to university.

"Aren't you coming round to our place, Bernard?" she asked after a while. It was obvious she had eyes only for him.

"We're off to the farm this afternoon," he said. "I come home so seldom that my folks insist on their pound of flesh."

"It's so boring in town," she complained with obvious disappointment. "There's just *nobody* to talk to."

"I'd bore you just as much," he teased her. "An old goat like me."

"You're not old! You're not even thirty yet!"

"In your eyes I must be positively hoary with age," he said, turning to me: "When her parents first arrived here she was only twelve or something. And I was twenty. She called me 'Uncle.'"

"I'm not twelve any more."

"You don't look much older."

"I'm nineteen."

Shrugging, he kissed her, like a brother, on the tip of her nose.

We still talked for a few minutes. When we said goodbye, she suggested, almost in exasperation: "Listen, Dad's going out to your place next Sunday for the service. Would you like me to come with him?"

"Fine," said Bernard. "We'll spread the carpet. Just wash your feet before you come." Pointing at her bare, dusty toes.

With that he shrugged her off. Perhaps it was in self-defense. For there was something quite shameless in the way the farmers' wives in the district found any conceivable pretext to bring their nubile daughters over to the farm while Bernard was there. Most of these daughters wouldn't survive closer scrutiny: even I, younger and more libidinous than Bernard, could see little hope for some of them. But there were others who were not only attractive, but ripe and more than ready to be bruised. Yet with superb diplomatic skill Bernard succeeded in getting through the ordeal without either giving offense or getting involved.

Elise came the next Sunday. The service was held in the large front room where some forty farmers from the outlying parts of the district were assembled. Afterwards we had coffee on the stoop and under the trees, while children ran havoc all over the place chasing chickens and pigs and dogs. Most of the visitors left after coffee; and when those who'd stayed for Sunday dinner had gone, Bernard's parents and the vicar and his wife turned in for an afternoon nap. The three of us remained on the stoop—without the devotional literature forced on us on Sunday in my childhood, but with the same feeling of drowsiness and boredom.

It was Bernard who finally suggested a stroll. We left our ties and jackets on the stoop; Elise kept on her hat as the sun was scorching, and she even retained her gloves in case it would upset her parents to see her without them. Lazily, with nothing much to talk about, we ambled through the farmyard in the April sun. The broken-down wagon, rusty ploughshares, unrecognizable parts of old engines, a meat safe with torn shreds of gauze still tacked to it, an upside-down wheelbarrow, everything strewn about in friendly confusion. In the barn we sat down on some lucerne bales, under hundreds of pigeons cooing and making love on lofty beams and ledges; outside, a hen was cackling behind some shrubs, and muscovy ducks waddled and hissed in a dirty puddle near the door. And all the time I remained disturbingly aware of her, so curiously out of place in her staid Sunday outfit.

We started out again, round the barn and the stable where the red mare stood looking out over the half-door, whinnying plaintively; past the cowshed, empty at this time of day and redolent of manure and hay, a row of upturned pails outside, waiting for the evening. Through the tatty orchard—it was a dry year—and past the row of pomegranates, down to the dam, an unsightly concrete structure below the windmill and surrounded by uneven patches of long green grass. We sat on the wall eating pomegranates, abandoning ourselves to the luxurious sun.

"Hell," said Bernard, "why didn't we bring our swimming gear with us?"

"It's Sunday," I reminded him.

"So what?" said Elise.

"But your father—"

"My father is enjoying the sleep of the just. And I can't see how a swim on a hot day can land one in hell."

Leaning over she scooped up a handful of water and watched it running glistening through her fingers. I look at her hand, smooth and wet, the long fingers, the delicate pattern of veins on the back.

"Do you always swim here?" she asked.

"Since I was a child," said Bernard. "My friends and I spent most of our summers down here."

"You're lucky," she said, almost wistfully. "If one grows up like me, all by oneself, with right and wrong spelled out on all sides—" She sucked some spilt pomegranate juice from her palm. "Even persuading my father to allow me to go to college was a major achievement. What does a girl want to do with education and all that crap?"

The word shocked me, coming from that lovely formal Sunday girl.

With a smile Bernard shook some pomegranate seeds into his hand and offered it to her: "Clean your mouth with this," he said.

She laughed, her cheeks still flushed with excitement; and holding his cupped hand in both of hers she ate up all the sweet red seeds, staining her lips. Then, jumping down from the wall, she kicked off her shoes. With that inimitably graceful gesture which comes naturally to women she put her hands up under her dress and stripped off her stockings, downward over pointed toes. I felt too self-conscious to look at either of them. (But I saw without looking.) Without any hurry or hesitation she took off her church hat, removed her bracelet, wristwatch and necklace, and turned her back to me.

"Will you undo the hook for me, please?"

My hands were dumb and fumbling. Still with her back to us, she peeled off the dress and kicked it from her feet; followed by her petticoat and suspenders. (God, the clothes girls wore those days!) I thought—and Bernard too, I'm sure—that she would keep on her underclothes. But as matter-of-factly as before, as if she were alone in a bathroom, she brought her hands up behind her smooth tanned back and unfastened the bra. She stepped out of her small white panties. Suddenly she was naked.

From the top of the wall she looked down to us. Sun on her high breasts.

Somehow we followed her example. I jumped in sideways, trying to hide my erection. Showing off like small boys we cavorted and played around for an hour and then began to mill around, embarrassed about getting out. Once again Elise took the lead. But she didn't run off to dress as I'd rather hoped she would. Wet and naked she sat on the edge of the warm concrete wall, her head thrown back to dry her hair and to relish the sun beating down on her upturned face. Bernard and I scrambled out on the opposite side and put on our clothes. With some pretext or other he disappeared into the orchard. I remained behind the wall, not sure about what to do next.

Then she called me: "Martin! Where are you?"

"Are you ready?" But when I came round the corner I stopped short. "Oh, I'm sorry. I thought you—"

"Like some pomegranate?"

"Thanks."

I went right up to her, until her knees, seated on the high wall as she was, were pressing against my chest. She held out a handful of seeds to me, just as Bernard had done with her before. (Was that her way of taking revenge on him?) Droplets of red juice ran down her wrist and spattered delicately on her full breasts. I ate from the cup of her hand, then, holding her wrist, impulsively kissed her palm. When I looked up she was watching me with the same imperturbable expression she'd had in church. This time, daring and defiant. I stared back: at her face, her breasts, her belly, and whatever could be seen in the shadow of her thighs.

"Never seen a girl before?"

From my throat came a croaking sound which meant: "Not one like you."

She shook her damp hair back over her shoulders, raising her face to the sun as before, impervious to my stare.

"I don't understand you, Elise."

"There's nothing to understand." Almost irritably she added: "Now go away, I want to get dressed."

She waited for me to go. I looked back once and saw her still sitting on the wall. Feigning lightheartedness, I waved. But she didn't respond.

When she was ready, we joined Bernard in the orchard and returned to the farmyard; he took us round to the back, where she could brush her hair in the bathroom before confronting her parents. And after some constructive conversation round the coffee table they went back to town, the boot of their car filled to capacity with carrots, mealies, cabbages and pumpkins, two chickens and half a slaughtered sheep. She kissed me when she left, her cool lips burning on mine until long after she'd gone.

In this dignified hotel room in London that distant day appears like an impossible mirage: the tall dark-blonde girl feeding me pomegranate seeds from her hand, unashamedly naked on the wall above me. And now my wife. Where, between then and now, did that girl disappear? Was it she who changed in the process, or I?

"Fallen for her, have you?" asked Bernard when we were lying in bed in his room that night, the heavy odor of the candle wax still lingering in the dark.

"She's fallen for *you*," I tried to defend myself.

"I told you I've known her since she was a knock-kneed child with freckles and buck teeth."

"Surely you can't think of her as a child any more!" The eyes, the breasts, that sly and secret mouth. "My God, she's beautiful. I couldn't believe my eyes this afternoon."

"I noticed." He chuckled in the dark. "If that old dam, hideous as it is, could speak! It knows more about me than my own parents. Ever since I was a small boy. Everything always seemed to happen on Sundays or holidays, when there were church meetings like today, or when neighbors came round. Dingaan's Days were the best of all. That's where I first discovered what a girl tasted like."

"Why aren't you interested in Elise?" I insisted. "If I were you I'd never leave her in peace."

He didn't answer.

"But of course," I said, feeling something grudging stir inside me, "you're spoilt by having all the women you want, I suppose."

"This is different," he said. "It's quite different. Nothing wrong with some mutual fun, provided neither is deceived in the process. But I know damned well if I started anything with Elise she'd take it seriously. She'll think I've fallen in love and all the rest. And then it becomes a way of committing murder. I just can't do it to her."

"Haven't you ever thought of getting married?" I asked.

"Of course. But I have no wish to become domesticated too soon."

"Is that all there is to it?"

He was silent for some time, before he said: "Look, marriage is marvelous for people who are prepared to become an indispensable habit to one another. If you're prepared to accept your mate as a key to your own existence. But I've still got too much which I can only do on my own. I simply can't limit my freedom of choice at this stage."

"You've got a larger range to choose from than anyone else I know."

He laughed. "That's not what I mean. I'm not talking about choosing a wife, but about one's *need* to choose from moment to moment as one goes on. The sort of choice which makes it worthwhile to go on living because you don't allow yourself to avoid or exclude anything beforehand."

"What has that got to do with marriage?"

"Well, if you get married you immediately exclude a whole series of choices because you assume responsibility for someone else's happiness. Then it becomes all too easy to avoid your other responsibilities by saying: Sorry, but I'm married, I've got a family, you can't expect me to do this or that."

"Suppose I told you," I said impulsively, "that I've decided I'm going to marry that girl?"

"You sure it isn't just your cock looking for a nest?"

"Bernard!" I sat up, scandalized. "How can you say that?"

"Because you're so bloody young and romantic. At your age it's natural to wrap your natural urges in a cloak of lofty ideals."

"I'm serious."

"She's a wild one, that child."

"I think I can tame her."

"I'm sure you can. You can also break in a horse. But then, what? Once you've had your way and the horse meekly accepts the saddle—perhaps the thing you miss most, then, is the very wildness you tamed. And once that's gone, it's gone."

"You're a pessimist."

"Or a realist," he said. "An idealistic realist."

He argued from the same point of view when, on one of our daily wanderings on the farm—in search of strayed sheep, or checking the jackal-proof fencing, or just exploring—I questioned him about his docile acceptance of his parents' religious obsession: why he, whom I knew to be so outspoken, lapsed so readily into the role of the obedient son in their presence, observing duties I knew he must find meaningless if not downright objectionable.

He merely shrugged. "Why shouldn't I ? You know how I feel about these things. And I never keep quiet about it when I'm with people one can argue with. But what's the use of hurting someone quite needlessly? They're my parents, they're old, I love them and respect them."

When it came to politics he did occasionally remonstrate with his father, but even then he never allowed a discussion to become too serious. Their most heated arguments had to do with Malan's persistent efforts to remove Coloreds from the common voters' roll.

"That's pure treachery," Bernard would say. "Isn't Malan the one who urged the Coloreds to vote Nationalist in the thirties because he said they were Afrikaners just like us? And then he calls himself a 'man of God'!"

The old man was irritable but couldn't really counter his son's accusations. "I admit there's a lot of sinfulness in our people," he said one evening after prayers (the Bible was still lying on the table, his folded gold-rimmed reading glasses on top of it). "We're just like the Jews, you see. I've often noticed the moment things go well with us, we get difficult. The Afrikaner has always been at his best in the wilderness, not beside the fleshpots of Egypt."

"So you agree one can't leave things as they are?"

"Of course we can't. But there's a right way to do a thing and then there's a wrong way. And it's not for us to turn against the leaders God gave us. If we pray as we should the Lord will provide."

"You had no qualms about sabotaging your own government during the war and going to concentration camp for it!" Bernard reminded him.

"I know, but that was because Jan Smuts had turned off the true way of the Boers to start a love affair with England."

"And suppose Malan also abandons the true way?"

"Don't talk nonsense, man!" said his father, pretending to be annoyed. Turning to me, he winked: "I don't know where this son of mine gets his stroppiness from. Been like that since he was a boy. You know, once, he was about eight or nine, he went for a swim one night, not knowing the dam was half empty. And when he dived in he struck the bottom and the piccanins who were with him pulled him out more dead than alive. He was ill for months. Half paralyzed and not right in his head. Then one day when I told him to do something for me he just looked up and said: 'I won't.' So I went to my wife and I said to her: 'Mum, you needn't worry any more. Bernard is all right for he's getting stroppy again.'"

Bernard grinned. But he was like a puppy who refused to let go once he'd got his teeth into something. "Don't avoid the issue, Dad," he said. "If it was right to turn against your government in wartime, it is right again now."

For a long time the old man just looked down on his large rough hands in the lamplight. Then, without raising his head, he said: "I won't say no and I won't say yes. For it's a deep thing which one can't solve with yes or no."

"When does one have right on one's side?" demanded Bernard.

"Why can't the two of you just leave it?" said the tiny old woman on the far side of the table, flicking her crochet needle. "We haven't even put away the Bible yet."

"I insist on an answer from Dad," said Bernard.

Uncle Ben looked up, his great grey mane wild and almost terrifying on his old lion's head. "The only answer I can give you, is this: one never knows in advance what road to take. All you can be sure of is that whatever road you take, you must be careful. And whatever you do, whether you get up or sit down on your arse, you place yourself in the hands of the living God."

His wife knew very shrewdly when an argument had gone far enough. Without the slightest faltering in the motion of her crochet needle, without even looking up, she called out in a voice out of all proportion with that frail body: "Rachel!" One of the three house servants appeared on the doorstep. "You may bring the evening coffee," said Aunt Lenie.

But Bernard was in a difficult mood. Unexpectedly he switched his attack to his mother. "Why can't you let the servants go home earlier at night?" he asked, staring sternly at her under the hanging lamp.

"They enjoy having their supper by the stove," she said, unruffled.

"And five o'clock tomorrow morning you expect them to start working again?"

"How else will you get your morning coffee?"

"I can make it myself."

"Don't be such a boil-in-the-arse, man," said his father, cleaning out the head of his pipe with a used match.

"There are some things we shouldn't tamper with," said Aunt Lenie, crocheting. "God brought us to a hard land where we must labor in the sweat of our brow. And then He gave us kaffirs to help us with our work."

"A hard land, all right," agreed the old man, stopping to blow through the stem of his pipe. "But we mustn't complain." His boy's eyes were watching me from under his broom-bush brows: "In the North-West where I grew up we really shat stones. I can remember one year it was so dry the sheep ate up all the soft rocks, leaving only the hardest ones."

"Now, Dad," said Aunt Lenie without much conviction.

"We still got a good life here, man," he went on. "There's only one thing you got to learn and that is you must take the Lord as you find Him. He's not the sort of man you can order about. If He wants you to suffer, you blerry well suffer. And if He decides to wash you away, it's a worse flood than the one that hit old Noah."

It really was a bad year. Several times, out in the veld, Bernard and I found sheep too weak to go on. Usually the Black laborers would load them on the truck and take them home to food and water; but sometimes it was too late and we had to cut their throats.

Most of the time it was good to be there, though. There was a quiet intimacy about our relationship. Eating, swimming, sleeping, wandering about. Occasional trips to the Co-op in town. From time to time neighbors arrived to talk "business" with Uncle Ben or just to share a cup of coffee: then the men would seat themselves on the stoop in a wide circle of pipe smoke and loud voices, while the womenfolk kept their distance inside the cool front room, in subdued conversation or eager listening, shuddering and swaying with laughter on their chairs whenever one of the men made a joke; interrupted by the soundless coming and going of barefoot kitchen maids serving coffee and fresh farm cream, and aniseed buns and rusks and milk-tarts and cakes.

The tone of our holidays was determined by our endless conversations, especially at night after the candle had been blown out. Discussions on religion and sex and politics, on the farm and university and the country and the world; and often on the future.

Bernard: "Right, so you're going overseas next year. But what are your plans for when you come back?"

"I don't even know yet for how long I'm going."

"Makes no difference. Sometime you'll be back, won't you?"

"Of course. I suppose I'll try for an academic job like yours."

"Don't be ridiculous. It's an artificial, claustrophobic existence."

"Why are you at university then?"

"I'm moving out at the end of the year," he said.

"You never told me that before!"

"I've only made a final decision during the past few days."

"Where are you going to?"

"To the Bar. As you know I've been defending cases in the Cape over the last few years. Now I'd like to have a go full time."

"Won't it mean sacrificing your security?"

"I can do without security. There are more important things."

"Like what?"

"Like getting involved in what's happening in the country. Before it changes into a sort of fate one has to endure without taking any responsibility for it."

"Things will change in due course, don't worry," I said.

His bed creaked; he probably sat up. "I wish one could be sure," he said. "But the sort of change we need in this country, going right down to the roots—I think of it the way I think of rain these days. Just rumors and no more." He was silent for a moment. "But of course," he added, "when it really starts raining it's like Pa said: a flood sweeping everything along with it."

Only later, when in my twelfth year I was sent away to boarding school in town, did I begin to react consciously to the difference between White and Black. Back on the farm during holidays my relationship with my erstwhile companions seemed to change automatically to that between master and subordinate. The only exception, up to a point, was the friend I referred to earlier; but even towards him I acted in a different manner. We no longer swam or played together. When we went hunting, he was my servant. Above all, I regarded myself as his teacher, conveying to him as much as I could of what Id learned at school during the term. Later my parents made arrangements with a missionary to have him sent to school and eventually to university. By that time he regarded me unequivocally as his master, and himself as the humble recipient of alms.

At university one of my first interests became a study of the theory of racial segregation, which at that stage appeared to me to provide the ideal solution to South Africa's problems. In due course I became the local chairman of the youth movement of the National Party. After obtaining my law degree I went to Holland for postgraduate research at the University of Leiden. There, for the first time in my life, I met Blacks on a basis of social equality. I had to sit down at table with them, something which, I found, required an enormous effort of will on my part. In fact, in the cultural and emotional sense, I believe it was the greatest shock I'd had to accommodate up to that point.

It forced me to spend many hours in thought trying to account for my strange revulsion. I remember how easy it had been to communicate with my boyhood friends. I'd never felt this embarrassment or resentment in their company. What became abundantly clear was that it was I and not the Black man who had changed; that I had developed an antagonism for which I could find no rational basis whatsoever.

I do not wish to burden the Court with personal reminiscences. But the outcome of my reflections in Europe was the beginning of a process which I had to see through to its logical conclusion—philosophically, morally and, in the final analysis, in practice.

4

THE WINDSCREEN WAS CLEAN and we were free to go. It was only half an hour's drive from Brandfort to Bloemfontein. From there it was five more hours to the farm, but knowing one had passed the halfway mark made it easier to accept the rest. Outside, the wind flattened the white grass to the ground; but inside it was warm and comfortable. The sun sank slowly, suggesting an infinite night ahead. Would the lights be working? For a moment I panicked and had to try the switch to make sure. It was still too light outside to notice the headlights, but the blue indicator on the dashboard was reassuring. Everything was under control after all.

As we drew closer to Bloemfontein the approaching traffic grew denser. And just after the Winburg road had joined ours—the way we would have come if I hadn't allowed the memories of Westonaria to distract me—the accident happened.

On a rise, soon after the single road had widened into a dual carriageway, a large, black, old-fashioned Chrysler came speeding towards us in the wrong lane. Like so many other times in my life I could see the disaster coming but was unable to do anything about it. There was a green sports car ahead of us. It missed the Chrysler by inches, swerving wildly, and disappeared over the hill, still zigzagging across the road. But the driver of the Chrysler lost control altogether, veered right off the road, struck a sandbank in the rough strip between the two carriageways, and started rolling, landing right in the way of an oncoming Volkswagen in the other road. With a curious impression of slow motion, bodies were flung from the Chrysler, landing in all sorts of contorted positions in and alongside the road.

"Jesus!" said Louis. "It's like that land mine we struck the day when—" He stopped.

"Bloody lot of Blacks again," I hissed through clenched teeth. "Might have expected it."

"Aren't you going to stop?"

"There's more than enough other cars on the road. If we stop now, it'll cost us another half an hour at least."

With the two wrecks out of sight, obscured by the hill behind us, the accident appeared as impossible and remote as the morning's suicide in the parking lot. Surely one *ought* to feel shocked. It seems to me, writing it down after so many months, that I'm shocked more deeply by it now than I was at the time. Then I kept my cool, as Louis would say; in fact, I was so concerned about making contact with him that the accident as such didn't upset me.

I remember saying something like: "You know, I have a philosophy about road accidents." Continuing, as he refrained from answering: "I mean, as a peculiar syndrome in the sort of society we have, where different races in various stages of development are forced to share the same space."

The sun was almost down by then, quite watery and weak; and traffic was increasing.

"I don't think your philosophy will bring those blokes back to life again," he suddenly said.

I turned my head to look at him, stung, but his face was expressionless.

"Can you tell me what earthly use it would have been for us to stop?" I asked angrily. "I can't wake up the dead and I know no first aid to help the injured. I didn't have anything to do with the bloody accident and I have no desire to gape at the misery of others. We would have been a nuisance to them, that's all."

"I didn't accuse you of anything, Dad," he said.

Ahead of us the monstrous concrete torch appeared, marking the entrance to Bloemfontein.

"Bernard would have stopped," Louis said, without looking in my direction: not challenging in any way, a mere statement of fact.

This time he really angered me. Not so much the remark as such (I can make allowances for youthful antagonism), as the familiar reference to his godfather. I'd been brought up to treat my elders with respect and I expected my children to do the same. I knew that he and Bernard had got very close during the years. Perhaps Bernard had used the relationship to compensate for the lack of a family of his own. At least twice a year Louis had spent his school holidays with Bernard in the Cape. Even so, it didn't give him the right to drop the "Uncle" in referring to him.

For the rest I had no quarrel with his statement. Sure, Bernard would have stopped. I don't think he ever missed an opportunity of getting involved in others' lives. What else did his whole career as an advocate come down to if not constant interference in the affairs of others? Not that I doubt for a moment the sincerity of his motives. But what did he get out of it in the final analysis?

It was this very tendency of his which first brought us together. (More than just a "tendency": it was as much a peculiarity of Bernard's to get involved with others as someone else might have big ears or bandy legs or moles.) It was after a weekend I'd spent in the Cedar Mountains with a girlfriend, early in my fourth year. Her name was Greta, and to her sex was as natural and as indispensable as water. She was my first proper lay; and with all the boundless enthusiasm of an explorer I became addicted to her the way others get hooked, as the phrase goes, on alcohol or drugs. Our weekend in the mountains was one long-drawn-out fuck (it's impossible to use euphemisms in connection with Greta) in all conceivable variations and postures and positions, in the cold of night and the heat of day, in rain which drenched us to the bone and sun which scalded the tenderest and most intimate spots of our bucking bodies. We returned in a state of total exhaustion, but it was worth it. Until the news leaked out a week later: then rustication, if not total expulsion, loomed.

Racked by worry and resentment and remorse (How could I face my parents? What was going to happen to my future? Why did the bloody little nympho broadcast it all over the place?) I neglected to hand in a major assignment to Bernard. After the lecture he asked me to stay behind.

"What's come over you, Mynhardt?" he asked. "I've never known you to do this before."

"I'm terribly sorry, Sir," I said. (By that time we were already on very good terms, but still formal.) "It really was—well, *vis major.*" I couldn't help grinning.

"Sounds interesting," he said. "But I doubt whether a court would accept it."

Without meaning to, I told him the whole story—or enough of it to give him a good idea of the gravity of my position.

"I see," he said at last. "Doesn't look good, does it? But I'll tell you what: if you promise to let me have that assignment by tomorrow I'll see what I can do."

"Hell, Sir!" I stammered. "I mean: thanks, Sir."

As I reached the door of the lecture room he said quietly: "Mynhardt, I'm not so much older than yourself. My name is Bernard."

"Yes, Sir."

The future still looked pretty bleak to me. Yet he managed to sort it out, with an ease—I should say a panache—which amazed me. I never found out exactly what he'd told the rector; all I knew was that I was let off with a severe reprimand and Greta was gated for a month.

Apart from anything else it cured me of Greta. I broke off the affair before she could land me in any further trouble. In any event, the self-assurance and technical know-how I'd acquired through her made it easy for me to pursue my explorations elsewhere.

As far as Bernard and I were concerned, the incident was the beginning of a lifelong—or nearly lifelong—friendship. How many times he got involved in similar situations with other people during the more than twenty years that followed, I don't know. I can specifically recall one very characteristic incident, about four years ago, when he was up North on one of his periodic visits. We'd just sat down to dinner one evening; it must have been about nine-thirty, and we had quite a collection of guests, all invited specially to meet Bernard. So I was annoyed when the commotion erupted in the backyard—doors slamming, followed by people shouting, screaming, cursing. It was before we'd acquired the Alsatians.

When I reached the back door the whole yard seemed to be overrun by police. A van and a car stood in the driveway, all doors ajar; from the servants' quarters a couple of constables appeared, dragging between them a struggling Black man, while one of our kitchen servants went on screaming and wailing until a Black policeman knocked her to the ground. Several others stood looking on.

"Good evening," I said, going nearer. "What is going on here?"

"This your place?" asked a young White officer, fiddling with his gun holster.

"Yes."

"Do you know this Kaffir?" He pushed the prisoner towards me.

"No," I said.

"We caught him in your yard."

The servant hurried towards me and grabbed my arm, sobbing hysterically: "He's my husband, Baas. He only came here to sleep with me."

"But you know it's against the law, Dora," I said.

"It's my husband, Baas!" she repeated blindly. "We were married by the *moruti.*"

"But it's against the law, Dora. He's not working in this area." I sighed, shaking my head, and turned back to the officer. "Well, I suppose that's that."

"Put him in the van," he ordered.

As they flung him into the back and slammed the metal doors shut, I discovered for the first time that Bernard had followed me outside.

"Just a moment," he said. "Isn't this a totally unnecessary thing you're doing?"

"The law's the law," insisted the sergeant.

"But there's no need to apply it in just this way, is there? The man is not a criminal. He didn't try to resist. So why rough him up?"

"Look here," the officer exploded, touching his holster again. "If you don't watch out I'll arrest you for interfering with the law, hey?"

"That'll be the last time you try to throw your weight around," Bernard said frostily. "I think I know the law a bit better than you do."

I could see trouble brewing: a few of the other White constables—none of them older than nineteen or twenty, it appeared—were edging nearer.

"Sergeant," I said hurriedly, "this man is an advocate. He's just trying to make it easier for all of you."

"You can come round to the station in the morning if you got anything to say," he replied scowling, turning away from us. "We're off now."

"Which station?" asked Bernard.

For a moment it seemed as if the officer wasn't going to answer. Then he said: "Randburg," and started revving the engine.

"See you there," said Bernard. He looked at me. "May we use your car? Dora, you come with us."

With a roar, tires squealing, the car and the van drove off, nearly taking one of my gateposts with them. All of a sudden it was quiet again. One could even hear the crickets in the garden.

"There's no sense in following them, Bernard," I said. "There's nothing we can do now which can't wait for tomorrow. Whether you like it or not, he did commit an offense."

"There's no reason why he can't be let out on bail tonight," he said.

Some of the other male guests were calling from the kitchen door to find out what was happening; behind them the women stood in a small nervous crowd, several of them clutching their glasses.

"We can't leave the party like this," I remonstrated with Bernard. "They've all been invited specially to meet you."

"They can wait a while." He went back to the kitchen and spoke to Elise for a moment, giving her a playful kiss before he returned to me. "Won't be long," he called over his shoulder to the assembled guests.

There was no sign of the van or the car when we reached the police station. Bernard, who'd memorized one of the registration numbers, went inside to make sure the vehicles really operated from that particular station. While I remained behind the steering wheel, listening to the small sobbing noises Dora made from time to time, he walked to and fro in front of the station's blue light, ten yards left, ten yards right. After half an hour there still was no sign of the van.

"Let's go," I said. "Look at the time."

But when Bernard had set his mind on something nothing would get him off it. He went into the charge office again. From what I heard later he insisted on speaking to the station commander on the telephone, and got permission to have the van recalled by radio. When it finally turned up and the prisoner was taken from the back, it was obvious at a mere glance that he'd been severely beaten up since we'd last seen him. Bernard was furious. When he was really angry, like that night, his self-control was quite formidable. With cool, quiet efficiency he telephoned the home of the station commander once again to report the matter; fifteen minutes later the officer arrived. Bail was arranged for the prisoner and a charge of assault was laid against the sergeant and his accomplices. Afterwards, Bernard insisted on driving Dora's husband to the district surgeon for a thorough medical examination and a signed report.

It was past midnight when we got home. All the guests had gone. Surrounded by empty glasses and dirty ashtrays and plates littered with bones and other remains, Elise was waiting for us. She didn't say anything in reproach; she even offered me her cheek for a kiss, her mouth taut in a weary functional smile. But I could see that she was mad at us. If Bernard hadn't been there she would probably have gone on nagging for hours to come. (But then, if he hadn't been there, nothing would have happened to start with.)

"Sorry, my girl," he said. "You know I hate doing this to you. But it's a matter of priorities." He poured himself a cognac from my cabinet and slumped into one of the large easy chairs. I recalled that he'd told me earlier he still had to prepare for the next day's court hearing; but I was too angry to care.

"To hell with your priorities!" I said, pouring myself a drink too; whisky. "All you did was to bugger up the whole evening for everybody."

"At least I got the man out on bail before they could beat him up any further," he said.

"Do you think they would have beaten him in the first place if you hadn't taunted them? That's all this sort of confrontation invariably leads to. All for the sake of soothing your conscience."

He said nothing. He merely sat there, watching me with a hint of a smile over his glass; both of us were too tired to argue. I can't remember what happened about the case later. I presume he proved his point. To what use? As far as I was concerned, at least I did something practical: at the end of the month I asked Dora to go, to avoid a recurrence of that sort of incident; and I bought the two Alsatians.

There is no letup in the London winter. Nothing to lure me outside or to influence me in here, so I can go on writing undisturbed. It's incredible, the things that come back to one once you abandon yourself to it like this—things you never even knew you remembered. In a way it's made easier by the game I'm playing with myself, half cynically, half in amusement: pretending this really is the "novel" I've always planned to embark on. It helps me to observe myself as an outsider. Objectively.

I'm trying not to judge or even to interpret too much at this early stage. My main concern, right now, is to get it all out of my system. Could it be argued that, like Pilate, I'm trying to wash my hands? Possibly. But I have no illusions about it at all. Years ago Elise's father and I had many arguments about it. Under normal circumstances I suppose I had a sneaking respect for the old man; however conservative and narrow-minded he could be ("Inside these walls, alone with Calvin and with God, I feel myself secure"), there was in him an essential and unmistakable humanity, a humility which couldn't but impress one. A man of love, one might call him.

As far as Pilate was concerned, he subscribed to the traditional view that the man was irredeemably guilty, something I have never been able to accept. I have just looked it up in the Gideonite Bible in my hotel room (St Matthew 27, St Mark 15, St Luke 23, St John 18 and 19) and I'm more convinced than ever that Pilate was completely justified in acting as he did in his particular circumstances.

What were those circumstances? The mob wanted Jesus dead; their leaders wanted him dead; He himself wanted to die in order to fulfill the prophecies. Pilate, knowing very well that the man was innocent, tried his best to save him. First he discussed the matter with the crowd; then he called in the accused, who told him that He had been born "to witness unto the truth." But when Pilate pressed Him to define what He meant by "truth," he received no answer.

So he came to a very sensible decision. He made it unequivocally clear to all concerned that he believed the man to be innocent. But because the circumstances demanded it, and because the crowd made it possible for him to comply by taking the blood upon themselves, he washed his hands calmly and fearlessly and gave the prisoner up to them.

To my mind it is the action of a reasonable man who has a clear view of the demands of his time and who refuses to be influenced by irrational considerations. Let us reflect for a moment on what would have happened if, as a matter of principle, Pilate had decided to protect Jesus. In all probability it would have meant his own downfall. Moreover, he would neither have saved anyone in the process nor done anyone a favor—because Jesus himself *wanted* to be convicted. He made a clear decision: one can have no doubt about the fact that he both despised the mob and believed in the innocence of Jesus. But at the same time he was sensible enough, having spoken out against the situation, not to be broken by it. I even find a measure of greatness in such a mind.

However, I want to make it quite clear that at that particular stage, during my studies abroad and for a considerable period after my return, I harbored no doubts about the system as such, the grand concept, the philosophy of apartheid. I still regarded the flaws as the unfortunate result of questionable implementation or excessive bureaucracy.

The gradual process of change within me was influenced by numerous factors and individual incidents and although I have no intention of providing the full catalogue I must beg the Court's indulgence for at least a summary of it and an indication of some of the more important moments from it, as I regard it as an indispensable part of my motivation.

Even on the boat on my way back to South Africa I encountered problematic situations. In this respect I must refer particularly to two friends I made during the voyage. The first was a young Indian doctor on his way back to Durban with his family after specializing in Edinburgh for several years. His name was Mewa Patel, and he was one of the most civilized people I have ever had the privilege to know. He is, of course, no stranger to this Court. On the voyage we spent much time together. Most of our discussions had to do with music in which we were both passionately interested; often we also talked about our country, which we loved in equal measure. What upset me about our relationship was a very mundane, even sentimental, consideration. The fact that, upon our arrival in Cape Town, good friends as we were, we would not be allowed to have a meal or a cup of tea together in any hotel or restaurant. What was more, if I ever had a son and if he were to fall in love with Mewa's daughter (one of the prettiest and most delightful little children I had ever seen), he would be jailed for it. Such are the small personal, subjective experiences which may prompt a change in one's entire view of life.

The second person I referred to was a young historian, Dennis Hunt, on his way to take up an academic appointment in Cape Town after receiving his D.Litt. at Oxford. In spite of an English background he was a fervent Nationalist: he even reproached me at times for not feeling strongly enough about certain issues. Shortly after our return I saw him again, a broken man, shattered by the realities of apartheid. Abroad he'd been able to rationalize it, but back in South Africa no evasion was possible any longer. Still, he loved the country too much to consider leaving it. Over a period of two years I saw him decline to the brink of a nervous breakdown. One day he came to me and revealed in the strictest confidence that he'd been approached to join an underground organization; but opposed as he was to all forms of violence he'd refused. However, that had made him feel that he'd betrayed both Black and White, and he was bowed down by guilt and frustration.

Presumably because of his association with "undesirable" elements he was placed under banning orders soon after, and his passport was confiscated. I tried to encourage him, but found him much too depressed to listen to any reason. And a few months later he fled to Lesotho, then still the colony of Basutoland, where his nervous condition deteriorated. One day a trivial incident brought about the final collapse: he broke his glasses, without which he could barely see enough to find his way. There were no opticians in Maseru. He lacked the money to fly to London; and he couldn't travel to Bloemfontein for fear of being arrested when he crossed the border. As soon as I learned of his condition I wired him money for an air ticket to London. But it came too late. That very morning he'd committed suicide by jumping from a cliff. He'd always suffered from an acute fear of heights.

There were numerous other incidents which contributed to my change of heart. Especially since I'd started practicing as an advocate in Cape Town I had an opportunity of acquainting myself with the innermost forces at work in our society, in a way which appalled me. During my years of doubt the one certainty I'd been able to cling to had been, through the very nature of my work, my faith in the independence and the impartiality of our judiciary. I do not intend it as any reflection on this Court if I confess today that the erosion of this faith was one of the most shattering experiences of my life. It was not restricted to isolated incidents: what was brought home to me over several years was, quite simply, the fact that, through the nature of our framework of laws, the judiciary in this country did not function primarily as an instrument of justice any more but only as an extension of power. It was no longer merely the practice of apartheid I found dubious and, in fact, abhorrent, but the entire system itself and the very principles on which it is based.

I can remember some of the cases Bernard must have had in mind when he wrote that, and his reaction to them. The fact that they were mostly ordinary criminal cases—involving straight decisions of right or wrong, guilty or not guilty, on the basis of factual evidence, far removed from the dangerous grey area of political persuasion or attitude or interpretation—made it all the more agonizing and obvious to him. And I must place it on record that in many respects I shared, and still do, his sense of outrage. The difference between us lies in the consequences we allowed our indignation. In his case the trials involved became, as he pointed out in court, factors contributing to his final decision in favor of active resistance. Whereas I, on the other hand, continue to believe that there are other channels for action available to one, aimed at a peaceful evolution from the inside of the system, as opposed to dramatic confrontation which can only lead to dangerous polarization and destructive conflict.

There were, for example, cases of rape and immorality, a few of which I may summarize here, chosen at random from several he discussed with me over the years. Right in the beginning of his career he acted *pro Deo* for a Colored who'd attacked a young White couple while they were making love in a car on Signal Hill one night. I believe he knocked the man unconscious with a length of lead piping or something, then dragged the girl into the bushes where he raped her repeatedly. Bernard produced psychiatric and social welfare evidence to explain the wretched circumstances in which the accused had found himself; in addition, if I remember correctly, he revealed a motive of vengeance, showing that the girl's father had sacked him and given him a severe beating the previous week. In spite of this the man was sentenced to death.

A year or so later Bernard was asked to defend a White man, a wine farmer from Paarl, who'd summoned a ten-year-old Colored girl to his house one Sunday morning when his wife had been away, and raped her. When she started screaming he broke her jaw. The case was postponed several times because the child had to spend months in hospital. When it finally came to court the farmer was given a suspended jail sentence and a fine of a few hundred pounds.

"All it proves is that you've become a much better advocate in the meantime," I told Bernard. "You know all the loopholes by now."

"How do you explain the fact that no White man has ever been hanged for raping a Black woman while the opposite happens all the time?"

"You must bear in mind the cultural and social differences at work in each case," I reminded him. "For a Black it means nothing to sit in jail for a year. For him it's a holiday with free food and lodging. In the case of a White even a few weeks can be traumatic."

"I'm talking about life and death!" he said. "And if you insist on social factors, fine. The other day I defended two people on an Immorality charge: not one of the disgusting run-of-the-mill little cases of a quickie in a garage or somewhere in the bush. This was a Colored teacher who'd had a relationship with a White secretary for over a year. If the law had allowed it, they would have got married."

"Why didn't they leave the country?" I asked.

"They did consider it for some time. In the end they realized they couldn't make a living anywhere else. They were too deeply attached to the only country they'd known from birth."

"In that case they went into it with their eyes open. So they had no reason to complain."

"They didn't complain. And they weren't ashamed to admit in court that they were in love. But when it came to the sentence, he got six months while hers was suspended. The judge found that she'd been punished enough already by the mere fact of becoming known to the public as a person who'd sunk so low as to sleep with a Colored." It took him a while to recompose himself before he added quietly: "When he came out of jail six months later they both committed suicide by gassing themselves in a car."

"You can't blame the court for that!"

"I only mentioned it as a piquant afterthought," he said. "Shall I tell you more?"

"Rather not."

"Hear no evil, see no evil!"

Much later, there was another trial in Johannesburg which upset him deeply. I must say, the whole thing struck me as an unfortunate and unnecessary mistake. (But surely not sufficient motivation for plunging the country into the chaos of revolution!) It had to do with a foreigner, an Italian if I'm not mistaken, who'd emigrated to the Transvaal shortly after the Anglo-Boer War, and married a Black woman a year or so after the Union had been formed in 1910. At the time such marriages were, of course, perfectly legal. Like other couples in the same position they settled in Sophiatown, where he stayed on after the death of his wife. When the suburb was declared White and the inhabitants were removed, he went to live with one of his daughters in another township; Albertsville, I believe. By that time the old man was already an invalid. A few years later, it must have been about '62, Albertsville was also proclaimed as a White area and the daughter, classified as a "Colored," was evicted from her home. The Resettlement Board, however, stipulated that the old man, then in his eighties and confined to bed, couldn't accompany her as he was White.

Bernard came to Johannesburg to handle the application for a court injunction. But before the end of the court hearing the old man died.

"So all your efforts have been useless," I told Bernard afterwards.

"My God, Martin! They knew he was old and sick. Couldn't they have waited just for a few months to let him die in peace?"

"I agree that the whole thing has been totally unnecessary and sordid. But you can't expect them to make a law covering every exception."

"How many hundreds and thousands of 'exceptions' do you think there are?" he asked angrily. "Whole societies uprooted and resettled. In this particular case we had the co-operation of the Afrikaans press, because it so happened the old man was White. But haven't you noticed the deafening silence about all the others who, unfortunately, are Black, which means they can't be measured in column-inches?"

At the time I thought of it only in terms of a difference of opinion in conversations, discussions, heated arguments. Only much later, the day he landed in court himself, did I discover, in retrospect, something of a consistently developing pattern, something "inevitable"—that is, seen from his point of view. Personally, I still feel convinced that it could have taken a different and more positive course, perhaps if he'd allowed himself to settle down and come to terms with himself and the world, relinquishing the unnecessary crusades; if, for instance, he'd submitted to the stability and discipline imposed by married life.

All right, I know he did get married in the end. But he was divorced after less than a year. In fact, it coincided with the case of the old Italian. But a marriage lasting only a few months is a far cry from getting settled. A pity. Because, in drawing up his balance sheet, the only finding one can come to now is of a tragic loss and an unnecessary waste.

There was another case I should perhaps refer to, one of the most sensational of his career. It involved a Cabinet Minister's son, accused of "salting" a newly opened mine in South-West Africa. I'd heard about it long before the news became public, because at one stage I'd also been interested in the mine in question. So I knew about the tremendous pressure exerted behind the screens to keep the case out of the courts. But after nearly a year of intense undercover activity the bombshell exploded (which confirms, doesn't it, the independence of our judiciary which Bernard so unfairly tried to implicate in his statement). When it became clear that nothing would keep the matter from being made public, Bernard was approached to defend the Minister's son. His first reaction was a point-blank refusal. I pride myself with contributing something to his final change of mind.

"The bastard is as guilty as hell," he said when the matter came up during one of his visits to us, late one night after Elise and the children had gone to bed.

"You've defended guilty bastards before now."

"Usually with good reason."

"Including that wine-farming rapist?"

"That was in the days when I had to gain as much experience as possible: and there's nothing quite as stimulating as a hopeless case. Perhaps there was the added challenge of trying to find at least something good in a man appearing so thoroughly evil. A question of morality."

"What's morality or immorality got to do with the law? Your duty as an advocate is to make a success, juridically speaking, of any case that comes your way. It's an intellectual exercise, like chess."

"Even so it remains my good right to choose whether I want to accept a brief or not."

"Suppose you manage to get your guilty bastard off the hook in such a way that it may later either help innocent victims or else make it possible for existing laws to be amended to eliminate present flaws? Don't you think that in itself may be a commendable achievement?"

Whatever his real reasons may have been, he finally accepted the brief and became responsible for one of the most brilliant performances in our judicial history. It seemed absolutely impossible to do something for the accused. Bernard did more than just that "something": in a dazzling display of juridical gymnastics he succeeded in getting the man acquitted—admittedly only on a series of esoteric technical points, but that was all that was required.

However, when I saw him a month after the trial, just after he'd been elevated to Senior Counsel (no doubt in recompense for his performance in that particular case), much to my surprise I found him in a deep depression.

"What's the matter?" I asked. "I expected to find you up in the clouds."

"Now you find me under a cloud." For a moment I recognized the old impish flickering in his eyes. Then he shook his head. "No, Martin. I'm afraid I've dirtied my hands with this sordid business. I feel a traitor."

"But you were brilliant!"

"If it had anything to do with brilliance it just confirmed what you said before: that the law is no more than a game of chess. And I'm sorry, that sort of academic exercise is not for me." He was too perturbed to sit down. After walking up and down for a while he turned back to me. "The worst of it all," he said, "is the sneaking suspicion that even if I'd fucked up the defense he would still have got off."

"But you *didn't* fuck it up."

"That's exactly why they'd hired me. They bargained on the fact that I'd be able to find some technical loopholes which could be used as an honorable excuse for an acquittal. And by accepting the brief I allowed myself to be prostituted." He stopped behind a chair opposite mine and leaned forward, clutching the back with his hands, his eyes burning into mine. "But I swear to God it won't ever happen again."

"Since when are you a God-fearing citizen again?"

For a moment he was off balance. With a brief flash of his boyish smile he corrected himself: "All right, then I swear to whomever may be present that every single brief I accept from now on will help me to strike a blow to the roots of their whole infernal system."

"'Their' system?"

"Yes, 'theirs.' I can no longer talk of 'ours.' I refuse to be associated any more with a nation that could devise a system like that with the simple, sordid aim of clinging to absolute power."

"So you're washing your hands of it all?"

"Certainly not." Once again he smiled. "On the contrary, I'm putting on my knuckle-dusters."

✧ ✧ ✧ ✧

Sharpeville and its immediate consequences also had a profound influence on my attitudes. My first reaction to the eruption of violence was emotional: a regime which depended for its survival on the massacre of peaceful demonstrators, including women and children, I thought, had no right to exist. By that time I was already firmly convinced that neither the Afrikaner nor any other group in the world could claim survival as a "right" on the basis of the simple argument that they existed. Survival had to be earned through the content and the quality of that existence.

After more reflection, I found I could argue more objectively: perhaps this terrible thing could still be atoned for in a way through the emergence of a new and humble discovery of the realities of the situation on the part of the authorities, and a sincere remorse for everything that had gone amiss.

Instead, a general state of emergency was declared, the ANC was declared illegal, over two thousand leaders were imprisoned and some ten thousand others were arrested.

This was the position when African leaders met in Pietermaritzburg in an all-in conference and decided to make one more peaceful call on the government to hold a convention, at least to discuss the constitution for the new Republic of South Africa, failing which there should be a three-day stay-at-home at the end of May. Again the appeal fell on deaf ears. Again instead of sympathy new oppressive legislation was passed, all gatherings were prohibited between 19 and 26 June; nationwide police raids were conducted; this time between eight and ten thousand Africans were detained, and the army staged demonstrations in the Black areas of our cities. In these circumstances a new era of violent resistance was born.

I want to say this about Sharpeville. It had a profoundly disturbing influence on me too, all the more so since I found myself on an extended business trip to Europe at the time. I was in London when the reports first hit the newsstands; I saw Trafalgar Square swarming with demonstrators. The situation seemed to grow worse from one edition of the papers to the next; it was as if South Africa was on the point of going up in flames.

There were some of my British acquaintances who said: "You can thank your lucky stars to have escaped the holocaust."

But my reaction was to suspend all my negotiations and take the first plane back home. Even if we had to go down, I thought, I had to be with my people in our shipwreck. It was one of the few wholly irrational decisions of my life. Yet I trust that in similar circumstances I will do so again. I hope so.

I don't mean to deny that there were serious wrongs in the system. But a government that yields to pressure in times like those, is asking for its own downfall. In any case I can't stand the attitude of people who, the moment things start going wrong, assume that all the blame must lie with us for the sole reason that we're White. This is an impression which can only be enhanced by starting to make concessions without proper reflection or restraint. Even if one gave the demonstrators everything they ask for at a given moment, they won't be satisfied, will they? It is imperative to first restore a context of law and order without which no natural progress is possible. And at that particular moment the only way of establishing law and order was by forceful action.

It pains me to think that Bernard couldn't see it like this. I can only assume that he'd never outgrown the romantic urge in him. But in a situation like ours there is no room for romanticism.

At the end of an exhausting court case in Johannesburg I drove an old

ANC leader to his house in Alexandria one night. On the way I propounded to him the well-worn theory that if you separate races you diminish the points at which friction between them may occur and hence ensure good relations. His answer was the essence of simplicity. If you place the races of one country in two camps, he said, and cut off contact between them, those in each camp begin to forget that those in the other are ordinary human beings; that each lives and laughs in the same way, that each experiences joy and sorrow, pride or humiliation, for the same reasons. Thereby each becomes suspicious of the other and each eventually fears the other, which is the basis of all racism.

He also asked: "How would Afrikaners react if ever my people were to say to them: 'From now on you may own land only in the Orange Free State, excluding the gold and coal mines in the area; if you go elsewhere in South Africa, where the majority of your people live and work, you must have a pass and stay out of our schools and universities and restaurants and theatres; you will be allowed to work in our industrial areas, provided you leave your families behind, you live in locations or in compounds, and you be excluded from performing skilled work, accepting that you are there on our sufferance only and that you can be sent back to your area whenever it suits us—'?"

5

SOON AFTER BLOEMFONTEIN THE SUN WENT DOWN; almost immediately it was dark, unrelieved by dusk.

"You hungry?" I asked Louis.

"Not really."

"Perhaps we can stop at a cafe in Aliwal North."

He nodded.

"I suppose you often went without food in Angola?"

"Sometimes."

I felt like taking him by the shoulders and shaking him to force some conversation from him. But it was no use. I had to find a way of gaining his confidence first. Would it help if I were to put my arm round him? (The last time such an idea had occurred to me was the rainy night with Bernard.) But with Louis it might have just the opposite reaction. I probably hadn't touched him, not even by accident, in years. For some reason I don't like physical contact with people. Women are an exception, of course. But only up to a point, really. When we're in bed it's all right; there I have no inhibitions at all. But once it's over I can't stand kissing and cuddling, or holding hands, or touching in any other way.

"At least we're past halfway now," I said.

"Yes."

Clenching my teeth, I looked at the clock on the dashboard. Three minutes to six. I switched on the radio. There was a silly piece of music. After a while it came to an end. The time signal. The dashboard clock was right, to the second, I noticed with satisfaction. The news, read by some young male voice thoroughly conscious of its own air of authority. New skirmishes in Beirut. The pound was down again. In the Pretoria Supreme Court Bernard Johannes Franken had been found guilty on twenty-three charges under the Terrorism Act and the Suppression of Communism Act, and had been sentenced to life imprisonment. In his verdict Mr. Justice Rossouw had pointed out that although the death penalty might have been appropriate in view of the gravity of the evidence—

Why had I switched it on in the first place? Perhaps just to make sure. One's sense of reality might have gone wrong or something. Now there really was no doubt. I switched off the radio and selected a cassette. Mozart. Ingrid Haebler.

Nkosi sikelel' iAfrika the moment after the sentence had been pronounced. That one moment, that one strange moment of utter astonishment in court as if a spell had been cast—only Bernard stood smiling, curiously serene, as if he was the only one not involved in it all, or the only one who really grasped it all—before the orderlies and the police began to react and cleaned up the public galleries. Even then they continued to sing outside, in the large pillared entrance hall and on the wide stairs leading to the street, and on Church Square where they stood gathered in a solid mass round the statue of Paul Kruger; singing *Nkosi sikelel' iAfrika*.

As for those who gave evidence against me, including some whom I once knew as clients or as friends, I have no wish to blame or reproach them in any way. I do not know under what circumstances they were persuaded to turn against me. There are facts of which the State knows, in connection with methods of interrogation used by the Security Police on detainees, methods through which the human personality can be twisted and distorted; these facts bring shame to our country, and in the light of what is known about them this Court will be competent to reach its own conclusions on the reliability of the evidence thus obtained. I must specifically remind the Court of the suicide of one person who had been approached to give evidence against me, a man of whom no one who had ever known him would have believed that he would try to take his own life; and of two other serious attempted suicides among those witnesses who were finally called by the State. In circumstances like these I suggest that the administration of the law changes its character. It ceases to have integrity. It becomes an inquisition instead. It leads to the total extinction of dignity and freedom.

My Lord, even if you should decide to impose the death penalty on me, I shall not offer any plea in mitigation. What I have done I did in the full awareness of my responsibilities, for the sake of a freedom greater than that of one individual. I put my self into your hands. I have no fear either of the future or of death. And now nothing can impair my ultimate freedom.

There was certainly no lack, in his trial, of the sort of "drama" journalists flourish on. In order to put it into perspective I have to summarize part of Bernard's biography: the "public" part, that is, of which I had as superficial a knowledge as anyone else.

When Bernard had told me, that far-off night, that he was going to put on his knuckle-dusters, he obviously meant it. In his first political case—which must have been in 1965 or 1966—he appeared for some fourteen defendants accused of conspiracy against the State, planned sabotage and anti-White propaganda. It became one of those judicial marathons which eventually lasted for more than a year. (When it started, Bernard stayed with us; but in spite of all our protestations he insisted that he couldn't "impose" on us, and found himself a furnished apartment, the owner of which, a lecturer at Wits, had gone abroad for his sabbatical.) In the end all the accused were found not guilty. In judicial circles it was interpreted as a triumph for Bernard. (Beyond those circles his life was made more unpleasant: ever since the day of the verdict he would regularly find his car tires slashed or his windscreen shattered; his house in Tamboer's Kloof was burgled more than once; his front door was painted with hammer-and-sickle motifs; one night an incendiary bomb was hurled through his bedroom window, fortunately without causing much damage. Needless to say, nobody was ever arrested in connection with any of these events.)

Even so his success was short-lived, since within a fortnight all the accused were rounded up again, this time under the Ninety Days Act (only two of them, probably warned in the nick of time, managed to escape to Britain); and after innumerable delays they all reappeared in court on a variety of new charges.

Increasingly severe legislation made it more and more difficult for accused in political cases to be acquitted, yet Bernard, indefatigable and undaunted, continued to accept their briefs, often, I suspected, for the most trifling of fees. Most sensational of all was the so-called "Terrorism Trial" early in 1973, in which all seven of his clients, including the Dr. Mewa Patel to whom reference has already been made, were given life sentences. The fact that they escaped the gallows, must be ascribed in equal measure to Bernard's by then almost legendary brilliance in court and (even though he wouldn't agree with me) to the remarkable moderation of the South African judiciary.

At the time the full irony of that trial wasn't grasped by anyone apart from Bernard himself. I'm referring to the circumstance that, in point of fact, Bernard was not only their counsel in the case but their accomplice. More than that, he was their leader. This didn't become fully clear until the day he himself appeared in the dock, although there had been rumors to that effect ever since the shocking news had been broadcast in December 1974, namely that

Bernard and three other Capetonians had been detained in terms of Section 6 of the Terrorism Act.

To act as counsel to people involved in an underground struggle against the government was one thing; to indulge in criminal action oneself was something totally different. (Perhaps I should have expected it? In the course of that first conspiracy case he'd defended and won he'd once told me: "Do you know what I find most upsetting about the whole case, Martin? The fact that although all fourteen of the accused, Black, Brown and White alike, are South African there isn't a single Afrikaner among them—whereas it was the Afrikaners who set the first example of fighting for freedom and justice in this country. Sometimes I feel I can only regain my self-respect if one day, among the Smiths and the Weinsteins and the Moosas and the Tsabalalas, there also appears a Jan Venter in the dock." In the end, as it turned out, it wasn't Jan Venter but Bernard Franken.)

As if that first shock about his detention hadn't been enough, it was followed, less than a month later, in January 1975, by the news that Bernard had escaped, together with one of his co-detainees, a Colored named Ontong. Until that moment I'd continued to believe that his detention had been no more than a ghastly administrative error. But I knew he wouldn't have escaped without good reason.

The two others who'd originally been picked up with Bernard and Ontong were held in detention in spite of predictable protests by NUSAS, the Christian Institute and academics with too much time to spare. And as it invariably happens, the reason for their continued detention became obvious in the end: they were to give evidence against Bernard. In comparison with him they were only very small fry.

It took no less than thirteen months before Bernard was arrested again in February this year. In the interim, it was revealed later, he'd even spent a few months abroad. That really shook me. If a man wants to get out of the country, let him. It's bad enough. But then to return knowing he's bound to be arrested, is quite beyond me. It just makes no sense at all. It's madness.

Three others were arrested with Bernard, including the Colored Ontong who'd escaped with him. At last everything seemed to be in order and the trial was scheduled to open in the middle of May. But that was where the "drama" and the subplots started, as if the main intrigue wasn't enough.

Two days before the opening it was announced that Ontong (from the very nature of things a key witness, especially as far as the period of their escape was concerned) had attempted to commit suicide in his cell. And before the Court had been in session for a week a second witness tried to cut his wrists. Still, the trial went on. Some of Bernard's earlier "clients" were brought from prison to give evidence for the State; and what they had to say about his leading part in the conspiracy of '73 belonged to the most sensational material produced by the whole case. Even so, one of them nearly wrecked it all by beginning to falter in the course of his evidence, until he lost all control and started sobbing. The Court had to adjourn to the following day, when the man appeared more restrained. But when the judge began to question him on his personal feelings towards Bernard, he suddenly broke down completely. An unwholesome spectacle, as far as I could make out from the newspapers.

"I shit on this Court!" he shouted, or words to that effect. Continuing in the following vein: "I shit on the lot of you! I shit on the whole sordid system which forces one to turn against one's friends." Then, apparently, he turned to Bernard and cried out: "I respected that man, I worked with him, I loved him, I still honor him in my heart. But I can't take it any more. They promised me a remittance of my sentence if I testified against him. I didn't want to, but if I don't do it I'll go mad. It's two years now that I've been in solitary confinement. They know how to break one down, all right. They piss on your food and then force you to eat it. They force you to listen to the condemned men singing in the death-cell before they go up to the gallows..." And much more emotional nonsense to the same effect.

And then, of course, there was Dr. Mewa Patel, also called by the State against Bernard. Something truly sensational had been promised by the newspapers. But unexpectedly it misfired. The morning before Patel was to have been called, he jumped from the tenth story of the Security Police headquarters in Pretoria. In itself it was unpleasant enough, but then all sorts of complications arose out of the post-mortem. A journalist who'd seen the body immediately after the examination (but how was it possible?), alleged that he'd noticed all sorts of other wounds on Patel—burns and cuts—not consistent with a fall. The next thing, the district surgeon's report on the inquest disappeared miraculously from his files. Et cetera.

With all this fuss the trial soon became something of an international *cause célèbre*, and in its own way a unique case in our legal history. One can only hope that the press, especially abroad, will realize sooner or later how out of the ordinary it all was, so that it will not continue to be used as a standard for judging our entire system. For Bernard himself, the lawyer *par excellence*, it was no good advertisement. He deserved something more dignified.

In short, my Lord, there came a day when I could no longer tolerate that history in our country be kept in a straitjacket. It meant that I had to turn against my own people: those very Afrikaners who in the past had fought for their own freedom and who had now assumed for themselves the historical vocation to decide utterly the lives of others.

In order to survive in South Africa, I realize today, more than ever before, it is necessary to shut one's eyes and one's conscience: one has to learn not to feel or to think, else it will become unbearable. In other words, the paradox obtains that one should really learn not to live, in order to go on living. And how can that be worth anybody's while?

Still it can never be easy for the normal citizen of a State to break the law. He has an instinctive tendency to obey the rules of his society. If, in addition, he has been trained as a lawyer, as I have, his instincts are reinforced by his training. Only profound and compelling reasons can lead him to choose such a course.

I have never regarded it as sufficient motivation merely to experience a vague "dissatisfaction" with one's situation. One must be able to formulate very specifically both one's objections and one's remedies. That is what I propose to do now.

Cool and sparkling the Mozart effortlessly ran its intricate course. The E-flat major sonata. In a life as busy as mine I find that music is really the only pure form of escape. Often, when I arrive home late at night, too tired to think and even too tired for sleeping, the most effective cure is to withdraw into my study and listen to Mozart. Invariably, when Bernard was visiting up North, he and I would spend at least one night listening to music. It was like a conversation without words. By abandoning ourselves to the music, we seemed to enter into an intensely private and profound communication extending far beyond language. It might have been a subjective and illusory experience like so many others; but then at least it worked the same for both of us, judging by our reactions of complete relaxation and renewed mutual confidence afterwards. In that world of ordered sound everything else would become unreal: the house around us, the dark garden and the swimming pool and shrubs and lawns surrounded by walls, the distant city, the land, all the concentric circles of the outside world. In the music ancient systems and certainties were reaffirmed as slowly the thousand natural shocks ebbed away from us. Something comparable to the splendid seclusion I'm experiencing in London at the moment.

My favorite Mozart has always been the B-flat piano concerto, K.595, preferably the Schnabel version. Above all, I love the

Larghetto. Unfortunately I didn't have a cassette recording of it in the car that day we were traveling to the farm. It occurred to me to ask Louis to tape it for me from the record. After all, he never seemed to be doing anything except fooling around with his sound equipment all day. Elise had started complaining that he was driving her up the wall. I'd tended to regard it as the sort of exaggeration to be expected of a housewife, until, during my convalescence at home earlier this year, I'd discovered how bad it really was. He would occupy himself with his tapes, with or without earphones, literally from the moment he got up (which, admittedly, was seldom before ten or eleven in the morning) until past midnight. The music as such was insufferable enough—he could never have acquired such a disgusting taste in my house—but what made it even worse was that he never listened to anything all the way. Every few minutes he would switch over to another piece, and the moment the barbaric rhythm began to work up towards an explosion at full volume he would either wind back to an earlier recording or forward to the next. Presumably he was constantly recataloguing the full extent of his cacophonic collection, switching cataloguing systems from day to day so that he had to start again from the beginning all the time. And this went on, not for days on end, but for weeks, for months.

Until I found it impossible to bear for another moment, so that I had to give him a choice between sending me to my grave with another coronary, or stopping forthwith. That was when he started disappearing from home. For days on end there would be no trace of him. And it was useless to question him about it. He would only shrug. Which wasn't acceptable from a nineteen-year-old any more, good God.

So it might be a good opening gambit to ask him to record the Mozart for me as soon as we were home again. Perhaps it would even restore some good taste to him. Before Angola he had proved quite susceptible to decent music. Even he wouldn't be able to resist the *Larghetto,* I felt sure.

I can remember very clearly where I heard the B-minor concerto for the first time. (I keep on surprising myself with the memories I retrieve now that I've set the process in motion: it's like bubbles rising from the bottom of the sea and suddenly breaking on the surface in small explosions of shocking, clear reality.) It was the night in my last year at university, when I'd discovered Charl Kamfer's body on the carpet in his lounge, with the blue circle drawn round his navel: a final act of defiance, an absurd and undecipherable message.

I hadn't even known him particularly well (Bernard had introduced me to him the year before), just enough to feel a youthful sympathy for an obviously lonely and highly gifted artist. Perhaps it was his cynicism which fascinated me, the attraction of opposites. He was an artist whom I regarded, with naive admiration, as "brilliant." But after a few highly successful exhibitions in Cape Town and Johannesburg he suddenly decided that he'd had enough of it, and packed away his paints. From then on he devoted all his time to lecturing and drinking, doing an occasional magazine illustration on the side.

"What's this nonsense about looking for 'meaning' all the time?" he often asked me in his mocking, provocative way. "Any search for meaning in a country like this is pure escapism. What is 'meaning' really? It's fuck-all. It's packing your books into a briefcase, or eating a sandwich, or buying a bottle of ink, or walking on the beach, or killing a fly, or laughing at a drunk, or wanking off."

"But surely one can't just take things at face value," I protested heatedly. "There must be something more. One's got to *achieve* something."

"Jesus, you're still haunted by lofty ideals. What's 'achievement'? Let me tell you, buddy: Everything we do is just a way of marking time. There's no bloody difference, *essentially*, between, let's say, peeling a banana or making love."

There was an undoubted homosexual element in his attitude towards me, but he never referred to it openly, let alone try to impose anything on me. In the end he became one of the key "influences" of my study years—his fiercely negative attitude, his incisive cynicism, his near-ecstatic nihilism acting as a corrective to Bernard's enthusiasm and indestructible zest for life.

When I phoned him that night—a week after the Easter vacation on Bernard's farm—to ask whether I could come over, he sounded particularly aggressive: "What's suddenly driving you back to me?"

"I just felt like dropping in for some conversation."

"I thought you had other people to talk to nowadays."

"What do you mean, Charl?"

"Nothing." A short bitter chuckle. "I heard you were going round with the daughters of clergymen lately."

"Oh, Elise, you mean?" I felt embarrassed.

"Do you just read *Song of Songs* together or is she a good fuck?"

"Charl," I said, "if you'd rather I didn't come over tonight—"

"Of course you can come. By all means. I'll have a conversation piece ready for you."

When I reached his home, he had already bled to death.

I'd seen enough of death and accidents by then not to be shocked by his suicide as such, but it was the way he'd done it—that blue circle—and the deliberate timing of it, which really shattered me. In my consternation I went to Bernard for help. Late that night, after the police and the ambulance had come and gone after I'd given them my statement, he took me back to his rooms in an old house in the Lane. He made us coffee. And sometime in the course of the night he put the B-minor concerto on the record player. That was the first of our long series of wordless conversations through the years. And perhaps that was why the music acquired some special dimension ("meaning?") for me. Without any conscious decision it became "our" music. (After all, I was still in my Early Romantic Period.)

And then there was another night: a night I've never thought of consciously until this moment in my room in wintry London. Have I tried deliberately to suppress the memory? I doubt it, though. One must maintain one's perspective and I don't think it was really all that important.

It happened soon after the marathon "Conspiracy Trial" had opened in Johannesburg, when Bernard was still staying with us. Much to my relief, really, because it made things easier for me with Marlene.

There isn't much to be said about Marlene (even though I can recognize her possibilities as a character for a novel!): she isn't of any importance in her own right. There had been others before her, ever since a few months after Louis's birth; and even more since her. The first time something like that happens, it still has the charm of the "forbidden" about it. But it soon becomes habit, like anything else. As one grows older, it offers the added satisfaction of confirming your prowess and bolstering your ego. But ironically, of course, it also becomes more and more easy with time, so one shouldn't put too much store by what can be proved by it. It's just a matter of increasing opportunities and perfecting techniques. Perhaps it becomes part of one's lifestyle, just as it would be unthinkable not to have a swimming pool or not to order one's red wine directly from the estate. And it's all so predictable: middle-aged businessman impresses girl with his importance, status, self-assurance, offering a sense of security; girl opens legs; both feel content: she, because an important man has taken notice of her insignificant existence; he, because his virility has been confirmed by this triumph over an absent and invisible younger man.

Back to Marlene. Six months earlier she'd started working for me as a secretary. I hadn't expected her to last very long: although she was twenty-five or twenty-six she was still much too soft for our sort of work, going through life with an expression of vulnerability on her innocent dark-eyed face: "Please hurt me!" Exploiting it while maintaining the illusion of being all virginal innocence: the defense of a woman who'd grown up too puritanically to admit to herself that she was no more than a delightful little whore. In addition, I suppose, her sensitive soul thrived on guilt feelings. In practice, her type is the most deadly of all predators.

She soon began to confide in me, and as time went on her confessions became more intimate.

On her birthday, I presented her with an expensive negligee from Paris. (One of the advantages of my many trips abroad is that I can always bring back "exotic" gifts to store away for the right occasion.) Accepting her thank you kiss I held her for just a moment longer than might have been expected of a father. And the expression in her dark eyes made it obvious that the matter had been all but clinched.

We dined out of town that evening, and I plied her with an excess of imported wine. Driving through a night flickering with lights, her head resting on my shoulder, we returned to my apartment in Joubert Park. (Originally I'd acquired it for the use of important visiting clients, but gradually converted it to suit my own needs. Elise, of course, knew nothing of it.) And so to bed.

The only complication was that Marlene soon became overwhelmingly possessive about me—"Oh Martin, no man has ever made me feel so intensely!"—"I've never had a lover like you before, you're so considerate!"—"Oh Martin, Martin, Martin, I love you!"— Bloody little fool. The moment a woman tells you she loves you, it's time to clear out.

But back to the great seduction scene. It was midnight when I finally persuaded her to put on her clothes so that I could drive her back to her own place—in Craighall Park, fortunately, which was on my way home. In her small bachelor flat she started slobbering all over me again and I was drawn into a new bout of lovemaking. It was another hour before I'd finally cleansed myself of the last sticky traces of her passion and went home.

The city was camouflaged in shimmering lights, as ugly as a Christmas tree. As if all the murder and violence and treachery and exploitation and God knows what else was nothing but illusion. I looked forward to getting back home, to a quiet hour with Mozart in my study. Perhaps Bernard would still be awake to share it with me. A glass of whisky. Then sleep.

It was before we'd bought the dogs, and the gates stood open. I drove into the garage, switched off the lights and sat for a while with my head resting on my arms on the wheel. My fingers still bore, faintly, the scent of the secretions of her undying love.

After some time I locked the gates, swung the garage door shut, and went into the kitchen. The house was dark except for a single reading lamp in the study. With my jacket flung over my shoulder and my tie loosened I went towards it. As I reached the door I discovered for the first time that both Bernard and Elise were still awake; and together.

I don't mean to suggest for a moment that there was any hint of impropriety between them; nothing vaguely resembling the vulgarity of what Bernard once referred to as "fragrant delight." And yet there was much, much more involved than that.

Elise was sitting in one of the deep easy chairs, barefoot and in her dressing gown, her dark-blonde hair loose on her shoulders, the way she generally wore it at night when we went to bed, but never in the presence of others. Bernard had just returned from the drinks cabinet to hand her a glass of brandy. They were still in that position when I appeared in the doorway: he with the glass held out to her, her arm outstretched to take it, like that gesture of Michelangelo's God creating Adam. Her face was raised towards him, her profile turned to me. Her mouth; her eyes. He was looking down at her with a little smile. In taking the glass her fingers brushed his, but fleetingly, barely touching.

On the record player the Mozart was playing, turned down very low, but unmistakable. The *Larghetto*.

Bernard saw me first, and turned to me with a smile. Elise also looked up, and said:

"Oh, hello. You're back."

"Hello. Yes."

"Finished your work?"

"Not all of it, but quite a lot. These option reports are a tedious business."

I went towards her, possibly because Bernard was present, and kissed her lightly on the forehead; then turned to pour myself a drink. All the time she sat quite still.

There was no embarrassment, no suggestion that I was an impostor. And yet I knew, prompted as I was by that music, that something of inestimable importance had happened or was in the process of happening; expressed in that simple action of handing her the glass.

After a moment I went out for some ice. When I came back, Elise got up from her chair.

"Past my bedtime," she said.

"Why don't you stay?" I asked mechanically.

"No, I'm tired. I never thought it was so late already."

After she'd gone I noticed her glass of brandy still untouched on the armrest of her chair. It occurred to me to take it to her. But why should I?

Bernard had seated himself on a corner of the desk; I sank into the chair she'd just vacated, feeling the gentle warmth of her body still in it. Elise. My wife. There was something strange about the thought. An ambiguity. A feeling both of possession and of distance, weary remoteness.

We sat in silence through what remained of the Mozart. I kept thinking of that gesture, that handing over, that reaching out to accept, their faces turned to each other. What I felt inside me was, I think, a sense of loss, a sense of waste, a dullness I couldn't grasp.

But what had I lost? What had gone to waste? Not Elise: how could I lose what I'd never had? Bernard then? Because he'd betrayed the exclusiveness of "our" music? Utterly ridiculous. Yet there was something, just in the way those two lovely, lonely people had been together in the half-dark room, in the raising of her arm, as if she would have liked to ask for more than just a glass.

He took off the record and put it away and switched off the player.

"Suppose it's time for us, too," he said.

"Sorry I was so late."

"Doesn't matter. We kept each other company."

"Yes, I'm glad you did."

With his hand on the switch of the reading lamp he looked up at me and asked: "Are you two happy together, Martin?"

"Why do you ask?"

"I don't know. You don't have to answer."

"Yes. I think we're happy. You know how it is. I've got to spend more and more time on my work, so we don't see all that much of each other. But we get along well."

"I understand."

"You're just feeling depressed about your own marriage." (It was just after his divorce.) "You know, you've never yet told me what went wrong."

"Nothing went wrong." He smiled in the semidarkness beyond the spotlight of the lamp. "We still love each other."

"Why get divorced then?"

"Because I shouldn't have got married to start with. I have no right to impose my sort of life on a woman."

"What do you mean with 'your sort of life'? You're comfortably settled."

"That's not what I'm talking about." For a while he looked at me as if he couldn't make up his mind; then he said evasively: "Here I have to spend months away from home on a court case."

"You could have brought her with you."

He didn't answer. Was there more to it than he wanted to trust me with?

"In that case I don't understand why you got married."

"A moment of weakness. Perhaps because of this sudden panic which strikes one just before you turn forty: knowing half your life is behind you and you're still in search of something, still alone. But one can't cancel loneliness by clinging to someone else. In the end one's got to acknowledge that everybody is lonely. And if you won't accept it you're only kidding yourself."

Without waiting for an answer he turned off the light and went out into the dark passage ahead of me. At the far end the dim light from our bedroom lay on the floor like something spilled.

"Well, good night, Martin."

"Night, Bernard."

Elise was still awake, even after I'd spent a long time in the bath. I had hoped to find her asleep.

"I don't know how you manage it, working so late every night," she said in unexpected sympathy as I got into my bed, although I could see that she'd moved up to make room for me in hers.

"You know how it is with my sort of work. People come to me with new options every day, in search of backers; and it's always urgent, they must have an answer before Friday, before Monday, or whatever. I've got to take all the decisions personally. One never knows when the great break will come. And so all the routine work must stay over for after hours. Unless there are still submissions or geological reports waiting to be studied—"

"I wasn't reproaching you, Martin."

"But you do feel neglected, don't you?"

"Not really. At least Bernard is here now."

"Elise." I wasn't sure whether I should go on.

"What is it?"

"Nothing." I pulled the blankets over me. "Did the children go to bed without trouble?"

"Yes. Louis said he wanted to stay awake until you could come to read him a story. But then Bernard told him one."

"Good."

"Is that all you can say?"

"I don't understand." I looked at her hair shining in the light on the pillow (hand-embroidered, from Lisbon). "What were you really trying to say?"

"When?" she asked.

"I'm too tired to remember," I said. But after a while, pushing myself up on my elbows, I asked: "Elise, haven't you ever had any regrets?"

"About what?"

"I mean about long ago—that you and I—that Bernard hadn't—"

"I married you, didn't I? That's all there is to it."

Long after she'd gone to sleep I was still lying wide-awake. There wasn't the slightest sound anywhere in the house. I could hear her breathing. I thought of Marlene, nestling against me and nearly drifting off to sleep in my arms, mumbling funny, incoherent things when I'd tried to wake her up. The strange panic I feel when a woman holds on to me like that, all her dampness and her warmth imposed on me.

And once again I saw Bernard and Elise as I'd seen them from the door, in their unbearable isolation, surrounded by music. The expression on his face as he'd looked down at her. How would one describe it?—tenderness, gentleness? It was something else. A suggestion that he cared, that it mattered to him, that he was involved. For a moment I almost wished I could feel jealous; I tried to imagine wild, banal scenes, but found it beyond my reach. Not because I was exhausted by Marlene: just because I felt untouched by it, completely unconcerned. Perhaps I even felt relieved. Surely it was the best and the most dignified for all of us in the circumstances.

We'd all of us chosen freely, years ago. That free choice which Bernard regarded so highly. If they had made a mistake, they couldn't blame *me* for it. I'd never stopped them. No one could point a finger at me.

The next afternoon Bernard announced that he'd found a place to stay in town, which he felt would be more comfortable for all of us.

6

I N THE DARK, AS WE DROVE over the high metal bridge at Aliwal,
the river was invisible below us. Or whatever would be left of
a river in that drought—probably only a series of muddy
pools, green with slime among the sandbanks and stretches of rock
and piles of driftwood below the tall eroded banks. But twenty
years before, when Bernard and I had set out from there with our
rucksacks and our canoes on the three hundred or so miles
downstream to the Aughrabies Falls, the river had been swollen
and swift, overflowing its banks for miles on end. I suppose it was
asking for trouble, in a way it was defying death; but the impact of
what we discovered on that trip remains with me to this day,
undiminished after all these years. The lean, brown, sinewy back in
the canoe ahead of me, speeding into the rapids, the white waves
splashing over his blonde head; the canoe going into a slow deadly
spin approaching the core of the whirlpool; the sausages we
roasted and ate in silence afterwards. The sort of experience no
philosophy can grasp or express: one can only live through it and
carry the memory with one, deeper than consciousness or
conscience.

In a depressing, seedy cafe Louis and I sat down and ordered
something to eat. Outside, greasy papers were blown about in the
dusty wind. A lean dog trying to steal into the cafe was scared off by

the Portuguese behind the counter, interrupting for a moment a raging argument with his wife who bustled about in the kitchen on her slippered feet, warming up our stale pies and chips. In the background, Springbok Radio was belching and bellowing out an interminable series of "hits" accompanied by inane comment, while Louis sat opposite me keeping time with the music by tapping his fork on the side of a ketchup bottle.

"Grandma will have something ready for us when we get to the farm," I said aimlessly.

"What sort of food do they give one in jail?" he asked without warning.

"How should I know?" I tried to be light-hearted, but it merely sounded fatuous: "I've never been inside yet."

"How long is a life sentence really?" he asked.

"Exactly what it says: for however long you manage to keep alive."

"Will they send him to Robben Island?"

"I don't think so. As far as I know that's only for Blacks."

"They used to send lunatics there, didn't they? And lepers."

"What are you driving at?" I asked, annoyed.

"Nothing."

The cafe owner went on shouting what sounded like abuse, without moving his heavy torso propped up on his elbows on the counter; from the kitchen his wife shouted back; and all the time the radio went on playing at full volume on a shelf stacked with dusty chocolate boxes and cigarettes. Opposite the counter was a rickety construction with piles of magazines and newspapers, pockets of oranges, cabbages, cold drink boxes. The top shelf sported an assortment of decorated ashtrays, tiny three-legged copper pots, slabs of wood painted with aloes and huts, lamps made of antelope horns, and toys: cars and plastic balls and a few dolls, of the naked boy and girl variety, strips of plaster covering their "parts" in order not give offense to up-country customers.

"Why didn't you go down to see him after the sentence?" asked Louis. "I'm sure they would have allowed it."

"How do you know I was there?"

"I was there too," he said calmly.

"You?"

"I went every day."

"I never noticed you."

"You weren't looking at anybody."

"But you never told us."

"You never asked."

Automatically I thrust my hand in my pocket for my cigarettes, forgetting for a moment that I'd given up smoking. Doctor's orders.

"I can't understand why you went," I said.

"He's my godfather."

I remembered how Bernard had flown up to Johannesburg for the christening. So much trouble for something so unremarkable. But he'd taken his godfatherhood incredibly seriously. To him it had been of the greatest consequence, no mere formality.

"Suppose I never get married," he'd said, "then this ugly little bastard who looks just like his father may be the only child I'll ever have some sort of say over. Just you try to mess him up and see what happens!"

"Don't worry," I'd said playfully. "We'll raise him in the fear of the Lord."

"That's exactly what I'm scared of."

The woman appeared from the kitchen carrying our two plates in her hands, and left them on the counter for her sullen husband to serve us. As he moved about rearranging everything on our table, enveloping us in a strong smell of stale perspiration, I tried to break the uncomfortable silence by asking:

"Is the river empty at the moment?"

"Pardon?"

"Is there water in the river at the moment?"

He gave me a blank stare. "Yes, very good," he said and went off to the kitchen where a new row erupted.

"Why did you ask him about the river?" Louis looked at me in surprise.

"No reason, really." With a strange feeling of embarrassment I salted my unappetizing chips. He seemed to be waiting for an answer. I shrugged. "Years ago," I said, "before you were born, Uncle Bernard and I"—I stressed the *Uncle*—"took to the river here at Aliwal in two canoes. All the way down to Upington and beyond."

There had been something timeless about the voyage along that stretch of water between high banks, through a barren landscape untouched by man. Occasionally we'd passed the patchwork patterns of irrigated lands, but even those had appeared temporary, a coincidence which might be swept away by a mere shrug of nature. As we went on it became still more desolate, a vast bare expanse in which everything was reduced to the mere elements of earth and water and fire and air, and nothing besides—until at last, after Upington, one reached the fertile Old Testament valleys of Keimoes and Kakamas.

It was somewhere in that arid, empty region that, in a moment of folly and recklessness, I managed to get my canoe capsized in the rapids, losing all our provisions in the process. In the deep, swift, muddy water it was out of the question to try and retrieve anything.

"What are we going to do now?" I asked, panting, when I finally dragged my canoe out on the bank. "We've lost all our food."

"*You* lost it," he said smugly. "So you'd better find a solution."

"We're bound to reach a farm or a village farther on."

Suddenly he had one of his enthusiastic, if suspect, brainwaves.

"Perhaps it's a good thing it happened," he said, reflecting. "Now we can try to make do without all the easy remedies of civilized life. Let's see if we can survive on our own."

"We're too old for Boy Scout games," I said.

"It's no game, I assure you," he said. It was clear that he'd made up his mind. "It's self-preservation. We're getting much too soft, relying on all sorts of extraneous things to survive. This is our chance of finding out whether we can really survive as men."

We survived the rest of that day on no food at all. We even managed to struggle halfway through the following day. But by then it wasn't funny any more. On a few excruciating expeditions into the thirstland we found some melon-like objects, but we were too scared to try them in case they were poisonous. All we had to eat was some honey, when, armed with smoking branches, we robbed a bees' nest, collecting scores of stings. To crown it all, we both got sick of the honey. Which wasn't altogether my idea of a Return to the Good Earth. Hunger and stomach cramps soon got the better of all philosophy. Consequently, when at last we saw a farm in the distance on the afternoon of the second day, we steered to the bank and, without any discussion, headed for the greenery. On our way to the farmhouse we came upon some grazing cows. And, once again inspired by the concept of Harmony and Nature, Bernard approached the nearest animal, a vicious-looking creature with long horns and an udder like that of a pinup. Quoting Gandhi's immortal reference to the cow as "a poem of mercy," and coaxing her with gentle words, he crept right up to the cow. But as he went down on his knees beside her, she made a fierce, sweeping attack with her horns, missing him by inches, and went galloping off. Grimly determined not to be outwitted by a mere animal, Bernard followed in pursuit and managed to grab her by the tail. Whereupon the recently praised poem of mercy started bucking and cavorting, covering his arm, from shoulder to wrist, in shit.

On the far side of a cluster of bluegum trees we noticed something which looked like a dam, and headed for it. I didn't dare say a word; and Bernard was unusually quiet, too, as he walked on, his arm bent away from his body at an odd angle, as if he'd tried to fly and then changed his mind.

After he'd washed himself, we set out for the farmstead again in a rather more optimistic mood. If it hadn't been for a watermelon patch between us and the yard, the farmer might have welcomed us with a show of hospitality. But by that time we were so hungry that we stopped to pick a watermelon on the way. And while we were greedily gulping down the sweet red watery chunks, the farmer suddenly bellowed at us from a stone wall nearby, a gun in his hand.

As we reached the fringe of the orchard on the river side of the watermelon patch, we heard the first shot, followed by two more; but by that time we were out of reach among the trees. And long before the farmer could come down to the river—if he'd been interested in pursuing us at all—our canoes had rounded the first bend.

Late that afternoon, ashen with hunger and fatigue, we reached Upington and went to the nearest cafe for a meal. I was only too grateful that the whole episode had ended without mishap, but Bernard had no intention of leaving the matter at that.

"My God," he said, halfway through his mixed grill, "one can't just go about shooting people like that!"

"This is the Wild West, didn't you know?"

"I'm going to get even with that farmer."

"The first thing you lawyers can think about is running to court."

"Who said a word about court?" asked Bernard. And as the meal progressed and he grew more relaxed, he started improvising. By the time he was having his second parfait, in hideous shades of pink and green, he'd already coaxed the attractive but tarty waitress from behind the counter to join us. (There was nobody else in the cafe at that hour; not even the owner.) She was a farm girl who'd come to town in search of adventure, and had obviously gained too much experience too soon; under her flimsy cotton dress she smelled of Lifebuoy soap and eau de cologne. Bernard chatted her up until she was like clay in his hands, divulging whatever he wanted to know: that the man who'd shot at us was Gawie Groenewald, one of the more prosperous, if also more "difficult," farmers in the district, secretary of the local branch of the National Party, etc.

When Bernard Franken was on the offensive—whether in a court case or in more secular affairs like the present—he left no stone unturned in his efforts to gather whatever might be relevant to his cause. Once he felt sure he had the situation in hand, he got permission from the girl to use the cafe telephone, and asked for Uncle Gawie's number.

"Mr. Groenewald?" we heard him say after a while. "This is the Upington Police Station. Yes, good day. Mr. Groenewald, I'm afraid we've got some bad news for you. Did you by any chance fire shots at somebody on your farm earlier today?" A longish pause. "No, no, Mr. Groenewald, that I really don't know. All I know is that man has just brought a corpse in to us. Pardon? Yes, two gunshot wounds. Yes. That's right. No, we'll have to wait for the doctor's report. But in the meantime there's a charge of murder against you." Another pause, even longer than the first. "Yes, Mr. Groenewald. Yes, I appreciate that. But you must realize it's very serious indeed. So if you would be so kind as to come in to the station as soon as you can—" A pause. "Yes, it would be wise to bring some clothes with you. We'll probably have to keep you here over the weekend. All right then, Mr. Groenewald. See you."

Was Uncle Gawie Groenewald still alive? Sitting in the dingy little cafe in Aliwal, I wondered what his reaction would be if he discovered that the man so much in the news lately was the same fellow who'd given him the fright of his life all those years ago. Would he realize that it had arisen from the same source of energy, only channeled in a different direction? How could he ever hope to understand the Bernard who'd made the long statement from the dock?

There has always, since the early days of slavery, been racial discrimination in South Africa. I suppose, at the beginning, when people enjoying a more advanced civilization came into contact and intermingled with those not so fortunate, this was inevitable. Today we know, from experience in other parts of the world, that it is possible to grow away from such a situation, through a process of "civilization" and a sharing of privileges, provided those in power are prepared to devote sufficient resources to it and to make sacrifices for it.

But in South Africa the White rulers hesitated for 150 years, before they finally chose a road which led in an entirely opposite direction. To preserve "civilization" one would think it prudent to spread it as rapidly as possible. Instead, our rulers elected as far as possible to retain it as a White monopoly. Deliberately we chose the path of "segregation" which, whatever changing appellations we may give to it, is a policy intended to keep the Blacks in a state of permanent inferiority and subjection, which is a political strategy based on economic considerations.

Inevitably this has led to a strong and ever-growing movement for the liberation of Blacks, which is obvious to anyone whose vision is not totally obscured by the myopia of the White South African, and which is supported not only by the whole of Africa but by virtually the whole membership of the United Nations, both West and East. However powerful South Africa may be in military or economic terms (and recent events have proved the country to be more vulnerable than had been wishfully thought before), the present minority group cannot maintain its position of absolute power indefinitely in the face of the natural historic development of the country's own inhabitants. The sole questions for the future of all of us therefore are not whether a Black majority will take over or when it will happen, but only:

(a) whether the change can be brought about peacefully and without bloodshed; and

(b) what the position of the White man is going to be in the new dispensation, after the years of discrimination and oppression and humiliation which he has imposed on the Black peoples of this country.

In both respects the Afrikaner finds himself in a decisive role. It is he who is in power; which means that it is he who is blamed for the evils and the humiliation of apartheid. But it also means that he is in a position to negotiate a peaceful changeover, provided he is really sincere about it; he can eradicate such wrongs as may later give rise to a justified call for vengeance. In this situation it has become imperative for me to act as an Afrikaner.

In the present struggle the Black man in South Africa finds himself in a remarkable position. If it is true that it is essentially a struggle for freedom—not merely freedom from political or economic exploitation but the freedom to choose for oneself—then it should be seen in the context of those situations in which it becomes possible for some people to discover that their personal choice coincides of necessity with historical inevitability. The slave who, in the USA in the nineteenth century, became conscious of his situation, had no option but to make the choice he made: and yet there was no coercion involved, he made his choice freely and proudly, and accepted full responsibility for it. The same applies to the Jew revolting against the Nazis in the Second World War. And this situation obtains in South Africa today where the Black man is concerned. It has become part of his normal human condition to find himself in revolt against his White oppressor: and from this very necessity the freedom of his choice is born. All that remains to be done is to prove publicly that freedom which he has already discovered for himself.

As a White, as an Afrikaner, linked through the color of my skin, and through my culture and my language, to that group which is in power in this country, my choice is different. I am free to reap the fruit of my White superiority while it lasts. Or I may choose to do nothing at all. But a third course is open to me. And as a thinking and feeling man my only freedom today lies in renouncing, for the freedom of others, everything I might otherwise lay claim to, not through any merit on my part, but through the condition of my birth—which is the epitome of bondage. No man is so completely oppressed by the oppressor as himself.

What does this mean in practical terms?

At first I tried to find solutions by using every "correct channel" available to me, either in the course of my duties or through my access to politicians and others in key positions. I had, for example, many discussions with a Cabinet Minister whose son I had once defended in court. The only result was the kindly and well-meant advice to confine myself to my work and not to interfere with politics.

When I realized that within my career I could do no more than help certain individuals without effecting any essential change in the overall system, I had to take my choice one step further. And while continuing to practice as an advocate, soon after the so-called "Conspiracy Trial" of 1965-1966, I founded the organization INKULULEKO on which this Court has already heard sufficient evidence.

In the beginning I insisted on nonviolent procedures: establishing organizations to initiate a campaign similar to that of the conscientizaçao *in Brazil—realizing the effort required to first convey to the oppressed the notion of his oppression, counteracting as it were the conditioning not only of a lifetime but of an entire history.*

This was soon expanded to embrace a program of carefully controlled sabotage, isolating targets which would have an impact on the mind and the imagination, yet without any danger of causing injury or loss of life.

But I believe the distinction comfortably drawn between violence and nonviolence to be mainly an academic one. Once one has chosen to rise up against an oppressive establishment, one should also be prepared to go all the way—in direct equation with the increasing power and violence of your opponent. There was a time when our organization could foresee the possibility of effecting, by nonviolent methods, a meaningful change in the attitudes prevalent in this country. But the authorities decided to react with increasingly violent measures, creating less and less scope for the most ordinary expressions of opposition. The result was that in due course we in INKULULEKO reached the stage where we also had to provide for urban terrorism.

I realize only too well that by killing one policeman one cannot overthrow a system. But through his death one can demonstrate that justice is not the prerogative of officialdom. It has become imperative for small groups of highly organized men to keep alive in the minds of the people, through dangerous and daring acts, an outrageous thought: the idea that the system is vulnerable, that freedom exists, that justice can be implemented by the people. And so I gave my approval to those forms of violent action through which one can affirm one's freedom and prove one's solidarity with the oppressed masses.

I am not ashamed of it. Had I remained inert or silent, that inertia or silence would have implied a condonation of what was happening. That I couldn't accept for a moment. I still cannot, even though I realize you will win in the short run because you have enough brute force at your disposal. But in the end your system must crumble. For in order to cling to power permanently one would require what you lack: right on your side, and justice in your system.

Today I find a special meaning in the words of the great Afrikaner leader, President Paul Kruger, expressed in 1881 and now inscribed on the base of his statue on the square in front of this Court:

"With confidence we expose our cause to the whole world. Whether we triumph or die: freedom will rise in Africa like the sun from the morning clouds."

I have copied out the whole piece of ranting rhetoric, even though I feel that Bernard harmed his own cause by turning a courtroom into a political tribune for the expression of his cliches. I was thinking of his statement as Louis and I sat beside our little table in the cafe in Aliwal North: I would have liked to discuss it with him, but the old sullen expression on his face suggested that he was not prepared to pursue our conversation.

"Let's go," I proposed, pushing aside the last few greasy chips on my plate.

Without a word he went out ahead of me while I stopped to pay at the counter. The radio started blaring again, after a brief interlude. In a pram against the far wall a baby began to cry. We got away just in time. Ever since Louis had been born I'd found the noise of babies intolerable.

7

I T WAS JUST AFTER EIGHT when we set out on the hundred miles to Queenstown; even the lights of Jamestown, in between, could do nothing to alleviate the monotony of that dreary stretch. The moon rose, revealing in its sepulchral light the prehistoric skeletons of *koppies* and ridges and hills against the stars. Now everything was reduced to the glare of the headlights on the road before us. The rest did not concern us and could be denied, even though it continued to threaten one with its subliminal existence.

The last time I'd passed that way had been just after the first news of Dad's illness. For the funeral Elise and I had flown to East London, where we'd hired a car. I could have done the same that weekend; for such a brief visit it would have been much more practical than the exhausting car trip. "In my condition." But I needed the time to think; to come to terms with myself; or simply to get away.

Dad had died at the height of day, at one o'clock. Almost exactly one year before that weekend. Then, as now, it had been winter. And as we drove on it felt as if we were approaching the farm not only in space but also in time.

Always traveling, on one's way from somewhere to somewhere, in transit. Dad's illness had also been a journey away from us. I hadn't been there when he died, only at the funeral. But the last time I'd seen him before his death, I'd already had the impression of taking leave on a station or at an airport: seeing him surrounded by all who had been nearest to him, one nevertheless had the impression that nothing was intimate that everything had been reduced to the banality of small talk. Because the traveler had already disengaged himself from the present, projecting himself into a dimension of which we others could form no concept.

The previous time I'd been on the farm, just after news of his illness had reached us, had been a surprise. Expecting to find him weak and exhausted, I discovered in him a tranquility incomprehensible to me, as if infinite space had opened up behind his eyes. He had Suetonius beside his bed, in addition to a pile of other books—biographies, travel books, even novels; in his grey eyes was a light of keenness and enthusiasm. "Now at last," he said, "I have the time to catch up with everything I've ever wanted to read." He talked incessantly, not only about his well-worn hobby but about topics I'd never expected him to be interested in. He even spoke about his illness, without a hint of self-pity. And when I said goodbye, he took my hand and said calmly: "Well, Martin, in case I don't see you again, good luck to you."

But that final visit was different. By that time he was so riddled with cancer that he could think of nothing else. The radiation had caused him to lose all his hair, jaundice had turned his face and hands into parchment, his voice had become high and shrill, and halfway through a sentence he would forget what he'd wanted to say. His skull appeared shrunken and fragile like that of a bird.

His only interest, now, was his illness and the variety of medicines he had to take; broken down, through pain, to this concentration on the irrelevant and the trivial. The total indignity of suffering.

And then the distance between us, our absolute isolation. Even his hand, when I was forced to take it, wasn't like his at all: it was a confirmation of all that kept us apart rather than of what ought to bind us. Exactly the same feeling I had about Bernard in court. He, too, was on the point of departing. A life-long voyage;

as final as death. Only the formality of dying remained. And there, too, I would be absent.

Even from his own point of view it must have appeared entirely unnecessary. He could have stayed in England, couldn't he?

It was to keep faith with all those dispossessed by apartheid that I decided to escape from custody. There was still work to be done. Through my arrest the organization had been caught on the wrong foot and I had to make sure it could be placed on a new basis in order to continue even without me. I owed it not only to those individuals who had been collaborating with me and whose lives had been endangered by my arrest, but to all those who had been imprisoned, or banished, or silenced for their beliefs. It is not the escape of an individual which is important, but the demonstration to others that the system is not invincible. And once again I derived a particular sense of obligation from the very fact that I was an Afrikaner.

During one of the cases I defended in Johannesburg I used to drive out to Alexandra early every morning to help transport people boycotting the bus services after an unreasonable increase in tariffs. Several times I was stopped at police roadblocks and threatened with prosecution. In the end they did institute proceedings against me, but abandoned it before it came to court. However, my most important recollection of that experience is that, of all the people I picked up—people who'd set out to walk ten or fifteen miles to work, starting at four or five o'clock in the morning—not one would believe me when I told them I was an Afrikaner. In their minds "Afrikaner" and "apartheid" had become synonymous. It made me realize, more than ever before, the obligation placed upon me by being an Afrikaner myself: an obligation towards all those suffering as a result of laws made by my fellow Afrikaners.

My only regret in connection with my escape is that the two young warders who had helped Ontong and me to get away were themselves appre-hended. I can only hope that in the long run they will reap some reward for the price they have had to pay.

Basically the same reasons which had prompted my escape from custody were responsible for my return to the country in November 1975.

I could have elected to stay in London after completing the organizing work for which I had gone there. Many of my colleagues tried their best to persuade me to stay there. But how could I remain a passive spectator while others were suffering? I was fully aware of the risk involved. Even in spite of disguising myself as an old lady the Security Police were bound to rediscover my tracks sooner or later. But I had made up my mind many years ago, and all that remained to be done was for me to follow my chosen course to the end.

I must emphasize that I do not believe in martyrdom and have no sympathy with masochism. South Africa has had more than enough martyrs as it is. What I did was not influenced by a consideration of what might happen to me if I were caught: I did it precisely because it did not matter to me what the consequences would be for myself. Freedom is infinitely greater than the individuals devoted to its cause.

I believe in life. I regard myself as a happy man because I have never deprived myself of anything meaningful in life, endeavoring to live as fully as I could at any given moment. Also, I believe it is much better to live for a cause than to die for it. But by the time I returned from London death and life as such were not really relevant any more. All that mattered was that I had to do whatever I could while there was still time to do it. Knowing that even if I were caught there were others whom I could confidently trust to continue the struggle.

My sole regret is that I wasn't able to do even more. Perhaps my arrest could have been avoided at the time it happened. But it is so easy to misjudge a situation, or a trivial detail, or a friend.

(Was he looking up at me when he read those words? Had he noticed me in the audience? It must have been my imagination.)

In any case I bear no ill feelings to anyone, and I blame no one, whether friend or policeman. They all did what they regarded as their duty.

❖ ❖ ❖

It was the news about Bernard which, in retrospect, brought that tedious evening into such startling perspective. If it hadn't been for that, I would probably never even have remembered it again. As it is, I find the memory obsessive.

I have never felt quite sure about my feelings towards Professor John Pienaar. In my student days I admired him, which was the obvious reaction of a young aspiring writer to the first live poet he'd ever met. At the same time I felt inhibited by his overbearing personality, aggravated by the suspicion that he and his wife had chosen me as a possible husband for their bespectacled, brilliant daughter Pippa (named after Browning's poem). Flattered as I was by regular invitations to meals in the home of the great man, I was wary about his real motives and about the daughter with her shapeless figure and astounding intellect. After Pippa had passed away on the slopes of the Jonkershoek Mountains (we'd all tried our best to dissuade her from coming, but she'd insisted: "You'll be there to give me a hand, won't you, Martin?"), the professorial couple remained devoted to me; while, from all the walls of the house, poor Pippa's beady eyes kept watching one through the fat lenses of her spectacles.

As Pienaar slowly turned into a literary potentate as a great compiler of anthologies and a member of prescribing committees and prize juries, he began to produce less and less original poetry, hobnobbing, instead, with Cabinet Ministers and accepting nominations to cultural commissions and the Board of Censors. Ever since his retirement and subsequent move to Pretoria, there had been persistent rumors about his elevation to the post of cultural attaché or to the Senate. Above all he remained a charming gentleman, a bon vivant, a patron of the arts, and an excellent host.

So it was with mixed feelings, as usual, that Elise and I accepted his invitation to an "intimate meal" to celebrate the publication of his *Collected Poems* in January last year.

At these "intimate" occasions the professor usually allowed himself a touch of eccentric nonchalance, wearing, over his evening suit and frilly shirt and velvet bow tie, a scarlet gown of Japanese silk, and soft black slippers lined with lamb's wool. (Bernard usually referred to him as "Monsieur Jourdain" and never went to any of his *soirées;* curiously enough, Pienaar remained very fond of him. Perhaps, in his heart of hearts, he was homosexually inclined.)

In this garb, all red and black, like a hierophant in some esoteric cult, the great man opened his solid teak door to our discreet knock. He was flanked by Mother, formidable in lilac and lace, an orchid bobbing on her bosom and the lower regions of her goitered throat obscured by pearls, redolent of powder and perfume.

"Oh, Martin. Oh, Elise. How good to see you."

With a soft white hand, all rings and nail varnish, Pienaar steered Elise through entrance hall and passage, past graphic work and the first intimations of dear Pippa on the walls, over Bokharas and Hamadans, to the lounge with the muted luster of silver and porcelain behind the glass doors of stinkwood armoires. The floor was covered with two Afghan carpets of extraordinary size, surrounded by a constellation of smaller Bakhtiaris and Isfahans; and on the walls one could admire, apart from the work of local greats and a life-sized study of dear Pippa, a Braque, a Matisse lithograph, drawings by Degas and Renoir, and an Ensor, while the glass shelves of alcoves, illuminated with subtlety and skill, showed off the work of Hamada and Leach and ancient Chinese craftsmen.

The guests were hand-picked too. The Church moderator, Dr. Koos Minnaar (widely known as Koos Cunt, after one of his unofficial pastimes), a university rector, a couple of MPs, a retired judge, a few literary critics. Almost out of place in their midst, the progressive newspaper editor Wynand La Grange. And the jet-set magnate, Thielman Pauw. All of them accompanied by their wives, except for Thielman, who'd turned up with a sexy blonde at his side (ever since he'd become a property millionaire he regularly served on juries choosing Miss Something or Other). His choice of companion was the only indication of the Thielman I'd known at university. In those days he'd been a likeable but totally irresponsible good-for-nothing known mainly for his prowess as a stud; in later years he became, in public at least, the epitome of bourgeois respectability. When he addressed a meeting it sounded like Koos Cunt in prayer. He donated hundreds of thousands to good causes, especially the Party, and he'd already been tipped as a future Minister of Economic Affairs. One problem he still had to overcome was a tendency to settle differences with his fists. Still, he had what was generally regarded as "a good heart"; an uncut diamond.

Copies of the *Collected Poems* had been placed, with studied nonchalance, all over the lounge, to be paged and fondled at leisure by the guests. Thielman was the first to break the ice when he exclaimed: "I don't understand a word of it, Prof, but I think it's damned smart of you."

"Why don't you also try to write poetry?" asked his blonde companion, massaging his biceps as an obvious surrogate. "I'm sure you can do it."

"No, writing isn't my line. But I *am* toying with the idea of publishing a magazine."

"We already have far too many papers," said editor La Grange.

"You needn't fear competition," said Thielman, giving him a companionable blow between the shoulder blades which sent him reeling. "Mine won't be a newspaper, but a weekly news magazine. Like *Time*, only in Afrikaans."

"Isn't it a very difficult field to conquer?" the rector enquired tactfully.

"Don't you worry, man," replied Thielman, winking. "The Department of Information has already promised to take ten thousand copies a week."

"What in God's name are they going to do with ten thousand a week?"

"That's not my worry. They can distribute the stuff or pulp it, I don't care. As long as the circulation goes up." He took up position squarely in front of La Grange. "Where you fail with your newspapers I'll succeed with my thing. You newspaper boys have gone all out to fuck up the whole of the Afrikaans press."

There were smothered exclamations of shock or protest from the ladies. Mother, fortunately, had gone to the kitchen to consult with her cooks and waiters.

"Criticism, that's all one sees when you open a newspaper these days," Thielman went on. "Otherwise it's just sex and sensation. What'll become of your paper if you drop the back page? Let me tell you, you boys are undermining Afrikanerdom worse than the Communists themselves."

"I cannot agree more wholeheartedly," said Koos Cunt, stern and corpulent in his black suit. "If our leaders can no longer rely on the unquestioned loyalty of their own press—"

"Since when is honest criticism regarded as disloyalty?" asked La Grange. "Do you expect me to shut my eyes or look the other way when things go wrong in the country?"

"Ah, but one should be loyal even in one's resistance."

I felt something stir inside me. My own sense of loyalty, perhaps—for Bernard had been arrested only a few weeks before and I was still convinced of his innocence. Irritated by Koos Cunt's attitude, and not entirely without deliberate provocation, I said: "You know, Bernard Franken once remarked that 'loyal resistance' was only the token resistance of a whore, knowing she'll get her money in the end." (He'd also said: "'Loyal resistance' is the sort of resistance you find in a man who tries to assert his freedom by keeping a mistress without the knowledge of his wife.")

Only after I'd spoken I became aware of the strange silence which had settled in the room at the mere mention of that name.

"Well, we all know what has become of Bernard Franken, don't we?" said Koos Cunt after a while, gulping down the rest of his brandy.

Editor La Grange was the only one to protest: "Wait a minute! Nothing has happened to him yet."

"He's being detained by the Security Police," said Thielman aggressively. "Do you call that 'nothing'?"

"He hasn't been accused of anything," La Grange persisted.

"So what?" asked Koos Cunt, as if he were pronouncing a blessing on all of us. "The Government knows what it's doing."

"In the old days," said La Grange, "a man was arrested and taken to court in accordance with the Rule of Law. Nowadays they can keep him for as long as they wish—and then they can let him go just like that. Hasn't that happened time and time again?"

"You amaze me," said Koos Cunt, staring at him through narrowed eyes. "I never thought I'd hear an Afrikaner newspaperman say that. Have you forgotten that in the war I was also imprisoned without trial? What about that?"

"There was a war on."

"Don't you think there's a war on right now?"

"Bravo!" said Professor Pienaar, raising a soft white fist. "I can assure you, I shall go on fighting until the blood rises to the bridles of our horses."

"Now there's a prophetic vision," said Koos Cunt. His voice was rising both in volume and in pitch. "We are engaged in battle with all the Forces of Evil. And what is at stake is the very soul of Afrikanerdom. What do you think will happen in this land if the Afrikaner renounces his identity?"

"I can't see that Bernard Franken's detention or his acquittal can have anything to do with identity," interposed one of the younger MPs. "We shouldn't lose our perspective."

"You won't repeat those words in public!" said Thielman, taking up the threatening stance of a boxer; but the blonde girl held him back.

"Of course I won't," said the MP. "But I trust we're speaking among friends at the moment, not in the caucus. I can tell you there's a lot of us who feel very strongly that this sort of thing can only harm the Afrikaner."

"Where can it harm us?" asked Koos Cunt. "In the outside world? But what has the outside world go to do with us? We've always managed to pull through on our own. If God is with us—"

"You're very sure of God's support, Uncle Koos," Elise said, quite unexpectedly. "You make it sound like catechism."

Her two steel-blue eyes were staring straight at him. He looked away. Everybody seemed to wait for an answer, but he only raised his empty glass, mumbling: "Got to fill up," as he walked off.

I was the only one who knew what Elise had been referring to. A low blow, really. When she'd attended catechism in her matric year in Bloemfontein, she'd had a rather unfortunate encounter with him. One night he'd summoned her to the vestry to "discuss her soul," to make sure that she'd been redeemed and that she knew her enemy, the Devil; to find out whether she had any evil urges in her and to impress upon her the sanctity of the "temple of the Lord." In the course of the interview he began to feel her up. She told him to stop his nonsense if he didn't want to be reported to the Church Council.

"We've really strayed very far from Bernard Franken," I tried to end the embarrassed silence in the crowded room.

"Bernard Franken is the one who strayed," said Thielman angrily. "Even back in our varsity days I could see which way he would be going."

"You certainly spent enough time at university to see a great many things," I said curtly. He'd been at Stellenbosch for eight or nine years, thanks to generous scholarships awarded to him year after year to make sure he retained his position as hooker in the First XV. To everybody's surprise, and probably to his own as well, he finally obtained a B.Comm. and left.

There was trouble brewing, but our host intervened. "What one should really feel," he said, "is a deep pity at the waste of such a talent. If one thinks of what Bernard might still have achieved for Afrikanerdom—"

"He no longer deserves to be called an Afrikaner," said the rector firmly.

"But look at the facts," I insisted. "What has he *done*? He's being detained, that's all. He hasn't been charged with anything."

Returning with a newly filled glass Koos Cunt remained in the background for a while, trying to catch up with the conversation.

"One should be most careful, though," said Professor Pienaar, with a benign smile on his flabby white face (only the cheeks were very flushed). "I mean, to be associated with someone like that if one doesn't even know for sure—"

"Do you discount friendship, Professor?" I asked with restrained anger, aware of Elise's approving eyes. "I think I know Bernard better than anyone else here tonight. I know he has never hesitated to speak out when he thought it necessary, whether one agreed with him or not. But he has never been underhand in any way. I refuse to believe for a moment that he would have got involved in anything sinister."

"I really don't think the man deserves so much discussion," said Koos Cunt.

"Isn't it time to put the whole matter in perspective," asked La Grange, "by beginning to ask questions about the mentality which makes this sort of action by the Government possible?"

"There are no questions in my mind at all," replied the moderator placidly. "The man is a shame on all of us. The sooner we forget about him the better."

"That's a very uncharitable remark for a man of the Church, isn't it?" said Elise quietly.

This time he was ready for her. "My child," he said, in a voice resonant with tolerance and goodwill, "when women start arguing with men in public, that in itself is a sign of something profoundly wrong. I think you are the one who should humbly start examining your conscience."

We were interrupted by the tinkling of a silver bell. The guests were invited to "powder their noses" before proceeding to the long table. Pienaar sat at the head, and Mother on the far end opposite him, where she could operate, with her foot, the button of a bell to discreetly summon the liveried waiters like a host of djinns.

It was her hour of glory. Since daybreak, she revealed demurely (encouraged generously by her husband), she'd been working in the kitchen to prepare the meal, being of the conviction that this noble task should not be left to servants. Shouldn't one concede that a well-prepared dish was as much an exquisite a work of art as a poem? Surely, what Van Wyk Louw had said about the balance of intellect and intuition in the poet, could be applied in equal measure to gastronomy?

The meal was as impressive as any Mass.

Kyrie: Mother's home-made pâté ("Elizabeth David can be so vulgar, don't you agree? To my mind Escoffier is the only one who—"), accompanied by a *Dom Perignon* to celebrate the *Collected Poems.*

Credo: Greek lemon soup and a very, very fine *oloroso*, the *Dos Cortados* of Williams & Humbert. ("Remember the little place in Jerez, Daddy? Such an *earthy* quality about it.")

Next, with a slight alteration of the usual sequence, the *Agnus Dei:* roast leg of lamb from the Karoo, specially provided by brother Sybrand and lovingly sprinkled with thyme and a soupçon of rosemary; served with *petits pois* and accompanied by a '65 *Roodeberg.*

("Don't you agree that all the subtlety and expanse of an entire Karoo landscape really finds its ultimate expression in a joint like this? I see it as a way of confessing the essence of one's Afrikaansness. Where else in the world would one—")

Sanctus: Mother's *pêches au vin*, marinaded overnight in Chablis. And how impish of Professor Pienaar to serve with it a *Swartberg Aristaat*, "that impudent little wine from Ladysmith" which he'd discovered all on his own, two years before, at less than fifty cents a bottle!

A brief interlude while the table was cleared. A flickering of candles. The discreet, contented rumbling of someone's stomach. Benevolent chuckling about a proposal for "intercourse smoking." And then the collective withdrawal to the lounge for the *Gloria:* home-roasted coffee, cream cake, and John Pienaar's cognac and port.

Editor La Grange had the bad taste of choosing that moment for a reference to the demolition of squatters' huts in the Cape, and malnutrition in general.

"*Ag*, no," said Mother smiling. "We all know that malnutrition is no longer a real problem in the world. Daddy and I were just talking about it yesterday, how our Bantus have raised their standards of living." A brief silence. "If anybody is still undernourished in our day and age," she continued, biting into her cream cake, "it's just due to the wrong eating habits."

The gastronomic orgasm had been reached. In the contented afterglow Professor Pienaar began to read his poetry to us, in the rich, sensitive voice which had caused generations of first-year girls to fall in love with him. It was followed by an appreciative murmur (Mother: "He has such a sensitive *organ* for poetry, don't you agree?") and enthusiastic discussion by the literary men in our midst. We had to restrain ourselves for an unconscionable time before there came a gap in the conversation, in which we could excuse ourselves gracefully and depart without breaking up the party.

At last we were outside in the sultry summer night. It was nearly eleven o'clock.

Driving home to Johannesburg I switched on the car radio for the late news. The news which suddenly, brutally, retroactively changed the tenor of the entire evening.

"The head of police in the Cape Peninsula, Brigadier Joubert, has confirmed to the SABC that Bernard Johannes Franken, detained by the Security Police four weeks ago, escaped from Caledon Square earlier today. With him was one of his co-detainees, a Colored man, Kerneels Ontong. It has not yet been established how—"

✧ ✧ ✧ ✧

Charlie Mofokeng had been the first to inform me of Bernard's arrest, four weeks before. On the Day of the Covenant, to enhance the irony of the victory of the Boers over the Zulus more than a century ago. I'd spent the day with Bea, and in the evening we had guests at a braai beside the pool until after midnight. I didn't know where I was when the phone suddenly rang at half-past two in the morning.

"Charlie?" It took a while to grasp what was going on. "What makes you phone at this hour of the bloody night?"

"It's Bernard." He said something which in my dazed state I couldn't grasp.

"What about Bernard?"

"Arrested. The SB."

"But why? How? When?"

"Anybody's guess. I just wanted you to know."

Slowly the confusion cleared. "Where did you hear it, Charlie?"

Did he hesitate for a moment? "Just got it from a reporter on *The Star.*"

"But it's impossible!"

"I'm telling you, man. I tried to phone his flat in the Cape, but no go."

"Perhaps he's sleeping out."

"Jesus, man!" He sounded angry. "Why d' you think I'm phoning you? You got to do something."

"What can I do?"

"You know all the Ministers and things, don't you?"

"I can't phone them at three in the morning, Charlie. Anyway, suppose it's just a rumor. How do I know—"

"Oh, Jesus!" he said. "Don't start with all that crap."

"Be sensible, Charlie. You know how easy it is for this sort of story to get out of hand. We've got to make sure in the morning."

For the rest of the night I couldn't sleep. I refused to believe what he'd told me. From eight o'clock the next morning I dialed Bernard's number in Cape Town at regular intervals. No use. His secretary couldn't help me either. But it was nearly Christmas, the Supreme Court had gone into recess, he might be anywhere. I didn't want to make a fool of myself by inquiring at top level about something for which there might be a very simple explanation.

Still it continued to gnaw on my conscience. I became irritable. At work I had an outburst when Charlie kept on insisting that I do something. With Elise I quarreled simply because I didn't feel like taking her into my confidence before something more concrete had come to light.

It was only three days later that the Minister made the formal announcement, without giving any reasons: several persons in the Cape Peninsula had been detained by the Security Police in terms of the Terrorism Act, among them the prominent advocate, Bernard Franken.

Once again it was Charlie who conveyed the news to me, when I arrived back at the office after lunch. It took me some time before I could focus my attention on anything.

Charlie was waiting quietly. I waited for him to say: *I told you so.* I swear I would have hit him. But he didn't say a word. And when I looked up—my God, how sentimental can one get?—he was standing there at the door, his black face ashen in color, tears running down from under his glasses.

I looked down and reached for the telephone. "I'll phone the Minister immediately," I said.

"Don't bother!" he spat out. Without waiting, he turned round and stormed out of my office. I was too shocked even to feel angry.

It wasn't until late in the afternoon that I finally got through to the Minister. We'd met at a few social occasions before and he'd impressed me as a very approachable person, but he sounded very formal and severe on the telephone.

"I appreciate your concern, Mr. Mynhardt, but unfortunately there is nothing we can do about it at the moment. I cannot interfere with the processes of justice in the country. But I can give you the assurance that my men had very good reason for doing what they did. The whole matter will be put into perspective in public at our earliest opportunity." It sounded like a prepared statement.

There was a feeling of numbness in my stomach. I must have known they wouldn't arrest such a public figure without grave reason. Yet I refused to believe anything negative about Bernard. He was my friend. I would stand by him. It had all been a ghastly mistake, no more.

I still had to face Elise with the news. And Louis too. ("Let me tell you one thing, Dad: they don't realize it, but if people like Bernard are turning against them their days are damned well numbered.") The entire holiday season was a nightmare. Lying awake on Christmas Eve; suddenly hearing Elise's voice in the dark saying:

"Martin, I just can't believe it. Not Bernard."

"I thought you were asleep."

"How can I sleep knowing that all the time we're lying here, he may be—what are they doing to him?"

"We must keep our faith in him. We know him well enough, don't we? We owe it to him not to doubt his integrity for a moment."

How ironical that in those circumstances we could proceed to comfort each other by making love. While he—

"Just wait," I assured her. "One of these days they'll let him go. This time they've made bloody fools of themselves."

But in the end *I* proved to be the bloody fool for having believed in him. It was not easy to come to terms with that.

People are essentially economic propositions. The way I see it, if I meet somebody he tries to sell himself to me; and whether I decide to buy him or not, is determined by his efficacy as a salesman. As far as Bernard was concerned, I'd never had any doubts before it was too late. But I never felt quite so easy about Charlie. Even if I did buy him in the end, wasn't it at too high a price?

In retrospect, our first meeting was not without comedy. When Bernard had phoned that morning, he'd only said:

"Martin, will you be at home tonight? I'd like to bring over an old friend of mine. Grew up with him."

"Gladly," I said. "We can always invite a few other guests as well."

"No, let's keep it intimate, shall we? Not like old Prof Pienaar's little soirées, remember?"

"I remember only too well. And he hasn't changed yet."

"All right, shall we make it about eight?"

As always when she knew Bernard was coming over, Elise prepared a splendid meal (artichokes; duck with orange) and put on a long evening dress, her hair in a formal chignon behind her head. And then, well: Guess who's coming to dinner.

For me personally the ice had been broken years ago when I'd studied in London; and in the course of my work I regularly had dealings with Blacks, including businessmen from abroad. But this was the first time a Black man had come to dinner at my house. And for a moment I could only stand and stare at him.

Bernard either didn't notice or pretended not to. "Charlie Mofokeng," he said. "Martin Mynhardt." Putting an arm round Charlie's shoulders: "My old pal. Played together when we were kids on the farm."

"You mentioned something to that effect on the phone." I put out my hand. "Pleased to meet you."

"Hi." He was smiling with bared gums. "So this is the Martin Mynhardt Bernard's been telling me about."

"Take a good look at him and tell me if you think there's still hope for him," said Bernard. "Between the two of us we may be able to sort him out."

"I'm not so sure," said Charlie with a straight face. "He hasn't even offered us a drink yet."

I laughed more loudly than was necessary. "Well, what would you like?"

Then Elise came in.

Bernard kissed her, held her at arm's length to examine her critically, then pulled her close to him for another kiss before he turned her round to face Charlie. On her beautifully made-up face I saw the momentary expression of shock, but she was much too civilized to lose her poise so easily. She took his hand. Soon afterwards she went out to the kitchen.

When we sat down to dinner, she brought in the dishes herself. "But isn't Evelyn—?" I started.

"Do sit down," she interrupted me pointedly.

Charlie wanted to go to the bathroom first and Bernard went to show him the way. In the brief spell when she and I were alone, she said angrily:

"For God's sake don't ask such stupid questions again."

"But what's happened to Evelyn?"

"I gave her the evening off, of course. You can't expect her to serve while *he's* here."

"I can't let *you* serve him!"

"It was you who invited him."

"It wasn't. It was Bernard's idea."

"What am I being blamed for now?" asked Bernard from the door, coming back to join us.

"You might have warned us, Bernard," I said.

"About what?"

"Where has he gone to?" asked Elise.

"Charlie? Oh, I went to say hello to the children and Ilse wanted a story, so she annexed Charlie. The Moon and the Mantis. Do you know it? His mother used to tell it to us when we were small."

"But how can you let a—I mean, you can't let Charlie sit there with Ilse while we're waiting to have dinner."

"He won't be long. He's marvelous with kids." Unperturbed, he unfolded his napkin.

Five minutes later, after Elise had kicked my shin a couple of times, I excused myself and went to have a look. Charlie was sitting on Ilse's bed and she was shaking with laughter.

"Food's waiting," I said, rather coldly I'm afraid.

He got up immediately. "Tell you another when I see you again, O.K.?" he promised Ilse, pressing her hand.

In blonde innocence she lay under the floral quilt looking up at him (how old was she then? eight or nine, I think). "You must come back soon," she demanded.

"Right, I promise."

As I stood to one side to let him go out, she asked: "Daddy, is he an uncle or an *outa?*"

For a moment I was completely at a loss for words.

Charlie burst out laughing, doubling up and wiping the tears from his eyes. "That's quite a problem, hey?" he said at last. "I think the best is just to call me Charlie. How about that?"

"Yes," she agreed, blowing kisses to both of us.

Back at the table it was he himself who repeated the story. Elise cast down her eyes. Bernard glanced at me briefly before he, too, began to laugh.

"When I had to shake hands with a Black man for the first time," he said, "I felt I couldn't touch food with my hand again."

"Don't worry," said Charlie. "Same here. When the first White man shook my hand in Cambridge I went out to buy a bottle of Dettol to disinfect myself."

"When we swam and fought bare-arsed in the dam," said Bernard, "we didn't even know that Dettol existed."

Something was easing up in the conversation. Soon we were talking and laughing so loudly that Louis peeped in to find out what was going on. He didn't unbend as easily as Ilse had, but towards midnight, hours past his bedtime, he and Charlie had become great friends.

Not that all was merriment and laughter that night.

"Why did you come back to South Africa when you were doing so well overseas?" I asked him—the question I was to repeat so often in the years to come.

"Because I'd left part of me here, man," he said. He laughed, but behind his thick lenses his eyes were serious. "You know, ever since I first went to school my whole life was one long denial: of my people, my culture, my language, the lot. I had to learn to look after myself through the White man's eyes. His history changed me into something different from what I'd been. Even at university. But

165

sooner or later I had to come back. To try and find that part of me I'd had to deny all the time."

"What makes you think you'll ever find it again?"

"Oh, it won't be easy, I know. But I'll get it, all right. I've got to—else it just won't be worthwhile going on."

"We all have to keep going on," I said. "After all, Sisyphus is supposed to be the symbol of our age."

"Ah, but don't forget: to a Black man Sisyphus means something different."

"Not existentially."

"Especially existentially," said Charlie. "Let's put it this way: your White Sisyphus operates in the dimension of metaphysics. My dimension is social."

"I'm afraid I don't understand."

"It's the social which determines the nature of my task, the nature of my rock. On my way downhill to pick up the absurd rock again, I don't see anything metaphysical: what I see is my social condition, my oppressors. You may think in terms of suicide, if you wish to stick to Camus. Not I, because I exist socially. I've got to make the jump from suicide to murder. And I don't think either of us can still start with innocence. To hell with William Blake."

"Dad," said Louis, "what does 'existentially' mean?"

"I think it's time for you to go to bed," I said sternly.

After he'd gone out, Charlie said: "You won't be able to evade him all the time."

"Who evaded whom?"

"You didn't answer your son's question about existentialism."

"Good heavens, he's only fourteen. What does he know about existentialism?"

"What do you or I know about it?" he asked.

I got up, smiling: "What we need," I said, "is some more wine."

"Indeed," he said. "Since we *are* involved in the Great Evasion."

Adding with a smile: "The latest version of the Great Trek."

"Now you're moving towards metaphysics," warned Bernard. He winked at me: "This invariably happens at about midnight. Like Frankenstein."

"You won't murder us in our beds, will you?" Elise asked Charlie.

There was a slight drizzle when we went outside in the small hours to see them off. I shook Charlie's hand. Bernard embraced Elise in mock passion and kissed her. Then, as if it was the most natural thing in the world, Charlie went to her to kiss her too. For a moment I saw her stiffen and I held my breath. Then she calmly offered him her cheek, and he and Bernard got into the car. The doors slammed, the tires swished down the driveway. The red tail-lights disappeared. From a shrub near us large drops were falling singly, with a small spattering sound.

She was the first to return to the stoop, where thin lines of rain were trembling in the light. I went to shut the heavy gates. Holding the cold metal in my hands I remained there for some time, dull and drowsy, more tired than I'd realized.

In retrospect the evening seemed to have been balanced precariously on a wave of excitement, on the edge of an extreme. Now it came washing past, leaving only a flood of dark water all round.

It was cold and wet and very quiet. It was like years ago, the sort of night in which I would find myself alone after a long evening of waging a seemingly endless offensive against a desired girl, breaking down her resistance, getting her to bed in the end; and then returning home in the small hours, hands deep in my pockets, whistling, the way one would in a cemetery. I had "conquered." I'd had "my way." But had I really? Or had I merely exposed something unbearable in myself, something I would have to cover up again as soon as possible by finding another girl, mounting an offensive against her, breaking down her resistance—?

Who'd mentioned Sisyphus? And who was it who'd said: *Nothing is more responsible for this weariness of life than the repetition of the passion of love?*

But what the hell did it all have to do with love, for me to think of it in such terms?

I had to go inside. It was getting colder and wetter all the time.

In the semi-darkness of the front entrance Elise said: "He turned out to be a very pleasant person, don't you think?"

"Did you like him then?"

"Didn't you?"

"Of course I did."

I wanted her to say something else. I would have liked to find something else to say myself. But why, really?

"Do you know the story about the Moon and the Mantis?" I asked her.

"No. Why?"

"I just wondered. I don't know it either."

She gave a small laugh. "You can say such silly things, Martin."

She was already on her way down the dark passage to our room.

I closed the heavy front door, trying to shut out the night.

8

QUEENSTOWN. THE LONG ROW of lights merely served to expose the desolation of the town at that hour. Garages, shop windows, here and there an open cafe, a group of people emerging from a hotel and talking on a pavement. The wide bridge on the far side of the town. The lights were farther apart now. In passing, they flickered across Louis's face like skins shed by a luminous snake. He crossed his legs, still staring ahead of him. A train approached, small squares of light in the dark, disappearing behind us. There were deviations in the road. Once we were forced to drive in the dust of a truck for several hundred yards. The Black driver deliberately tried to prevent us from passing. Bastard. Probably derived a sense of power from knowing he could block my way. In the end, accelerating suddenly and swerving dangerously, I managed to pass; then it was my turn to force him off the road before leaving him behind for good.

"Now there's only Cathcart left."

Louis said nothing.

The landscape, starkly beautiful in daylight—wide yellow plains and blue table hills in the distance—had a fantastic aspect in the moonlight. Perhaps it was just as well, softening the scars of drought. In a recent letter Ma had written: "The Eastern Cape has never been so dry before even the aloes are beginning to shrivel up I always knew the Lord was going to punish us one day."

Every week her letter came, unfailingly through all the years, even when she was ill: not that that happened often—Ma had the constitution of an ox and all the fierce strength of will inherited from her French and Dutch ancestors.

If she got it into her head to block the sale of the farm, there would be trouble. But I tried to reassure myself: in the past I'd always succeeded in getting round her, perhaps because we were so similar by nature. Theo had always been different, something of a softy like Dad. Of course, if Dad had lived, there wouldn't have been any problem persuading him to sell. He would have been only too glad to get rid of it.

Or would he? When it mattered least, during his last illness, he'd suddenly showed an illogical affection for the place, insisting he wouldn't be buried anywhere but there.

Bernard's parents had also been dead for a long time now. It must have been at least ten years since his mother had died peacefully in her sleep one night. And her husband—that magnificent old man, lord and master on his domain, undaunted by drought or floods, locusts or depression, war or rumors of war—he couldn't survive the death of his frail wife and followed her within six months, of a broken heart the doctor said.

But it was perhaps just as well they'd died in time, to be spared the upheaval and agony of Bernard's trial. I doubt whether they would have been able to come to terms with it. Of course, one shouldn't underestimate them. He'd often said and done things which must have shocked them, yet they'd never reproached him or lost faith in him or altered in their love of him: they would pray for him, but never reject him. Even so, the trial might have proved too much for them.

Useless speculation. Equally useless as wondering whether I could have changed the course of events.

Still, there had been one night, during the Terrorism Trial in '73 (when his clients had been the men who later turned out to be his accomplices and subordinates). I hadn't even realized that anything special was involved in our discussion that night: it was only afterwards that he told me, and by then it was too late.

That time when, as a child, I'd been so ill—the night the lampshade tinkled against the wall and the doctor said: "Don't worry, he'll pull through"—I'd never even known how serious it had been. By the time I realized it, the crisis had passed. Perhaps it generally happens that way. In which case that night in '73 may have been the true moment of crisis.

What happened had been decided by totally insignificant events. For instance, it would have been quite different had Bernard stayed with us at home as he usually did, with the exception of that early marathon trial—but at the time Elise's parents were visiting us. We had more than enough room for him as well, but he didn't want to intrude and so I'd put him up in my private apartment.

Or: if I hadn't gone to Aunt Rienie's birthday on that night of all nights. Or: if Bernard had accompanied me as we'd planned. Or: if Bea hadn't been there. All those *ifs*.

It was soon after the court case had started and we hadn't had much time together yet. On that particular Monday afternoon I came from work rather late (the auditors were working on my books); I was flaked and not in any mood for a party, so I decided to go round to the apartment first and have a drink with Bernard. Perhaps he would agree to go with me. He'd always been fond of the old lady, since the time when, in my final year at university, I'd rented a room in her old eighteenth-century house in Dorp Street. Aunt Rienie had been born and bred in Stellenbosch; for five generations her family had been living in that house and nobody had ever expected her to move. But both her daughters had settled in Johannesburg and the only way to be close to her grandchildren was to sell her house and move north. In her flat in one of the rambling old buildings in Parktown she tried, perhaps with too much obvious effort, to keep her spirits up by clinging to everything that constituted life for her: music, people, laughter, poetry. Slowly wasting away as she pined for oak trees and mountains and water furrows beside the streets and the laughter of young people, she tried to cover up by assembling a *salon* around her. I doubt whether I ever visited her without finding strangers in her flat, people she'd picked up in buses or museums or at exhibitions or in restaurants and brought home with her to overwhelm them with love and attention. Petite and delicate as she was, Aunt Rienie could be a most demanding old lady, always ready to take control of one's entire existence. What she loved above all was to act as matchmaker and plan marriages for all her young friends. Bernard was the only persistent recalcitrant: which was why she tried harder with him than with anybody else.

The climax of her social life was her birthday every April. Then all her friends and acquaintances were assembled in her cramped little flat to celebrate and drink and run amok until daybreak; and invariably, in the course of the wild night, she would take up position in the middle of the floor, her silver hair specially "done," her ears and wiry little neck adorned with pearls, her eyes as lively and intensely blue as cornflowers—and then she would start reading poetry to her guests.

It was on that particular day of the year, that Monday afternoon, that I went to Joubert Park to see Bernard. The pleasant, peaceful, elegant apartment furnished and decorated to my own taste, on the top floor of the tall modern block, where at night, relaxed in the double bed, one could lie listening to the leaves of the plane trees outside. One always remained aware of the city—moving, dynamic, a never-ending throbbing presence on the threshold of one's consciousness—not as a threat or an intrusion, but familiar and intimate, an affirmation of life.

Bernard had just taken a shower when I knocked, and he came to the door wearing only a towel round his waist.

"Am I in the way?" I asked. "Are you going anywhere?"

"Not at all. Come inside." On the way back to the bedroom he took off the towel and began to dry himself. I remember thinking, as I followed him, that although he was five years older than me, his body looked younger.

"How do you manage to keep so fit?" I asked, not without envy.

"Play squash. Drop in at the gym once a week or so. Nothing much." He threw down the towel and started dressing. "But if you neglect your machinery"—his familiar smile—"well, then you tend to lose respect for yourself and for others, don't you agree?"

"I've come to pick you up for a party."

"Good. Where?"

"Aunt Rienie's birthday."

"Oh my God, yes, I've forgotten."

"She heard you were in town, so she insisted I bring you along."

"I suppose she's found just the right wife for me again."

"How did you know?"

"Every year she finds a girl 'destined' for me. Poor old thing, I've broken her heart so many times. But never say die." Picking up his shoes and socks he came to the door. "Let's have a drink first. I suppose there's time enough."

"Sure. We needn't go before eight, or even later. You know she never stops before dawn."

"Will you pour or shall I?" He was standing beside the old Cape yellowwood *jonkmanskas* which I'd changed into a cocktail cabinet.

"Go ahead. You know the place as well as I do."

"Gorgeous set-up." He opened a bottle. "Haroun al Raschid."

"Not quite."

"Matter of degree. Do you ask the girls to tell you stories?"

"No, usually it's I who spin the yarns."

He handed me my whisky and sat down with his, still barefoot. "Cheers."

"Up yours."

"I wish you *would* start telling stories again," he said unexpectedly. "I can still remember the stuff you brought me years ago."

"Once you flushed it down the toilet."

"Never mind. You had talent, all right."

"But now that I've become a man—how does the phrase go?— I've put away childish things."

"Like faith, hope and charity?"

"I'm still going strong on the love bit."

"I'm not talking about fucking."

"What makes you so evangelical tonight? One would almost think you were the one with a clergyman father-in-law, not I."

"Don't mock him, he's a good man."

"Having regrets?" I asked lightly. "About the snows of yesteryear?"

"Not the snow. The droughts perhaps." Suddenly he was very serious. "Those wonderful, terrible droughts that stripped the veld so you could see the very bones of the earth. Like a sheep's skeleton. Until you arrived at a point beyond despair and cursing and fear, in a stillness you'd never known before. I remember there was something so utterly clear and pure about the feeling. And only then, usually, the rains would come."

"You're in a sentimental mood."

"Yes, I suppose I am."

Dusk was gathering outside. Inside the apartment it was getting dark, and the outlines of furniture and paintings became blurred. Neither of us moved to put on a light. After some time he got up and refilled our glasses, then stopped at the record player and switched it on. There was a record on it already. The Mozart, of course.

We entered into another of our wordless conversations, phrased in the metaphors of music, the clear and precise sounds of the piano which didn't hesitate to spell out the simplest of truths.

The years in between didn't matter any more. For the time being

I'd also put away the things of a man, purified by the music in the way he'd talked about drought. A sweeter, gentler, more considerate way, but not, in the final analysis, less inexorable. Returning to beyond faith and hope and charity, to the truths of sun and stone, in a land where rain was no more than a rumor or an intimation of mortality.

That holiday on the farm. Elise. (*Never seen a girl before?*) The nights in his room, in the dark, heavy with the smell of wax after the candle had been put out, and exposed to the sounds filtering in from outside: frogs, crickets, bats, a night owl, a dog sighing or moaning in its sleep or licking its balls; the eerie howling and laughter of jackals; a voice calling from the huts; the gnashing of the windmill straining against its chain in a sudden gust of wind.

"Sorry, man," said Bernard after the record had stopped. "I suppose it's this case I'm working on which depresses me."

"I don't understand why you keep on getting involved in that sort of thing."

"What sort of thing?" he demanded.

"Defending people like that."

"What do you know about 'people like that'?"

"I know enough of you."

"Do you really know me?" He was staring at me in the dusk.

"Only too well," I insisted. "I know you're trying to free yourself from your own Afrikaansness, but you won't ever succeed."

"Really?"

"You're still prompted by all the same motives."

"What do you mean, Martin?"

"Well, you've spoken so often of the Afrikaner's 'masochistic ecstasy': his way of drawing inspiration from his sense of standing heroically and alone against all the world. But aren't you doing exactly the same? You're standing alone against the establishment you've rejected. The 'ecstasy' is unchanged. The 'masochism' too. Your position continues to be determined by the group you've tried to break away from. And so you're really only confirming what you're trying to escape from."

"Is that your diagnosis?"

"Yes. There are other symptoms too, of course."

"Please tell me the worst, Doctor."

"I'm serious, Bernard. You've chosen the role of rebel for yourself. Fair enough. But you're forgetting something: in history, the only rebels able to succeed have been young men. A young man can afford to rebel, he has nothing to lose, he can go all the way. But in this country most of our rebels have been in their thirties, if not in their forties. They're people who run the risk of losing a lot. And so they can never go far enough. Do you see what I mean?"

"Yes, I agree. But suppose you do come across a man of thirty or forty prepared to sacrifice the lot? Like the ones I'm defending at the moment: people who are ready to risk everything one normally associates with the 'good life'?"

"It just can't work. It goes against nature."

"Do you really think it can't work?"

"If it happens, it's absurd. It's sick."

After a while he got up. It had grown quite dark inside. I could see his silhouette against the dull glow of the city at the window.

"Martin, these people I'm talking about: they would also like to relax in this lovely flat and have a drink. Some of them have wives and children."

"Then they're grossly irresponsible."

"Don't you think a man, especially if he's a highly sensitive and intelligent man, can be driven to the point where he sees violence as the only solution for a situation in which he has become expendable?"

"Surely it's no excuse for becoming as evil as the thing you're opposing? Then your man begins to regard his opponent as equally expendable. That's the basis of terrorism, isn't it?—the conviction that the end justifies the means. How can any revolution succeed without extremism and an aesthetic of violence for the sake of violence? And how can you defend that in the name of 'humanity'? You're glorifying an ignoble cause, Bernard."

"And then you pretend to know me," he said from the window. He was looking at me but his face was too dark for me to see his eyes. "Martin, I want to talk to you. I've been meaning to for a long time now, but it's so seldom we are together like this."

"What's the matter, Bernard?"

"What we need is to spend a whole night talking, as in the old days." His voice sounded dull all of a sudden; there was a vulnerability in the frame of his shoulders. He looked up. "I think I need you. Just to help me to see clearly again. To regain my faith. One reaches a stage—"

I wanted to go to him, but something about the tone of despair in him inhibited me. I wasn't sure how to handle him. In the past I had been the one to go to him for help. It was unnerving to discover that he suddenly needed *me*.

"Don't be so depressed," I said. "Let's go to Aunt Rienie's party. That will cheer you up."

"I can't face a party just now."

"But I thought you said—"

"That was when you came." He walked away from the window, approaching me in the dark. "Please stay here with me, Martin. I've got to talk to you."

"But she's counting on me." I got up and moved towards the door. "Do come with me."

"No, I'd rather stay. Perhaps it's a good thing to sit down and think about it all on my own."

I opened the door. Blinding light filled the room from the landing. He looked up, startled.

"Please come back soon, Martin," he said. "Give Aunt Rienie my love, enjoy yourself for a while. But then come back. I'll wait for you."

"All right." I smiled. "We can talk about it when I'm back. Don't be so morbid. We'll sort it all out, whatever it is."

But of course it didn't go as we'd planned, and the conversation never took place. It's senseless, as I've said before, to speculate on all the *ifs*. Things happen the way they do because they're meant to happen like that. If we deny that certainty we'll all inevitably end up with blue circles round our navels.

I may add that there are some things which appear to go against nature, against one's natural urge to live safely, protected by the security of a career, a house, a wife, children. But once one has made the discovery that there are millions of others living in one's own country, deprived of those basic elements through laws enacted by one's own people, one can no longer claim that way of life as a "right." Then one is forced to free oneself from the security and the bliss of ignorance. In my own case, if I may be subjective for one last time, it demanded of me to sacrifice even my own marriage before it could turn into bondage for myself and the woman I loved—at the expense of the lives and the happiness of others.

I couldn't understand it at all, much as I tried; and my incomprehension was aggravated by the fact that I'd never known his wife, which made it impossible to conjure up an image of Bernard as a married man. There was no visual context in which to project him in order to understand him "in situation." Perhaps that was why neither his marriage nor his divorce touched me very deeply—until the day she arrived at my office.

There hadn't been any warning before their wedding. As I might have expected of Bernard, the first I heard of it was when he phoned to say: "I thought you'd like to know I got married this morning."

"Bernard! I don't believe it."

"I'm a normal red-blooded male."

"That's not what I mean. But—out of the blue like this?"

"I've never been one for trimmings. *Veni, vidi, vici.* Except that, in this case, the *vici* turned out to be *vicimur.* Anyway, we're both as happy as can be. And firmly resolved to grow old together."

But only months later, just before he came up to Johannesburg for the conspiracy trial, they were divorced. He didn't want to talk about it when I saw him, and I respected his privacy. Still, I couldn't help feeling that, for the very first time, a gulf had come between us: for something momentous had happened in his life which he hadn't shared with me and of which I had no grasp. Was it that feeling of being out of touch which paved the way for those other, later, silences in his life to which I found I had no access?

It was more than a year later, as the trial was drawing to its close, that she turned up at my office. The name, Reinette Franken, meant nothing to me; I was intrigued only by her refusal to mention to my secretary the reason for her visit. When she came in, she made an immediate impression: not only because she really was beautiful—tall, blonde, athletic, tanned, with wide blue eyes—but because of her undeniable "presence." Very young, she couldn't have been more than twenty or twenty-one, but nothing about her suggested girlhood or ignorance: she was unmistakably, and disconcertingly, a *woman.*

"How do you do?" I said. "Please sit down."

She hesitated. "You are Martin Mynhardt, aren't you?"

"Of course. What can I do for you?"

"Didn't Bernard—I mean—"

"Bernard?"

"Aren't you the Martin Mynhardt who was at university with him? He always spoke about you."

"It's me, all right. But—" Suddenly it hit me. "Good heavens, are you his wife?"

"I was." With a slight, sad twitch of her mouth.

"I'm so sorry."

"Why should you be? It had nothing to do with you."

"No, but he's always been very close to me and I was awfully pleased when I heard about the marriage last year. Then, suddenly, well—"

"Are you very busy?"

"Not at all. I'm very glad to meet you at last. Shall I order us some tea?"

"No thanks."

Now that she'd come and I knew who she was, she suddenly seemed less confident of herself. In obvious embarrassment, she explained that she'd made up her mind to come and talk to me about him. Everything had happened so quickly. Perhaps he'd had time to think about it again. Perhaps they could—but she didn't want to upset him in any way. At first she'd thought the mere surprise of coming back to him would be enough, but then she'd realized how childish it was. So she'd decided to first discuss it with me.

"Please forgive me," she said. "I won't bother you any longer. I've just realized how presumptuous it was of me to think that anyone else—"

"I'm not 'anyone else.' Bernard and I have always been completely frank with one another."

"Did he say anything to you? I mean—while he's been up here in Johannesburg?"

"No. In fact, your marriage was the only thing he never discussed with me."

"Then I must have hurt him very deeply." There was nothing emotional in her attitude: she was simply stating a fact.

She took out a cigarette. I got up to light it for her.

"Thanks."

There was something disturbingly familiar about the way she raised her head when she blew out the smoke: as if I'd watched her do it for years.

"He never blamed you for anything."

"If only one could be sure." She inhaled smoke and held her breath for a while before blowing it out. "You see, I had the impression we were very happy. He never looked unhappy. He was so relaxed and full of life. Then, quite unexpectedly, he just said—"

After another minute she got up resolutely, with a firmness which, once again, appeared disturbingly familiar. "I didn't mean to burden you with it," she said. "If you could only tell me quite honestly: Do you think I should go to him and discuss it, or will it upset him too much? At this stage of the trial—but perhaps it might help him. What do you think?"

"I wish I could be sure. You've caught me totally unprepared."

"I'm in no hurry." She added, with cool and quiet emphasis: "There's a whole lifetime ahead, isn't there? I wouldn't like to fuck it up by doing anything rash."

The crude word startled me—like another, years ago. And suddenly I realized why so much about her appeared familiar. It was of Elise herself that she reminded me. Not the Elise of the present, but the defiant and positive young woman of many years ago. The girl who, one Sunday afternoon, had calmly taken off her Sunday hat and gloves and her Sunday clothes to dive, naked, into the concrete dam. Something about the discovery made me breathless.

"I'll phone you again tomorrow," she said. "Or whenever it suits you."

"Why don't you have dinner with me tonight?" I suggested, wondering whether she had noticed anything. "Then we can talk about it unhurriedly and at length."

After a brief hesitation: "All right. What time?"

"Eightish. Where are you staying?"

"The Carlton."

"I'll pick you up."

"Thank you very much, Martin."

"I should thank *you.*"

"Why?"

"Just, well—" I took her hand. "Because you came."

For a moment her eyes were watching me, keenly but unperturbedly.

"Goodbye," she said.

"See you tonight, Reinette."

As I closed the door behind her I discovered that my hands were damp. I didn't feel like work. Instead, I went to a window and stood looking out over the smoky city.

✧ ✧ ✧ ✧

"All I wanted to do," she explained when, long after dinner, nearly midnight, we were enjoying a final drink on a terrace, "was to make him feel at home, to give him peace and quiet, and children in due course. He'd always been so restless, always in search of something. So I thought—"

"Perhaps he'd waited too long before he got married. He'd got too set in his ways. He'd become used to being his own boss."

"Some people get married even later than he did, and they're happy."

"Bernard's is a different sort of independence."

(I felt like saying: "If you'd been less like Elise, it might have worked out better." But I didn't.)

"So you think I should rather go back without seeing him at all?"

"How can you expect me to give you a straight answer? How can you expect me to take responsibility for your whole life?"

She sat looking down at the glass she held on her lap. "Perhaps that was the mistake I made in the first place," she said. "Leaving it to him to take responsibility for both of us."

"You must give me a chance to broach the subject with him," I said. "I won't tell him you're here. I'll just try to find out how he really feels about it."

"Will you do that?"

When I went home, she impulsively kissed me.

It wasn't that I deliberately postponed discussing it with him even though I saw him every evening. But in those final weeks of the trial he was very excitable and I didn't want to wreck it all by choosing the wrong moment. So it was about a week before I brought it up. He was worn out. Perhaps that was why, his defenses down, he unburdened more readily than he'd done before.

"You wouldn't have been so tired now if you had a wife to look after you," I said as lightly as I could.

"Maybe I would have been more tired. Having to give everything I've got on two fronts at the same time."

"I'm not sure you gave your marriage enough chance to prove itself, Bernard."

"What do you know about it?" he asked quickly.

"I'm just drawing my own conclusions. A year isn't long enough for a marriage to get going."

"I don't think time has anything to do with it. It's a matter of knowing clearly enough that you made a mistake. For some it takes a lifetime; for others it happens sooner."

"Didn't you love her?"

"Of course I did."

"When you phoned me that day, you said you wanted to grow old together."

He looked past me. "I can't think of anything I'd like to do more than just that," he said after a long pause. "But for a man in my position, with the choices I've made, marriage is pure selfishness. It's an escape. I allowed myself to be blinded temporarily. My God, don't you think I'd love to settle down and have a normal family life? But I can't think of myself only."

"Have you ever thought of Reinette?"

He looked at me: "I've thought mainly of her."

I didn't want to make him suffer any more. It was obvious how deeply the conversation had perturbed him. For my own sake I would have liked to find out more, but I couldn't do it to him.

It was equally difficult to report back to Reinette. (What was there to report? What did I dare tell her? How could I presume so much as to decide the course of both their lives?)

I tried to be as evasive as I could. "Just give it a rest," I suggested in the end. "He's very tense at the moment."

"You're hiding something from me. You're sorry for me."

"It's not that at all, Reinette."

I poured her another drink from the bottle I'd ordered earlier. We were in her hotel room. After dinner we'd gone for a walk, but it was cool outside and she was tired; she made no protest when I came up with her. By that time there was a strange (should I say: dangerous?) intimacy between us, as if in his absence Bernard had caused an electrical current to flow between us. Then there were those gestures, attitudes, intonations which reminded me uncannily of Elise but which, belonging to another person, had a curious intensity all their own. As if I were courting my own wife again; as if I'd miraculously cancelled ten years of my life to return to someone I'd lost, a girl in cool water on a torrid day.

She began to cry. It came without warning, and she seemed to collapse completely on the bed where she was sitting, with a lostness about her which startled me. At the same time I couldn't just let her cry like that. I went to sit beside her, taking her in my arms and comforting her as if she were a child like Ilse. Holding her more and more tightly, and caressing her, soothing her, I slowly became conscious of desire stirring inside me, quite uncontrollably. Rocking and swaying, clinging to me in despair, something was changing in her too. Our embrace became the agonized writhing of love, and when I entered her I felt her nails tearing into my back. It felt as if we were trying to strangle and tear apart and kill each other in the wildness of our efforts to obliterate ourselves.

There were moments when all was confused in me, when I really thought it was Elise I had in my arms, as in those first days of our love, long before our marriage. But with the strange discovery, not of possessing her more completely than before, but in fact of doing so for the first time.

Deep in the night, I remember, I was sitting on the edge of the bed with my head in my hands. Reinette lay behind me, her torn and crumpled dress pulled up to her breasts, her bruised thighs wide open, exposing the grimace of her sex.

I wanted to say: *I'm sorry.* But why? No one had been injured by what we'd done. We were adult, both of us; we were responsible. We'd gone into it together. And yet I was appalled by the finality and the irrevocable quality of it.

I drew the spread up over her. She still didn't move. For a moment I thought in panic: *My God, suppose she's dead?*

But then she opened her eyes and asked: "Are you going away?"

"It's very late."

"Of course."

"I promise you I'll come back tomorrow. I—"

She moved her head on the pillow, from side to side, her eyes closed: "No, please don't."

"I mean—"

"I know. But it won't be necessary. I'm going home tomorrow."

"But Reinette, you still haven't—"

A small, weary smile flickered through the smudged lipstick and saliva on her mouth. "Perhaps you've made it easier after all. Now it really is finished."

I wanted to argue or protest, but her closed eyes shut me out. Putting off the light as if that would cancel her image both for me and for herself, I went out and walked down the four flights of stairs, avoiding the lifts for some inexplicable reason.

Perhaps it really had been the best thing that could have happened, I thought in the car on my way back home. I had saved Bernard the upheaval of a new confrontation and a new painful decision; for her as well. There was no need for anyone to feel guilty. How could I be held responsible? I'd merely wanted to comfort her.

The strangest thing of all was to see, as I came from my hot bath at home, Elise sleeping peacefully in bed. Somehow I found it inexplicable to see her so untouched and immaculate. Until, in my sleepy stupor, I realized: *Of course, it's as it should be. No one has raped my wife. Not even I.*

9

O N THE SLOPE BEHIND US, reflected in the rearview mirror, lay the lights of Cathcart. The road became misty, and it grew denser as we went on. By the time we turned off the main road, a few miles from Stutterheim, I had to slow down to forty miles an hour. Occasionally the narrow dirt road rose above the mist on the slopes of the high round hills, from where one looked down on the silver clouds in the valleys and kloofs below, a magical, incredible sight. But I was no longer susceptible to irrelevant beauty. The farm was weighing heavily on my mind and my memories.

I stopped at the farm gate on the narrow ridge of a small plateau. Louis got out, walking stiffly past the headlights, and tugged at the chain for a few moments before he could push the gate open. He was forced to lift the loose end of the gate bodily, as the little wheel on which it was supposed to run was missing. Stolen by one of the piccanins, most likely. Unless one kept an eye on them all the time one would end up with nothing.

As Louis opened the door to get in again, I could hear dogs and voices from the huts on the slope above the house. There was a flickering of fire. Two years ago they'd burnt off all the winter grazing with their fires. We had to buy fodder for the cattle at enormous expense. One of the children had also got killed in the fire.

The narrow farm road was in an appalling state, all potholes and loose stones. I felt a surge of anger as a large stone hit the body of the Mercedes. No matter what Ma said, the farm needed a man's hand.

Where the road made a sharp bend to the right, the lights shot out into the void beyond. There was a very sudden drop there, invisible from as close by as fifty yards: a rift torn into the guts of the earth, probably long before the advent of man. Presumably it had either exposed deeper, fertile layers, or else in the course of time the sides of the valley had caved in, bringing down the humus of rotten plants and opening up courses for streams. For the valley was luxuriant, perennially green, and in the daytime one could follow the fingers of virgin forest along the beds of fountains and a hidden stream; there were even ferntrees and palms, apart from a jungle of cycads and plumbago, euphorbias and brushwood and enormous wild figs, and an incredible variety of aloes.

Approaching the bottom gate at the beginning of the lane of flamboyants, I slowed down to stop for Louis once again, but someone had already opened it. Ma's three large mongrels came running from the house, barking and wagging their tails, looking like young lions in the car lights. I pulled into the garage next to the shed, beside her dilapidated little van and the tractor. On one side lay a broken harrow, under a tree covered with the nests of weaver birds; a couple of old wagon wheels; farther away were the fowl run and the low wall of the pig pen.

As I turned off the lights, I saw Ma waiting beside the water tank at the kitchen door: tall and erect, tough, sinewy, her grey hair gathered tightly behind her head. Over her working clothes she was wearing a soiled white apron. The calm, practical, indomitable woman I'd known for so long, never showing her age, even now that she was past seventy. At the same time, standing there in silhouette against the light from the kitchen, she also appeared lonely, the loneliness characteristic of people who never allow one to look past an active or proud exterior. Perhaps she wasn't even aware of it herself.

In her arms she held a bundle, like a baby. And going towards her, I discovered that it was indeed a baby, held comfortably in her arms as she stood there waiting for me, regal and self-assured in her back door, with her apron.

I kissed her. With one hand—the other still held the bundle—she pressed me against her with an urgency contrasting strongly with her proud bearing. Drawing back, I even caught her wiping off tears. But for her sake I pretended not to notice.

"You're late, sonny," she said. (Even when I'm sixty I'll be "sonny" to her.) "Been held up?"

"Not really. We couldn't get away from Pretoria earlier."

"What were you doing in Pretoria then?"

"Business," I said laconically, turning back to the car to call: "Will you bring in our things, Louis?"

"Is it only Louis with you?" asked Ma. "You didn't say anything in your telegram, so I was wondering." I couldn't make out whether she was disappointed or relieved.

"It was impossible to bring the whole family."

"Didn't Elise want to come?" she asked, with a suspicion born from her possessiveness.

"Ilse has to go to school, Ma."

She turned away from me to look at Louis as he approached. "Goodness me," she said, "you've grown into a man since I saw you last, haven't you?"

He frowned, yielding for a moment so that she could kiss him before he went into the house.

"He's become very difficult ever since he came back from Angola," I explained briefly, keeping my voice down.

"His grandpa would have been proud of him. They really gave those terrorists hell, didn't they? He helped to make history."

"I'm not so sure of that." I followed her into the kitchen. "Whose baby is this you're holding?"

She turned back to me, opening one corner of the bundle, revealing a Black child with enormous eyes.

"His mother brought him down this afternoon. Gastro. I'm just trying to calm him down a bit. These people, you know, they always wait for the last minute."

"Evening, Baas," said a voice from the far side of the kitchen. In the dusky corner I recognized the old Black woman in a blue headscarf.

"Evening, Kristina. How are you keeping?"

"No, good, Baas. Thank you, Baas."

"Come on, hurry up," Ma told her. "Take the food to the table. Don't stand there like you got the lame sickness."

There was another woman in the kitchen, behind Kristina. All I could see of her in the dark was a gleam of eyes and a glimpse of a youthful face with high cheekbones. She cast down her eyes the moment she noticed me looking in her direction.

Ma handed the baby to her. "Take him now, Thokozile." She spoke in Xhosa. "If he wakes in the night, give him some medicine. You can bring him back to me in the morning."

She followed me through the dining room and down the front passage to the spare room.

"I prepared the double bed in my room in case Elise came with you," she said. "But I think you and Louis will be all right in here."

The white crocheted bedspreads were drawn tightly across the two beds; brass knobs shone dully in the half-dark. The room smelled of floor polish and soap. There were white towels draped over the pitcher on the washstand.

"Make yourselves at home, sonny. Dinner's ready when you are."

"I'm not hungry," said Louis after she had gone out.

"Have something anyway. You know what Grandma is like."

In the dining room we stopped for a while to gape at the collection of dishes on the large table under the gas lamp.

"You've come a long way, you need strength," Ma said calmly. "Will you say grace for us, sonny?"

Mechanically I recited Dad's prayer. "For what we are about to receive, may the Lord make us truly thankful. Amen."

Ma carved the leg of lamb—even when Pa had been alive she'd done the carving—and filled our plates without asking what we wanted. Sweet potatoes, roast potatoes, rice with raisins, stewed peaches, vegetables; heaven knows where she'd found it all in the heart of winter.

In the kitchen the baby whined.

"Close the middle door, Kristina!" called Ma in a loud voice, without looking up from her duties.

The gas lamp was hissing peacefully.

"What's happened to the generator?" I asked. "Don't you have electricity any more?"

"Broke down day before yesterday," said Ma. "And that Mandisi does things in his own good time. It's useless to speak to him, he just looks at you with those eyes."

"I'll have a look tomorrow."

She laughed. "What do you know about machinery? Rather let Louis have a try. He's good with his hands."

"I'll speak to Mandisi anyway."

"If he'll listen to you."

"What can you expect, living here all on your own like this?" I said. "It just can't work out in the long run."

"Don't let's start on that again, sonny," she said. "Your Dad's grave is here on the farm and that's where I want to be buried too one day."

I decided not to pursue the subject any further for the moment. We ate in silence. Louis just pecked at his food.

"You still haven't told me what you came for," said Ma when Kristina came in to collect the plates. "All this way for only a few days."

In the passage the clock struck the half hour. It must be half-past eleven.

"We can talk about it tomorrow, Ma. We're much too tired now."

"It's a bad thing to travel so far with that heart of yours."

"I'm perfectly all right."

"You look much too thin to me."

Kristina brought in the coffee pot, and three large white cups and saucers.

"No sugar for me, thanks, Ma."

The night pressed down heavily on us. Through the kitchen door we could hear the child whining again. Ma got up and went out. I tried to focus on Louis's face opposite the blinding spot of the gas lamp.

"Tired, Louis?"

"Not too bad."

"Time to turn in. Tomorrow isn't going to be an easy day."

"What am I going to do all the time?" he asked.

"Oh there's more than enough to do on the farm. Take a good long walk."

"Why did you bring me along?"

"I thought the change might do you good."

He didn't answer.

After a few minutes I got up and went down the passage, through the front door to the lawn outside. The clear black rumps of the hills stood placidly all around, defined in the moonlight. Where the valley sloped down towards a dark, dense kloof running through two rows of hills, the silver mist softened the stark outlines. A nightjar shrieked. Going towards the row of tall cycads I opened my fly and watched the moonlight glistening on the thin jet of water. Louis approached from the house and stopped a few yards from me, following my example. In the dark, fleetingly but reassuringly, through that mundane little action, we became allies again.

In the direction of the valley, past the dairy, lay the family graveyard. Stifling a ridiculous urge to go down there, I turned back with Louis. The house stood staring out at the night through blind black windows.

"I brought you a lamp," said Ma, waiting in our room.

"I prefer the candle," I said. "It's more homely."

"As you wish. Good night."

"Night, Ma. Now please don't lie awake worrying."

"I have nothing to worry about," she replied calmly.

Her proud grey head held high, she went down the passage to her own room, her shadow showing the way. A few minutes later our candle was out, leaving the intimate and heavy smell of wax behind in the dark. Slowly the night took possession of the house.

I was too tired to sleep. There were too many memories taunting and troubling me. All the things conjured up by the smell of the candle. Holidays on the farm of my boyhood friend Gys; or on this same farm, visiting my grandparents with Dad and Ma and Theo. Sleeping either in this room or in the one built on to the stoop; sometimes, when the whole house was filled with uncles and aunts and cousins, I'd sleep on a mattress stuffed with dried mealie leaves, on the floor in the corner of my grandparents' room. The comforting rustling sound it made when one stirred or turned in the exciting strangeness of the oppressive dark behind the wooden shutters closed for the night. The candle on the table beside their great canopied bed; the two bodies kneeling for prayer on the down mattress, like two blanket-covered loaves set out beside the fire to rise.

Bernard's room in the outbuilding, and our interminable conversations. The Sunday night after Elise had been there. *Suppose I told you I've decided I'm going to marry that girl?—She's a wild one, that child.—I think I can tame her.* The young lecturer who'd saved Greta and me from rustication after the weekend in the Cedar Mountains: simply because he hadn't been able to resist the temptation of getting involved in others' lives. Just as he'd interfered in the backyard squabble about the servant's husband. A conversation about a suicide with a blue ring round his navel (and all the blood on the shaggy carpet). Music: Mozart, the *Larghetto*, Schnabel. The urgency in his voice as he spoke from the door of the apartment: *Please come back soon, Martin. Give Aunt Rienie my love, enjoy yourself for a while. But then come back. I'll wait for you.*

The lean, straight back and the blonde hair in the canoe in front of me, the slow spinning motion in the whirlpool; a small fire on the bank, the smoke drifting upwards in the clear still air. Shots fired by an angry farmer; a little cafe tart, a telephone on a counter with rows of bottled sweets.

Deep in the night, a man and a woman in a half-dark room, that emblematic moment: two hands touching the same glass, a head upturned, an awareness of irrevocable loss. Images from half a lifetime. A man pursuing me like a conscience, even to this dark and distant farm where I'd hoped to be rid of him.

Are you washing your hands?—No, I'm putting on my knuckle-dusters.
Loss, loss, waste. All of it, one slow diminishing.
(How long is a life sentence?)

But in recalling all these memories I was merely postponing the inevitable, the one thing I'd prefer not to remember, but which, in that tired, defenseless hour, I could no longer resist.

It might have been easier if he hadn't spoken those words in court. But he had to make sure that I, too, would be forced to face it all and come to terms with it. *Perhaps my arrest could have been avoided at the time it happened. But it is so easy to misjudge a situation, or a trivial detail, or a friend.*

I'd been working on a takeover contract that night when the

telephone rang on the corner of my desk: the private number known only to Elise and Bea and one or two of my staff. Mechanically, as I put out my hand, I glanced at my wristwatch. Twenty to twelve.

"Martin? Thank God you're still there. I tried to reach you at home."

"What's the matter, Bea?"

"Will you pick me up at the witchdoctor place?"

"The witchdoctor place?"

"Don't you remember? I took you there once."

"But what are you doing there at this time of the night?"

"Will you come straight away, please?"

She rang off without waiting for an answer.

In all my years in Johannesburg I'd never bothered to stroll through Diagonal Street on foot before the day she'd taken me there. I might have expected it of her. The witchdoctor shop with its *muti*, its vulture eggs, the skins and hair and nails and horns and unmentionable excretions, its useless whorl of incense; and the Indian owner glaring at one like a dark wooden mask. Outside, the din of street vendors and pennywhistles, the pimps and contacts and con men; the sinister characters pretending to stand dozing against pillars covered in graffiti and peeling paint. It was bad enough in broad daylight. At night it was inviting swift and certain death.

Annoyed and worried I pushed aside my work—another half hour and I would have been finished—and went down to the parking garage in the basement. Emerging like a shadow from behind a pillar, the nightwatchman shuffled to the entrance to remove the chain barrier.

"Thanks, George. I may be coming back."

The streets were warm and wet. Not the sort of rain to end a drought: a dirty little drizzle, just enough to make everything filthy and unpleasant, the musty February heat clinging stickily to the dark buildings; the lamp posts surrounded by dull spheres of murky light.

Diagonal Street. I slowed down, making sure the car doors were locked. A few empty fruit carts stood abandoned in the gutter, some of them covered with tattered canvas. All the windows were protected by bars and railings and steel mesh, with glimpses of mysterious and certainly malodorous wares behind them. Just as well the whole street was due to be demolished soon.

I stopped at a safe distance from the curb, very reluctant to risk it outside. Something moved behind a pillar. I kept my foot on the accelerator, ready to drive off fast. Someone approached in the dull drizzle. A woman, slightly crippled. Not Bea: this stranger appeared elderly and stocky.

Was it a trap of some sort? Had someone else been imitating Bea's voice on the phone? But it had been unmistakable, the Italian roundness of her vowels, the slight pause on double consonants. I had no doubt at all that it had been she who'd phoned me.

Turning the window down a few inches I called: "Where's Bea?"

"I'm taking you to her," said the woman in a curious falsetto voice.

Something was wrong somewhere. However, my anxiety about Bea forced me to lean over and open the door on the passenger side for the stranger to get in. She brought with her a smell of wet feathers.

"Will you please tell me—"

"Let's get away from here first." This time it was a male voice. I was paralyzed.

"Don't worry, Martin," the stranger assured me. "It's quite all right."

I refused to believe it. In such a night, in such a place, one could expect any sort of treachery, if not witchcraft.

"Don't tell me you really didn't recognize me?" By that time we were several blocks away. The woman was fumbling with her hat; a wig was removed.

"Bernard!"

I would recognize that chuckle anywhere.

"Just drive out of the city first."

Aimlessly, in a daze, I turned up and down all sorts of streets until I could start thinking coherently again. Along an old abandoned road I drove out to a mine dump. There were trees on either side, frayed and miserable in the drizzle. The wipers were buzzing to and fro, evenly, unobtrusively, monotonously. At last we stopped. The drops running down the side windows seemed to insulate us like fish in an aquarium.

"Where do you come from, Bernard? Where have you been all the time? Where's Bea?"

"At home and quite safe. She couldn't tell you more on the phone, one never knows whether it's tapped."

"But where have you been? What have you been up to?"

"I need your help."

"How? With what?"

"I'd like a cigarette first."

"You never smoked before."

"One gets used to many things." He took the cigarette. I pushed in the lighter and waited for it to jump out.

"Now you must tell me everything."

"Not everything," he said, keeping the smoke in his mouth for a while, without inhaling, before he blew it out again.

"Why did you escape from custody last year?"

"Had no choice. I had to finish a job."

"What job?"

"Business." I guessed he was smiling in the dark. "Don't ask too many questions, Martin. Just listen to me. I don't want to keep you out of bed for too long."

"Well, go ahead then. Tell me."

"You must help me to hide for a while. They're hard on my heels."

"I don't understand."

"The SB infiltrated one of their men into our organization."

"So there *is* an organization?"

"Of course." He pulled at his cigarette again. "I never trusted the bloke completely, but I couldn't find anything to put a finger on. Then, last month, I found irrefutable evidence that he was a plant. I couldn't confront him with it, of course. I didn't dare to let him find out I knew, so I had to keep up the facade. You follow me? While he thought we were working in a certain direction we were really involved in something quite different. But it's nerve-racking. And I believe he's now got wise to it. They're watching our place near Pretoria. I can't go near it. But if I can disappear for a week or two, I'll get them off the track completely. It's absolutely vital to shake them off."

"But how can I—"

"You needn't know about anything. I don't want to drag you into it. Just give me the key to your apartment and let me stay there for a fortnight. Then I promise you I'll disappear from the face of the earth."

"But why come to me?"

"Who else is there to go to?"

"Jesus, Bernard—" I couldn't think of anything to say.

"You remember that night, three years ago, during the Terror Trial?" he suddenly asked. "The night we started talking in the apartment and then you went to Aunt Rienie's party?"

"What about it?"

"There was something between us that evening—I may have been mistaken, but I felt I wanted to talk to you. I wanted to make a clean breast of it so that you could help me. I was beginning to have doubts. Everything seemed to be heading for the rocks. I was wondering whether I hadn't made a terrible mistake—" He broke off. "But that's beside the point now. I don't want to burden you with particulars."

"Was that why you were so insistent that I had to come back after the party?"

"Yes."

"And then I—" Everything came back to me. I felt sick.

"Don't worry, it's all long past now. The very fact that we weren't able to talk it out helped me to make up my mind. For better or for worse. At least I had more than enough time, that night, to sort things out for myself."

"And now you're asking me—"

"Just the key, no more. You needn't go near the place. For all you know I could have broken in there."

"Why didn't you just go ahead and do it?"

"Too dangerous, I suppose. But above all"—in the dark the strange elderly woman was looking at me—"above all I have to be fair to you. You've got to make your own decisions, I can't impose anything on you."

"It would have been better if you hadn't told me."

"I only told you enough to help you make up your mind."

"Suppose I refuse?"

He shrugged.

"Bernard, do you realize the risk I'm exposing myself to if I—"

"Everybody gets a chance to decide with open eyes," he said. "And then there comes a day—or a night—when it's too late." The familiar teasing tone was in his voice when he asked: "Well, what will it be?"

"Bernard, if I'd been free like you—"

"Isn't it up to yourself to decide on the measure of your own freedom?"

"I'm married. I have children. I have a responsible job. Don't you realize—"

He said nothing.

"My God, man, you know very well that if there's anything I can really do to help you—"

"You can let me have the key and then forget about it. That's all I'm asking of you."

"And if anything goes wrong?"

"Then you deny all knowledge of it. I'll take all the blame."

"You must have known all the time that sooner or later you were bound to get caught if you got involved in—well, in whatever it was."

"Don't start moralizing. I didn't come here to go on my knees to ask your favor."

"But I'm going on my knees before you. Please, Bernard, why don't you drop the whole wretched thing?"

"Now you're being very naive."

"If you gave yourself up—you could turn State witness—I'm sure—"

"Is that what you think of me, Martin? After all we've gone through together?"

"Well, if that's your attitude, you can't expect me to—"

"I don't expect anything of you any more." He turned down the window. The miserable night air came flapping into the car like a moist rag. He flicked away the dead stub of his cigarette and closed the window again. "Let's go now."

"I can't take you back just like this."

"Then I'll get out right here."

"Don't be stupid, that's not what I mean."

"I don't care a damn about what you mean or don't mean. Just drive on."

Never before in my life had I felt such a burning urge to talk and talk, but there was nothing I could say.

On the outskirts he asked me to drop him.

"Can't I take you somewhere?"

"No. I don't want you to take any risks."

I couldn't make out whether he was being sarcastic or whether he really felt concerned about me. I stopped and involuntarily thrust my hand into my pocket, touching with my fingers the cold metal of my keys. But he'd already closed the door and gone off, without a word. In the rearview mirror I saw him for the last time: the tired old woman with the drooping shoulders and the wide hat, in the drizzle sifting down over the sordid world.

Two days later he was arrested.

In any case I bear no ill feeling to anyone, and I blame no one, whether friend or policeman. They all did what they regarded as their duty. Those had been his own words. So why should I go on brooding over it all? It was done. No one could have expected me to get involved in such a business. I had duties and responsibilities of my own. Surely it would be ridiculous to suggest that I'd been responsible in any way for what had happened. He'd made his own choice, years ago and without me.

There is so much I still have to write down. I must come to grips with Dad, with Louis, and with Bea. But at least I've finished with Bernard. Thank God. I'd been reluctant to attempt it, but now it is out of my system. Now his name need never be mentioned in this document again.

The night was cold but under Ma's eiderdown I was snug and satisfied. I could hear mice scuttling in the attic above the heavy varnished beams of the ceiling. On the front stoop one of the big dogs stirred and groaned in his sleep. Floorboards creaked from time to time. And from outside came a sound straight from my childhood and still inexplicable: like a bucket scraping on stone. Some nocturnal bird or small animal? I'd never been able to find out. It was something unearthly, belonging to the night.

Here I was back on the farm, surrounded by all the familiar and good and comforting things I'd known from childhood; my people sleeping, in canopied bed or graveyard; an entire history. I ought to feel safe and protected. And yet I knew—or rather, writing here in London, I know in retrospect—that, just as the doors were unlocked and the windows left open to the night, I too was vulnerable and exposed, unable to escape from anything any longer. And succumbing to sleep, it felt as if I were sinking, sinking into mud and water; and soundlessly I cried for help, but no one came towards me from the bank.

Saturday

1

AND HAVE NOT LOVE. I have just looked it up in the hotel Bible again, but somehow it seems pale and meaningless compared to the sonority those words had when I was small. Everything about my suspended existence here in London, however immediately I am involved in it, appears as pale and unreal beside the intensity of my memories. I have embarked on this project, trying my hand at writing, not without a sound measure of cynicism. Now I cannot but go on. It is disturbing, and yet the mere act of writing down everything has become, in a sense, compulsive.

And have not love—in the booming voice of my grandfather, his reading spectacles on his nose, the table lamp placed beside the large Dutch State Bible with the brass buckles (now an ornament on the bar counter in my lounge): every syllable emphasized separately. When we were very small, evening prayers at table meant abandoning oneself to the grown-ups' ritual of reading and praying and singing. I didn't understand a word of it, nor did it even occur to me to try to. Yet there was something profoundly reassuring about the experience of great words thundering past one, protecting one like a solid wall of sound from the night outside. But from the day we turned six, first I and then Theo, it was required of us to repeat to Grandpa something we'd memorized from his reading. From that day religion ceased to be something dark and comforting and became, instead, something terrifying. In a state of panic one would desperately try to clutch some phrase drifting past in the slow and steady current of Grandpa's reading; paralyzed with fear if you discovered you'd lost a word and had to grasp at something new. Even if it were only a series of meaningless names: *Adam, Sheth, Enosk, Kenan, Mahalaleel, Jered.* It wasn't necessary to understand anything of what one had memorized: the mere act of remembering was enough. In our minds it made the difference between heaven and hell: and high on the dining room wall behind Grandpa sat the picture of *The Broad and Narrow Way* in confirmation and admonition, the fierce Eye of the Lord burning above.

The first time it happened, Grandpa pounced on me without warning. As always in our farm holidays I'd been sitting at table, subjecting myself to the flow of his slow, thundering voice, anticipating the warmth of my bed, when suddenly, the Book still open before him, he looked at me over the top of his glasses and demanded:

"Well, Martin, can you remember anything I read?"

"Grandpa?"

"I want you to repeat something I read tonight." Dad tried to intervene: "But you didn't warn the boy to prepare himself for this."

"I wasn't talking to you, Wim. Well, Martin?" I looked at the lamp burning steadily on the table; and beyond it at the Eye staring down on me.

"Can't you remember anything at all?"

I started trembling. For the first time in my life I felt exposed to a grown-up world of ruthlessness and confusion, all my early certainties beyond my reach.

"The Lord will be deeply hurt by this, Martin." I gulped.

"I hope you'll do better tomorrow night. Let us pray."

We moved back our chairs; I pressed my face against the leather thongs of the seat as the steady waves of Grandpa's prayer began to break over us. But it wasn't comforting as before; it was a judgment condemning me to hell.

The next evening I hardly touched my food. From the moment Grandpa opened the Bible I sat in a sweat trying to memorize one phrase after the other, as if they were pieces of flotsam drifting past me on Noah's flood. One by one they sank away from reach again, until I managed to grasp that one line and hold on to it in desperation. And when once again he put down the Bible and looked at me, I recited stuttering:

"And have not love, Grandpa."

I was saved. But that night I had one nightmare after the other, and at irregular intervals I woke up with those words burning in my mind like fire and brimstone.

From a lifetime of confused memories that was the phrase to come back to me when I awoke from a restless sleep to hear Ma's strong, flat voice singing the morning hymn the way she'd been doing it all the years. *And have not love.* The words were so real that, momentarily, all the dead returned to me: Grandpa and Grandma, and Dad himself.

It must have been from sheer fatigue that I'd slept so badly. In addition, I couldn't shake off the thoughts of Bernard. And I was irritated by Louis's deep, regular breathing. It was still dark when I heard the first sounds of the servants from the kitchen; outside the cocks were crowing. I turned over and tried to sleep on. There were at least another two hours before breakfast; even more, considering that I'd come to have a proper rest on the farm. But then, hearing Ma's voice, I knew I wouldn't be able to doze off again.

It was an eerie sound, that voice singing in the dark in painful exultation; yet there was something deeply reassuring about it at the same time—the resolute and invincible quality of it, affirming her ability to survive in spite of suffering and loneliness and death itself. Pushing myself up against the pillows I sat listening to her, thinking about her and the way she'd kept us together all those years without one bitter or reproachful word about Dad's lovable but unpractical ways. She'd always been so much more positive and self-assured and strong than him, but she'd been careful to keep her place behind him and never to take control openly. From the shadows she kept him going, even though he must have driven her to despair more than once. Her way of managing our affairs had been so unobtrusive, in fact, that one only really became conscious of it after his death—from the way she began to grow and blossom like a tree which suddenly, after many years of mere existence, started sprouting new branches and leaves as if the roots had struck a deeper layer of fertile earth below.

After the funeral I'd wanted her to come and live with us, assuming that she would be relieved to leave the farm after so many years of struggling. But I hadn't reckoned with her tenacity. In the beginning it hadn't been all that obvious:

"Just give me some time to find my feet first," she'd said. "I think I'll manage all right."

I'd let her have her way, assuming it would he a matter of only a few months. But she became more and more obdurate, and after a while I discovered that the solitary life on the farm had indeed become indispensable to her.

In short, Ma had begun to flourish. Ma, but not the farm. That continued the steady decline of the previous years and on several occasions I had to invest large sums of capital just to keep it going. An irking responsibility, since she would never ask for help herself. In the past, when Dad had been alive, she'd always been the one to warn me when things weren't going well ("It's not that he's ashamed to ask, sonny. It's simply he doesn't realize when he needs something"). Now that, because of the drought, she needed more help than before, she never said a word. If I hadn't inquired on my own initiative from time to time, God alone knows what would have happened to her.

The crunch had come one Saturday (I only learned about it months later and quite by accident): all the laborers had been drunk and not a soul had turned up for work. Instead of resigning herself to the inevitable as most others in her position would have done, Ma took a sjambok from the stable and walked up to the huts, half a mile uphill from the house, where she promptly started flailing left and right among them. One of the men, swaying on his feet, grabbed the sjambok and hurled it away. The next moment he pulled out his knife. Even the women had stopped wailing and screaming and suddenly it was deadly quiet on the hillside. The man came closer.

Ma waited until he had planted himself right in front of her. Then, looking him in the eyes, she said: "Now put away that knife and go down to the milking shed." Without waiting for a reaction she turned her back to him and walked away. And he followed.

It was that episode which had finally anchored her to the place, as if it hadn't been the unruly laborers only but the farm itself she'd tamed that morning.

Her people, the Neethlings, had an old-established reputation in the Sandveld for taming the land in the face of marauding animals, and Bushmen, and the vagaries of nature. By the time *I* met them, in my earliest childhood, they'd already settled in Malmesbury, where we regularly went for holidays.

One thing I'll always remember about those visits is how, every Sunday afternoon after coffee, we would all set out to the graveyard in our church clothes. The two old people had selected a spot for their dual grave years ago; even the hole had been dug and remained there in readiness, covered by iron sheets. And on Sundays we would pay our solemn family visit to "Oupa's hole" to make sure everything was still in order. In the attic of their old house on Hill Street their coffins stood waiting, filled with dried apricots and raisins and figs for the time being. A family steeped in death, almost voluptuously conditioned by it.

✧ ✧ ✧ ✧

In the cold dark dawn, listening to Ma's morning hymn, it all came back to me very vividly. On the bed opposite, Louis was still asleep. I could hardly see him in the dark; but I could hear his peaceful breathing. From the kitchen the noise of the servants was increasing. In the yard outside, and from the direction of the dairy, came deep, cold voices; a calf lowed plaintively. And in the dining room, Ma. I felt a sudden urge to be with her. In my childhood she'd always been the first to rise, serving Dad his coffee in bed and scurrying about in the kitchen to prepare breakfast for us. Then I'd often get up too to have my coffee in the kitchen with her—seated on a windowsill or on the table in summer, and in winter in the corner at the coal stove, beside the pail of dough which had been set out the evening before to rise overnight. There had always been an intimacy about our early morning conversations not superseded by anything else in my life: it had been a form of mutual acknowledgement and of recognition, immediate and frank, an attitude inconceivable at any other hour of the day, when we'd both have entrenched ourselves in the routine of our respective lives.

I got up, shivering in the cold, my hands fumbling with my clothes. In the bathroom the icy water took away my breath.

Ma had just pushed the Bible aside on the table when I came in. Kristina, placing a cup of coffee before her, looked up.

"For the Baas also?" she asked.

"Yes, please."

"I'd hoped you would get up," said Ma, content. "But I thought you'd be too tired after the long drive."

"Actually I was too tired to sleep."

The first dark grey light was just beginning to filter through the windows; it was as yet impossible to distinguish anything outside. The lamp isolated us at a corner of the large table. Kristina brought in my coffee, bringing with her a whirl of warmer air.

"Why don't you stay in bed a little longer in the mornings?" I asked Ma. "You're not getting any younger."

"What'll become of the farm?"

"I'm sure the laborers can cope."

"What sort of respect will they have for me if I lay in bed till all hours?"

"It's no life for a woman, Ma."

She shrugged. "In dry times like these it isn't easy, I admit. But one still scrapes through. We're used to it. It's only the English people in the district who can't take it. There have been many stories of selling up and moving out lately." Her eyes scrutinized me as if she were reading my thoughts: "But you know what an Englishman is like, sonny: he thinks a farm is only a piece of land he can get rich on. He knows nothing of the earth itself."

"You say people have started selling?" I asked cautiously.

"Yes, all over the place. Even old Lawrence on the next farm."

"He's always been such a help to you."

"Yes, I know. A real Christian, even though he's an Englishman. Pity he's such a communist."

"What are you talking about?"

"Well, it's true. You should hear him. Blaming the government for not doing enough for the Blacks." She grunted. "You should see what he pays his own laborers. Worst wages in the district. But I don't want to say anything bad of a neighbor."

"Is it because of the drought they're selling their farms?" I deliberately feigned ignorance.

"Yes, what else? Just wait till you get outside. I don't think you've ever seen the farm quite as bad as this. Even the stream has dried up."

"Down there in the kloof?"

"Yes. And the borehole is getting weaker too. There's a man coming today to look for water. Perhaps we can sink a new hole."

"Is it really as bad as that?"

"I tell you. But one can't give up just because it's dry. The Lord knows His own time." And before I could interrupt, she was off on one of her reminiscences: "I remember, in the Sandveld when I was small, it used to get just as dry as this. Once it lasted for years. Pa was nearly finished that time. Then the hail came. It started from the north, then it turned south. And after a while it came from the east and the west too. Sonny, I tell you, in the end it seemed as if the hail was coming up right from the ground. There was nothing left of Pa's orchard. You know what the Lord is like: He got no respect for anything a man has made on his own."

I had to use the opportunity before the day grew older and Ma more obstinate: "Perhaps there's more reason than just the drought for selling the farms around here." Seeing the lines round her mouth deepen as she looked at me, I continued: "I understand the government is buying up farms to add on to the Ciskei Homeland."

"Is that why you came?"

The grayness outside had grown lighter. From the dairy the calves were lowing more insistently: the milking must be nearly done. One felt less protected in the small circle of the lamp as the daylight slowly intruded.

"You know I often get confidential information in my work, Ma. And I can assure you it's true. They want to consolidate the Ciskei."

"As long as they leave our farm out of it. I hope you told them so."

"If we sell now, we can get a decent price for it, Ma. But if we put it off and they decide to expropriate it, we'll have to take whatever they offer."

"What do you call a decent price, sonny?"

"Two hundred and fifty thousand rand."

"If that's the truth you must be lying."

"It's true, Ma."

She looked at me for a long time before she asked quietly: "And every man has his price?"

I knew my face was flushed. "That's nonsense!" I said sharply. "It's you I'm thinking about. I know you love the farm life, but you must be reasonable. You're not young any more and you can't go on like this. Apart from anything else, it's becoming much too dangerous for a woman on her own."

"I've never had any trouble so far."

"You'll be very comfortable with us."

"That's not the problem." She remained quite calm. "I'm just not the sort of person you can transplant at my age."

"Think of the expense to keep the farm going, Ma," I said, trying another approach. "It's never become profitable enough to make a proper living."

"Can't you afford it any longer?"

"Of course I can afford it, but—"

"Well, if it's not that, we needn't discuss it any further. We've pulled through other bad times and we'll do it again."

"But you don't understand. If the government—"

"You're a man with influence. You just tell them."

"Don't be so damned pigheaded, Ma!"

She pushed back her chair and went to the dresser to put away the Bible. At the window she stopped to look out.

"It's not just a piece of land you can sell like that, sonny," she said after a while. "There's your father and all his people lying in their graves. This place has been ours for generations."

"I'm just as attached to it as you are, Ma. But let's try to look at it in a practical way: neither Theo nor I will ever come to live on the farm. Our lives are different. And it's foolish to let it go to waste."

"Perhaps Louis would like to come back here one day."

"Nonsense!" I had to laugh. "He's become quite unmanageable as it is. Angola messed him up completely."

"You never know." Her back remained straight and unyielding. "Things have looked bad for the farm before this. But there has always been someone in our family prepared to come back to it, and it will stay that way. Our roots are here." She turned round, pushing back a few loose strands of hair behind her ears. "Now forget about this silly business and enjoy your weekend. We won't talk about it again." And she went through to the kitchen.

2

EVER SINCE MY STUDENT days I'd known Charl Jansen, the secretary of the department headed by Minister Calitz. We'd never been close friends. We were probably too ambitious, both of us (at university we'd competed fiercely in events like the annual orator's competition, for example, taking turns to win the cup), but after each had chosen his own career, excluding the possibility of further rivalry, we'd established a firmer footing for our relationship. He could benefit from my confidential information on shares etc., in exchange for help with permits and other favors. We were, in fact, looking after each other's interests quite well.

With Calitz's predecessor, Peet Louwrens, Charl had had an excellent understanding. Louwrens had been one of the Old Guard who'd spent many years in the political wilderness with his party; finally rewarded with a Cabinet post, he was content to sit back and reap whatever benefits came his way, leaving the run of his department to his secretary, which suited Charl's ambition and initiative perfectly. And the department itself prospered as a result.

Then the old man resigned (after an unfortunate incident with a Colored cleaning girl in his office in the Union Buildings) and the Hon. Jan Calitz proved a very different boss altogether. The day he became Minister he announced—his silver Hitler moustache trembling with emotion—that he was firmly resolved to "leave his own

imprint" on the department. Chad's freedom to maneuver was dras-
tically curtailed, and from the outset there was a clash of personalities. That was the position when he telephoned me in May this year.

He didn't want to talk on the phone. I was forced to cancel a date
with Bea in order to meet him for lunch, but it proved to be more
than worth my while.

He came straight to the point: "I've got a tip-off for you.
Cigarette?"

"No thanks. Tell me."

He lit a cigarette. "I've had enough of His Excellency's shit."

"I know. But what can I do to help you?"

"It's straight from the hand of God." And then he told me about
the government's decision to transfer more land to the Ciskei. It had
been decided in principle only and no final choice of land had yet
been made. Calitz had set to work immediately, profiting from the
drought to buy up, through intermediaries, a vast block of farms at
ridiculous prices. Almost in the centre of the block was our family
farm. In fact, it had been the knowledge that the farm belonged to
me which had prompted Calitz to decide on that area in the first
place: in the light of dealings he'd had with me in the past, he was
under the impression that I'd be willing to "cooperate." Five farms
had already been bought, at an average of about R40,000; but he was
willing, I learned from Charl, to offer me up to R50,000. He had
already signed a contract with the Department of Bantu
Administration, in terms of which they would buy the whole block
from him for half a million rand, leaving His Excellency with a net
profit of about R250,000 (to be divided between him and the
responsible official in Bantu Administration).

Everything was in the bag. All that remained was for me to sign
a deed of sale, a detail of which Bantu Administration was ignorant.

"I thought I'd warn you in time," Charl said, winking. "So you
can have time to think it over."

He didn't want anything for his trouble, but I insisted on offering him R10,000. And when His Excellency invited me to lunch barely a week later, I was well prepared. Throughout the meal, while he was making polite conversation, I kept my cool and pretended to be greatly astonished when finally, over coffee, he mentioned casually that he was prepared to offer me a good sum (R40,000) for my farm.

"But Mr. Minister, I won't think of selling the place. It's been in our family for generations."

"Fifty thousand," he said calmly.

I shook my head.

"Mr. Mynhardt," he said, "surely you know how badly the drought has hit the Eastern Cape. I know of people who would be eager to sell at half the price."

"Then it's a matter for their own conscience, Mr. Minister, not mine."

"I'll tell you what, Mr. Mynhardt." In a show of confidence he leaned over to me. "I am prepared to pay you sixty thousand cash."

"But why should you be so interested in a farm in a drought-stricken area?" I gave him no time to reply. "Or does it form part of a plan to consolidate the Ciskei?"

He grew pale, but his face remained expressionless; he even managed a hoarse laugh. "In these times of economic recession, Mr. Mynhardt?"

I looked him in the eyes. "I shall be frank with you, Mr. Minister. Your offer did not come as a surprise to me."

"Really?"

"No. A friend of mine, a newspaper editor, mentioned it to me yesterday. I believe they're working on the story at the moment."

"Impossible!" In the pale blue flickering of his eyes I could see both fear and fury. "Which newspaper is it?"

"You will appreciate that it was told me in strict confidence, Your Excellency, so I'm afraid I'm not in a position to tell you more. It's possible, of course, that they're on a wild goose chase."

"Oh, undoubtedly."

"In which case it would be better to leave it at that." I paused for a moment. "But in case you are really interested, my price is a quarter of a million."

"Ridiculous!"

I shrugged.

We picked up our coffee cups simultaneously. A few minutes later he said: "I'm sure we can come to some sort of an agreement, Mr. Mynhardt. You are a reasonable man."

I knew I'd won.

In the career of an entrepreneur, as in some highly competitive sports, there is that element known to boxers as the killer instinct. If you lack it, it's better to clear out as soon as possible: then it's simply not your scene. You need a tennis player's "hunger," otherwise you cannot win. And winning is the name of the game. Nothing else. No fancy labels. Just winning. I think I inherited it from Ma: but in her it still assumed a different, old-worldly form. In my generation we have discarded the niceties. We call it by its Christian name.

His Excellency knew only too well that to save his reputation— compromised by concluding that contract with Bantu Administration before he had all the cards in his hand—he had no option but to clinch the sale. The price had been named. It would leave him with a new net profit of only R50,000, half of which still had to go to his accomplice. Peanuts. Still, he wouldn't be left penniless. That, too, was part of the game.

He pretended that the matter was closed: he wouldn't even consider such a preposterous proposal. I assured him that I would be only too glad to drop the whole thing, and on that note we went our separate ways.

I waited for his telephone call, knowing he had no choice but to come back. Without my farm his transaction with the government could not go through and he would be exposed to the worst kind of publicity. The government, of course, could still save face by acquiring an entirely new block of farms—but then Calitz would be left with the five he'd already bought for R200,000; and he wasn't the sort of person to play it that way.

Within a week we had another business lunch, and three days later we signed the contract. Smiling stiffly, he agreed it would be better for himself in the long run to keep his own profit as low as possible: it would avoid tricky questions in the press or in parliament.

But when we shook hands after signing the deal, I knew very well that I'd acquired a new enemy, one who was in no mind ever to forget what had happened.

What he didn't know was that I had to settle the sale with Ma before the news was made public. Dad had left the farm to me in his will all right, but Ma was entitled to the usufruct for life and there had been an explicit codicil to the effect that it could not be sold without her written consent. That was why I had to go to the farm without delay. If Ma decided not to cooperate, Minister Jan Calitz would finish me off very efficiently, and with glee.

3

MA WAS BUSY WITH THE Black baby again when I came into the kitchen. The child was screaming as she went her imperturbable way, administering medicine, washing, changing a nappy, uttering small comforting sounds until the baby became quiet in her arms. She'd been a nurse before her marriage.

"Morning, Baas," said Kristina from the stove.

The young woman who'd been in the kitchen with her the previous night was there again, at the corner of the table, looking at me without saying a word. There was neither insolence nor limp passivity in her attitude. Serenity, really, if the word wouldn't sound out of place here. Now that I was able to see her properly, I was quite impressed by her face, which reminded me of some of the Black women painted by Tretchikoff in his youth. But what really caught my attention—because I must admit that most Black women look alike to me—was the swollen wound on one cheek, partly exposing the flesh.

"What's happened to her?" I asked Ma after she'd handed the baby back to its mother.

"It's her husband. That foreman, Mandisi. Beat her because she came here last night to get medicine for the child."

"Why has she come back then?"

"She waited for him to go down to the cows. The baby was very sick during the night."

"But what's the matter with the man?"

"You know how they are. He doesn't trust White medicine. He wanted to take the child to the witchdoctor." She sighed. "You should have seen how he beat her up last year, just after Dad died. Just because I gave her an old bra of mine and she put it on. She came crawling down here in the middle of the night, a collarbone and one of her arms broken. I didn't think she would make it."

"Why doesn't she leave him?"

"I suppose she loves him." Taking the poker from Kristina she started stirring up the fire in the stove. "I've spoken to her many times. All she can do is smile. One day, I remember, she said: 'I know he'll kill me sooner or later but he's my husband.' Can you beat that?"

"Why don't you give him the sack? He's a menace."

"Without him the farm would have been down the drain long ago. He's a difficult customer—he's the one who pulled the knife on me when I hit him with the sjambok that time—but he's a good worker. He drives me up the wall with his insolence. But he's my right hand and one must take it as it comes."

"I can't understand why you continue to put up with it all."

"We've already talked about that, haven't we?" she said calmly before turning to Kristina to go on with her work.

Opening the back door I was struck viciously in the face by the cold. A clean, incisive cold cutting one to the bone. My breath forming small white clouds in the air, I walked through the backyard, past the water tank and the electricity plant. The chickens had come down from their slats and were eagerly pecking up the mealies someone had thrown out for them. A group of chilly geese and muscovy ducks were messing about in the shallow ditch running from the water tank, shattering the thin layer of ice.

Beside the house stood the enormous wild fig tree under whose widespread branches the members of our family had gathered for generations, on holidays or festive occasions. There were still a few rotten boards and dangling ropes left of the treehouse Dad had built years ago for Louis and Ilse (and then he'd fallen from the tree and hurt his back, so he had to spend the long December holidays in bed). A broken plow, some old worn tires, the axle of a wagon. The place had always been a jumble, but now it really seemed to be falling to pieces.

I went round to the front of the house, looking out over the valley. And for the first time I discovered the full truth of what Ma had said. I'd seen the farm in other droughts, but never as ghastly as this. The lawn was reduced to dry tufts, now covered with frost, leaving large bare patches of red earth in between. Beyond the stalks of shrubs and cannas the hill sloped gently down to the dairy and Dad's outbuilding. The lower reaches of the slope and the valley itself, normally a lush green even in the harshest of winters, appeared arid and scarred, the remaining euphorbias looking like black charcoal smudges on a dirty sheet of paper. Where the two rows of hills met at the far end of the narrow valley, the thickets surrounding the stream still showed a touch of green, but even that was dull and lifeless compared to the luxuriant virgin forest I'd known before.

Going down to the cowshed and the dairy I could feel the brittle grass and twigs snapping under my smooth-soled shoes. The bell of the separator was tinkling regularly. A few laborers were washing the pails as another poured skimmed milk into a trough for the calves. I inhaled deeply, relishing the smell of dung and milk, the warm odor of life. As I came nearer the men looked up, murmuring a greeting: *"Molo, nkosi"* their white teeth sparkling against the dull blackness of their faces.

As the cows were chased out I had to sidestep smartly not to be trampled by the front ones. In passing I recognized the man following them.

"Molo, Mandisi."

"Molo, nkosi." He didn't smile like the others, but looked me straight in the face; nothing submissive about him.

Struggling to scrape together individual words from the bit of Xhosa I'd picked up through the years, I said: "Is everything still all right on the farm?"

"*Ewe.*"

I wondered whether I should say something about his wife, but decided against it for the time being: there were too many others listening.

"The Missus told me the electricity plant is broken." I gestured in the direction of the small shed behind the house. "Do you think you can fix it?"

"*Ewe.*" Without waiting, he went off after the cows, driving them downhill much faster than he should. At a turn in the road he looked back, shouting something at the other laborers, who promptly burst out laughing, one or two with a furtive glance in my direction. I couldn't make out what he'd said: something about me? Whatever it was, it made me furious.

"Don't stand around like that!" I said. "Get on with your work."

They fell silent immediately. The separator was still tinkling inside. Far in the distance I could hear Mandisi's voice again, shouting at the cows.

In spite of myself I had to admit that there was something appealing about the man. He wasn't really provocative. It was, rather, a positive if disturbing affirmation of independence; there was something regal and assertive about the very movement of his legs as he strode on, in the attitude of his shoulders and his barrel chest: as if all the world belonged to him, as if nothing could contain him; a man carrying the fire within him.

On an impulse I went to Dad's small outbuilding. But the door was locked and the faded green curtains were drawn behind the windows.

What I did next, had been unavoidable from the beginning. Following the narrow path, hardly more than an erosion ditch, I went downhill to the stone wall of the small graveyard below. My smooth leather soles were slippery on the rough surface: I hadn't thought of bringing along my veld shoes and these Italian ones were most uncomfortable, the sharp-edged stones pressing right into my footsoles.

A small formation of hadedahs, four or five of them, flew past overhead, shrieking their wild death cries across the valley. The sun was rising above the hills.

The wooden gate in the wall got stuck as I pushed against it. The rusty top hinge had broken, so the gate had to be lifted before one could open it. Then a silly thing happened. Leaning forward to force the gate, I stepped on a loose stone and lost my balance, stumbling against the wall. My glasses fell on the ground. And turning round to retrieve them, I heard a crunching sound under my foot. One of the lenses was shattered and the frame itself broken in two places.

Well. Another of those entirely unpredictable mishaps, this time much more serious than the previous day's. Squatting on my haunches with the broken spectacles in my hand I stupidly tried to fit the shattered bits together. In the process one of the splinters cut into my palm, sending a thin needle of pain up through my arm. In a momentary blind rage I threw the useless thing away and got up.

In the distance the vague shapes of hills were huddled in large simplified patterns of ochre and brown and olive green. All precision had disappeared from the landscape, leaving me lost and angry in the midst of it. Damn it! Suddenly my own farm had become strange to me. I could still see well enough to find my way, but all detail was lost, all definition blurred, all familiarity gone. I felt isolated, abandoned among the dull hulks of things.

The remarkable thing is that everything should appear so startlingly clear to me now that I'm writing about it, whereas it seemed so distant and vague to me then. I can almost see myself in that landscape, on that farm, enclosed in the small graveyard.

My first impulse was to go back home. But I'd wanted to come down there, so it would be better to stay until I had regained my grasp on the world. Moving haltingly past the other, older, graves I picked my way to the shining new stone which I hadn't seen before. It wasn't difficult to read the large capitals of the inscription:

WILLEM JACOBUS MYNHARDT

Born 5.9.1908–Died 11.5.1975

followed by a text. Gravel, a glass container with imperishable plastic flowers, an empty jam jar.

Willem Jacobus Mynhardt. I found it impossible to relate the formal names to him. The whole pretentious grave had nothing to do with him. I looked up, across the stone wall, at the hazy world in the distance, then back to the headstone. Was it only the loss of my glasses which gave me that feeling of total isolation, of being remote from where I was, wholly out of touch with that grave? I felt no emotion, nothing whatsoever. And even though I'd learned to eliminate emotion long ago, nevertheless I had expected to feel *something*, to come one step closer to the enigma of my father.

Perhaps I can explain that sense of absence in terms of an experience Elise often spoke about in connection with our children: her feelings for Louis have always been profoundly different from what she feels for Ilse. Not only because, after the first miscarriage, she was exceptionally possessive about Louis when he was born, but also, and perhaps especially, because it was a particularly difficult birth, two full days of almost unbearable agony: and afterwards it took over a year to recover from the complications. Which was quite a shock to both of us, since we'd always regarded that beautiful body of hers as infallible. When, four years later, the doctor predicted a second baby as big as the first, a Caesarean was recommended. Elise was pushed into the operating theatre in the morning and only saw the baby several hours later. Afterwards it was as if she could never quite accept the fact that Ilse was her own child—because she felt she hadn't been "present" at her birth.

Would it have been different for me too if I hadn't missed Dad's death? Surely it would be a purely sentimental argument. Or had the bond been broken in advance, during those long months when the ravages of cancer had torn him out of our reach? He'd been so untouchable in his agony; death had replaced all other landscapes in his eyes long before he actually breathed his last. But this argument presupposes that there had been a strong bond to start with, and I'm not sure that I ever really understood him. Who was this man I called Dad? And what are the real implications of the relationship father/son? Is there sense in assuming that something is handed on from generation to generation?

I must return to his death. I'd been up in the Northern Transvaal, inspecting a small chromium mine I'd just taken over near Tzaneen, and I'd arranged with Elise and my office that I would be back on the Thursday morning. But in fact I'd already returned on Wednesday evening and spent the night in my apartment with Bea. It was something I did quite regularly: the easiest for all concerned, as I had no wish deliberately to hurt Elise. I presume she was intelligent enough, and woman enough, to suspect that, like any other man, I had women on the sly from time to time: but as long as it remained unrevealed and unsaid it could be ignored since no one was injured by it. I can state with a clear conscience that I am a good husband to Elise; I give her a bigger household allowance than anyone else I know of, I allow her the freedom to indulge in all the hobbies she's had over the years: painting, weaving, pottery, gardening, batik, the whole gamut. (All I fail to understand is that every time she becomes proficient in something she loses interest and gives it up: anyway, that's her worry, not mine, although she knows very well I don't approve of vacillation.)

However, to return to Dad's death. (After so many years of being concise and to the point in reports and memorandums, I can now enjoy the liberty of indulging myself by digressing whenever it suits me.) When I arrived back home at about ten o'clock that Thursday morning—"from Tzaneen"—Elise awaited me with the news that Ma had been phoning constantly since the previous afternoon. Pa was dying. We took the first plane that afternoon and hired a car in East London to drive out to the farm, but when we got there he was already dead. If we'd come the previous evening, or even early that same morning, we would still have been in time: but the South African Airways service to the Eastern Cape leaves much to be desired. And there is no point in blaming myself for the night with Bea. If I hadn't spent it with her I wouldn't have returned home before the Thursday anyway. Any argument on "liability" in this connection is senseless.

During the last hours, Ma said, he'd been very clear and calm, with no pain. They'd just sat there, she told us, holding hands and talking about the times they'd had together. She'd been a nurse in Paarl where he'd studied for his Higher Primary Diploma; after their marriage they'd started together in Calvinia before he got the history post in Griqualand West.

Those last hours, according to Ma, they had been like two young lovers again, and age and suffering seemed miraculously to disappear from his face as if an old skin had been shed. And while they were laughing about something they'd remembered—how, soon after their wedding, he'd dropped a stud on the floor and went down on all fours to look for it when she stepped on his hand—he suddenly gave a curious little sob, and when she looked at him he was dead. I still think that maybe it was a good thing after all that we hadn't been there to intrude into their intimacy.

The body had already been removed by the undertaker when we arrived on the farm that evening. The next day I went into town with Ma, "to say goodbye." There, again, I felt that strangeness between him and me. I hardly recognized him, his face looked quite different, relaxed and unfamiliar, wearing the hideous makeup like a mask; and then that ridiculous frilly shroud.

It wasn't death as such which put me off. Even as a child there had been something natural about it. Our village barber had also been the undertaker: and often it happened, when one arrived for a haircut, that his shop would be empty—then the accepted thing to do would be to go through to the backyard surrounded by a tall, red, corrugated iron fence, a real scrapyard filled with the wrecks of old cars, a decaying lathe, jacks, piles of firewood, tarred beams, sheets of iron and rolls of wire. Chickens. And wild birds. Oom Koot had the most remarkable collection of birds I'd ever seen, and when one arrived in the backyard all those hundreds of birds would be singing their little heads off and hens would be cackling behind the pepper trees in which cicadas were shrilling uninterruptedly. From the row of tumbledown iron garages one would hear the sound of hammering. That was where one invariably found Oom Koot in his black trousers and waistcoat and greasy dotted tie with a gold pin, the top buttons of his shirt undone. One had to pick one's way through the rows of coffins—the expensive black ones with silver handles, simpler brown or stained ones, and the cheap pine ones for Blacks. The corpse would be laid out on a trestle table, and there Oom Koot would be working, whistling or humming like a truly happy man.

"Come for a haircut? I'll be with you in a moment. Just hand me that hammer. No, over there, beside Uncle Dirk's left hand." He always referred to the dead as if they were still alive; sometimes, working on a corpse, he would address them directly and carry on long one-sided conversations with them.

Usually I stood on the threshold waiting for him to finish and to put on the white dustcoat he wore for cutting hair. What held me spellbound was not Oom Koot's fascinating activities but the collection of pinups on his iron walls, among the coffins and the tools of his macabre trade. There was no titillating literature available in our village in those days (the hours it took to find a picture even remotely sexy in one of the agricultural magazines or in

Ma's *Femina*, to stimulate one's pubescent fantasies!—a glimpse of anything above the knee was enough to raise a hard-on, a bare midriff was paradise; the mere sight of bra or panties almost unthinkable): my only contact with that world of forbidden delight was Oom Koot's garage—those cuttings from old calendars or imported magazines brightening up the unsightliness of his walls among the stacked coffins.

And when I found myself standing beside Dad's coffin that day, so many years later, the night with Bea fitted curiously into the whole situation, taking the place, as it were, of those pictures of my boyhood.

The memory didn't bring Dad any closer where I sat on a stone beside his grave. The distance between him and me remained unbridged. If I couldn't even reach out to touch the man who'd been my father, what about all those others who had preceded him? I *had* to make the effort. I had to make sure, I suppose, what I was really giving up in abandoning the farm which had been ours.

4

THE FOUNDER OF OUR TRIBE, Marthinus Wilhelmus Mynhardt by name, arrived at the Cape of Good Hope in 1732 as a standard-bearer in the employ of the Dutch East India Company. A restless spirit, no doubt, for within a year he deserted from the service of the company and, leaving behind him his young pregnant bride, joined an inland expedition in search of Monomotapa, that fabled ancient kingdom of gold somewhere in the heart of Africa. We have no record of his death: he simply disappeared. Perhaps he found his golden city. More likely not. What matters is that he rooted our tribe in the land. And, I suppose, that he left us the substance of his dream.

His only son, Marthinus, became the Nimrod of our race, a man who stood nearly seven feet tall and lived to the age of ninety. In his youth Cape Town was a wild and merry place, the "little Paris" of the vast commercial empire, drifting towards bankruptcy while the burghers enjoyed every moment of it. Marthinus, however, had no taste for town life. Eloping with what was reputed to be the prettiest girl at the Cape, he moved to a frontier district and became a stock farmer, which meant that he had to spend his life trekking this way and that, his wanderings determined by available pasture, the onslaught of Bushmen or predators, and rumors of rain which lured him inland as surely as Monomotapa had done with his father.

As an old man, after the death of his wife, he returned to the Cape with his twelve or thirteen children. But he soon ran into trouble with the new British authorities of the colony and went off on his own again to measure off a vast farm in the barren North-Western region of Namaqualand. The image I have of him is of a deaf and nearly blind old giant sitting in front of his wattle-and-daub cottage, an open Bible on his knees, a mere speck on the endless plains. And at regular intervals he would grope for his gun, and blindly take aim, and pull the trigger, just in case anybody was approaching from the horizon. After the shot, when the chickens and goats had settled down again, everything would once more become deadly quiet, except for the shrilling of the cicadas and, in the kitchen, the gentle bustling of the solitary slave woman who kept house for him.

In the meantime, his two oldest sons had moved to Graaff-Reinet to stake out farms in Bruintjieshoogte, the most turbulent part of the frontier district. The elder brother was soon killed in an expedition against the Bushmen. The second, Wilhelm, married a cousin of the Van Jaarsveld who later became the noted rebel leader. A feature of the wedding was that invitations were addressed, not to "Mr." or "Mrs." or "Miss" So-and-So, but to *citoyen* or *citoyenne*: incredible, the way in which germs of the French Revolution had spread to that outpost of the civilized world. Wilhelm, in effect, played a notable part in the upheavals of the following years and it comes as no surprise to learn that, in 1801 or 1802, he spent nearly a year in the Dark Hole of the Castle in Cape Town. Upon his release, as irrepressible as ever, he went into Kaffir Land to negotiate with the Xhosa chief Ngqika some scheme for a joint attack on the British rulers.

But he returned to find his farm deserted—the cattle stolen, his house and kraals burnt, his family massacred by the marauding Black tribes of the Suurveld. Only three of his sons had been saved by neighbors.

Beside the grave of his wife and children Wilhelm took an oath of vengeance; and without waiting for the funeral meal, he jumped on his horse and galloped off towards the Suurveld, where his body was found a week later, bristling with assegais.

The three orphans were brought up by the neighbors, a Badenhorst family, until they were old enough to acquire their own farm near Uitenhage.

The middle one, Lewies, happened to be in Algoa Bay for some buying and bartering when the first British settlers of 1820 were brought ashore; and his wagon was among those commandeered to convey the immigrants to their farms in the interior. He was reluctant to comply, but the journey proved to be the turning point of his life, because one of the members of the family he transported was a young girl, Melanie Harris. He first really noticed her when an old chair fell from the wagon and was broken—irreparably, it seemed. The chair, with barley-sugar legs and exquisite wood-carving, was an heirloom Melanie had inherited from her grand-mother and the girl was grief stricken. But Lewies promptly set to repairing the damage, using his hunting knife to cut pieces of indigenous wood which he inserted so skillfully among the splinters of the chair leg that it was impossible to feel the joint with a finger. In the process, inevitably, he won Melanie's heart. And today the chair has pride of place in my study, after the many years Dad used it in his outbuilding.

Within a year Lewies and Melanie were married. For a while they prospered, but the proclamation of Ordinances 49 and 50 brought a radical change in their lives: Kaffirs were no longer restricted to their own land beyond the Fish River, and Hottentots could roam throughout the Colony without a pass. After the brothers had twice lost all their possessions in raids, and after Sybrand had been shot dead by a Hottentot he'd tried to scare away from his kraal, the two remaining brothers and their wives moved across the border. There they bought a piece of land from a friendly Xhosa tribe and settled on the farm which was to remain in our family for nearly one and a half centuries.

But Lewies became restless. On his regular business trips to Grahamstown he met Piet Retief; and when Retief and his company decided to trek in search of a Promised Land of their own, Lewies joined them. And in the end he, as well as three of his four children, shared Retief's fate in the massacre of Trekkers by the Zulu *impis* of Dingane.

After the annexation of Natal by England in 1843, Melanie was among the women who insisted they'd rather cross the Drakensberg barefoot than live under British rule again. With her only surviving son, Hermanus, then a young man of nearly twenty, she once again loaded the wagons and moved off to the Transvaal. But on the way she fell ill and soon after their arrival at Potchefstroom she died.

Hermanus, true to his history, didn't settle down easily and soon moved off on his own. For many years he made a life as a big game hunter in Matabeleland and Mashonaland, allegedly penetrating as far as Kilimanjaro. In the end he did return with a wife he'd found on the way: curiously enough, Dad never spoke about her. Hermanus became involved in the political strife of the young Transvaal Republic but soon withdrew in disillusionment; and after the death of his wife he loaded his meager possessions and his two children on a mule wagon and rode off, lured by incredible tales about the diamond fields of Kimberley.

It was an alternation of good times and bad. A few sound diamonds; then nothing for months on end. After an altercation with his Griqua helper, resulting in the latter's unexplained death, Hermanus had to flee from justice—which he did none too reluctantly, as by that time rumors were rife about a new annexation by Britain.

One day in 1880 or thereabouts he and his sons arrived back on the Eastern Cape farm his father had left so many years before.

His uncle had died long ago and the latter's son Gert had inherited the place. It was a joyful reunion with the old wanderer, who promptly accepted the invitation to stay on. But the newly found peace lasted for less than a year. Then there was a hunting accident. Going off into the bush with his elder son in search of a lion that had killed two Black children on a neighboring farm, Hermanus came staggering back home in the last daylight carrying on his broad shoulders the body of his son. He got as far as the stoop. There he was felled by a stroke; and he died, weeks later, without having uttered a word.

The remaining son, Karel, didn't remain on the farm for very long after his father's death. Attracted by rumors of gold in the Transvaal, where, in addition, it was possible to breathe free air again after the First War of Liberation, he loaded his wagon and went off.

In Potchefstroom he stopped for a few months, long enough to meet and marry Helena Wepener, the daughter of a wealthy farmer; then he proceeded to Pilgrim's Rest in response to the old call of Monomotapa.

Life in the gold fields turned out to be hectic, depressing, and unprofitable, and soon Karel was following the example of most of the other diggers, spending more and more of his time in the canvas-covered tavern known as "Stent's Cathedral." What finally pulled him to his senses was the death of Helena's first baby. The local doctor, who also acted as barber and tentmaker, was drunk most of the time and nearly succeeded in knocking off Helena too.

Still, Karel wouldn't heed his wife's pleas to return to the tranquil farm life of Potchefstroom. When news came of a new gold reef discovered at Barberton—it was in 1884—he set off in search of his fortune once again, with all their earthly possessions in a single iron trunk on a donkey cart.

This time he struck it rich. And before the end of the year, just in time for the birth of their son, they were able to leave their tent and move into a corrugated iron cottage.

In less than three years the Barberton reef was exhausted. The locust swarms of fortune seekers packed their carts and wagons or set off on foot with their bundles on their backs; the drink stopped flowing, the prostitutes flocked to the Witwatersrand, and once again silence descended on the little ghost town in the Eastern Transvaal.

At last Helena had her way and they returned to the district of her parents to buy their own farm near Boskop. Their wanderings seemed to have come to an end. Then came the October night in '99 when a neighbor knocked on their bedroom window to announce that war with England had broken out.

In the beginning the prospects looked good. But within a few months of Magersfontein and Colenso and Spioen Kop the tide turned. Kimberley was relieved. Pretoria was taken without a shot. It became a foretaste of hell. Riding on horseback on the hard white winter veld, attacking and withdrawing immediately afterwards, shivering with cold in the rainy nights, stumbling along for days on end without food. Still the tattered group of men went on, singing, mornings and evenings, their dark hymns of hope and despair and listening to the commandant reading and praying with somber, sullen faith. Then back to the horses.

At the end of 1900, when Karel's commando was back in the Western Transvaal, he was allowed to return home for one night. But there was no farm left. The house was a blackened, burnt-out heap of rubble, the fields destroyed; on his approach vultures rose up like a swarm of flies from the chickens and pigs and sheep slaughtered by British bayonets and left to rot. Only much later did he learn that Helena and her five children were still alive, in the concentration camp at Heidelberg. But a fire had been extinguished inside him. Perhaps he no longer cared. Whatever it was, just after Christmas he and his companions were surprised by the enemy and taken prisoner. In open cattle trains in the violent summer sun they were transported to Durban, where they were herded on the boats to Bermuda.

On the barren, rocky island where they were dumped, he spent his days writing in a leatherbound book, committing to paper the history of his life and of those of his father and grandfather, as far back as he could remember. After the war the book was brought back by friends and restored to the family, for he himself had died before he could finish his story.

Three of Helena's children belong to the statistics of 26,000 who died in the concentration camps of the war. The two who came out with her after the Peace of Vereeniging were mere skeletons, but with the help of her mother they survived. Times were terrible. Helena wanted her children to have a proper education, but at school they were branded "dirty Dutch" and forbidden to speak their own language. The last straw was the death of her mother.

In her distress Helena took a desperate decision and returned to the family farm in the Eastern Cape, now managed by cousin Gert's bachelor son Johannes. He welcomed them with open arms and when Helena died in 1904, never having recovered fully from the effects of concentration camp life, he adopted her children as his own: by that time Coen was eighteen and Lenie only seven. Soon after Coen's marriage about two years later he was allowed to take over the management of the farm. In this way it returned to our line: for Coen was, of course, my grandfather.

He appeared to thrive as a farmer, but when war broke out in 1914 and the rebellion started against the government's decision to support England, the ancient fire flared up in him. Leaving his wife behind with four small children to look after, Coen took the train to the north and joined General Beyers.

But, of course, everything was over so soon that he never even took part in a proper battle. The commandos were disorganized and confused, and after a few half-hearted skirmishes Grandpa and his group were taken prisoner. After a year in jail he returned to the farm. It was not the end of his restlessness, however. Whenever the old family urge got hold of him, every ten years or so, Grandpa would simply pack his things and go off. Grandma soon learned to let him have his way. He always came back, usually after a couple of months or at most a year. Once he stayed away for two years, but that was the last time. It was during the Second World War, and what he did then and where he went, we still don't know. Most likely it had something to do with the underground activities of the Ossewa-Brandwag, but Grandpa would only smile if one tried to prod.

He always remained something of a lovable rogue. All his life he continued to prepare his illegal white lightning down in the kloof, distilling peaches and prickly pears and even onions, a brew more potent than battery acid. Still, he had a feeling for "higher things" and he acquired a formidable reputation for his skill in interpreting the Bible. When he died in 1949 there weren't many unfulfilled prophecies left in his reckoning, and he was pleased at the prospect of not having to lie in the earth for too long before Judgment Day.

Because he'd never had a "full-mouthed education" himself, he made sure that his sons received one. The eldest, Aalwyn, was sent to the agricultural college at Elsenburg as it was a foregone conclusion that he would take over the farm one day. The second, Dad, was earmarked as a *dominee*, but after heated arguments he was allowed to go to training college.

But there was something curious about Dad as a teacher. Although it was obvious at a glance that he would never make out as a farmer, he himself always spoke wistfully about his desire to become one. He probably felt quite safe, knowing Uncle Aalwyn had been destined to take over the farm. There was something depressing and almost unnerving about the way Dad would talk about his silly dream, as if he'd been cheated out of an ideal and so decided on teaching as an alternative.

Then, of course, the blow struck, when barely a year after Grandpa's death Uncle Aalwyn landed under a tractor and was killed. Both of the sisters had settled elsewhere long ago. In order to save the farm there was only one way out: Dad had to give up teaching and become a farmer. Everybody was elated for his sake: after all, he'd dreamed about it all his life. But it struck him like a life sentence. He'd needed the farm to dream about, not to cultivate it. Now he was no longer its master but its slave. And as the years went by we saw him going downhill slowly and sadly, until he finally came to rest in that grave, below the ostentatious headstone which said:

WILLEM JACOBUS MYNHARDT

Born 5.9.1908–Died 11.5.1975

5

LOOKING BACK ON IT NOW, the impression I have is not so
much that the vagueness of myopia causes one to feel
isolated and remote from everything, but rather that one is
exposed to space and left without any protection against objects
invisible in the distance. It was almost in panic that I began to look
among the graves for the spectacles I'd thrown away, until I found
the right-hand section of the frame with the lens still intact; and,
after a while, among some shriveled weeds, the other, empty,
eyehole. I realized how futile it was; nevertheless I clung to the
pieces as if that would ensure a grasp on the world.

This time I closed the gate very carefully. I didn't expect ever to
return that way. What had I come to look for in the first place?
Whatever it had been, I certainly hadn't found it. Sooner or later,
inevitably, one had to discard one's tribal romanticism. A form of
liberation, Bea might have called it.

Who and what had they been, anyway? Losers, all. Every one in
his own way a victim of the land.

I fastened the gate with a length of wire to make sure it would
stay shut.

The sun was much higher now above the grey hills in the
distance. It made the day look even more bleak than before; and
from behind a thin wind was cutting into me.

As I passed the cowshed, the dogs came running down from the house, barking and jumping up against me.

"That's enough, now, go away!" I scolded them.

The noise brought Ma from the kitchen.

"Oh, it's you." She laughed at my helpless anger, surrounded by the wretched beasts. "I was wondering what had become of you. Come on, Bull, come here! Leave the Baas alone, will you?"

Tongues hanging out and tails wagging, they ran up to her. She fondled their ears and stroked their enormous heads.

"All right, all right, good old doggies, down you go."

"One of these days they'll kill somebody," I said, annoyed.

Ma laughed. "I don't know what I would have done without them." she said. "And they adore their Madam." She went on fondling them for a while before she looked up. "But what's happened to you, sonny? Where are your glasses?"

Pulling my hand from my pocket I showed her the broken pieces.

"Shame," she said sympathetically. "That's bad, isn't it? Just as well you won't need them this weekend."

"How am I going to get back to Johannesburg on Monday?" I asked. "I can't drive like this."

"Can't I try to stick it together for you?"

"One of the lenses is smashed."

"Oh dear. Then Louis will have to drive. He'll be all right, won't he?"

"Not in the Mercedes."

"Now don't get so upset," she said. "It's time for breakfast. Where have you been all the time?"

I put the pieces back into my pocket. "Down to the graveyard."

She stared at me more intensely, obviously expecting me to elaborate, but I didn't.

"I'm glad to see you haven't started digging your own hole yet, like Oupa and Ouma Neethling," I remarked, to change her mood.

"Oh the soil is much too hard in this drought," she replied with a cryptic smile.

Kristina was busy in front of the coal stove. This time there was no sign of the young woman Thokozile and her baby. We went through to the dining room.

"Louis is still in bed,'* Ma said, noticing my glance in the direction of the passage.

"I'll go wake him up."

"No, let him sleep. I'm sure he can do with a bit of holiday too."

"He's been having one long holiday ever since he came back from Angola," I said resentfully.

"It can't be so bad."

"It's worse. He refuses to go to university or anywhere else. You know he'd always wanted to become an engineer."

"What does he do then?"

"Nothing. Stays in bed until ten or even later. Never leaves his room for days on end. And when he does come out, he just disappears for three or four days or even longer."

"What sort of friends has he got?"

"I wish I knew. No use asking him. Easier to get an answer from a stone wall. He's impossible, I tell you."

Sitting down, she called to the kitchen: "Kristina, bring in the porridge!" Adding quietly and sensibly: "You were a difficult boy too when you were his age."

"But not like him!"

"Will you say grace for us?"

Mechanically reciting the short prayer I recognized, with a shock, in my own voice the very intonation with which Dad had always spoken the words. For the moment the pretentious headstone down in the graveyard had become irrelevant as I made the disquieting discovery that, in subtler ways, Dad was still alive. I wondered whether Ma had also recognized his voice. It irritated me.

He could be very absentminded at table, especially when he'd been working on some new "research." Then it had been Mother's duty to remind him to say grace, which he would promptly do without even giving us time to close our eyes. But it had happened regularly that, a few minutes later, it would suddenly occur to him to recite his prayer, oblivious of the fact that he'd already said it: and without any warning he would start again, catching us with forks in our hands, or in the middle of a conversation. Then we all had to keep our composure and pretend we hadn't noticed anything amiss. Because if anyone started giggling or dared to remind him that he'd already said grace before, he would fly off the handle: those were the rare occasions when Dad really lost his temper, accusing us of having no respect for either himself or the Lord; and he would begin to hold forth on the decay of societies in which religion was on the decline: *If you go back in history—*

At the time, we merely found it odd, or endearing, or amusing. But writing about it now, it has a touch of great sadness about it. He was such a stranger in our world; there were so few certainties he could cling to. Those first months after they'd moved to the farm must have been sheer hell to him. We weren't there to give a hand—I'd just entered university and Theo was finishing his Matric in Griqualand West—but Ma told us all about it. He refused to touch a sick cow, let alone one that was having trouble in giving birth: she was the one who had to take over. He had a talent for breaking things, but then he would insist on mending the broken implements himself, invariably damaging them even worse than before, so that, in the end, they had to be replaced at great cost.

One night the dogs woke them up with a frenzy of barking.

Ma nudged him with an elbow: "Wim! Wim, wake up!"

"Huh? What's the matter?"

"Listen to the dogs."

"What about the dogs?"

"They're barking like mad."

"They bark all the time."

"There must be something among the cattle. You'd better go and make sure."

"Why me?"

"Who else is there to go?"

Grumbling, he got up. She didn't want him to light a candle lest there were thieves who could be scared off by the light. He bumped his head against the bed trying to find his shoes in the dark. It took a while before he cooled off sufficiently to continue the elaborate preparations. Finally he took his gun from the cupboard. The dogs went on barking furiously.

Ma accompanied him through the back door and round the house. It was new moon, so dark one couldn't see the outline of the hills against the sky. After he'd stumbled over a paraffin tin in the backyard, they realized it would be senseless to go any farther without a light, so reluctantly Ma went back for the lantern. Holding it as high as she could, she led the way.

Once again he stumbled, this time over a stone; and as he fell against her, she dropped the lantern, which immediately went out. By that time they were halfway down to the kraal and the dogs were still barking. Realizing the danger she was in, Ma hurled herself headlong to the ground—not a moment too soon, for at that very instant Dad pulled off a shot behind her, missing her by inches.

"Wim, for God's sake, you're killing me!"

The dogs went berserk. The cattle trampled down the wooden gate of the kraal and stampeded off into the night. It was late the following afternoon before the last ones were rounded up. No one ever discovered what had caused the trouble: thief, marauder, jackal or whatever. Fortunately there had been no damage apart from the broken gate. But from that day Ma preferred to investigate on her own, with or without the gun, whenever there was a noise at night.

And Dad had the little outbuilding behind the dairy restored and repainted; inside, he fitted it out with shelves and filled them with his books and as time went by he spent more and more time in study, withdrawing increasingly from the outside world.

It was more than mere eccentricity. He sometimes tried to communicate to me what he really felt and thought about: it wasn't easy, we were so far apart, but he tried. One afternoon, I remember, we were sitting in his study. Outside, the piccanins were cavorting with the calves, and there were birds in all the trees, a summer's day.

"If you go back in history," Dad said (I'm trying to reconstruct the general content of the conversation: the actual details escape me—but so many of his monologues had the same drift), "if you go back in history, you generally find two kinds of people. They are the doers, the Caesars and the Attilas and the Napoleons and so on. And then there are those who come later and who try to find the meaning of what the others have done. An act isn't something clear and defined and tangible like a stone you can pick up from the ground. And if you look at our people"—for sooner or later all his discussions returned to "our people"—"you will see the same thing. Ever since the first Marthinus Wilhelmus Mynhardt arrived here—remember what I told you about his travels and explorations? I've just got a new book on eighteenth-century explorers at the Cape, remind me to show it to you—anyway, ever since he first came here, our people have had their hands full just trying to survive. You can check up for yourself, not one of them was a learned sort of a man. They could barely read and write. Because the land was still so wild, you see, it had to be broken in like a horse. Every new generation did it in their own way. But it can't just go on like that, blindly. Sooner or later one has got to sit down and try to find out: What have they really achieved? I mean, if you look at them from one point of view, they've all been losers. But were they really? Or did each of them go a little bit further with the long process of breaking in the land? That's why I think the work I'm trying to do may not be so useless after all."

That whole long-winded explanation to justify himself.

"Yes, of course, Dad." It was better to agree with him.

"I mean, the farm isn't doing as well as it should, is it? But it's not because I'm a bad farmer. It's just that I have a more important vocation in life. Do you understand?"

"I can understand that very well, Dad."

"Actually I rather like farming. I think I've got it in me to become a prosperous farmer. But it's a matter of priorities. And if you go back in history, you'll find it's always been the same. Every man must define his own priorities first of all."

"Undoubtedly, Dad."

"One has got to open one's heart to history, you see, to find out what it really wants to say to you. You can't just sit down and read it like a book. Even though it may all be printed in books, you need a code, as it were, to decipher it. A matter of interpretation. And perhaps posterity will realize that what I've done hasn't been all in vain. I mean, trying to reshape and hone one's definitions. What does it mean to be a Mynhardt? What does it mean to be an Afrikaner? That sort of thing. If you go back—"

"You're quite right, Dad. It's a most important function."

Thinking back now, I suddenly get the impression that what he really tried to say to me that afternoon was, quite simply: *Help me.* But how could I help him ? What did he really want of me? I couldn't light his lantern, like Ma had done, or carry his rifle, or help a cow deliver her calf. I don't think that was what he'd really wanted of her either. But what was there I could possibly do for him?

On the afternoon in question I gave him a check to help him cover some of the recent farming expenses. He thanked me profusely and, in his meticulous way, put the check in his shirt pocket and fastened the button. It wasn't the first time I'd helped him, nor the last. Ever since I'd started earning my own money I'd contributed money to the farm, usually when Ma told me things were going badly. Nineteen thousand seven hundred and eighty-five rand in all, to be exact: I've kept a note of it. I did it, fully realizing it was throwing it in the water, because Pa just did not know how to handle it. But I never complained. It was only in the light of recent events that, when I went to the farm that particular weekend, I felt I'd reached the point where one couldn't go on casting one's bread upon the water without ever getting anything in return for it.

Perhaps I should mention that the check I'd given Dad that afternoon never came back to me with my bank statement. He never cashed it. That's what I'm trying to make clear: his complete irresponsibility in financial affairs. It was, after all, a matter of several hundred rand.

I cannot, of course, swear to it that I consciously thought of all that as I sat at the breakfast table with Ma that Saturday morning; but I was certainly thinking of Dad and the failure he'd been on the farm. However, I deliberately avoided talking about the sale again, knowing Ma well enough to realize that she needed time to accommodate the idea.

To make conversation, I said: "You know, I really had a fright when I came outside this morning. I never thought the drought could get as bad as this."

"I told you, didn't I?" She seemed almost smug. "You know, the day of Dad's funeral was the last time it rained."

"And then it was a flood."

"Yes, we were nearly swept out of house and hearth. Old Lawrence up there had five thousand rands' damages." She smiled. "But you know how it is: when a farmer tells you he's had this or that amount of damages, it means he's included his drowned laborers in his reckoning."

"Were some of the laborers drowned?"

"Of course. Three up there by his place. Two of ours. Not that they really were ours. They just keep turning up on the farm all the time, and squatting."

"It's because you're too good for them."

"Well, you know what the Lord said about one's neighbor."

"But what's going to happen to you if the rains don't come soon? Those poor cattle, they look like sheets of corrugated iron."

"I'll manage." She was looking right into my thoughts again. "One must just go on praying."

"And if God doesn't listen?"

"He'll listen when the time comes." Her mood was expanding now. "You remember that time in Griqualand West when it didn't rain for three years? Then we held the prayer meeting and I took my umbrella and my raincoat to church with me. They all looked at me as if I was out of my mind, in that blistering heat. Even *Dominee* was joking about it. But I just said to him: 'I thought we'd come to ask God for rain? Where's your faith then?' And as we came out of church, it started raining. I was the only one of the congregation who got home dry."

"Haven't they tried firing rockets into the clouds around here yet?" I asked.

"No, why should they? It's a bad thing, that. Trying to twist the Lord's arm, they are." She was picking at a sliver of meat between two of her strong white teeth. "That's what's wrong with our world today, sonny. In the good old days one prayed for rain and shot at one's enemies. Now they're shooting for rain and praying for their enemies. Isn't that just asking for trouble?"

"But you don't think it's a sin to drill for water?"

"No, why should it be a sin? The water's in the ground already, isn't it? Just waiting to be taken out." As we rose from the table Kristina looked in with the news that the "water man" had arrived and was waiting outside.

6

HE WAS STANDING AT THE back door, a big, flabby man with an infinitely sad face, wearing a black tailcoat as if he were on his way to church, and holding his hat in both hands, pressed against his ample stomach. Behind him stood his Black helper, an old man with graying peppercorns, a small iron trunk on the ground before him.

"Morning, Mrs. Mynhardt," said the stranger, as if to commiserate with a death in the family. "Name's Scholtz. I've come about the water." His voice was high and hoarse, and he spoke so softly that one had difficulty in following him.

"Good day, Mr. Scholtz," she said. "You're early. This is my son."

"Yes, I came early," he said sadly. "There's no pull in the water after noon, you see." He offered me his hand. It lay limply in mine, cold and damp like a death sweat.

He seemed to be able to divine not only water but thoughts as well, for with a pained look on his face he withdrew his hand. "I'm sweating," he announced. "That's always a sign of water." He looked around slowly. "Won't surprise me if this house is built right on an underground course. Now if you don't mind, Missus, I'll put on my hat again. Bad for the brains."

"It will be a good thing if you could find something near the house," said Ma. "It'll make it easier to irrigate the fields. Our borehole is a mere trickle, and one of these days winter will be over."

"Any willows nearby?" he asked, obviously without having paid any attention to her. "Quince is all right too, but my hands operate better with a willow fork."

"Behind the dairy," said Ma.

"Will you go and cut me a forked stick?" the man asked me, studying me in great sympathy.

I turned to fetch a knife from the kitchen, but stopping me with an impatient gesture as if he'd expected nothing better of me, he handed me his own pocketknife.

He and Ma remained behind, talking, while I went down to the dairy in cautious, measured paces: without glasses, the earth seemed to be farther away from me than normally, as if every step carried me across an abyss.

"I prefer you without glasses." Bea.

"And I prefer you without your dark glasses too."

It is shocking, the acuteness with which she suddenly returns to me, a burning loss. So often in our relationship there were moments of an almost unbearable intensity, an awareness of existing *in extremis*. The day we met at the hole where Dullabh's Corner had been. The week in the red hut at Ponta do Ouro. The night I returned from the Northern Transvaal, just before Dad's death. Would it really have been our last night if he hadn't died just then? Everything seems to interlock with disconcerting, almost uncanny, precision.

I can recall her in sensual detail. That night in my apartment. The short dark hair and narrow face with the wide mouth; the small hollows formed by her collarbones as she bent over to refill my glass. The slight trembling of her breasts in the open muslin blouse: narrow pear-shaped breasts, the most vulnerable thing about her, drooping slightly, the elongated nipples: woman-of-thirty.

Her words on the telephone, in that final conversation before the weekend: *"Martin, is it really quite impossible to postpone this farm business just for one week? I must see you."*

"But I told you."

"Oh well, if it's out of the question. Oh, God."

"Goodbye, Bea. See you Tuesday."

I wish I could scrap the rest of the weekend and proceed to Bea. But in this attempt to reconstruct the increasing complexity of what was happening I have no choice but to move with the time. Saturday was only Saturday, with no foreknowledge of Sunday or Monday or today. Otherwise everything will start running like watercolors on a wet sheet of paper. And it is imperative to keep it all apart.

Perhaps I really stood thinking of Bea while I was selecting and cutting a firm fork from the willow tree. I know I must have been absentminded, because the knife slipped, nicking me across the web between thumb and forefinger. Tiny specks of blood appeared on the skin. Instinctively sucking it off, I returned with the fork.

"Oh well," said the big man with the drooping shoulders when he took it from me and inspected it morosely. "Oh well, it'll have to do." He started stripping the bark off the fork, exposing the bare white wood.

"Will you go with me, Missus?" he asked. "There's more pull in the water if a member of the family goes with one."

"I have my clinic this morning, Mr. Scholtz," she said. "Martin can go with you."

I would have preferred not to accompany him, but could think of no excuse to get out of it. He turned to me, obviously resigned to the inevitable.

"What about some coffee before you go?" Ma offered.

"No, no," he declined. "It only works on an empty stomach."

Ma went round the house to the front stoop. The small built-on room, where Theo and I had slept when we were small, had been converted into a simple dispensary years ago and on Saturdays she ran her clinic for all the Blacks in the neighborhood who required medical attention. There were already ten or twenty of them waiting in the meager sun against the front wall, ranging from suckling infants to shuffling and half-blind old men. The more seriously ill would be driven into town, any day of the week, on the back of her little van. There had been occasions when Ma had got up at two or three in the morning to take someone to the doctor. I'd often tried to dissuade her from continuing with these time-consuming, irksome duties, but in vain. It probably satisfied some deep need inside her, the urge which originally had made her become a nurse.

"Shall we go?" said the old man, like a clergyman announcing the hymn to be sung. "Bring the trunk, Philemon."

I followed him up the hill behind the house, past the cluster of laborers' huts, Philemon bringing up the rear with the small metal trunk. It had no handles, so he had to carry it like a child's coffin.

"Isn't this too high?" I ventured after some time.

"One can never be too high," he said cryptically, his breath coming from his chest in short asthmatic gasps.

From behind, probably because of the black outfit on his large boneless body, he looked familiar—like Elise's *dominee* father. The broad-minded, benevolent old man with whom I'd had so many interminable arguments, on predestination and Pilate, churches and prophecies and the Word made flesh. I remembered him saying: "One thing you should always bear in mind is that God must have an enormous sense of humor too, else He would never have made man." He and Bernard had been great friends in the past. His wife had been more cautious, but between the two men I'd sensed a profound bond of sympathy. *All I ask of life is that I won't ever grow too old to kick a sacred cow in the balls—before she shits on your head.* The old man had often chuckled about those words; perhaps he's even approved secretly. But to his wife's liking Bernard had been too "worldly," too much of a threat to her daughter's peace of mind and purity of body. She'd probably preferred me as a son-in-law not so much because she's liked me as a person but because I'd saved Elise from a worse fate. The *dominee*, it seemed to me, had been rather disappointed, although he was much too loyal ever to make it obvious.

What would his poor wife have done had she known about the nights Elise had spent with me in my room in Aunt Rienie's house during that final study year? The first Sunday afternoon when, after long and passionate petting, she'd pushed her hands up behind her back to undo the hooks of her bra, gasping through wet and open lips:

"For God's sake, Martin, what are you waiting for? *Take* me!"

In those days, after my lusty initiation with the voluptuous Greta, I'd regarded myself as a man of "experience"; and that first time Elise had still been a virgin. But it was a virginity troubling and oppressing her, so that, in the end, it was really she who seduced *me*. And I became infatuated with her body, those large firm breasts, the tension of her taut belly between her hip bones, the golden hairdust at the bottom of her spine, the smoothness of her tanned skin. Amazing how such a skin, exposed to sun and air, can age and become wrinkled and dry; how heavy and pendulous the breasts can grow with the years. The hideous disfigurement of stretch marks after a birth, the discolored weal of a Caesarean. Strange how one can be enraptured by a body in youth simply because it is a body: and how one can be revolted by it later for exactly the same reason. A body with flaws and scars, fallible, withering and wasting all the time.

Her parents, too, had changed with age. Even her father had become more narrow-minded that last time they'd spent their holiday with us: the time Bernard stayed in my apartment. That was when we'd had the discussion about Pilate and he'd disappointed me with the conventionality of his opinions. I remember it particularly well, for that had been their last night with us. The next day, on their way back to the Free State, they were both killed instantly in a head-on collision. He'd become much too old to drive, his reactions had slowed down, but he'd refused to listen to my warnings.

High up on the slope the old diviner stopped, his pale unhealthy skin shining with perspiration.

"Put it down, Philemon."

"What do you keep in that trunk?" I asked.

He shook his head, looking mournfully across the scorched valley.

"I can feel it running that way," he said, pointing. "Can you see it?"

I couldn't see anything but pretended to be pleased.

"It's these underground courses which keep a farm alive," he said. "You don't see them, but they're there all right." It sounded like the text of his funeral sermon. "If it hadn't been for them, nothing would have grown. One has got to *know* about them and heed them."

"I understand," I said demurely.

He didn't look at all happy with my response.

"Down there, Philemon."

"Are you from these parts?" I asked him, trying to make the depressing silence more bearable.

"Yes, I've always had this gift," he said, panting, as if that was a comprehensive and satisfying reply.

He stopped again. Philemon put down the black trunk, but made no attempt to open it. On an even strip along the slope the old man began to pace up and down, the white forked stick in his outstretched hands. In the long, measured strides of a secretary bird, his face taut with concentration, he walked ten yards to the right, stared at his feet for an instant, then went ten yards back. Repeating the move, without any pause, for about fifteen minutes on end, while Philemon remained standing, more or less at attention, beside the trunk.

The old man began to heave. His eyes widened. I could see perspiration on his neck and the backs of his hands. The stick began to twitch and turn in his hands. It was a very strange thing to watch, as if that dead piece of wood had suddenly acquired a life of its own, touched by some hidden source of power reaching up from the recesses of the earth itself. I was scared that the stick might hit him in the face. He was holding his breath now, his head turning a deep purple for as far as one could see under his black hat. His neck seemed to swell like a bullfrog's. And then, suddenly, he let go, breathing out like a punctured tube, dropping the willow fork, panting for breath.

"Found something?" I asked, intrigued in spite of myself.

"No," he said, looking happy for the first time that morning.

For a moment I had a ridiculous, unreasonable wish for Bernard to be there with me to share the moment.

But there is no sense in bringing Bernard back into it. I've dealt with him. It is imperative for one to organize one's material, keeping the different elements apart, otherwise there can be no system in one's thought. I have a lifetime to interpret in terms of the events of four crucial days. Without a system the only result can be anarchy.

"I'm going home," I announced as the old man stooped, with obvious effort, to retrieve his fallen implement.

He stared at me in surprise and sorrow.

Without waiting for an answer I turned back and began to walk downhill as fast as I could risk it without my glasses. From the bottom of the hill, at the edge of the farmyard, I looked round, but everything was reduced to a dull smudge. The old man himself might have been an illusion.

7

LOUIS WAS WASHING THE car when I arrived home. He'd pulled it behind the kitchen door where he stood hosing it while ducks and geese were quacking in the mud around him.

I was angry on the spot. "Don't you know how scarce water is?" I scolded him. "This isn't the city where you can just open a tap."

"Morning, Dad."

"Morning. Did you hear what I said?"

"All right." He went to the tank to shut the tap. "I only wanted to—"

"Trouble with you," I said angrily, "is that you never think of other people. As long as you can just go on messing about you're dead happy."

"How should I have known?"

"If you'd opened your eyes for a minute you'd have seen how dry it was."

"Well, I've closed the tap, haven't I?" Taking the chamois from his shoulder he started cleaning the Mercedes. I was irritated by the possessiveness of the gesture.

"How did the car get here?" I asked.

"I drove it here, how else?"

"Suppose you'd hit a gatepost or something?"

"I didn't."

"But just suppose—"

"Oh Jesus, Dad, it's just a car, not a woman or something!"

"Mind your tongue, Louis!"

"It's time you realized I'm not a child any more."

"You're behaving like one. You haven't shown the slightest sense of responsibility these last months."

He didn't answer, but I saw his jaw tighten.

"Lying about at home like a tramp, refusing to lift a finger to do anything, expecting us to wait on you. And why? What for?"

From the other side of the shining pale grey car he glared at me, a small contemptuous smile on his lips, as far as I could make out.

"You're not the first person to go to war, you know," I went on.

"What do *you* know about war?" he asked with a sneer.

"That's got nothing to do with it."

"If you knew—"

"Hundreds, thousands of young blokes went up to Angola with you. Don't tell me they all came back as punch-drunk as you."

I had to restrain myself before I went too far. If I hadn't gone too far already. I was wrecking the whole weekend. I'd brought him along with the intention of trying to "find" him; now I was compromising the chances just because I felt frustrated by Ma's obstinacy and by the breaking of my spectacles and the futile superstitions of the old diviner trying to find water we wouldn't need. All the months since Louis's return we'd been trying to handle him with understanding and patience: something traumatic had happened and we had to help him re-adapt to life, however much our nerves became frayed in the process. More than once I'd felt like exploding, but for the sake of Elise and Ilse I'd controlled myself. Now my restraint was wearing thin. Damn it, I'd been close to death myself, I also needed some consideration.

"The other soldiers came back to become useful citizens again," I said. "But you don't care a damn."

"Why should I try to become a useful citizen in this goddamned country?" he asked viciously.

"There is no need to swear," I said coldly.

"I'll swear if I want to! You realize it's you who are responsible for the mess the country is in?"

"Oh no, I'm not," I said. "For heaven's sake don't try that naive little argument on me."

"I'm talking about your whole generation!"

"That's what I mean. But it's too easy to get out of your tight corner by starting to accuse me."

"I didn't ask to go to Angola!" he said.

His aggressiveness caused mine to subside into a feeling of wry and reasonable superiority. "Listen, Louis. I regarded this whole Angola mess as a foolish blunder from the beginning. We should have stayed out of the war altogether. It was their business, not ours. In all of this I'm with you. But whether we liked it or not, we did get involved. And once one lands in a stew like that all you can do is to see it through. No sense in trying to get out."

"I didn't chicken out. I went all the way," he said, flushed with anger. "But it's easy for you to talk. When one's right in the middle of it, one wants to know why it's happening. You want to know what you're fighting for, what you're getting killed for. You don't want to get your head blasted off just to keep this shithouse standing."

"What you call this shithouse is the country you were born in. It's the only one you have. What would you do without it?"

"Don't lecture me, Dad. It's not a political meeting."

"Louis!" For a moment I felt like clobbering him. What he needed was a bloody good hiding. But even in my rage I realized he was quite capable of resisting and I wasn't sure how that would turn out. (My heart.) In hopeless anger I stared at him. For the first time in my life I had to acknowledge that I had no physical control over him any more. It took a great effort to calm myself. "If you don't like the country," I said as acidly as I could, "you can either leave it or try to change it for the better. But you're not helping much by just sitting on your arse."

"And what happens when one does try to change things?" he asked. "What happened to Bernard?"

"You leave him out of this!"

"Why? I think he's very relevant."

"There's no need to provoke a confrontation like he did. There are other ways."

"Like elections? Working from the inside? D'you think there's still time for that sort of thing?"

"There is always time for doing the right thing." I was regaining control now, of myself and of the situation. "I know what the world looks like when one is young, Louis. There was a time when I felt just like you—"

"What did you *do* about it?"

"I told you there are more ways than one. You saw the uselessness of violence in Angola, didn't you? You left a greater mess behind you than you'd found."

"That wasn't what I asked you, Dad."

"I'm not sure you're really interested in an answer."

"Don't you understand what I'm trying to say?"

I looked at him, calm and composed by now, confident that I knew how to handle his impetuousness. "Finish the car," I ordered, and walked away.

"What happened to your glasses?" he suddenly asked behind me. I swung round, but he was too far away for me to read his expression: was he trying to placate me, or merely taunting me again?

"I broke them," I said laconically.

"What are you going to do about driving back home?"

"I'll manage."

"But you can't see properly without them."

"Of course I can. In any case, what else can we do?"

"I can take over."

I looked at him, a misty figure behind the shimmering shape of the Mercedes. Without answering, I walked off.

A small group of Blacks still sat clustered on the front stoop waiting for Ma. With some hesitation I went nearer, and they made way for me to pass. The smell was overpowering, but Ma didn't seem to notice. She went on attending to her patients, questioning and examining and carrying on long conversations in Xhosa, which I could follow only with difficulty. I tried to help by handing her whatever she required from the large cupboard in the corner: ointment and powder and tablets, medicine for diarrhea or cramps, cough mixture, plaster, occasionally a syringe or vaccine.

"It's going to take you all morning," I remarked after some time.

"There's more and more of them every week," she said.

"Breeding like germs."

"I'm waging a running battle with them about it. Next week I'm rounding up all the women again for injections. No use giving them the pill, they just throw it away or carry it in a bag round their necks for *doepa*."

"You need a more drastic solution than that."

"It's the men," she said. "Think it's a disgrace if their women don't have babies, so they don't want them to use anything. We've nearly had murders on the farm because of that."

Of course contraception wasn't the answer. She was approaching it from the wrong end. What was involved, was the standard of living as such. A sense of responsibility to be instilled in them. And they wouldn't acquire that by living off Ma's charity on the farm. One had to start in their own homelands, raising economic standards: how often must I repeat this?

I felt irritated by all the bodies and dumb faces surrounding us.

"Let's go and have some tea first," I suggested. "You need a break."

"I'm all right." But when I left, she followed me, instructing the patient human bundles to wait for her return.

I went to wash my hands; even my clothes felt dirty. But Ma went straight through to the kitchen. Kristina brought in the pot of bush tea which had been left to simmer on the kitchen stove.

"What about Louis?" Ma asked.

"Kristina can take his outside. I don't think he'll come in right now."

"Why not?"

I shrugged.

"Something wrong?" she insisted.

"Not really. We had a bit of a tiff."

"About what?"

"He was wasting water." I took my cup. "I suppose I'm a bit overstrained. This tension isn't good for me." (An unfair blow, I had to admit, but I had to use the opening.)

"What tension?" she asked innocently.

"This farm business. I've been worrying about it for so long, and it's bad for my heart. Until you've made up your mind—"

"Why should you worry about it?" she said. "We spoke about it this morning, didn't we? I don't think there's anything more to be said."

"You know very well we can't leave it like that."

She sipped her hot tea. Only after she'd put down the cup again did she look up: "What does Theo say about the whole idea?"

Did she suspect something about the conversation I'd had with Theo just after Dad had fallen ill? Had he gone to her behind my back? But her face didn't give away anything.

"I didn't discuss it with him," I said as calmly as possible.

"Surely he has a say in it too."

"Theo has nothing to do with it, Ma. You know very well he's interested in nothing but demolitions and new skyscrapers and stuff."

"He's your brother."

"But Dad left the farm to me. It's something between you and me only."

She shrugged her shoulders.

I knew I had to keep calm and not lose my temper as with Louis. The weekend was beginning to turn sour and if Ma got angry, all would be lost. In silence I finished my tea, aware of a slight trembling in my hand.

Come on, I told myself. You're used to dealing with delicate matters. You've learned all the rules of the game and know how to improvise and improve on them. You've been specially mentioned in the *Financial Mail* for your qualities as a negotiator. It's a matter of knowing when to hold back and when to give the impression of putting all your cards on the table while keeping a trump up your sleeve.

The problem was it didn't work so well within the family context. With others I could remain imperturbable; with Ma I tended to get emotionally involved. It wasn't only because she knew me so well she could predict all my reactions, but also because the nature of our relationship required of me to respect her however much I resented her opposition. And since the coronary I'd been more excitable than before anyway.

"It's all in your hands now," I told her when I put down my empty cup. "By acting now, we can retain the initiative and score a deal at the same time. Or we can let it pass, to face a loss if we're forced to sell at a later stage."

"I must go back to the clinic," she said calmly. "My patients are waiting."

I didn't answer.

At the door she asked: "Oh Martin, won't you drive up to old Lawrence's store for me? Otherwise I won't get any mail today. And take the eggs with you. Kristina will give them to you."

I wasn't sure that it really was all that urgent. She was probably just trying either to prove her goodwill or to remind me of her maternal authority.

"All right, Ma. I'll go when I'm finished." It was my turn to establish my independence by pouring another cup of tea.

"Take the van," she said. "The key's in it." She disappeared into the passage.

When I came outside with my basket of eggs Louis was just emerging from the garage where he'd put away the Mercedes. He stopped, as if expecting me to say something.

"I'm going up to the store," I said, doing my best to sound affable. "Want to go with me?"

"But I've just cleaned the car."

"We're going in Grandma's van."

"You can't go without glasses. Shall I drive?"

"I'm not an invalid yet." Why did he always manage to say the one thing he knew would make me flare up?

He hesitated, then decided against it. "I'd rather have a look at the generator." He gestured towards the small shed housing the electrical plant.

I didn't answer. The mere fact that he'd offered to do anything on his own came as a surprise. Perhaps our brief sparring had done him some good after all.

The van was cold and took some time to warm up. Driving up the hill from the row of flamboyants, the engine sputtered and died twice. I glanced in the rearview mirror, but couldn't make out whether Louis was watching me. With a roar the van shot forward the second time, the rear wheels skidding on the loose gravel. The road was narrow and scarred, winding upward between boulders and grey euphorbias and the bright smears of red aloes. I had to hold the steering wheel with both hands to keep the vehicle on the road. Perhaps it would have been better to bring Louis along, but it was too late to turn back now.

Once I'd reached the top of the narrow plateau above the deep valley of the farm, it became easier to drive. As I approached the top gate a group of piccanins came running on to open it for me. One was covered by what must have been his father's jacket, the sleeves dragging on the ground; the pants were missing entirely. Two others were wearing tattered sweaters which revealed rather than concealed their bodies, and baggy pants down to their knees. The last one was completely naked, ashen-grey with cold. While the others were tugging and wrenching at the gate, he stood on one side, casually sucking two worms of snot from his upper lip into his mouth, his hands cupped in my direction.

"Cent, Baas. Cent, Baas," he whined, without much conviction.

It wasn't from any lack of sympathy that I shooed him off. But what sense was there in giving him money? He would either buy sweets, which in his state was the last thing he needed, or hand it over to his father to buy liquor.

Above all—I do find it important to make my point quite clear—my main consideration was that one couldn't base an economically independent nation on begging and charity. It would only strengthen the Black's suspicion that all he had to do to obtain something was to ask for it, without any effort on his part. It robbed him of the motive to achieve something in order to be rewarded. There should be no doubt about this: man is inherently a competitive animal. Reward without effort is as negative as effort without reward. (Here I'm off again! But it's important.)

Let me state unequivocally that I have no objection against promoting Blacks to more responsible positions—provided it doesn't happen only because they're black, but because their achievement warrants it. At this stage of their development "responsible positions" would involve, for example, the supervision of more expensive equipment. But one cannot proceed too fast. (In the mining industry I see it every day: it is useless to expect mathematical thinking from a man incapable as yet of distinguishing a straight angle.) I refuse to write off an expensive bulldozer just because in a crisis its driver panicked and lost his head. One has got to start with basic skills and basic responsibilities. And in their own areas, among their own kind.

As far as my own laborers are concerned, I pay them proper wages in exchange for proper work. They are mine and I assume responsibility for them. But the sentimentality inherent in charity is nothing but economic short-sightedness. I hope I have made it quite clear now.

The winter sun was warming up a bit, but the thin white grasses were still shivering in the wind. As I drove on, I thought of Ma again. She would just have to yield and accept the inevitable. One of her objections, it occurred to me, might be her reluctance to live either with Theo's family or with mine. On the other hand we couldn't let her go to an old-age home. One had obligations towards one's family. And anyway, it would provide Elise with much more freedom to come and go if she knew Ma was at home to keep an eye on the dogs and the house and the servants.

If only Ma and Elise had been on better terms. From the very beginning there had been tension between them: nothing unhealthy, just the sort of electricity to be expected when two women with strong personalities believed they had to compete for the love of the man between them. Especially if one of them had had him all to herself for more than twenty years and was reluctant to see a young and inexperienced girl take over.

When I'd brought Elise home the first time, in the July vacation after our encounter on Bernard's farm, Ma had been her warm, hospitable and generous self. Elise was the prettiest and the nicest and the best girl I'd ever introduced to her. But from the moment the word "marriage" was first uttered, the tension began to build up. Nothing overt. Ma had always prided herself on her "intuition" and her "tact," even though it was the sort of peasant tact a blind man could feel with

a stick. Ma was quite happy with the prospect as long as it was rele-
gated to a vague and distant future. But as soon as a date had been
mentioned, she launched her fierce—but "tactful"—campaign:

"You know, Elise, what I like most about you is that you're so
sensible. Other girls can't think of anything but getting married, but
I know you'll never enter into anything head over heels. I've noticed
that you respect Martin's need to find his feet in life first. It's obvious you love him and you won't try to bind him too soon." And
much more in the same vein.

A few months after I'd gone to London I asked Elise to come over
too. Not that I'd struck it badly with girls in England (on the
contrary!), but I'd become agitated at the thought that in my absence
Bernard might change his mind about her. I knew she would marry
him the moment he asked her. And in spite of the intentions I'd
voiced so confidently that Easter, in spite of the nights she'd spent
with me, in spite of all our fervent promises for the future, I knew I
still hadn't "tamed" her. Something wild and passionate in her had
remained beyond my reach. One landscape inside her had been kept
intact. For Bernard. I knew it. And I wanted to possess that too. How
could one hold a woman in one's arms knowing that far behind her
eyes she carried the image of another face? And so I urged her to come
over for a holiday. Once she was with me it was easy to pursue the
campaign and not to allow her to go back without marrying me.

Her parents felt reluctant because she was still so young, barely
twenty-one; but in the end they were persuaded. They even came over
so that her father could marry us in the Embassy. The only real
problem was Ma. Not with me (after her first cautious letters she'd
admitted, with her customary generosity, that "it's your decision,
sonny, and you should know what's best for you"); but as far as Elise
was concerned Ma used an approach which shattered me when I first
learned about it three years later, when Elise showed me the letters.
Nothing as blatant as reprimanding her or quarreling with her, just

an endless series of "tactful" reminders about how easy it was to spoil a young man's whole future by tying him down too soon, etc. ("I know Martin, my child. I know he loves you dearly and I'm sure you love him. But I know he's the sort of man who can easily be blinded by love"—sic!—"and you are the one who must keep your head and help him do what's best for both of you—")

Of course, when she saw we were serious about getting married, Ma resigned herself to it. But after our return from overseas there was a constant undercurrent of conflicting interests. Mere trifles would upset Elise, especially when she was pregnant. For example, Ma would come to watch her while she was preparing a meal: "Oh, is that how you make your *bobotie?* Looks good. Of course, I always add raisins too, Martin adores them—" Or Ma would look on as she sat weaving, or making pots on the wheel, or doing batik or whatever: "You're so clever with your hands. I can see why you prefer to do this rather than waste your time cooking or looking after a home—"

Louis's birth brought on an early crisis. We had arranged for Elise's mother to be with us for the occasion, but a month before the time she'd fallen ill and I asked Ma to take her place. Just as well, in view of all the complications after the birth. And I don't know what we would have done without Ma's help with the baby (I already had to work late quite regularly, or go off on option deals etc.). But Ma had a way of taking over completely, and she changed the whole routine of our household. Elise accepted it without a murmur, being much too ill to care. But then Ma also tried to take over the baby. In order to allow Elise some rest at night, Ma moved the child into her own room. Feeding was restricted to the strict schedule she herself had followed when we'd been babies: "You can't feed a child every time he starts crying, Elise. It upsets his stomach. Even worse, it spoils him. He must get used to a four-hour routine from the beginning."

In her weakened condition Elise, I suppose, was much more sensitive than normally. Whatever it was, one day when Ma again insisted on leaving the baby to cry in its cradle until its "proper" feeding time, Elise got out of bed, dragged herself to a cupboard and started bundling clothes into a suitcase. I can well imagine the scene:

"What are you doing, Elise?"

"Packing. I'm going away."

"But what has come over you?"

"You know everything about everything, don't you? All right, so now you can take my child and do with him what you like. I'm going. I've had enough. I'm not wanted here any more."

I had to rush home from the office to resolve the matter. To preserve the peace—although I couldn't but feel a grudge against Elise for forcing me to do so—I had to send Ma back to the farm the next day and replace her with a trained nurse. It was then that Elise, in a sort of emotional clearance sale, showed me all Ma's letters of long ago and gave vent to everything she'd suppressed for so long. I did my best to make her realize that Ma had acted with the best of intentions, but she was in no state for logical argument.

As time went by the quarrel was forgiven, the emotions subsided, Elise grew more mature, and they learned to tolerate one another—although there always remained a certain deliberate correctness in their relationship, in which the territory of each was very carefully defined and respected. That was why, that weekend on the farm, I had enough confidence, in spite of what had happened in the past, to expect them to get along if Ma were to come and live with us.

With Dad, on the other hand, Elise had had a remarkable rapport from the very first day. That was something else which might have contributed to Ma's attitude towards her. Although she was too proud ever to say a word about it, I suspect that Ma felt a tinge of jealousy because Elise obviously understood Dad so much better than she ever had. When we'd first arrived on the farm, he'd kept his distance as always, withdrawing into his study at the earliest opportunity. In the afternoon, while I was helping Ma on the farm, I noticed Elise walking in the direction of the dairy, but when I went to look for her an hour later, there was no sign of her. One of the laborers remembered that he'd seen her go into Dad's study. My heart sank, as I knew it was the one sacrosanct place where he was not to be disturbed by any means. He would never react aggressively, of course, but any person who had disturbed him once, would be written off for ever. He had a way of quietly turning away and stalking off if anyone arrived he didn't like.

But when I cautiously looked through the window, I was dumbfounded by what I saw inside. Elise was sitting on the desk among his litter of open books and scattered papers—with the same nonchalance she'd shown that warm Sunday afternoon, perched naked on the wall and swinging her legs—and Dad was talking. It was never easy to get him started, but once he was under way it was almost impossible to stop him. The rest of the family had learned, rather painfully, to occupy our thoughts with other things once he'd drifted into one of his rambling discussions, but Elise had the same faculty so characteristic of Bernard: to listen to one in enthusiastic attention, making you feel that whatever you were saying was the most important thing in the world to her. And it was no mere pretense. She really was enthralled by what Dad told her.

For the rest of the holiday I often had trouble tearing her away from the study. Often, when one passed outside, one could hear them laughing together. And when he finally got so far as to start putting up new shelves—a project he'd been postponing for years—Elise was the one to encourage and actively assist him. She could saw a straighter line than he could; and in her slender hands a plane worked miracles. The first shelves he'd made when he'd moved into the study were nothing to look at and one always expected them to come tumbling down at any moment. But she made sure the new ones were properly joined and glued and screwed together; and between the two of them they did a most respectable job. I'd never seen him as relaxed and happy as when Elise was on the farm.

I remember how surprised I was when, shortly after that first visit, she spontaneously confided in me: "You know, your Dad is a real gem."

I grinned good-humoredly, like any other member of the family when Dad was discussed, and said: "Oh he's a lovable old plodder. One gets quite fond of him."

She looked at me attentively for a long time, almost as if she felt amazed and hurt by my reply; and then she said: "I don't think you realize what you've got in him. He's a very remarkable person."

After our children had been born, she succeeded in bringing to light another concealed dimension in Dad—because I'm sure it was mainly for her sake that he gave so much attention to the kids. He would spend hours with them, telling them stories, carrying them on his back, helping them to make things. In spite of the fact that he'd never in his life been able to drive two nails through a board without hitting his thumb, he made them little cars from fish tins, and minuscule tractors from cotton spools and candlewax, and furniture from matchboxes; as well as exquisite clay cattle, which Elise baked for them in her kiln. He was just as interested in all her successive ventures and hobbies. In her weaving period he supplied her with mohair—during the brief spell he tried to farm with angora goats, before they were all killed off by the cold one winter. When the pottery bug bit her, he brought her loads of clay from the farm on his little van, and helped her to sieve and clean and knead it. Sometimes he would stay awake all night to feed and watch her kiln, or spend days burning wood to collect ash for the glazes. In his shy, retiring way he would try to devise new tools for her: a sifting screen one could tread like a sewing machine, a clay mixer, and so on. More often than not the implements were so clumsy or cumbrous as to be practically useless. But she would always show the greatest enthusiasm for what he'd done, and together they would laugh about it and try to improve on it.

Small wonder his death was such a blow to her and that she was in such a state when I came back too late to be in time to say good-bye. I think something in our own relationship died with Dad: as if, through him, she'd been able to touch something indefinable in me which couldn't be grasped in any other way. That something was changed irredeemably. And it seems to me now it was one of the last things which we'd still had left to lose.

The store was an unattractive little building just off the dirt road after one had passed the turnoff to the neighboring farm of Mr. Lawrence; but if I shut my eyes in this splendid hotel room, I can recall every detail of it. Against the side wall, the two petrol pumps and the phone box with all its windows smashed. On the roof covering the stoop, the big advertisement for Joko Tea. Years ago the stoop itself, invariably swarming with idle Blacks, was used as a stacking place for bags of flour and mealie meal, and paraffin tins, and boxes of soap, but later, on account of theft, everything had to be kept inside. Which wasn't easy by any means, since the place was cramped to start with, and crammed to capacity by wares illuminated by a single bare 25-watt bulb suspended from the ceiling. Rolls of German chintz, bags of dried beans, samp, rolled tobacco, bicycles, transistor radios, coffee, Sunlight soap, *velskoene*, dip and dubbin and leather thongs, tea, bottled sweets, snuff and cigarettes, medicine (Vicks and Aspro and all the thin bottles familiar from Ma's dispensary: red and white dulcis and Haarlem drops, chlorodyne, wonder essence, Jamaica ginger, chest drops, cascara); a special section of ladies' clothing, with some old-fashioned pink XOS bloomers suspended from nails, a pile of old Viyella patterns, knitting wool and needles—disappearing into the deeper recesses of the fragrant dusk. In that same darkness, behind bags of coffee beans and piles of blue soap, I'd petted in my boyhood days with the eager little Lawrence girl while her father, oblivious of it all, stood reading his *Dispatch* at the far end of the counter; and one day things became so hectic that afterwards we weren't able to find her panties again among all the tumbled goods; and self-consciously keeping her thighs close together under the gay floral print of her crumpled dress, she shuffled out while I stayed behind for a while to get my fiercely fondled hard-on down. The urgent caresses in the half-dark, the scuttling of mice behind shelves, the smell of groceries and shoe-polish and hides, dust, her warm breath as she whispered wetly in my ear, the scent of her sweat and more secret secretions: all that returns to me now, over years and continents. Sweet, sweet Cathy!

Mrs. Lawrence was attending to a group of Black women in frilled shawls, passing the material from hand to hand to feel and loudly comment on before they removed their tall turbans and unfolded them to produce small, crumpled bundles of notes; after the transaction the change would be restored to the turban and the latter tied round the head again, before the next purchase was embarked on in the same tedious way.

I greeted her and we chatted for a while. She took the eggs from me—in some inscrutable way it would be entered into the complicated bartering transactions between her and Ma—and handed me the mail: a few accounts, an announcement from *Reader's Digest* (Your Sweepstake Numbers Inside!!!), a farming magazine, an airmail letter from Pretoria, presumably from Theo's wife.

"And how are you keeping?" I asked mechanically.

"Oh, I'm not complaining." Mrs. Lawrence was a tiny, mousey woman with the pointed nose of a shrew and the inquisitive eyes of a *meerkat*; I'd never been able to understand how she could have produced a pretty, lusty girl like Cathy. "I suppose you heard we're going to sell up?"

"Yes, Ma told me. The drought's really bad."

"It's not just the drought. We're getting on, you know, and we thought we'd like to move closer to the children. Both Cathy and Doug are living in the Cape now."

"I should never have allowed Cathy to get away from me," I joked, winking. Until two years before I'd often seen her during holidays, playing tennis on their farm or having sundowners; pleasant husband she had, outdoor-type surveyor; and once, on a New Year's Eve, when we'd all had rather too much to drink, she and I disappeared among the shrubs to consummate, for auld lang syne, the remembered passion of our childhood.

"Doug doesn't want to take over the farm?" I asked.

A hopeless question, I knew. As Ma had put it once: "Poor Doug. The Lord gave him only one talent and that was to play rugby. Now he's gone and hurt his back, so all he's got left to do is drink." At one stage he'd almost reached the Springbok team. Now his old man regularly had to bail him out of jail.

"It's just not pleasant any more, Martin," confided Mrs. Lawrence. "I used to enjoy working in the store, you know. We always got along very well with the Kaffirs. I mean, they were noisy and all that, but they knew their place. Nowadays they're so cheeky, one doesn't know what to do any more. I've got to keep a gun in the shop, just in case. One never knows." She pulled open a drawer to show me the pistol. "Oh, it's a real problem. They're getting too white, is what I say."

"Well, time to go, Mrs. Lawrence. Goodbye, then. Give Cathy my love when you write again." Adding, for the sake of propriety: "And to Doug as well."

✧ ✧ ✧ ✧

I drove back with my eyes narrowed in concentration as the little van bucked and danced on the corrugated road, kicking up a cloud of dust behind it. Soon I was back at the top gate. The piccanins came running on from the distance, but stopped when they recognized me, obviously reluctant because I hadn't given them money the first time. I hooted loudly. They seemed to confer among themselves until I opened the door. That got them moving all right.

Mrs. Lawrence had been right, I thought as I drove through. They were becoming cheeky, even at their age. This time I chucked a handful of cents at them, grinning to see them fighting and rolling in the dust for the money. It wasn't to confuse or spoil them that I'd done it, but to reward them for the little service they'd performed without begging like the previous time.

Straining my eyes, I could see the deep red gashes of erosion ditches running down the side of the road. If this drought lasted for much longer, Ma would have no choice but to pack up and leave. Not only Ma, but everybody else in the district. It seemed as if the drought was bent on getting rid of us. Beyond buying and selling, beyond economics and politics, beyond White and Black, lay the land itself, and in times like these one discovered it was only by its leave and by its grace that we were tolerated there.

It was unnerving to realize how easily we could be dispensed with. When I'd left Aunt Rienie's home after completing my studies in Stellenbosch it had taken me an afternoon to clean the room and pack up and dispose of the accumulated waste. Afterwards, a stranger might have walked in without an inkling of the man who'd lived there before him, so completely had I eradicated all signs of my existence. And in London it had happened again, when Elise and I had left our basement flat in Islington to come back home. Two years of our lives had gone into that miserable little place: yet, after a single day's packing and cleaning there hadn't been anything left of us at all. How much worse it would be, one day, when the earth itself began to clear us away. One never knew when it would happen. The worst of all was that it might have been predestined in the very core of the earth since millions of years before one's own birth. Like a shooting star that became visible aeons after it had already burnt out.

There had been the disaster at the mine near Carletonville, two years before: a rockfall caused by the pressure of earth on a geological fault, a displacement of less than one micron, creating shock waves which caused the whole mine to collapse. An event prepared a million years ago: a disaster predestined without our slightest knowledge (Calvin would have relished the thought). By the time we became aware of it, the earth was shaking and the tunnels and shafts were caving in. More than two hundred men buried, four of them Whites. I shall never forget the scene. The crowd gathered in the cloud of red dust, the four White women praying on their knees, the hundreds of Blacks to one side—first in deadly silence, then erupting in ululations of grief, lasting all night. The floodlights, the bulldozers and cranes, the Women's Auxiliary serving coffee. Even the Salvation Army turned up for prayer meetings, separate services for Blacks and Whites. The brave little choir singing in the wind, the bulging red cheeks of the old men blowing their trumpets. And the journalists. Pages and pages of interviews with the four White women. In the end the operation had to be called off, after some thirty bodies had been found, all of them Black. The others remained under tons of rock and rubble. It was useless to continue the search, and extremely dangerous as well. I had to write off the mine. A loss of several hundred thousand.

Driving back to the farm, I thought: When will it happen again, to us? When will the continent decide to throw us off, like an old dog shaking himself to rid him of fleas?

I was getting morbid. It was time Ma made up her mind. The

273

farm was no good to us any more.

How long would it take to clear out everything that belonged to us? Perhaps a week, at the most. Only the graves would stay, of course.

In the backyard the old diviner was preparing to go and Philemon was just putting his small black trunk on the back of their van when I stopped. Unfortunately I was still in time to shake the limp, damp paw of Mr. Scholtz.

"Found any water?" I asked perfunctorily.

"Yes," he said in his mournful way, as if he were blaming me for it. "Yes. Just as I thought. Running down from the ridge up there and passing right under the house." For a brief moment there was a flickering of malevolent glee in his lifeless eyes: "But it's very deep," he said. "And solid rock. Almost impossible to reach."

8

LUNCH STARTED PEACEFULLY ENOUGH, even with a hint of good humor. But there was a more ominous undercurrent. There we were, halfway through Saturday, and Ma hadn't budged yet. I would have to start turning on the pressure before long. There was too much involved not to feel tense. But I had to wait for the right moment, or all would be lost.

I was annoyed to see Louis sitting down with unwashed oil-covered hands, but feeling Ma's eyes on me in silent warning I decided not to make a remark, although I felt sure he'd done it deliberately. My silence probably unnerved him; also, he may have felt some guilt about the morning's scene, or otherwise his involvement with machinery had made him more approachable: whatever it was, he was much more relaxed at table than he'd been for a long time.

"Do you think you'll get that engine going again, Louis?" asked Ma, handing him his loaded plate.

"Don't know, Gran. I'll have to strip the whole thing. But I think it'll be all right. Just needs a proper cleaning."

"Wouldn't you like one of the laborers to help you?"

"Yes, it'll be useful."

"I'll ask Mandisi," said Ma. "It's Saturday and he's got nothing to do before milking time."

"But isn't it his afternoon off?"

"Yes, but he'll be only too glad to earn something extra." She called Kristina to give her the message for Mandisi.

"I noticed some of the boys up there running about without clothes," I said after Kristina had left.

"I just can't keep up with them," Ma sighed. "I keep dishing out old clothes. Some of the men just sell it for liquor. What can one do? I'm doing my best to supply them with mealie meal and things, but every month new squatters arrive, God alone knows where they come from. The farms are getting blacker all the time."

That was the opening I'd been waiting for.

"Why do you put up with it?" I asked. "It's going from bad to worse. Be honest, Ma: isn't it better to clear out while you can still do it with some dignity?"

"How is running away going to solve the problem?" she asked.

"It's not running away. It's using your common sense."

"You're just being stroppy today, Martin."

"It's you who refuse to understand reason."

"Oh I understand very well, sonny. It's just that I won't sell out so easily."

"What's this about selling?" asked Louis.

"Your father wants to sell the farm under my feet," said Ma.

"First time I hear of it," he said in obvious surprise.

"If you'd been home more often you'd have known about it," I said coolly, annoyed at his interruption. "But one never sees you around any more."

"And when I'm seen you tell me I mustn't be heard."

I refused to be baited by him again. Turning back to Ma, I asked her: "Can you give me one sound reason for staying on here?"

"I told you before. Dad lies buried on this farm."

"Listen, Ma." I knew I had to phrase it very carefully; at the same time I couldn't be too gentle: "Dad is dead. We are the ones who must keep on living. What's a grave if you really think about it? Just a hole and a bundle of bones."

For a while it was very quiet. From the kitchen came the clattering sounds of washing up.

"One can't grind all bones to make bonemeal," said Ma. After a while she looked up: "What will become of us if we start deserting our bones? It's just another way of saying we don't need the land any more. That's the sort of pride the Lord brings before a fall."

"Leave the Lord out of it!"

"Now don't kick up another row, sonny." Her voice was soothing, but I could hear the deeper passion stirring in it. "What will become of this place if we leave it?"

"We're talking past each other, Ma. It's not our concern what happens to the farm afterwards. What matters is that you can't stay on here."

"Oh no. What matters is that you want money for it."

"Don't you think it's high time? How much money has it cost me over the years to keep you and Dad going? And what has become of it all? As far as I'm concerned the farm is nothing but a gaping hole into which I've been pouring money all the time."

She was very pale. "Are you sure that's all it's been to you?"

"What's the use of staying on if the farm is going downhill all the time?"

"I'm not asking any help from you. All I ask is to be left alone. I'm just fine right here."

The moment had come, I decided, to confront her with the full finality of the fact.

"I've tried to be as cooperative as possible," I said. "But you won't listen to me. All right, then I won't go on pleading and begging. I'll just tell you straight: the documents have already been signed."

Taking her time she put her knife and fork back on her empty plate and wiped her mouth with the large damask napkin. "Then you'll just have to cancel it again, sonny. I'm staying here. And without my written consent you can't do anything."

It was time to become aggressive. Getting up I kicked out the chair behind me, sending it toppling backwards. "That's all it amounts to!" I shouted at her. "Plain, ordinary selfishness, and nothing else. Whatever I've done to help you survive on the farm means sweet blow-all to you. You can't care less if I want to be freed of this burden. Because deep down I don't mean anything to you. I know Dad would have understood, but you don't."

"There's still coffee to come," she said quietly behind me as I got to the door.

But I refused to submit to kindness. It would just take us back to where we'd started, and now it was time to bring the whole thing to a head. I slammed the door behind me. In the kitchen I was conscious of old Kristina's startled glance from the wash-up basin, but without paying attention to her I stalked out to the yard. Under the spreading wild fig with the decayed remains of the treehouse I stood for some time in the clear, biting cold.

After a while I went round the house to the front door and took the bunch of keys from the hook in the passage. Allowing both the front door and its covering frame of wire mesh to slam behind me, I went off in the direction of the dairy and the stables and Dad's study. His sanctuary. The door was stuck, as if it hadn't been opened for months, and I had to force it with my shoulder.

For a moment I waited on the doorstep. There was a musty smell inside and everything was covered in dust. It was obvious that the room had not been used for a long time. I opened the curtains to let in the wintry, watery sun. The room had a second-hand look about it, depressing and down-at-heel, irrelevant. On the wall was a calendar of two years before. Here and there the paint had peeled off. The curtains, the chair cushions, the mohair spread on the divan (woven by Elise many years before) looked faded.

The rickety shelves were filled with books, interspersed with some of Elise's pots; one still had a few dried grasses stuck into it. A small collection of semiprecious stones from South West. The shelves running from the door to the far wall were sturdier: those were the ones Elise and Dad had built together. Everything in the room appeared disconnected, an assortment of totally unrelated objects, tokens of an existence which had no relation to mine at all like a bunch of old keys which no longer fitted any lock.

When Pa had still been a teacher our village carpenter had fitted his study shelves: Oom Hennie with his baggy shorts and checkered cap, his wiry grey moustache and two bright beady eyes; aided by his old Black helper, Freddie, shriveled and hoary with age. I'd watched them at work for days on end, relishing the smell of sawdust and shavings, the hissing sound of the plane, the noise of the drill entering the wall. Oom Hennie was a miserable little runt of a man, more or less despised by everybody for his cringing ways. But when he was working with wood, his whole aspect changed. He would handle every plank as if he knew it intimately, as if he actually respected it. I'd never seen a dovetail fit as tightly as his: one couldn't get a thumbnail into it. Once he'd started measuring or sawing or shaving or hammering he appeared to become taller than before, his back straightened out, and his eyes were gleaming as if they could see invisible things in the wood. His clumsy hands with dirty fingernails moved gently across the grain as if he were caressing it. And the wood seemed to understand him, yielding in advance to the magic touch of his tools.

He and old Freddie formed a perfect team. Their four hands never got in each other's way; each seemed to anticipate what the other would be doing, adapting to every move effortlessly. Oom Hennie was a very ordinary old Boer. When he'd reluctantly pushed aside his tools for a few minutes to share a cup of tea with Ma and Dad, he would complain endlessly about the unreliability of Blacks. But when he and Freddie were working, they were like twin brothers.

On the last day but one of their job in our house Freddie fell off the stepladder and seriously injured his back. Dad and Ma helped Oom Hennie carry him to the truck to take him to the doctor. He had to stay in bed for a month. And every single day Oom Hennie drove to the location to visit him with some food and to chat for a while. In our presence he would good-naturedly fulminate against "the stupid bloody Kaffir," but it was plain for all to see how helpless he was without his assistant. And when they returned at last to finish the shelves, it was pure joy to watch them again, as if it were a new lease of life to both of them.

Both Oom Hennie and old Freddie had died long ago; and there I was, on that Saturday afternoon on the farm, in Dad's study, looking at his own crooked shelves, made with much love if without any skill. Rickety as they were, he'd been proud of them. They'd supported his little world.

Without knowing what I was really looking for, I went nearer to scan the titles. All the books showed unmistakable signs of extensive handling. Theal, Cory, Walker, Preller, the Cambridge, Archives Year Books, the Van Riebeeck Series. European history too: Fisher, Hayes, Robinson, Shotwell. Toynbee. Older leather-bound tomes. Carlyle's *French Revolution* in three black volumes. A dark brown series of Gibbon. Without much interest I began to pull out books, leafing through them. There were notes in all the margins, in Dad's small, neat handwriting. Holding a book close to my eyes I tried to read what he'd written: a running conversation with the author, agreement, approval, questions, refutation. Once again, as in the course of the prayer at table, I became conscious of his living presence. I could hear his voice again. *If you go back in history*. But it didn't bring me any closer to an understanding of him.

Returning one of the Gibbons to the shelf I felt an obstruction and when I pushed harder something fell from behind to a lower shelf. Going down on my haunches, I removed several books to retrieve a brown file, one of the old-fashioned type fastened with faded green ribbons. And an old dusty cane, the end frayed and worn. It must have been the one Dad had used to intimidate the children at school. Including the girls, I remembered. They'd received their stripes on their hands or bare legs while the boys had had to bend over a desk: one cut for every question unanswered. I'd always found it beyond my comprehension that he should have resorted to such violence while he'd never beaten either of his own children at home (that had been left to Ma, a task she'd never neglected). But why had he brought the cane with him to the farm? A souvenir? Of what?

I placed the cane on the desk before blowing dust from the file cover and opening it. Old circulars of the Ossewa-Brandwag. 1940. Captivated, I turned the yellowed pages, but there was nothing remarkable really. Boring motions. Agendas. Circulars. Rhetoric. An oath, underlined:

> *If I advance, follow me.*
> *If I retreat, shoot me.*
> *If I die, avenge me.*
> *SO HELP ME GOD.*

With a strange feeling of wry sympathy I put down the file and picked up the frayed old cane again. I was much more intrigued by it than by the dull contents of the file. How had it landed behind the books on the shelf?—had it fallen in by accident, or had Dad hidden it deliberately? The thought was ludicrous. Unless he'd felt guilt about it for some reason. But what then? The meager sense of authority he'd been able to enforce with it? A touch of perverse pleasure? A depressing feeling of "sin" because he'd derived some joy from it? Our Calvinist heritage?

There was a knock on the door. I froze, as if caught in an indecent act.

"Baas!" a voice called outside.

Hurriedly I pushed the cane in behind the Gibbons on the shelf again. It was Dad's secret, I had to keep it for him. The shelves swayed at my touch: some of the pegs anchoring it to the wall had come away and fine plaster dust was sifting to the floor.

"Baas!"

I felt what he would have felt if someone had disturbed him in this room.

When I opened the door irritably, Kristina was waiting outside with my coffee on a tray.

"The madam sent me, Baas."

"I don't want any coffee."

She looked uncertainly at me.

"All right, give it to me." Taking the cup from her, I closed the door again and returned to the desk, sitting down on the beautiful old hand-carved chair our ancestor had repaired for his Melanie. It had come a long way, that chair; and there were many people sitting on it with me. But Dad above all.

Absently, I stared at the books on the opposite wall, too far away now to distinguish any titles. And I wondered: How shortsighted had Dad been? Not in the literal sense, but in his interpretation of everything he'd read. The history of man, of this country, of our tribe? How much of it had he really conveyed to me—and how accurately would I hand it on to Louis one day? How much of it had he really grasped and understood?

How much of him was there for me to understand?

Pa's conscience had always troubled him. Not because of the cane (that too, perhaps): but a more profound anxiety surfacing at regular intervals. Very predictable intervals. Something like a spiritual menstruation.

In my childhood I'd been unable to understand it, but when I'd discussed it with Ma one day, many years later, her explanation was very simple:

"It's the *Broederbond*, sonny. The Band of Brothers, you know, that secret organization everyone knows about."

"What's the *Broederbond* got to do with it?"

"It's been going on all these years now. You know, except for one short period in the war, your father has never been one for mixing with others. Prefers to keep his own company. That's the way he's made. But now there's this *Broederbond* business, with their monthly meetings. And every month, from the day the notice arrives until the meeting is over, he's impossible to live with. Dissatisfied with everything: we're not good enough Afrikaners, we're neglecting the Cause, all that nonsense. As soon as the meeting is over, it's all right again—until next month."

I'd seen the humor of it and, like her, learned to accept it. *(Lovable old plodder.)* And one always knew, before broaching an important subject with him, to first confer with Ma. If she said: "No, sonny, your Dad's in his bad time again," one simply postponed the matter for a week. One of his charming eccentricities.

But had it really been so simple? Here I was sitting in his chair having my coffee, isolated in the room with its hidden cane, closer to him than I'd ever really been. And for the first time I began to understand—no, it was less than understanding; a mere intimation— something of his anxiety about being left out of the mainstream of his people; a shift in the relationship between the individual and his context. Under normal circumstances it suited him fine. But at regular intervals there came the reminder that all was not well. He couldn't put a finger on it—hadn't he spent all his life trying to determine just that?—but he knew it was there, it existed: something was lacking, something which might prove of immeasurable importance.

Mechanically I started paging through the OB file again. That, I assumed, represented the "one short period in the war" Mother had referred to. I couldn't imagine him ever getting involved in anything of real importance; after all, he'd never been prosecuted, and during the war, I knew, they'd kept a close watch on teachers. The most he'd done was probably drawing up a few insignificant reports like those; translating a couple of documents from German; no more. He must have resigned from the OB quite soon, because I knew he'd become a Malan supporter at an early stage and, of course, Malan had never approved of any underground organization.

But perhaps he'd been left with a sense of loss. The way I saw it, he'd been involved, however fleetingly, with something great: he, Wim Mynhardt, had been able to transcend his own insignificance by immersing himself in a noble, national cause. And then, drifting away from it, he'd returned to the paltriness of his solitary existence, with only that thin brown file to remind him of what might have been. And his passion for history had become the unsatisfactory surrogate for all that.

I must pursue the thought. Did Dad have some presentiment, perhaps, in his brief monthly anxiety, of an apocalypse, of a great general fall in which he would once again be part of his people? An all-embracing death wish? In which case that apocalypse would have been a fate prepared through all our preceding generations, like a trembling of the earth. Destruction and apotheosis at the same time. Apotheosis *because of* destruction, since that would be a vast, collective experience, fusing all the minute meaningless particles into one great mass, a heap of clay in the hand of an angry God.

That would explain the obsessive nature of his work, of his efforts to understand what had happened in the past and what was inevitable in the future. In order to be prepared more fully for that Judgment.

There had been nations in history before, he told me, who'd disappeared from the face of the earth without leaving any trace at all. The Avares, for example. And it might happen again.

It is a strange and awesome thought: if such an apocalypse were really imminent and unavoidable, then every day or every trifling action we perform, brings us closer to it. And, looking back, whatever I was doing on that farm, wandering up a hill, or having coffee with Ma, or chatting in a store, or remembering long-lost little girls, or recalling in the dusk the words of years ago: *And have not love*—or sitting in that chair of Dad's—all the time, around me, below me, deep inside me, there would be a current moving inexorably in that direction. It was as inevitable as the flood that would end the drought. And suddenly the mere sound of a teaspoon against an empty cup acquired a terrifying significance.

There is a morbid streak in us. Not only in our family: in all our people. Even our anthem sounds like a funeral hymn. Oom Peet, the undertaker/barber in the village of my youth, once expounded his philosophy of life to me:

"The way I see it, Martin, everything in the world keeps changing all the time. Farms, horse-drawn carriages, churches, markets, the lot. There's nothing you can really depend on. Except for death. Death is a man's best investment, and it keeps one close to God. That's why I chose it as my career."

It is applicable to more people than just Oom Peet. I think that was why Ma, and even an otherwise sensible woman like Elise, found it so shocking that I should have been absent at Dad's death. What difference could it really have made? I'd taken my leave of him long before that, before his cancer had dragged him beyond our reach. And today, I think, I know better than they ever did the comfort death must have become to him. Not as an escape from suffering, but as a way of being reunited with his own: in the death of the individual he was able to experience the death of his kind.

The whole family returned to the farm for the funeral. Elise and I, Theo and his wife; and also Dad's sisters with their husbands, and Ma's brother from the Sandveld. The previous occasions on which we'd all been assembled like that had been the funeral of Dad's elder brother and that of Oupa Mynhardt. It took death to bring us together.

The old family home was filled with people again, as in the holidays of my childhood when there had been uncles and aunts and cousins sleeping in all the rooms, even in the dining room and the lounge. Only this time it was very somber, without the exuberance of children on holiday.

The *dominee* came to the farm for the service; and many other townsfolk too. It had been raining since the previous afternoon and the earth was soaked, the grass as green as in the best of summers and the soil as red as blood. Under the black umbrellas we assembled in our black clothes in the muddy graveyard, for the final prayer and the lowering of the coffin. I spoke on behalf of the family, and old Mr. Lawrence on behalf of the friends and neighbors. Then, unexpectedly and unannounced, old Danzile came forward too— he'd been foreman on the farm for years, before Mandisi took over—launching into a long mumbled discourse on how good the *baas* had been to them, and how they were mourning the death of a father: rendered in a mixture of Xhosa and Afrikaans, rather rambling and annoying in the discomfort of the rain. He spoke about the rain too, I remember, calling it the blessing of the Lord: "Where He buries, He also gives new life"—or something to that effect. In the end I had to ask him to cut short his speech, and motion to the vicar to get on with the hymn, otherwise we would have been there until dark.

Afterwards all the guests went up to the house to sit down at the enormous funeral dinner Ma had been preparing since dawn. She still believed in the old-world thoroughness of leg of lamb and yellow rice and sweet potatoes, all the way through to milk tart and coffee for everybody—including the laborers assembled at the back door.

Elise was inconsolable. At the graveside I had to support her when she dropped her handful of mud on the coffin. Quite indecent, I thought, such a public display of grief. Ma herself never shed a tear during the two full days we spent with her. And after the guests had left, late that same evening, she went out in the rain to tidy the study and get everything in order; none of the servants, not even old Kristina, was allowed to give her a hand. When I went down to look for her shortly before midnight, she was still on her knees, polishing and shining floors and furniture, clearing the desk, stacking away the books. I offered to help, but without a word she motioned me out of her way; and I sat waiting on the divan until she finished just after one. Then she drew the curtains, made sure nothing was out of place, turned off the light and locked the door behind us. It was still drizzling faintly outside. For the first time I felt that now, for her, Dad had really died.

"Well," Ma said. She sounded weary, but there was a deep satisfaction in her voice, as if she felt relieved beyond words; as if she had finally got rid of an unbearable burden.

Later that Saturday afternoon, I'm not sure about the time, Ma came to me in the study. She'd opened the door so softly and I'd been so wrapped in thought that I only looked up when the door clicked shut behind her.

"What are you doing here all by yourself?" she asked. Without making it obvious, she was surveying the room to ensure that everything was still in its place. I felt relieved that I'd hidden the cane again, although I didn't know what earthly difference it could have made.

"I was just looking round."

"Of course."

I pushed the brown file towards her. "I found this."

"What's that?" She opened it and began to page through it, frowning.

"Dad's old OB papers."

"I thought he'd thrown them all away years ago."

"Doesn't look very interesting."

"Oh well, you know what he was like." She closed the file and tied the faded ribbons.

"Don't you come here any more?" I asked her.

She looked up at me, but didn't reply at once. "Not really," she said at last. "I have more than enough to keep me busy."

"Were you happy together, Ma?" I asked in spite of myself.

"Happy?" In her characteristic way she pushed back a few loose strands of hair. "What a question. We were married for more than forty years, you know." She sat down on a straight-backed chair.

"We knew so little about him."

"*Ag*, well." She seemed to be looking for an explanation, or an excuse. "What does anybody know about anybody else?" She looked directly at me: "Even one's own children."

Ignoring the hint, I asked: "Had he always been so secretive? Or did it only come later?"

She reflected for a minute. "When we were young, somehow it seemed easier to get on with him. We were talking and planning all the time, he had so much ambition for the future."

"Ambition?"

She gave a short laugh, and I wasn't sure whether she'd heard me. "You know," she said, "in the war he once went out to a farm—those days he loved to go hunting whenever farmers invited him—and when he came back, he told me about it. He was all red in the face, but he couldn't help laughing at himself."

"What happened?"

"He was out in the veld, you see, when he had this sudden, well, call of nature. And while he was sitting there in a nice sandy patch, he wrote with his finger, in large letters on the ground before him: GENERAL WIM MYNHARDT. Then he forgot all about it.

But by the time they went home, one of his friends came to him, one who'd been in the OB with him, and he said: 'Wim, it's time you buried that general of yours, he's beginning to smell.'"

"You think that was his ambition?" I asked after a while. "In the OB?"

"I don't know anything about becoming general and that sort of thing. It's just that—*ag*, I suppose he just wanted to be recognized, you know. By somebody. But he left the OB very early, it was in '41 I think, and since then there never was much life in him." She got up, quite unnecessarily, to pull a loose thread from the hem of the spread on the divan. "But people easily misjudged him," she said with sudden vehemence. "There was more to him than met the eye, let me tell you."

"In what way?"

She continued to wander through the study for a while, pushing the books into an even row with the palm of her hand, wiping away a line of dust from the edge of a shelf; and almost casually she began to tell me the story of Dad's encounter with the police. He'd been on the point of leaving for a secret OB meeting, one day, she said, when there'd been a knock on the door. Two sergeants from the Security Police.

Dad invited them in, glancing at his watch. When it became clear that they were in no mood to leave soon, he came straight to the point.

"Do you mind coming back tomorrow?" he asked with disarming candor. "I'm rather busy this afternoon."

"Oh?" they asked. "What sort of business?"

"Well, I'm going to a meeting."

"Really? What sort of meeting?"

"We have a regular prayer meeting every Tuesday," Dad explained without batting an eyelid. "Discussing texts from the Bible and so on, you know."

Finding it most interesting they offered to go with him. He tried to get out of it by hinting that they might get bored, but when they remained adamant he quietly fetched his Bible and left with them in their official car.

At the house where all the OB men sat waiting, Dad went in ahead of his escort and introduced the visitors. "Friends," he said, "we have two newcomers to our prayer meeting today. Sergeant Grobler and Sergeant Henderson of the Security Police. On behalf of all of us I'd like to welcome them in our midst."

Before much more could be said, he opened the meeting with a prayer which lasted, according to Ma, more than half an hour. Then one of the men fetched another Bible from a bedroom in the house and somebody began to read from Romans or Corinthians or something, going on for four or five chapters. Followed by earnest discussion. After the first hour the sergeants were beginning to shift uneasily on their seats, but the brethren became so absorbed in the discussion that the visitors were not allowed to say a word. After two full hours, when the end was still not in sight, Sergeant Grobler rose with an expression of desperation on his face:

"Mr. Chairman," he said, "you must please excuse us, but—"

Whereupon Dad promptly asked him: "Sergeant, have you been born again?"

"Have I been what?"

"Born again. Redeemed by our Lord Jesus Christ."

"Well—I—yes, I suppose so, I—"

"Brethren," said Dad, "I propose we pray for the soul of our friend."

And before the sergeant could protest any further, they proceeded with passionate and seemingly interminable prayers again.

It was growing dark outside when Dad finally said: "Sergeant, if you give us your addresses, we'd like to visit you at home to pursue the business of the Lord."

According to Dad's subsequent report to Ma, the policemen paled at the mere thought and never gave the group any trouble again.

"But of course," said Ma, "from the time we moved to the farm, he lost all interest. But I tried to make things easier for him, that I can swear to God."

"I know very well, Ma."

"And when he finally came to rest, down there—"

I sat stroking the carved wood of the chair.

"We're all beginners, all the time," she went on, impetuously. "One never learns. That's why we've got to start from scratch again, every time."

I didn't want to look at her.

"The day he went to lie down in his grave, sonny, it was as if for the first time in many years I could feel solid earth under my feet again. As if we'd finally settled down. As if we'd taken root at last."

A dog was barking in the yard. At the far side of the house an engine began to sputter, stopped, then droned on. Louis must have got the generator started.

The sound immediately brought her back to the practical present.

"I didn't mean to disturb you here," she said. "I just wanted to have a little chat."

"Thanks, Ma."

"I must be going."

"Please stay if you want to."

"No, I've got work to do. And I suppose you've got a lot to think about. Please put Dad's file away when you've done with it, will you?"

It seemed so easy to follow Ma's advice and go back to Johannesburg and cancel the contract. I could always excuse myself by referring Calitz to the stipulation in the testament about Ma's written consent. I would have the peace of knowing she was free to enjoy her old age on the farm. And, even more important perhaps, the farm would remain in the family for the future. Even if it had no practical value, the mere fact of its existence would be reassuring, like a wholesome conscience, a form of emotional security, a guarantee of perspective.

But of course it was more complicated than that. The Minister and I were both checkmate. He had to conclude his transaction with Bantu Administration or his whole maneuver would be exposed. And I was forced to sell, otherwise he would make quite sure that I was destroyed.

It was, really, too late for argument: the decision had been made, and I had come to the farm merely to confirm it.

Even if a choice had still existed, the situation was impossible. For it was not a matter of balancing two comparable elements, but two essentially different contents, two different value systems. The farm was an ideal, a dream, a sentimental quantity: involving, let us say, our history, our pastoral past, our tribal tradition, perhaps our freedom. In other words, everything I'd grown unaccustomed to handling. For in practice my life comprised the opposite, the calculable: compromises and studied risks, profit, achievement. Simply in order to survive I had to stay on top. There was no alternative. It was either that, or go under. The same choice which had confronted my ancestors in one generation after another, but in a totally different dimension. And I refused to consider the prospect of going under.

The question was: how much of the sentimental, or the ideal, how much of my atavistic romanticism, could I allow myself without relinquishing my hold on survival? How far could I indulge myself? Because it had indeed become a luxury. In my context luxury did not mean the house Theo had designed for us, or the Mercedes, the yellowwood, the red wine, the cycads on the lawn: all that was part and parcel of my existence itself. True luxury was: the freedom to dream; the freedom to be unpractical. And freedom as such had become a romantic notion.

There was no need for me to believe in the sort of life I led. I only had to live it.

In order to survive I had to regard all the components of my life as relative and adaptable. Without cynicism one had no hope of retaining one's hold on reality.

I was tired. Why shouldn't I admit it? I had chosen an exhausting and demanding way of life. For that very reason it was so tempting to accept what Ma had offered me: the peace and quiet of an illusion. But having recognized the illusion as such, I had no right to yield to the temptation.

Oh, I would have loved to believe in freedom and hope and faith and charity. But above all I wanted to survive. And in order to survive I had to stay on the winning side, one better than my opponent. In me was the hunger to succeed, the instinct to kill. Dad had never had it. (Neither had Bernard.)

✧ ✧ ✧ ✧

I looked up when Louis appeared on the doorstep.

"Hello!"

"Have you been here all afternoon?"

"Yes, indeed."

"What are you doing?"

"Looking through Grandpa's things. To make sure it's all in order."

I saw his quizzical, ironic glance as he looked at the solitary closed file on the desk, but I made no attempt to explain.

"Isn't there anything I can help you with?"

"Are you bored?"

"Of course."

"I heard the engine a little while ago," I said. "So you got it going?"

He smiled, looking like a boy again, briefly. "Yes, it's working all right." After a moment: "Mandisi helped a lot, though. Nothing wrong with his hands."

"You don't feel like taking up that engineering course again?"

For a moment his eyes lit up with enthusiasm, but he quickly closed up again, shrugging his shoulders.

"Why do you want to sell the farm?" he asked without warning.

"It's just not a viable proposition any more." I decided to be as frank and reasonable with him as I could. "You can work it out for yourself. Let's say the market value is—what?—forty thousand. That means a return of R4,000 per year at the normal rate of ten percent on your investment. But what happens instead? Not only does it fall far short of four thousand, but in actual fact it costs me several thousand a year just to keep it going. All right, I admit I can deduct it from my income tax. But it remains a very bad investment. And I'm a businessman."

"Is that all you are, Dad? Just a businessman?"

"What do you mean?"

"Surely you should consider Grandma too. It's her life."

"I *am* thinking about her!" I protested. "Haven't you noticed how she's aged in the last year? And all her neighbors are selling out. It's dangerous for her to stay here all on her own on the border of a Black homeland."

"So the old Eastern frontier is becoming a frontier again, isn't it?" he asked. I couldn't make out whether he was joking. "We're creating more and more frontiers all the time."

"Don't tell me you have any interest in the farm," I said, interrupting his nonsense. "We haven't been here for a full day yet and already you're bored."

He came past the desk to look out through the window on the valley side. Outside, the lowing of cattle was coming closer.

"Strange when it's getting dark," he said without turning round to me. "At home, somehow, one doesn't notice it so much. But here on the farm it's as if one suddenly feels all alone in the world."

I'd been just as sentimental when I'd had his years. In the gathering twilight I sensed a fleeting new closeness between us.

"We just don't belong here any more," I said.

He turned round abruptly, as if upset by something he'd seen outside: the returning cows, the increasing darkness in the valley down below, the hadehahs coming over the hills, something.

"I suppose you're right," he said, with a readiness that caught me unawares. "It may be better to sell the place after all. But Gran is holding on, isn't she?"

"Stubborn as a mule."

"I'll talk to her if you want me to."

"It's all right, I know how to handle her."

"But she discussed it with *me*, I think she feels—"

"What did she tell you?" Suspicion added an edge to my voice. I didn't want Ma to draw Louis into this.

"Nothing much," he said evasively. "Still, I think I may be able to talk her into it."

"You're asking for trouble if you try to push her."

He lingered for another minute before he went out again, leaving the door open behind him, I considered calling him back to close it. But in the end I got up quietly: it was getting late anyway. Pushing the exquisite old chair back into position I rested my hands on the backrest for a moment. We should take the chair home with us, it would look good in my own study.

The file I put away in one of the dusty drawers of the desk before drawing the curtains. Outside, the dusk was deepening. From the stables came a pungent smell of manure. Just as I was leaving I remembered something and returned to the bookshelves on the far wall to remove the cane from behind the Gibbons. It would be better to dispose of it somewhere in the farmyard: I didn't want Ma to discover it when she started packing to clear out.

9

THIS TIME I FOUND MANDISI alone with the calves. I didn't
like the idea of interfering with their way of life, but as I
was in the position of authority I felt obliged to talk to him.

"Mandisi," I said, "what's this thing I hear about your wife?"

"*Nkosi*," he asked sullenly.

"A man shouldn't beat his wife."

He poured a pail of skimmed milk into the trough, not
bothering to reply.

"Your child was desperately ill, you know. It needed proper
medicine."

"*Ewe.*"

"Then why did you beat her like that?"

He said nothing.

"Mandisi, I don't want to hear this sort of thing about you again,
you understand?"

He picked up the pail and turned to look at me, still refusing to
say a word. He stood a head taller than myself, with the muscles of
a gladiator: I could see them rippling through the tears and holes of
his shirt.

"If ever you hurt your wife again, you must get off the farm. Did
you hear me?"

He began to walk in the direction of the dairy.

"Answer me when I speak to you!"

Half turning his head, he grinned before he went on. Arrogant; but not impertinent. The suggestion of superiority in his bearing, as if I had to be forgiven for not knowing what I was talking about. Perhaps he hadn't understood me properly.

Disgruntled, I went away. His ways, his superstitions and his primitiveness were no concern of mine. But surely I couldn't turn a blind eye where a child's life was involved. And if he'd made up his mind to come and work for Whites, he had to learn to adapt. In the final analysis it was for his own benefit.

It was so much easier to get along with a person like Charlie. Our frames of reference were similar. He'd said so himself. (Ironically, I had been the one to protest at the suggestion.) It had been a strange and disconcerting day, about a month before.

That morning, on behalf of the South Africa Foundation, I'd had to show a couple of Canadian businessmen around—two highly intelligent and pleasant gentlemen who'd revealed a reassuring insight into our national problems—and, as usual, I'd arranged to take them to the Ndebele village near Pretoria.

As I was still taking it easy after my coronary, Charlie was driving; on the way we had a relaxed and informative discussion in which he also took part.

The visit was, predictably, a success. There was nobody to accept our visitors' forms, so we strolled about on our own, admiring the neat houses painted in fascinating geometrical designs. A picturesque scene which never failed to impress our foreign visitors: the bunch of old women stringing beads under a tree; two or three men pushing a car down the "main street" to get it going; children prancing around us wherever we went; a group of young girls kicking a soccer ball. As soon as they noticed us, they ran behind the nearest houses to remove their clothing, returning with beaming smiles: "Photo, Baas, photo, Baas!" The Canadians eagerly photographed their bare breasts and paid the requested fee without a murmur—whereupon the girls put on their clothes again and resumed their soccer game in the balmy May morning.

Charlie waited for us in the car; and when we returned I could see he was in a bad mood. On the way back he hardly said a word. He didn't feel like joining us for lunch at the Carlton either, but I persuaded him that it would be in the firm's best interest: it always made a good impression on foreigners. But after we'd taken our leave of the two Canadians, as we drove back through the heavy afternoon traffic, he looked very glum indeed.

"What's the matter with you, Charlie?" I inquired after some time, when it became clear he wasn't going to volunteer anything on his own.

"Nothing."

"Oh, come on. Don't be childish."

"I'm not childish, Baas Martin." He knew very well how it piqued me to be addressed like that.

"So your guests enjoyed their bit of local color, did they?" he finally asked.

"Of course."

"Nice slide shows they can arrange for their families and friends when they get back home. All these uninhibited children of nature. I suppose you'll be taking them to the mine dances on Sunday?"

"What have you got against 'uninhibited children of nature'? Nobody forced the girls to undress."

"I'm not even referring to that."

"I wish you would say what you mean."

"It's bad enough fooling a bunch of foreigners," he said angrily. "But how the hell do you manage to go on fooling yourself?"

"In what way am I fooling myself?"

"Why don't you show them what the land really looks like for a change? See South Africa and die."

"Where do you want me to take them?"

"Have you ever set foot in Soweto?"

"Of course not. Why should I?"

He accelerated suddenly, driving through a yellow light, and went straight on instead of turning right where he should.

"Where are you going now?"

"Today you're going to Soweto," he said with a grim smile.

"What's got into you?"

"Regard it as an initiation. How the other half lives. The other eight percent."

It took me a few moments to regain my composure. "Fair enough, Charlie," I said. "But I can't go there without a permit."

"Oh fuck it," he replied, turning his broad smile to me. "How many of us are going about without passes every day?"

"I still don't understand what you really want me to see."

"Let's call it a bit of history."

"That's not history. That's today."

Charlie laughed, his eyes almost closing behind his thick lenses. "That's *our* way of making history, Martin boy. In this country you and your people think you've got the monopoly over history. I've got to make my own from day to day."

"I've never denied your right to your own past."

"Sure. As long as it could be read between the lines. Nothing official." Swerving to pass a loaded truck he said: "Did you know my great-grandfather was a counselor of King Moshesh—a *moeletsi?*"

"Really?"

"That's right, man. I don't know anything about further back: we must have come out of the *difagane* somewhere. But he was a *moeletsi* all right, in the time of President Brand—if you want to approach it from your White side. Gave the Free State farmers hell."

"And then, what happened?"

"Downhill all the way. His son, my grandfather, became a

soldier—a *molaodi* in fact, a commander—but he got wounded in a battle near Ficksburg. The missionaries got hold of him and healed him. That was the end for us. In later years he went to work as a laborer on a Free State farm. There my father was born. And I myself."

"But you broke away."

"Yes, I broke away, man. Just like you." He looked at me, light flickering on his glasses. "Have you ever thought about how similar you and I really are?"

"You're exaggerating."

"You think so? We come from the same sort of place. Then we both went overseas." More subdued, he added: "And then we both came back. What the hell for? What did we really hope to find? We don't belong any more, man. You're just as bloody detribalized as I am."

"I'm still an Afrikaner."

"That's where the similarity ends and the difference begins." He nearly doubled up in a sudden spasm of laughter.

"Surely you have no desire to go back to what you once were?"

"Of course not."

"So why are you complaining?"

"You think I'm complaining?" He shifted into a more comfortable position behind the wheel. "I just made a statement of fact. And today I'm going to show you something."

"*What* do you really want to show me?"

He laughed. "The inside of hell," he said.

After supper and evening prayers we spent the evening in front of the fire—Louis on the floor, fondling one of the dogs; Ma and I on two of the heavy easy chairs. There was no uneasiness in our conversation. Outside, the wind had come up, causing the chimney hood to spin this way and that with an unearthly screeching sound. Inside, we relaxed in front of the dancing flames, in which, from time to time, small bits of bark exploded sending sprays of sparks up into the chimney; on the ledge beside the grate the kettle of bush tea stood hissing tranquilly. Ma had switched off the generator just after supper, and the only light we had was the gentle flickering of the flames. The day with its harsh, forbidding wintriness seemed to have subsided like a sea, leaving us stranded in silence and peace. Even our skirmishes appeared insignificant at this distance.

Later, Louis selected a few magazines to take to bed with him; Ma and I remained, she with her crocheting. Even at her most relaxed she couldn't leave her hands unoccupied. Occasionally one of us said something, or a dog groaned. Otherwise it was silent.

Deep inside the blue and orange of the glowing coals I discovered Dad's face, sallow and shriveled as it had been the last time I'd seen him, wearing the odd little knitted cap to cover his hairless head, his nose disproportionately large in the sunken face and protruding like a beak, his eyes sunken. I'd looked in at his room once or twice a day and dutifully sat with him for a few minutes at a time; there was nothing left to talk about. At night, Ma and Elise took turns to watch him—not without some hidden tension, because, exhausted as she was, Ma didn't like the idea of Elise taking over. But one night Dad called me in and insisted I stayed with him, refusing to allow one of the women near us, not even Elise. I spent the night in the chair beside the bed, half-dozing most of the time, going out occasionally to relieve myself or pour a drink. He appeared to be sleeping, yet every time I stirred he would open his eyes. Whenever he tried to say something in his shrill, hoarse whisper of a voice, it sounded disjointed if not totally incomprehensible. But by three o'clock in the morning a curious, unnatural clarity came over him and for the first time I had no difficulty in following what he said, however slowly and haltingly it came out.

"That you, Martin?"

"Yes, I'm here with you, Dad. Don't worry. Go to sleep."

"No, I don't want to sleep. One of these days I'll have enough time for sleeping."

"You're not afraid, are you?"

"No, I'm not afraid." A long pause. "Not afraid. I've made my peace." Another pause. "I'm just sorry, that's all. Such a pity."

"What is?"

"Everything. I've been a failure, Martin."

"That's not true, Dad." I had to comfort and encourage him.

He persisted, weary but with stubborn effort. "No use to pretend. When one's got as far as I have, one can afford to be honest. I've been a failure, all right. In everything."

I felt the urge to put out a hand and take his, but something like revulsion held me back.

"There was one short time," he said, "during the war, you know. Just a few months. When it seemed, when I felt, I was going somewhere. But then I got scared. That's what it was. I simply got scared. I could lose my job. I had a wife and young children. And so I left. I was a coward."

"It's all in the past now, Dad."

"It's never past. That's why I wanted to talk to you tonight. Only, I'm so tired."

I offered him some water. He seemed to have forgotten what he'd been talking about. But after a while he took up the thread again.

"Now it's your turn. I've had mine and I failed."

"Don't worry, Dad. I'll—"

"You must go on, Martin. I want you to succeed. For my sake too."

"Of course I will." I had no idea what he really meant.

"You know, when I get to the other side, God may ask me anything He wants. I won't mind pleading guilty and asking for His mercy. But I know there's one thing He'll never forgive me."

I prepared myself for a deathbed confession, not sure of what it would be, but certainly expecting something grave.

And after a long time he came out with it: "I haven't been a good Afrikaner, Martin. I failed. I left my people in the lurch."

"But what was it you *did*, Dad?"

"Nothing. That's what. I did nothing at all." Another long pause followed, in which he seemed to drift off to sleep. Then he spoke again: "And I resisted. When I had to take over the farm, I resisted."

"Every man has the right to decide about his own life."

"No, Martin. History decides for us. And history is the way God has of making His will clear to us." He made an effort to raise his hand, as if he wanted to reach out to me; then dropped it. "Whatever you do in your life, Martin, you must never let this farm go. It's ours. It's our sin and our redemption. You must promise me that."

"I promise, Dad." After all, there were only the two of us. And his thoughts were already wandering.

He refused to go to hospital. During his last months he clung to the farm he'd never wanted. Unable to live there, he seemed to have made up his mind to die there. And sitting at the fire that evening, with Ma crocheting peacefully and the chimney hood grinding outside, I think I understood something more of that irrational urge in him: something of that for ever incomplete, defeated man who'd been a stranger all his life but who, through his death, had finally reconciled himself with history and with the earth. To him it had been the only way he could atone for an obligation towards the past which he'd been unable to fulfill.

The fact that he'd tried to transfer it to me had been quite unreasonable, of course: how could I be expected to compensate for whatever, in his view, he'd done wrong or left undone? I had my own life and my own responsibilities to look after. And there was nothing in his testament to stop me selling the farm—apart from the clause about Ma's consent, that was. Juridically that was all that mattered.

✧ ✧ ✧ ✧

Going to my room later, I took Ma a hot water bottle. With the plait of her chignon undone, her grey hair fell over her shoulders down to the middle of her back.

"Thank you, sonny." She took the bottle from me. "You've always been such a considerate child."

Behind her the door of the wardrobe stood half open. Inside I could see one of Dad's jackets, the faded corduroy ones he'd always worn on the farm. What struck me was that, even suspended among the other clothes as it was, the material had retained the shape of his body, the slope of his shoulders, the bending of the elbows, the slight stoop of the back.

Louis was asleep already. I undressed and got into bed and blew out the candle.

For the first time I realized just how tired I was. The long journey to the farm the previous day, the nearly sleepless night, Saturday with all its hidden tensions: everything seemed now to press down upon me with its accumulated weight. Voluptuously I abandoned myself to the sensation of sinking, sinking through layers of sleep. But suddenly there was fear too: the old panic because I was sinking into mud with no one near to hear me or to help.

I felt overcome by the myriad of small superficial events of the day. The water diviner, lowing cattle, the breaking of my spectacles, the quarrel at table, Dad's study, the frayed cane. Now all that appeared no more than the signs of a deeper anguish I couldn't fathom. And beyond those incidents were others: Elise giving birth to Louis; a Caesarean scar; Cathy shuffling self-consciously from the many-flavored shop, her panties lost among the groceries in the dark; Ndebele girls with bare breasts; Charlie offering to be my guide through hell. Bernard. (No, Bernard had to stay out of this.)

I tried to pick at all the thoughts stirred up by the day; just as, writing it down now, I pick at the scabs on the wounds of the past.

Stern old men marching across the barren veld of history: a giant with innumerable children, setting off into the wilderness in search of Monomotapa. A deaf, half-blind old patriarch with a Bible on his knees and a gun at hand to shoot at invisible foes on the horizon. A rebel taking an oath of vengeance beside the graves of his family and dying with an assegai in his heart. A Trekker looking for the new Canaan, and murdered in the night. A hunter stumbling home with the body of his son on his shoulders. A digger of gold, painstakingly writing down the story of his life in exile, dying before he'd uncovered the meaning of it all. An incorrigible dreamer, disappearing at intervals and reappearing unannounced whenever the lure of the farm had become too strong. Pa shrunken and shriveled on his deathbed.

Had they really all been losers only as I'd thought? Or had each in his own way succeeded in taming his small portion of the wilderness, paying for it with his life, as, gradually, they won the land for those who came after them? Conquerors of a farm, of a piece of Africa. Not calculable in terms of money; and therefore indisposable.

In the end I must have drifted off into uneasy dreams, for suddenly, through the escape of sleep, something hauled me back to consciousness: a voice calling. For a while I had no idea of what was happening or where I was. Outside the dogs were barking. There was a deep man's voice speaking to them on the stoop, calming them down. At first I didn't recognize it. As I slowly woke up completely, a dull headache throbbing in my skull, I began to grasp what was happening.

On the stoop the voice went on calling softly but insistently:

"Nkosikazi! Nkosikazi! Nkosikazi!—Madam!"

At last Ma's voice, sleepy and surprised, answered: *"Yintoni, Mandisi?*—What's the matter?"

Mandisi. So something must have happened. I sat up to listen more clearly.

"Kukho inkathazo enkulu ekhaya—There is big trouble at home."

Almost eerily in the night came her calm query: *"Umlibazile na umfazi wakho?*—Did you hurt your wife?"

"Ewe."

"How bad is it?" she asked.

"Ufile, nkosikazi.—Dead."

I got up quickly. When I reached the passage door, Louis's startled voice stopped me:

"What's happened, Dad?"

"Trouble with one of the laborers."

Ma was on her way down the passage to the front door, carrying an oil lamp. I wanted to follow her, but the cold forced me to turn back first and put on something warm. I lit our candle. Louis got up too. Outside the chimney hood was still grinding away.

When I arrived in the passage again, Ma was already turning the handle of the telephone beside the door to the sitting room.

"Where's Mandisi?" I asked.

"I sent him home. He'll wait for us in the hut. I told him I'd send the police up."

"He can kill the lot of them in the meantime!"

"No, he'll wait. Don't worry." After a few more turns of the handle the exchange answered and Ma asked for the police. In another minute a sleepy voice replied.

We rekindled the fire in the grate with pinecones and firewood. Ma made some coffee, and the three of us sat drinking it beside the fire, waiting for the police to come. We didn't talk. All round us darkness lay heavily in the rooms of the house and outside too, under the tiny pinpricks of the stars.

Soon after the clock in the passage had struck three we heard a distant rumbling. The van stopped in the yard. The clear, loud clang of a metal door. Voices.

A White sergeant and a Black constable appeared in the doorway.

"It's just up there on the hill behind the house," said Ma. "The first hut you come to. You show them the way, sonny."

But I kept on stumbling in the dark, and twice my myopia made us lose the path up the bare slope.

I'd expected to find everything in turmoil at the huts, but all was quiet. When the sergeant shone his bright torch into the first hut, we were paralyzed for a moment. The body was lying on the ground, covered by a blanket, only one arm visible, stretched out above the head. Beside her lay four small children, fast asleep, one of them the baby. And next to them, Mandisi, sleeping just as peacefully.

The Black constable pulled away the blanket. It was Thokozile, the young woman I'd seen in the house, with the high cheekbones and delicate features. She was completely naked, her body like a bare brown statue, washed clean of all traces of blood—except for the bad bruise on the one cheek and the small dark slits of knife wounds in the breasts and arm and belly.

Bending over, the sergeant took Mandisi by the arm and shook him gently, almost as if he were reluctant to wake the man. Mandisi sat up and blinked, looking about him in surprise. Then he nodded. "It's all right, *nkosi.*"

Louis and I helped to carry the body downhill, wrapped in the grey blanket with the white stripes. Mandisi carried the baby. The three other children were left to sleep.

There was something quite unreal about our small procession going down the slope in the immensity of that night: the sergeant leading the way with the torch, followed by the tall gladiator with the sleeping baby in his arms, then the constable and Louis and myself with the body. Unreal: not only because of my shortsightedness, but because of the solemnity and the quiet dignity of the occasion, as if we were moving in a silent movie.

As we reached the gate to the yard, Ma came from the kitchen to take the baby from Mandisi.

"Don't worry about him," she said. "I'll look after him."

"Thank you, *nkosikazi.*"

The Black constable opened the back door of the van for Mandisi to get in. Locking it, there was the rattling sound of a chain on metal. The engine started. A minute later the lights disappeared over the ridge of the rise.

Ma had already gone inside with the child. Louis and I remained behind in the utter darkness of the yard. The wind had died down. It was very cold.

Then Louis said, in a voice I barely recognized, almost in awe: *"Nkosi sikelel' iAfrika."*

Sunday

1

WHAT HAPPENED THAT WEEKEND, including the murder, was not very important in its own right. I realize it more and more clearly. Not the events as such that were significant, but everything drawn into the whirlpool by them. And if I experience a sense of urgency in writing about it all it is not through any desire to come to the end of the weekend (there is no "goal" towards which I'm striving; and what awaits me at the end I am, in fact, reluctant to face). My urgency is of a different nature altogether: an awareness of the massive clearance involved, and of the fact that it cannot be done in haste, even though every moment is placed under pressure. My time is running out: I have been writing for five days now.

I have never subscribed to the prognoses of the Club of Rome. But in their first report there was an image which expressed admirably my own feelings as I am writing here now. A children's riddle, to be exact, used to demonstrate the suddenness with which exponential growth within a finite system reached its fixed limit: Suppose you own a pond on which a water lily is growing. The lily plant doubles in size each day. If the lily were allowed to grow unchecked, it would completely cover the pond in thirty days, choking off the other forms of life in the water. For a long time the plant seems small, and so you decide not to worry about cutting it back until it covers half the pond.

On what day will that be?—On the twenty-ninth, of course. By which time you have exactly one day left to save your pond.

✧ ✧ ✧ ✧

It was deadly quiet on the farm that night. Not a floorboard or a beam on the ceiling creaked; no dog sighed in its sleep; no nightjar shrilled in the silence. I couldn't even hear Louis breathing. I must have slept for some time, troubled by confused and oppressive dreams; but then I woke up again. Fatigue pressed me down on the bed with a heavy hand, yet I found it impossible to fall asleep again.

A few hours before someone had been murdered in this same dark, yet it now seemed improbable if not wholly impossible, part of the far-fetched dreams of the night. And yet I'd helped carry the body down the hill.

Beside the sleeping man and the small sleeping children, that naked young woman with the symmetry of her limbs, the full firm breasts and smooth belly, the satisfying curve of hips and long legs; the wounds like small wet mouths. There was a simplicity about the scene which had shaken me. Call it innocence.

There had been no sensual motive in the back of my thoughts: my appreciation of the fine sleeping face and beautiful body had been detached, "aesthetic." What had shaken me was, simply, the discovery that a Black woman could be as beautiful as that. Thinking back, lying in my bed, I found it difficult to believe the memory.

As the night wore on, small smothered baby sounds could be heard from Ma's room from time to time, followed by her own soothing voice in the dark, stirring up something atavistic in me and confirming the reality of what had taken place. It really was true, it had happened, the woman was dead.

Would it have happened if I hadn't reprimanded Mandisi? The thought was preposterous. Irrelevant.

What intrigued me that night (what intrigues me now) was the mere fact of what had occurred: something so wild within a few hundred yards of the house. As if an entire primitive, invisible world had reached up, through that simple, barbaric act, to momentarily reveal itself. It was more than a discovery of "their" world, "their" way of life. It was something darker and more profound: something belonging to the very guts of the farm itself, as secret and as dangerous as the subterranean water courses beneath the house, of which we'd never been aware before.

It is difficult to identify it more closely. All I know is that, in writing down the events of Saturday, it eluded me. I was blinded by Dad and our history. But there are other forces beyond him, different from him—forces related more closely, perhaps, to the boy-man who was sleeping on the narrow bed opposite me that night.

My own childhood: holidays on the family farm, long weekends with my friend Gys on their farm ten miles out of town, among iron-stone ridges and bare *koppies*. There had always been something cruel about my experience of life, but not the sort of cruelty one could judge morally. More elemental. Walking across the veld to where one'd seen the vultures circling; finding the springbuck wounded yesterday and now dead and half devoured, the smelly green dung in the guts exposed, the tattered white-and-brown skin smeared with dirt. Or finding sheep that had strayed or fallen ill, the eyes gouged out by claws, bleeding holes gaping in the obtuse head; occasionally a tongue torn halfway from a mouth still groaning. Christmas in the village, when the farmers brought in lambs to be slaughtered for the Women's Auxiliary, so that the meat could be distributed to the poor—tied in neat brown paper parcels and packed into paraffin boxes, together with flour and sugar and coffee, candles, condensed milk, oatmeal and sweets and oil. For some reason—Ma must have been chairlady or secretary of the society—the lambs were generally slaughtered in our backyard. A laborer would be brought from the farm to do it, but I was always present; and sometimes he allowed me to hold the lamb's head and pull it back, exposing the throat to the quick flash of his razor-sharp knife. The warm red blood spurting over one's hands and arms and clothes. There was something voluptuous about the very horror of it. That smell of blood and manure and piss: death. At the same time there was a remarkable discovery of *life* in this encounter with death, something rich and stimulating. Primitive innocence. (That word again.)

The day I so nearly drowned in the dam, sucked into the slimy mud, then saved by Mpilo. As the sun was setting I went up the slope behind the house; no one had noticed me. There was an urge in me somehow to offer thanks to someone for being alive still. The God of the Old Testament, who gave and who took away, who burned in thornbushes and consumed sacrifices in fire and brimstone. "God" was simply the name I gave to it because it was all I knew: but the urge as such had a deeper chthonic source.

On a small, even patch in a dry streambed high up on the hill I built an altar and stacked some firewood on top. It wasn't easy to decide on a sacrifice. I looked at the fox terrier which had accompanied me, an eager little bitch with gaping mouth and an excitable stump of a tail. But I felt reluctant to give up my dog. In the end I decided on my new pocketknife, the one I'd promised Mpilo. Opening both blades to prove to God it was no ordinary knife, I put it on the altar and fell on my knees to pray for fire from Heaven—making sure I was a good distance away in case God didn't aim accurately.

Every few minutes I opened my eyes briefly to examine the sky for any sign of descending fire, with no doubt in my mind at all about the imminence of the event. Then, seeing the sky still clear, I would return to prayer, more fervently than before.

I recited everything I'd ever heard Dad or Grandpa pray—about the poor and needy, the authorities appointed over us, those near and dear to us, the *dominee* and his council, road workers and servants, the preaching of the Gospel in heathen lands, the lot. But nothing happened. Was I lacking in faith then? Surely not. I started right from the beginning again until my knees were aching on the hard ground. The Lord's Prayer, the Ten Commandments, *And have not love*, everything I had memorized in my short life, including a few secular recitations. Still nothing. And night was beginning to fall.

I was beginning to be plagued by memories of the priests of Mount Carmel, but I resolved to give God a fair chance, in case He was otherwise occupied at the moment. I decided to leave the knife on the altar for God to consume with fire sometime in the course of the night: perhaps He was reluctant to make it happen in front of my eyes. More or less by way of ultimatum I gave God a full and final brief on the whole situation, and then set off at a fast trot in the disquieting dusk.

During the night one of the typical Eastern Cape storms came up, raging and thundering over the farm, uprooting trees and tearing the earth open and sending wild streams of red water gushing down the hills. By morning it had cleared up, only the wind was still blowing. I slipped out of the house to investigate. The streambed on the hillside was littered with rocks and stones and driftwood swept down by the sudden short-lived flood. There was no sign of either the altar or the knife.

I was left with a disturbing uncertainty: had God heard my prayer and consumed my sacrifice, not in the manner prescribed by me but in His own inscrutable way? Or had He poured his wrath over me and my little altar as He had done with Cain's? Or hadn't He been involved in it in any way: had the storm wreaked its destruction blindly and on its own? (Or was wrath and love so closely related that I couldn't yet distinguish between them?)

One thing was certain: never again in my life would my faith be as fervent and as fierce as on that day. It was as if a source of energy had been extinguished inside me. And thinking back that night I realized: somewhere between the child I'd been and the man I was something had changed irrevocably. Somewhere I'd lost that wild innocence. What made it happen? And was it really quite inevitable?

The first faint dawn was filtering through the stoop window. Cocks had begun to crow. In Ma's room the baby was whining again and she tried to comfort it.

I got up to pour myself some water from the earthenware carafe on the washing table. The glass tinkled against the neck of the carafe.

"Are you awake too?" asked Louis.

I turned round, but it was still too dark to see him in his bed.

"I thought you were asleep?" I said.

"No, I can't."

"It's a bad thing that happened, isn't it?"

"Wasn't she a beautiful woman, Dad?"

Protected by the dark it was easier to admit than otherwise: "Yes. One felt quite shaken."

It was very cold and I crept back into bed. In a strange way it unnerved me to find that he had also found her beautiful. It was different from the day beside the swimming pool or the day in the crowd encouraging the man to jump.

Without being able to explore it or to explain why, I remembered a day when Louis, a small boy of five or six, had come running into the house from the garden, his blonde hair dusty and unkempt, shouting excitedly: "Dad! Dad, you know what?"

"No, what?"

"I was standing against the tree. You know, the pear tree. And suddenly I could hear my heart throbbing inside the trunk."

Somewhere between that day and this early dawn he, too, had changed. He'd never wanted to talk about it. But perhaps, in this newly discovered intimacy in the dark, he might let his defenses down.

"I suppose you've seen more than your share of dead bodies in Angola?" I ventured, as casually as possible.

He didn't reply immediately. In fact, I'd already given up hope of getting an answer, when he said in the dark: "Yes. A lot. But I don't think it makes all that much difference. Before one has seen a corpse you expect it to be something terrible. Then it happens, and you discover it's—it's very ordinary. So vulgar, really." He fell quiet for a while. "That's what I can't understand, Dad. That *everything* should seem so ordinary."

"You've changed a lot," I said.

"Naturally." Briefly, the bitter, defensive tone returned to his voice: "They say war makes a man of one, don't they?"

"What really happened, Louis?"

"I don't know. Perhaps one just gets blunted. Or initiated. Or something."

"Women?"

He laughed contemptuously. "How can you be so Victorian, Dad? Do you really think 'initiation' means one thing only?"

I didn't answer. The conversation was balancing on such a fine edge that I hesitated to prod it in either direction.

Without warning he relented again: "It was part of it, I suppose. Women." And after a long silence, as if he'd had to think it over first: "That day we passed Sa da Bandeira. We'd been driving for twenty hours nonstop. I was on one of the Unimogs. They'd already cleaned up before us, so there wasn't really any danger, except for the occasional landmine or sniper. Then we reached one of the villages. Almost nothing left of it, all blown to bits. We set up our HQ, in a tumbledown little municipal building. It was just papers and torn files and things all over the place. We were like zombies, we dropped down to sleep wherever we could find an open spot. Then, some time in the night, there was a rumpus. They brought in some women—the Black soldiers who were with us, the Unitas. One young Portuguese girl. I don't think she could have been older than fourteen. I heard someone say she'd got caught when her folks were trying to escape from Luanda. There were refugees wherever we went, those days. She didn't cry or anything. She didn't even plead to be left alone like some of the others. Perhaps she was a bit soft in the head. Her eyes stayed wide open all the time. She never seemed to blink at all. They passed her on from the one to the other. She didn't have any clothes left, just a bit of frayed collar round her neck where they'd ripped off her dress. And a small golden crucifix between her tits. Tiny little tits, not even the size of apples. Her legs were streaked with blood, not badly, just a bit messy, you know."

"And then?" I asked, when he fell silent again for a long time.

"You know, Dad, I actually felt like taking off the top of my tracksuit or something, to cover her up. But what use would it have been? If one's been going for so long and if so much has happened to you, you no longer really think about what you're doing."

"I suppose it's inevitable if you want to survive," I said, as sympathetically as I could.

"Hell," he said, without appearing to have heard me, "there isn't much left of a girl when she's taken off her clothes, is there? Some of them looked so tough, but once you had the clothes off them— And that little one, Jesus!"

I waited in silence. It took some time before he spoke again:

"There were other occasions too. In other villages. Not often, for the PFs kept a close watch on us. But from time to time a few of us would break out. Just for the hell of it, even if we knew there was short-arm inspection coming up afterwards. We usually found liquor somewhere, and Black women." Suddenly he sounded irritable. "But that wasn't important at all. It wasn't that."

"What was it then?"

"I wish I knew. I don't think it was anything in particular. No, it wasn't as easy as that." He sighed. "It's just that—everything was such a bloody farce. We were cheated. Right from the first day when the PFs in the camp told us to volunteer."

"How do you mean?"

"I don't mean they used force on us or anything. But, hell, there's only two things in the army: it's either 'in' or it's 'out.' And not to go to Angola was 'out.' You know the sort of argument: 'If you boys got any guts, then sign here. Any bugger not signing up, is lower than the shadow of shark shit on the fucking bottom of the sea.' You think any of us would like to be shamed in front of his pals? So we went, the lot of us, *boknaaiers* and *pansies* and *cannon donkeys*, the lot. I mean, Jesus, what did we know about where we were going? They just spoke about 'the border' all the time. It sounded like one hell of an adventure."

"But you liked camp life last year. The weekends you came home you couldn't stop talking about it."

"What does one know about war while you're in the training camp? You shit in the pump and they give you hell, especially while you're still a blue-arse and some old man's slave, but it's the army and it's all right, and in a way you even learn to enjoy it. But Angola—" Another pause; another unexpected start: "Do you know what one feels like in that godforsaken bush, within farting distance of Luanda, when a group of *ous* are sitting round the fire listening to the radio, and you hear the Minister or some other top cunt telling the public not to worry, our men are just on the border protecting our installations at Ruacana and Calueque, we're not interested in occupying other people's countries—Then you sit there and you think: Jesus, they're pretending we're not here. They're pretending we don't even exist. Even if we bloody well die here in the bush they'll just pretend it didn't happen. And that's when you start asking yourself what the fuck you're doing there."

I restrained the impulse to scold him about his language. Perhaps he wouldn't even have heard me, for now that he'd got started he seemed unable to restrain himself any longer:

"One day a group of Top Brass arrived to look around the 'operational area.' We slaved away to make everything shine and then they arrived in their helicopters. Big booze-up. All smiles, the lot of us. Oh what a lovely war and all that shit. But late that evening, when I took some more booze to the big boys, I heard one of them saying—he was rather far gone by that time: 'Hey, listen, General, there's one thing. I'd appreciate it if you could cut down on all the bodies you're sending home, you know. I'm getting sick and tired of attending a bloody hero's funeral every week.'"

The dawn had grown lighter and I could see Louis sitting up.

"Let me tell you, Dad, that's when one starts feeling all sour inside. You start thinking again: 'It's for all you cunts down there in Pretoria we're getting blown to pieces in this *bundu*. It's your bloody war, not ours. We don't want to have anything to do with it. But we're getting killed while you keep your fat little hands clean.'"

"I think I understand your feelings, Louis," I said, uncomfortably, not really knowing how to handle his anger.

"How can you understand?" he said. "I haven't told you anything yet. You know nothing!"

It was unnecessary to coax him into talking any longer. Nothing could stop him now. It was like a dam bursting inside him, and all I could do was to allow the flood to go its own cascading way.

"Don't get me wrong, Dad. I didn't feel sorry that I'd gone. One always wonders, you know, especially in the training camp: 'If it really comes to the push, if war broke out, how am I going to shape? Will I shit in my *santamarias* or get through to the other side?'"

"You got through all right."

"Yes, I got through. I never shat in my pants. I wasn't a coward after all. I suppose it makes some people feel good. But it did nothing to me. How can I explain it?—I mean, when I got there and the mortars started exploding and the bombs bursting and the bullets whizzing like bloody flies past my head, I found it was quite irrelevant wondering about cowardice. It's not a matter of courage or that sort of crap at all. All that matters is whether you can switch off all right. Not that I stopped *thinking*—it wasn't that. If only I *could*. But—well, you know, emotionally, sort of. I didn't care about what was happening. I couldn't feel a thing. And then, when I got on the other side, I realized that *nothing* could shock me any more. Nothing. Death, wounds, filth, atrocities, I couldn't care less. I could take it all. I'd become a man, hadn't I? And then there's something else you discover. You find out that this whole country depends for its survival on the fact that you can shut off your conscience. Otherwise it wouldn't last for another day. And just because I'd succeeded in being cold-blooded and fucking callous enough, I helped to keep this country going."

"It seems a very natural reaction to me. You're still suffering from shock. Just give it time."

"Shock has nothing to do with it. It's the opposite. *Nothing* shocked me and nothing can shock me. Don't you understand?"

"But what happened to change you so much then?" I repeated.

And once again he said: "I told you: there was no isolated incident. It was the whole caboodle as such. Some of my pals came out all smiles on the other side. No scars on them at all. They're the same good and solid *ous* they'd been before. Because they managed not to think."

"Think about what?"

"Anything. Just the plain, simple act of thinking as such. I told you. I could handle the feeling bit. But *thinking*—Jesus, that was different. One day just after we'd passed Pereira d'Eca, right in the beginning, I killed my first enemy. One just knows it, the moment you hit him. Quite some satisfaction it gives you. After all, you're a soldier and a soldier's got the right to kill: and if you don't kill him, he'll blast your brains out. And anyway, you don't think of him as a man. It's the enemy. So you feel fine. You even swagger a bit and the *ous* pat you on the shoulder: Well done, old chap. But you can't smother your thoughts. Soon you start asking: *Why* has a soldier got the right to kill? Who gives him that right?—And once it's started you can't stop it again. Never again."

The early, innocent light had grown stronger. Louis went on talking, uncontrollable. And I let him go on, waiting for—what? I couldn't define it: I only hoped I'd recognize it if it came.

In Ma's room the baby began to cry, but it was soon comforted. I could hear her moving about as she got up and dressed and went to the bathroom. There were sounds in the kitchen too. Water running, wood being broken, the clanging of cups and saucers. And soon afterwards, from the dining room, the sound of Ma's voice in prayer, followed, like the previous day and all the mornings of my childhood, by the measured morning hymn, each note awarded more than its full value of painful sincerity. Then it was silent for a long time. I knew she was waiting for me. But I lay listening to Louis who went on talking without interruption; following him on all the tedious detours of his senseless campaign, through skirmishes and full-fledged battles, past shorter or longer halts in camps and villages along the way—moved by the violence and death of his tale, yet waiting all the time, in vain, for that revelation which would cause all the jumbled pieces to fit together in a pattern. I knew it would remain with me all day. I would have to return to separate incidents again and again to grope for their sense; in search of Louis and perhaps of myself. Somewhere there must have been a moment, in both our lives, when the final turning point had been reached and passed. Had we both lost something in the process—or was it a form of gain? Was it something to be sad about, or profoundly thankful? What was the real sense of this irritably recurring word, *innocence?*

"I don't think you understand, Dad," he said when he finally stopped, looking at me. Outside, the sun was already lighting up the pillars on the stoop. Down by the dairy the calves were lowing violently. He shook his head. "You still don't understand," he said.

✧ ✧ ✧

"Do you really think 'initiation' means one thing only?" Perhaps it *is* characteristic of my generation; I'm not sure. Why should this one particular memory return to me?—the stag party in Thielman Pauw's house, one weekend when his wife had gone away; thirty of us, each contributing ten rand for the liquor and the stripper. She encouraged us to cover her in oil, the full length of her lithe body, her disappointingly small breasts, between her legs, everywhere, while she was writhing like a snake among us. Obviously knowing her job, she stripped and danced to maximum effect. But the curious thing was that, while one was rubbing the oil into her—the smoothness of her shaven mound—one could feel her trembling under one's hands, a persistent, incessant shudder; while her eyes were staring vacantly past us, her mouth drawn in a fixed and rigid smile. Almost as if she were terrified of us. Which was quite incomprehensible: we were respectable gentlemen, all of us, no one would think of hurting her. And if she had chosen to earn money in that particular way, there could be no hint of exploitation. In fact, we helped her.

2

THERE WAS NO ONE in the kitchen when I came in, only the thickset old Kristina, preparing the porridge on the stove with Thokozile's baby tied in a bundle on her back.

"Morning, Kristina," I said. "Are you looking after the orphan now?"

"Ma, Baas." She poured me some coffee from the pot on the stove. "Thokozile she don't even cry out, Baas. We never hear anything. All the years she just take what Mandisi give her. It come from far away, this thing."

"What's going to happen to the children now?"

"Thokozile's ma she come fetch them. The Missus phone early this morning."

"What's happened to the Missus now?"

"She go down to the cows, Baas. There's no man to work on the farm today. It's only Mdoko."

"Why didn't she come and tell me then?" Annoyed, I went to the bathroom to call Louis. He was washing his face, bent over the basin, bare to the waist. A boy's body still, smooth and lean; but the muscles were sinewy and tough. "Louis, there's no one to do the milking today, we'd better give Grandma a hand. Kristina will pour you some coffee in the kitchen, then you can come down afterwards."

Outside the back door three small children were sitting huddled in the sun. Probably Thokozile's.

"Go and sit in the kitchen by the stove," I told them.

But they just stared at me with large dark eyes. I gestured towards the kitchen, but they didn't move. Oh, well. They were probably used to the cold anyway.

The dogs came charging round the corner of the house to greet me with their usual boisterous enthusiasm, and I first had to chase them away before I could go down to the cowshed. From a distance I could make out two figures among the cows, but was unable to distinguish them before I reached the gate of the enclosure: Ma, and a young Black laborer who grinned widely when he saw me, but without saying a word.

In strong, regular movements she sat pulling at the teats as the milk purred into the pail, the foam bulging over the sides in small whispering sounds.

"Why didn't you call me, Ma?"

She chuckled. "I don't like to wake sleeping dogs."

"If I were you, last night's business would have been the last straw to me, you know."

She looked up at me from the low milking stool. "Just as well you're *not* me then."

"You're being difficult."

"Did you come down to help or to criticize?" Without waiting for an answer she switched to Xhosa: "Mdoko, come and tie up a cow for the Baas. I want to see if he still knows how to milk."

Pushing aside his pail, her young helper got up to tie a cow to the manger next to Ma's. He brought me a pail and a stool, and held out the round tin of dubbin for me to grease the teats. Much to my annoyance he didn't return to his cow straight away but remained behind me to watch.

I had trouble with the first few tugs, unable to get a proper grip on the leathery teats; and the cow fidgeted, swiping with her horns in my direction from time to time. But when the first thin jet came spurting from the udder, missing the pail and squirting over my trousers, she began to calm down and soon I rediscovered the easy rhythm of long ago.

"Well done," said Ma. "If you go on like that you may still become a farmer one day."

After a while I didn't feel the cold so badly any more. The milk steamed from the pail clenched tightly between my knees, and I breathed in the warm, comforting odor of cow and milk and dung and fodder. In a singular sensation of relaxed luxury I felt the weariness slowly draining from my body and my mind.

(As children Theo and I had regularly milked straight from the udder into our open mouths.)

As soon as she'd finished with her cow Ma got up. "Now that you're here I'm going home to keep an eye," she said. "I see Louis is also coming down to help. Don't bother about separating this morning, the calves can drink their milk full-cream for a change."

"You look like an old stable hand!" said Louis as he came into the shed. "*Molo*, Mdoko."

The boy greeted him and they started talking. I was surprised by Louis's easy way of speaking Xhosa. But of course, he was still young, he hadn't forgotten what he'd picked up during holidays.

"How come you know his name?" I asked as he sat down on Ma's stool beside me.

"Don't you remember him then? We used to play together when I was small. Then he went away."

"And you recognized him just like that?"

"He came round to the outhouse while I was working on the generator yesterday. It was good to see him again after all these years. He said he'd left because his father had died and so he'd gone to live with his mother's family."

It really didn't interest me, but I made no attempt to interrupt. He still seemed in the expansive mood induced by his long confession about Angola.

"He became a man last year," said Louis. As the milk rose in his pail the sound became more subtle. "It's quite a business. Did you know about all their initiation ceremonies and things?"

"You mean circumcision and so on? Yes, I know." I remembered the light fear with which, in my youth, we'd used to watch the groups of wandering *amakweta* on the farm, covered in white clay from head to foot and without a shred of clothing, except for a loincloth or a small penis sheath. Usually they'd fled into the bushes at the first sight of us. And what happened there we could only guess. At night we heard the singing and dancing from the kraals, but in the daytime life went its customary way as if nothing had happened.

"Did Mdoko tell you about it?" I asked after a while.

"Yes. He said he'd really wanted to wait until this year, but it was just as well he went through with it last year when the *incibi* came, because that was before the drought. He says they're not allowed to be circumcised in times of drought."

"Who's the *incibi?*"

"The old man who comes from the bush to do the job. At new moon, I believe. It's got to be new moon for some reason."

I sat listening like a few hours earlier, amazed at rediscovering in him all the enthusiasm of his boyhood which had been absent for such a long time. Even though there was hardly anything new in what he told me, I made no effort to stop him but sat listening passively as he eagerly spoke on. About the *amakweta* hut built by the men in a lonely place where no one had lived before, and furnished with soft grass inside by the women, like birds preparing a nest. And about the first goat sacrificed in the kraal; the shaving of the *amakweta*, leaving their heads and bodies as smooth as those of babies, and burying the hair in the veld. Afterwards, one had to submit to the mockery and vituperation of the old men: and if you so much as blinked, you weren't allowed to continue. Once you'd passed the first test, you received the ritualistic belt for your waist and an *ubulunga* for your neck, made from the tail hairs of a pregnant cow. And then you were taken to the secret hut in the bush where the old men sat waiting in a circle of silence.

Next would come the going down to the water, to be cleansed of all your wrongs; returning, washed and smooth and naked, with a kaross over your shoulders, to sit down on the ground with knees wide apart, for the *incibi* to perform his duties. Holding the prepuce between the fingers of his left hand the assegai in his right hand would move very swiftly to and fro; and if your face revealed the slightest expression of pain you were dismissed. Wiping his assegai on your kaross, the *incibi* would hand you the severed skin to be exposed on an antheap; and once it had been consumed, you would be required to drink water in which the soil of the antheap had been dissolved. The wound would be bandaged with leaves, and the following day your body would be covered in the white *ifuta* clay. Now you were ready to go out hunting and looking for food in the veld, far away from all human beings. It might last for weeks, until the next goat had been slaughtered in the kraal. It was then the nightly singing would begin, as the *amakweta* trekked on from kraal to kraal. And when finally everything was ready, they returned to the water to be washed anew; and each boy received from his father the penis sheath confirming his manhood.

The secret hut would be burnt with all the earlier possessions of the *amakweta*, so that they could start like newly born, even with new names. In the cattle kraal a great celebration would be held, the Dance of the Big Bull. And covered in red clay the young men would make merry with the girls till dawn—for now they were initiated; now they were men. And round them sat their elders clapping their hands rhythmically and shouting like peals of thunder in the night: *Siya vuma!*—So be it!

Listening to Louis's eager narrative, it occurred to me that there was something reassuring about this form of initiation leaving nothing to the initiative or the uncertainties of the individual. It was so much easier than Louis's, or my own. What had he known about what was in store for him upon entering Angola?

Aided by Mdoko, he chased the cows through the bottom gate down to the veld, even though there wouldn't be anything for them to graze there. Late in the afternoon they would come home again to be fed.

Remaining behind at the trough of the calves I watched them push and ram each other taking their turns. But my thoughts were still wrestling with what Louis had told me earlier that morning.

We crossed the border at Oshikango in a large convoy after a week at Grootfontein. Jesus, you should have seen the mud up there. We were grey from head to feet. Anyway, then we crossed the border. Strange feeling, you know. Suddenly everything is different. We'd crossed the Kunene a few times during that last week, and that was strange enough, that wretched little concrete bridge over the enormous river: a sudden feeling of really being in Africa now. Still, it hadn't been all that different. At Ruacana and Calueque one still had the feeling of being among our own people, that sort of thing. But the day at Oshikango it was different. On our side of the border everything was normal. The petrol pumps, the ugly little buildings, the police station protected by sandbags. But on the other side, at Santa Clara, hell! There was almost nothing left, you know. Buildings with roofs torn down, doors missing or hanging on one hinge only, empty holes for windows. Even the petrol pumps in front of the garage were uprooted and burnt. The streets were littered with bottles and tins and paper and junk. And then the slogans: ABAIXO MPLA! *Or* POVO UNITA! *Or* POVO SAVIMBI! *All over the walls and right down to the tarred road with its potholes.*

We pushed on. No one felt like talking. The veld opened up again, but there was something strange, something sinister and horrible in the air. It was very hot and quiet, and the grass and bushes and trees all had this deep sort of venomous green. Here and there we passed a farmhouse, most of them in ruins, doors and windows broken out and blackened by smoke.

In some of the yards we still saw chickens running about. If we'd known what the world looked like farther on we'd have caught them and taken them with us, even though they were just skin and bones. Even a pig in the road. And white-and-black cattle with long fierce-looking horns.

Then we came to Pereira d'Eca with its ramshackle stores looted and plundered, the windows boarded up. And the miserable little houses with their verandas torn down. A bank building with the whole front missing. Streets ankle-deep in rubbish. And a restaurant with its name still showing— Restaurante Ruacana or something—with painted walls and fancy arches among the rubble. Once again there were slogans everywhere you looked:

VIVA MPLA!

VIVA FNLA!

ABAIXO NEOCOLONIALISMO!

VIVA ROBERTO!

And, in the middle of all this mess, the enormous church with its broken roof sitting there like a great wreck of a stranded ship, completely out of place.

That's where we stayed over. Even at that early stage, before we'd fought any battles, it felt as if something had closed up inside one. Still, there was, I don't know how to explain it, a sort of excitement. Suddenly the "operational area" had got a name, you see. It was no longer just a place far away. It was a country with landscapes and villages. It wasn't just talk any more. We'd really crossed some sort of border.

But there was something else too. A feeling, well, that there were still other borders to be crossed ahead. Different sorts of borders.

We were still full of talk about how we'd give them hell, all eager to meet the "enemy." But Jesus, it was a sad place to be in. From the next day there were the refugees, the trucks stranded without petrol along the road, the old toothless grandmothers, the children swarming all over the place gaping at us, the Blacks. Still, we were full of confidence. We thought:

*Don't worry, boys, we're going to clear this mess up for you. We'll blast the
bloody enemy right out of your country.*

*But as one goes on one sort of talks less. Especially after you've seen the
enemy face to face for the first time. I mean, it's all right while you're lying
in your trenches and he's over there in the bushes; it's all right if you can
get to his PM-46s in time and pull out the detonators. But once you've really
seen* him *it's a different story.*

*It was just short of Benguela we first found the Cubans. By that time
they were already falling back, but here and there they'd dug themselves in.
Once, just before we got to the railway line, we were held up for three days.
Supplies were running low. In the end we hardly had any food left. Bit of bully
beef we ate out of the cans in the trenches; a gulp of water, that was all. But
we blasted them right out of their holes and they started running, leaving most
of their tanks and Scanias behind. It was there I saw my first dead Cuban,
lying half under one of the abandoned jeeps. Clean shot in the chest. His shirt
was soaked with blood, but for the rest he looked just like he was sleeping.*

*He was very young. My age, I think. Not a day older than nineteen. In
his shirt pocket we found a snapshot of a girl. Not particularly attractive or
anything, but quite a sweet little face. I suppose it sounds soppy. But it
wasn't. I didn't even feel shocked or anything. But I can remember thinking: Shit, who's going to tell her about it now?*

*While we were pitching camp and fixing trenches in the late afternoon—
I was one of a crew digging the latrine ditch for the row of green plastic
seats we carted along everywhere we went—we saw a few of those long-
horned cattle grazing among the trees, some of them with calves. We rounded
them up and started milking into our mouths. A bloody mess, but it was
worth it. Two or three of the ous would hold on to a cow while the others
took turns to drink. We were covered in milk, our shirts were soaked. It
was as if we were trying to bloody well wash ourselves in milk.*

*That night in my sleeping bag I kept on thinking about the Cuban,
although I was exhausted after those three days. I couldn't help myself. I
thought: What was that little bastard doing so many thousands of miles away*

from home? Perhaps they hadn't even told him where he was going or whose war he was going to fight. Just as they never told us. All we knew was that the Angolans were fucking one another up and we had to move in before the Commies took over. But hell, it wasn't our war either. Like that young Cuban we were fighting someone else's war for them.

And that was when I knew, that night: Now we'd really crossed a border all right. A worse one than just the Kunene. Now we really were in a strange country not meant for humans. And milk alone wasn't enough to clean oneself any more.

3

THEY WERE DIGGING THE GRAVE, beyond the huts where the slope of the hill was leveling, near the spot where the water diviner had stopped the day before. There was a small enclosure of aloes, tenaciously clinging to the hard earth and aflame with flowers even in that drought. The picks and spades made little impression on the baked red soil, ringing with a loud metallic twang as they struck what appeared to be solid rock. In spite of the early-morning cold the men were working with bodies bared to the waist and shining with sweat, hiccuping at every blow. Here and there within the aloe enclosure lay the small stony humps of older graves.

On the farm of my boyhood friend Gys there had also been a row of old Griqua graves in the open veld among the *swarthaak* thorn trees, far from the house—small mounds of stone, piled up and eroded by sun and wind. Once, hunting hares with the dogs, we'd arrived at the graves in a state of near-exhaustion. I was on the point of flopping down on one of the heaps to rest when Gys shouted in panic:

"Hey, Martin! Watch out! Those are graves, man!"

"So what?"

"If you sit on one of those graves the ghost of the Griqua buried there will come and haunt you tonight."

"*Ag*, nonsense." Too tired to care I sat down. Gys and Theo squatted a little way off in the sparse shade of a thorn tree, staring at me fearfully. In that dazzling sunlight it seemed ridiculous to heed his warning. To prove my disdain, I even peed on the grave before we left, grinning at the dismay of the others.

But at bedtime that evening it was beginning to weigh uncomfortably on my conscience, although I refused to let on. Long after Theo and Gys had gone to sleep I was still lying awake, the blankets pulled over my head. In the end I dozed off too. But when I woke up, somewhere in the hollow of the night, all hell was loose: a commotion in the yard outside, and something sitting on my chest trying to throttle me.

Afterwards it was all explained. A couple of jackals had ventured in among the fowls where the dogs had got hold of them, and the din outside had awakened Gys and Theo. Gys had immediately grasped what had happened, but Theo's first thought had been that the dead Griqua had come to avenge the desecration of his grave, and seeing that I was making no movement, he'd jumped on me to find out whether I was dead or alive.

Once the confusion had been cleared up, all three of us collapsed in hysterics, which brought Gys's mother to our room (his father had already gone out with the gun by then). We were all bundled off to the kitchen where she made us coffee with lots of sugar. But I remained shivery until daybreak. And ridiculous as it might seem, I'd borne within me, for many years afterwards, a feeling of awe for all those dark forces lurking in the earth, ready to intervene in the lives of the living without any warning.

When one is eighteen years old, you see, one thinks one is bloody well immortal. It doesn't matter that you're in the army and shooting enemies from dawn to dusk and finding corpses behind every bush. You just go on believing it can't happen to you.

But then it changes. One day it comes so close that you discover it's possible after all. You can die any moment. You're not worth a turd. And it makes a difference.

By that time we'd passed Benguela on our way to Novo Redondo. On a stretch of open road one of the trucks struck a mine. Not the front one. In fact, I think two or three had driven over the mine unharmed. Then, all of a sudden, it was just bodies catapulting to all sides. The moment the convoy stopped, the machine guns started. And the grapeshot exploding in the air. And those big Russian RPGs. An ambush. We dived off the jeeps and trucks and scuttled into the bushes like bloody rats. Ten minutes ago one could still hear the insects humming in the grass, and the birds and monkeys and things in the trees. Now it was like a fucking thunderstorm. The mortars went on the attack while the cannon donkeys tried to get the 88 mms ready. Jesus, they were shooting so fast even the auxiliary charges exploded.

Our crewie decided a few of us had to try and get through to the left to attack the enemy from the side. Old Gouwsie and ten or twelve of us. There was one patch of open veld with no bush or stone in sight. All we could hope for was that the other boys would be distracting the attention of the Commies. Gouwsie was the first to run. He got through. Then two of the others. And then it was my turn, and Ronnie's. You remember Ronnie, don't you? Started camp with me. We were together all the time, rowers, blue-arses, old men, all the way. Marvelous ou, *not scared of the devil himself.*

The moment we moved into that open patch, they started shooting right at us. Must have seen the front ones and waited for us to come out. I never thought I'd make it, but I did. Ronnie wasn't so lucky. When I looked back from the bushes on the other side, I saw him lying there.

Gouwsie and I went to get him. Funny thing is one isn't afraid when you're right in it like that. It's only afterwards you realize what a bloody fool you were. We just ran back and got him. Thought he might still be alive, but he was dead all right. On our way back Gouwsie got a shot in the shoulder. By time that our 88 mms had found their target and drawn the fire off us. Another hour and it was all over. Our little outing had been quite unnecessary. Only Ronnie was dead.

That's the worst, you know, Dad. There's no one you can blame for it, no one you can take it out on. It's "the enemy." But who's he? You see his tanks and his jeeps, you blow up his trucks, sometimes you find his dead bodies like that young Cuban. But you know that's not really the enemy. He's different, he hasn't got a name, you can never reach him.

And yet old Ronnie was dead. I'd helped to carry back his body. Nothing special about it, like a roll of blankets, you don't feel it. But you know Ronnie's dead. Old Ronnie who could take the mickey out of the PFs. Old Ronnie who nearly trod on a snake last night, taking his shower under the mango tree. Old Ronnie who used to brag about all the women he'd had. Good old wind-bag Ronnie, who always shared his biltong *with you. Who showed you the letters from his girl and told you what her tits looked like. Old Ronnie who sawed through the latrine seat on the shit trench just before the sergeant-major took his spade for a walk, that night outside Pereira d'Eca. Old Ronnie is dead all right.*

I knew they would send his body back. He would get a hero's funeral and the top cunts would be moaning about wasting their time again. The papers would splash all about him and perhaps his mother would be offered a medal— his father had died a long time ago. I knew how they would announce the news. They'd say he'd been killed in the "operational area." "On the border." No one would be told he'd been here. Officially we weren't here. We counted for nothing. He was as expendable as the whole fucking rest of us. They'd lie the same about all of us. And that *killed Ronnie for me, good and for all.*

❖ ❖ ❖

I hadn't been aware of him following me. The first I noticed was when I saw his vague figure entering the aloe enclosure.

Coming up to me he stood watching the digging for some time. The picks were still hitting the earth with their dull thuds, going

335

deeper inch by inch; but it would be many hours before the grave was deep enough. Their digging was accompanied by a rhythmic, monotonous chant with hypnotic effect, maintained without a moment's rest:

"Ndiboleken' inipeki ndigaule.

Nobaselitshisa ndigaule.

Goduka kwedini.

Goduka kwedini.

Goduka!"

"That's why there's no one at work today," I said to Louis.

"I suppose they had no choice."

"The whole thing was unnecessary, right from the beginning."

"Isn't anything that happens unnecessary?" he asked dully, with the total rejection characteristic of his adolescence.

"It could have been avoided. If Mandisi hadn't been such a savage, if he'd had a grain of civilization in him."

"What has civilization got to do with it?" he asked, a new tone of rebellion in his voice: not vague and general any more, but specific, directed against me.

"Everything," I said laconically. "For three centuries we've been trying to civilize this land, and all the time these people are still gnawing at the roots."

"I suppose we also tried to civilize Angola," he said. "With our cannons and mortars and things."

"Those Angolans had been exterminating each other long before you ever got there," I said. And without giving him a chance to reply I went on the attack: "Say what you want, Louis, but our country has always been the most stable in Africa. One of very few in the world still ruled by law and order."

"You call this stable?" he asked, looking me in the eyes: "What I'd like to know is how you manage to go on living so peacefully as if nothing had happened."

"I think we can still control what's happening here." (Would I have said the same the next Tuesday or Wednesday? But then, of course, it was still Sunday.) "In spite of the balls-up we made in Angola we're still all right. There's a lot to be done, I grant you that, but it will all come in due course."

"We've been waiting too long as it is."

"You're oversimplifying, Louis. You're just against everything."

"There isn't much in this country one can be *for*, is there?"

"Are you sure? If you had to work in the sweat of your brow you would have thought twice before speaking. Things are too easy for you, that's what. Now that we've tamed the land for you—"

"What do you call 'tamed'?" he asked in sudden rage. I could see his eyes burning. "You grew rich out of the land, you're just taking from it all the time. Have you ever tried to give anything in return?"

"Wait a minute," I said. I couldn't help smiling, knowing he'd chosen the wrong territory for his attack: I'd found the answers long before he'd even dreamed up the first question. "What I possess today, I've achieved in a system of free enterprise because I've been prepared to take risks. And now I can offer all my capital and my experience and my know-how in return. I never stop ploughing back. Our whole system depends on individuals prepared to create job opportunities and training for others, and accepting responsibility for them. Where do you think the capital for development would come from if people like me weren't prepared to furnish it?"

"And on whose labor do you base it all?"

"What would their labor have been worth without my capital and my guidance?"

"But you're not prepared to *share!*"

"Good heavens, Louis," I said, "are you really expecting me to give up the race so that the loser may win?" I couldn't help feeling contempt for his argument: it was so superficial. "You want a race where everybody can reach the winning post at the same time. Balls!"

(His language was proving contagious.) "The day you deny a man the chance of being rewarded for his effort, you can dig a grave for our civilization. And achievement is based on competition. That's all there is to it."

"Survival of the fittest?" he asked furiously.

"No. I didn't get here at the expense of others. I use my position and my capital to teach them to be self-sufficient themselves."

"There are many ways of buying a conscience," he said fiercely.

"Do you regard prosperity as a disgrace?!"

Throughout our argument the rhythmic chant accompanying the picks and spades went its droning way.

"Don't you feel afraid sometimes?" he asked unexpectedly: it came like a blow below the belt.

"Afraid? Of what?"

"Of everything suddenly coming to an end. Exploding."

"They'll lose much more than we would, if they tried. They know only too well that they depend on us for their economic development. And if you take a look at what my companies are already doing for them—"

"It didn't sound very peaceful at Westonaria."

"We've already settled those riots."

"But for how long, Dad? When will the next ones break out? And where? Doesn't that scare you? You and your whole generation, Jesus, Dad: you organized everything so neatly, made a law for everything. But surely you know it's only a temporary arrangement. One murder like last night's threatens the whole edifice. You can't understand it. You feel scared. And the more scared one gets the more power you need to keep it nicely covered up. Until one gets addicted to it."

I controlled myself as well as I could. "You're young," I said. "You've got nothing to lose yet. So it's easy for you to criticize and attack."

"And you've got everything to lose, so you're scared. Is that it?

So you'd rather cling to what you've got, no matter how bloody sordid it is. And no matter in what sort of a mess you leave the place to us."

"What do you think will happen if we just let go? Don't you think it's the very function of civilization to keep pruning and checking and controlling the world? I mean, look at nature: it looks beautiful enough when it's wild and primitive and innocent or whatever you might like to call it. But if you don't control it properly it becomes a menace."

"Don't you think law and order can also get out of hand? If it stops acting as a means to become an end in itself?"

"*Ag*, Louis." I sighed. "Really, you can be so terribly naive."

"I'm not trying to make you mad. I'm *asking* you. If I don't say anything, you think I'm sulking. But the moment I start asking questions you refuse to answer." He looked at me in silence for a moment: not defiant, but with a curious new assurance in his attitude. "Today I won't be quiet," he said. "Today I want some answers, because I've got to know."

"I appreciate it. Provided you are constructive in your approach."

"Do you really not understand what I'm trying to say?"

"Not if you come out with such sweeping statements."

"You mean what I said about law and order? But I'm not making it up, Dad. I see it every day. What do you think you're doing to Ilse and me? All these years we *had* to be first in our class every term. I had to choose a career that flattered you, no matter what I wanted. Ilse has *got* to take ballet and piano and speech training and God knows what else. What for?"

"For your own benefit, of course. To develop your talents."

"Oh no. Just because it's achievement. No other reason. Not to get anywhere. Just achievement for achievement's sake."

"Well, if you don't try hard, you sink back. How long do you think it took our people to find their feet in the cities? It's a full-time job to maintain our position. All around us are English and Jews just waiting to push us aside again. They've never forgiven us yet for beating them at their own game."

"Why do you always talk in terms of 'our people,' our little tribe?"

"Because this land itself makes it impossible to think in any other terms."

Suddenly, like the previous morning when I'd recited the prayer, I could hear Dad's voice in my own, saying: *"Martin, we Afrikaners have had to put up with a lot in our lives. There's still people looking down on us just because we're Afrikaners. But we must show them. Every day of our lives we've got to show them. Until they learn to respect us."*

Louis stood looking right past me as if he'd lost all interest.

"It took us three hundred years before we received any recognition in our own country," I told him. "No one can expect us to give it all up without resisting."

"Do you think it's still a question of 'giving it up'?" he asked aggressively. "Or is it just a matter of time before it's simply *taken* from us—unless we learn to share?"

"Let them try to take it. We'll see who gets blown into the sea!"

"Oh Jesus, Dad!" he said. "Who's being naïve now?"

"What you need is some ordinary old-fashioned respect for your elders!" I said, momentarily losing my temper. "What you're saying here today is exactly what Bernard has been saying all these years. And what good did it do him?"

"For everyone like Bernard who's silenced there are ten others to take his place," he said, defiant.

"I hope *you're* not toying with the idea of becoming one of them!" I said. "I thought you had more common sense than that."

"What Bernard said didn't sound so senseless to me."

"For God's sake think of what you're saying!" I warned him. "I never thought I'd live to see my own children turning against me."

There was no end to his impertinence: "I'm only being a good

Afrikaner, Dad," he said. "Haven't we always turned against our authorities in the past?"

"Not against our own kind. You don't know what you're talking about."

"And I get the impression that you don't know what you're trying to defend, Dad."

For a while we stood opposite one another, balanced on the unpredictable see-saw of our argument. Only the picks went on thudding into the stubborn red earth, accompanied by that monotonous chant:

"*Goduka kwedini.*

Goduka!—

Go home, boy.

Go home!"

I became conscious of a pressure in my chest. I had to be careful, it was becoming a vicious circle: because I'd had the coronary I got upset much more easily; and because I got upset it affected my heart.

"Louis," I said at last, making an effort to control myself. "Surely you're not suggesting that you approve of what Bernard did?"

"I can't find any fault with what he represented either."

"You were in court yourself. You heard the shocking indictments against him. And he didn't deny anything. He was guilty. He was as guilty as any murderer."

He merely shrugged, turning away from me. Without answering he walked off. In sudden anguish I saw him grow dimmer before my eyes. I'd thought I'd done with Bernard.

As if supervising the work, I stood beside the gravediggers watching them attack the earth in dull, thudding blow after blow.

4

MA WAS SITTING ALL BY herself beside the large bare table in the dining room, the transistor radio in front of her, with the aerial pulled out to its full length. She had straightened her hair again, I noticed, and was wearing her black hat and a Sunday dress, navy blue with a small white pattern.

"Are you expecting visitors then?" I asked.

"No, I just got ready for the service." She nodded towards the radio. There was choral music playing.

"Where's Louis?" I asked.

"Gone in to town for the Sunday papers."

"In the Mercedes?" I was on the attack immediately.

"No, in the van." She smiled patiently. "Come and sit with me. There's enough time for a cup of tea. Kristina!"

For a while we sat drinking our tea in silence in the muted light of the dining room. Turned low in the background, the choir went on singing.

Behind her on the wall I could make out the shadowy outlines of two pictures. At that distance I couldn't distinguish any details, but I knew them well enough. *The Broad and Narrow Way* hung on the left. Without seeing it I was aware of the presence of the staring, all-seeing Eye in the center at the top. To its right was the bluish, yellowish amateur oil painting of aloes at sunset. The Women's

Society in our village had given it to Ma as a farewell present years ago when she and Dad had left for the farm.

For the moment the events of the night were stowed away and I could forget about the persistent chant on the hillside. I didn't even wish to bring up the farm for the time being: there would be time for it again, later. For these few minutes the two of us were left in peace together, like so many other times in my life, a scene repeated endlessly, reassuringly. In the comforting familiarity and predictability of our togetherness I relaxed again, feeling the dull pressure in my chest subside. One had to learn to live with it. It was no more than an occupational risk, like ulcers.

The music came to an end. A voice took over.

Ma turned up the radio. "Time for the service," she said.

I would have preferred to find a sunny spot outside rather than to submit to Ma's church service. But I knew it would irritate her. And if I allowed her to have her way now, it might be easier to have mine later.

The vicar was preaching and praying from Pretoria, obviously relishing the opportunity of impressing not only his own congregation but the rest of the country with the modulations of his voice. I submitted to 1 Corinthians 13, Grandpa's favorite, *And have not love*, in its modernized form *(but if I am without love)*. In his long prayer the preacher sounded profoundly moved, with carefully rehearsed use of the tremolo.

Ma was listening with closed eyes, passively prepared to accept implicitly whatever he wanted to say. And as I sat watching her, her noble face tense with concentration, I had the curious impression of actually envying her that faith as deep and dark and narrow as a well—the one quality which had made it possible for her to survive for so long, and still to hold on.

Outside there was the sound of a vehicle stopping, a door slamming. Probably Louis. For a brief moment Ma opened her eyes in irritation before she returned to her absorbed listening.

There was a knock on the front door.

She frowned and, without opening her eyes again, motioned with her head. I went through the small dark lounge to open the door. There was a police sergeant outside, a different one from last night's, his red crew cut as stiff as the bristles of a toothbrush.

"Morning, Mr. Mynhardt," he said, taking off his cap and offering me a large freckled hand. "We've just come for a statement on last night's business."

"Come inside."

He waved to a young blonde constable who had been waiting at the end of the stoop.

"Ma," I said from the middle door as we entered, "it's the police. They've come for—"

"Sit down," she said. "We're just listening to the service first."

"It won't be long, Missus," the sergeant apologized.

Ma pointed to two chairs opposite the table. "Sit down. The world can wait for the Lord."

Clearly flustered, the two policemen glanced at one another, but her commanding gesture didn't leave them much of a choice. Pulling out the chairs they sat down, their caps on the bare shining surface of the dining table. And without another word the four of us sat listening to the service.

In spite of myself I thought of the way Dad had deceived the Security Police in the war. But Ma had nothing to hide. With closed eyes, her head held high, she sat unmoving to the end. And writing it down now I can again imagine the light from outside respectfully modeling the prominence of her cheekbones, and her nose, and chin, the web of wrinkles of suffering and laughter around her eyes and mouth, the delicate brushwork of her hair.

Something in her attitude reminded me of Elise's father. He'd had the same forceful yet gentle quality about him; to him the formalities of the church had been equally indispensable. Yet he could be surprisingly broadminded and generous.

Those last holidays they'd spent with us, just before their accident. The senior vicar in our congregation had been on leave and Elise's father had volunteered to lend a hand with some of the services and prayer meetings. In this way he'd established a firm friendship with our junior *dominee*, Rev. Cloete. Often they would sit up talking until midnight or later; and several times Elise invited the Cloetes over for a meal. We found him quite a sympathetic person, in spite of his tense and nervous attitude: he was very young, barely thirty, with an exaggerated awareness of his "calling." Extremely intelligent, very pale, with intense dark eyes rather too large for his narrow face. Apparently he'd been an outstanding tennis player in his time, but in their previous post in a very small backveld congregation, people had objected to the idea of a *dominee* taking part in something as worldly as sport, so he'd had to give it up. He had several blind spots too: for example, he was much too dogmatic for my liking, insisting on the Biblical foundations of apartheid. (Why justify from the Scriptures a system explicable in terms of basic economics?) Still, all things considered, he was quite a pleasant man, burning with ambition—the sort of stuff church moderators are made of.

But we were less taken with his wife. She certainly was attractive, perhaps even too beautiful for her role as mother of the congregation; and impressing one with a very cold and correct sense of propriety. Hardly a week before the catastrophe Elise had complained about the woman's unsympathetic attitude at a meeting where the sisters of the congregation had assembled to discuss a young "fallen" girl's plea for help. ("It's no use being gentle and forgiving just because she's one of us. The Afrikaner has a duty to set an example to others." Etc.)

On the night in question I'd just arrived home from working late when the telephone rang. The rest of the family had already gone to bed.

"It's the Randburg police station," said the formal voice on the phone. "Sergeant Van Wyk. I'm looking for a Reverend Rautenbach."

"Yes, he's staying with me," I said. "But he's asleep now. Why do you want to speak to him?"

"Man, can you please call him for me?" He sounded ill at ease.

"If it's really urgent. But what's happened?"

"We got a Cloete here, says he's also a *dominee*."

"Yes, I know him. But—"

"He asked us to call Rev. Rautenbach to the station."

"Certainly. But what's the matter?"

"If you don't mind, we'll talk when he gets here, all right?"

Fortunately the old man was a light sleeper and he awoke the moment I touched his shoulder. After I'd left the room I could hear him conferring softly with his wife before he came out, in his gown and slippers. Ten minutes later we were on our way.

Some visual impressions seem to remain with one for ever; and in the heart of this London winter I can recall all the small particulars of that disturbing summer night. The blue lamp in front of the face-brick building. The flat white light in the charge office. The brown counter; the tables marked with white stenciled numbers; the files tied with pink ribbons. A few wooden cupboards and steel cabinets. The notice board with a map of the area and an assortment of official papers pinned to the green felt. Rev. Cloete on the wooden bench. He was wearing his black suit, but it looked as if he'd just crawled from a mealie bag. His tie was missing, his normally straightened hair disheveled and the tail of his white shirt protruding, half torn off, over his trousers. He looked up quickly as we came in, then dropped his head. Elise's father sat down beside him, putting an arm round his shoulders, as I went up to the counter. On the other side of a wooden partition a constable was painstakingly taking down a statement dictated by an immaculately dressed Black man. He seemed to have trouble with his spelling, as he scratched out every third or fourth word; and as he wrote his mouth soundlessly formed every syllable. Behind the counter a group of other policemen were lounging on and behind their tables, most of them in uniform, one wearing a black tracksuit.

"Mynhardt," I announced briefly. "I've brought Rev. Rautenbach."

The big man in the tracksuit came to the counter, offering his hand. "Evening, Mister. Sergeant Van Wyk. It was I who phoned. Sorry to bother you this time of the night, man." He had an open, friendly, boyish face, with one front tooth missing. The zip of his tracksuit top was unfastened, revealing, through the dark tangle of hair on his chest, the blue and red outlines of a tattoo. He appeared generous to the point of joviality, like a compére at a sports meeting.

"What happened?" I asked again.

He motioned me to come closer, as if he didn't want the two clergymen on the bench to hear us.

"Immorality," he said.

"My God!" I couldn't hide my shock. "But it's impossible!"

The sergeant pulled up his bull shoulders. "I wish I could say so, Mister. But in our sort of job you soon find out that nothing is too impossible to be true."

"But—how—?" I still couldn't believe my ears. Involuntarily I turned round at the very moment Cloete looked up in my direction. Those dark eyes burning in the pale narrow face. He quickly looked down again, but I still remember that expression of complete bewilderment, and the cringing attitude of a dog expecting to be beaten.

"We've been suspecting it for a long time now," confided Sergeant Van Wyk in his hearty way, as if to say: "This way, boys, this way. Come and enjoy yourselves." Propping himself up on his elbows on the counter he leaned even closer than before: "Been watching him for a month, you know. Once or twice a week. Regular as anything. Just after he's done his rounds. Same servant girl every time. Picks her up at the back gate, house of one of his elders. Then it's off to the bluegum plantation."

"What's going to happen now?"

"Well, he kept on asking for *Dominee* Rautenbach, so we'll let them chat for a while to calm him down a bit. Then we'll have to lock him up. Too late now to bother about bail and all that. Better to arrange it in the morning."

As I turned round again, at a complete loss about what to do, my father-in-law was just getting up from the bench to come to the counter. Cloete didn't look up.

"Well?" I asked. "Did he tell you?"

He nodded. He, too, was looking pale.

"Sergeant Van Wyk says they can arrange bail tomorrow. He'll have to stay here for the night."

"Oh, no, no," he said. "It's quite out of the question." He came to the counter, his white hair shining in the unmerciful light. "He must go home tonight, Sergeant. Please."

"Just look at the time, *Dominee!*" For the first time the policeman's friendly face became sullen, suggesting an altogether different side to his character.

"I know, Sergeant. And I hate to give you any unnecessary trouble. But it's imperative to arrange bail straight away. Here and now."

I knew him well enough to predict that he wouldn't leave the charge office before he'd had his way. In that respect he was just like Bernard.

Now I wasn't being inhuman or anything, but to my mind, if a man went in for that sort of thing, he had to face the consequences. He'd gone into it with open eyes, knowing it was forbidden. In such circumstances sympathy was quite misplaced; it became a sickness. But I knew it would be useless to argue with my father-in-law.

In spite of all his protests, and openly resentful, the sergeant had to comply. The forms were filled in and signed. But even that wasn't enough for the old man.

"Now for the woman you caught with him," he said calmly.

"What about her, *Domineer*?"

"We can't bail one of them out and not the other. After all, they were together."

"But really—!"

"Please, Sergeant. We're expected to do something for our neighbor, aren't we?"

Not having enough cash with us for bail for both of them, we first had to drive all the way back home so I could fetch some money. And it was past two when we stopped at the vicarage.

In a way that was the worst moment of the night: seeing that normally so correct, prim woman coming from the house in a shapeless old gown, with curlers in her hair. The shock on her face as she recognized us. At first she thought there'd been an accident. When she saw her husband emerging from the car and approaching in the dark, her beautiful face hardened, distorted in denial and disgust.

My father-in-law put his hand on her shoulder. She tried to shake him off but he held on.

"Now, my girl, you're going to make us all a nice cup of tea," he said, "then we can calmly talk about it all and ask the Lord's guidance."

"What happened?" she asked her husband. "What have you done, Hendrik?"

"Don't worry," Elise's father said soothingly. "We'll get it all straightened out. And whatever we fail to understand we'll entrust to God."

My memories of the following hour or two are very confused. The comforting, imperturbable voice of my father-in-law. The hysterical tirades of the woman. The pale young man bursting into ignominious tears. I was bone tired. The best we could do, I thought, was simply to leave the two of them to fight it out on their own. The old man could come back the next day when they'd had time to sort things out. But he insisted on staying until, out of pure exhaustion, a weary, blunted calm was restored.

The day was already beginning to break when we returned home. Because of my fatigue I was irritable.

"It's just a waste of time," I said, resentful. "The harm has already been done. That's a nice sort of *dominee* for you! How do you feel about having to work with a man like that?"

"It's a great help to one," he answered tranquilly, to my surprise. "You know, one builds up an image of a *dominee* just as you build up images of an 'Afrikaner' or anything else. Then a thing like this happens to teach you the humility to revise all your definitions and leave room for more understanding in future. It's a great help to one, should the temptation ever arise to become too proud or too sure of oneself. Don't you think so?" I wonder whether he was still so convinced of it when, two days later, Cloete committed suicide.

Of course, it depended on how close we were to the enemy. If there was any fighting, Sunday would be just like any other day of the week. But on quiet Sundays there was church parade and it felt just like home, really. Except of course for the destroyed villages and the tropical scenery and the blown-up trucks and things on the road. Actually, the church routine made one feel O.K., sort of reassuring.

But gradually it changed, I'm not sure how or when, but it changed. Some time after the first battles, after the first landmines. The day I really became aware of the difference, Ronnie had already died.

We were camped on the outskirts of a dead village in the tropical jungle. It was steaming hot, we were sticky with sweat all the time, and there were bloody millions of flies and mosquitoes and things. And birds kicking up a row in the trees.

The day before, the Saturday, two of our jeeps'd been blown up by mines. And it was then, when church parade was called the Sunday morning, as if nothing had happened, I felt as if something was going to explode in my guts. There was a new soul-tiffy to do the job for us. You know, we used to call the mechanics "tiffies," so the doctor was a "cock-tiffy" and the chaplain a "soul-tiffy." Anyway, there was this new cunt, an elderly uncle with glasses, nothing could wipe the smile from his face: as if he wanted to sort of demonstrate to every-body that Jesus had saved his miserable little soul. And when he preached, his voice went up and down all the time like he was practicing his scales. When he prayed, he damned near yodeled. There was nothing special in what he said: all the old crap about being in a heathen land to fight for our religion and our civil-ization; and that everybody was fucking proud of us; and that we had to put on the whole armor of God, that sort of thing. And when he prayed, he asked the Lord's blessing on our campaign against the enemy, the servant of Satan.

He prayed for "these young men in the prime of their youth, who have answered Thy call to take up arms against the forces of Evil." Plain and simple shit. We hadn't answered anybody's fucking call, we were thrown headlong into it.

I sat thinking of Ronnie, and of that dead Cuban with his silly little snapshot. Perhaps his blokes were also having church parade that morning, asking for God's blessing against their enemies, the servants of Satan. Us. And then—oh bleeding Jesus—it became fucking impossible to take it any more: that old soul-tiffy with the smile plastered on his face saying: "We're here because the Lord called us to establish His kingdom in the wilderness."

I thought: How? By destroying people the way we'd done with the Blacks who'd happened to cross our way the day before? By blowing up bridges and tanks and maiming people? Some kingdom!

You know, Dad, I never used to bother much about religion before I went to Angola. I mean, it was all right, it didn't hurt me. But over there God began to sort of worry me. I was a good Nationalist when we crossed that border. But when I saw what sort of war we were really fighting and what was behind it all—sorry, Dad. It taught me to puke on everything I'd believed in before.

❖ ❖ ❖ ❖

People like Louis really tend to make life impossible for themselves. Perhaps it's just a stage. One gets through it. You've got to, if you want to survive. A man like my brother Theo, for instance, has never encountered this type of problem in his life.

As a child he was never precocious or impudent. He never tried to take the initiative in anything. He was quite happy to follow me wherever I went and to do whatever I ordered him. Sometimes with nearly catastrophic consequences (when I told him to jump from the tree), often resulting in some loss to himself (poor chap, in our high school days I regularly took his girlfriends from him). Perhaps that is why he and Ma have never really got along very well. She once called him "a toes-together sort of man." With her more aggressive nature she simply couldn't understand his retiring ways, his tidiness, his gentleness: he must be as strange to her as Dad used to be.

Not that Theo is a weakling, don't get me wrong. He is much too ingenuous for that. Or, if he is weak in any way, he knows how to camouflage it with organization and planning and efficiency. Sometimes I get the impression that he became an architect only because it offered him the means of transforming his innate timidity into a lust for power, expressed in terms of the demolition of old buildings and the construction of colossal new edifices.

Dad sometimes blamed him for his lack of a 'sense of history,' because of his lack of respect for old buildings. But Theo had no difficulty in refuting the accusation:

"What is 'a sense of history' in a country like this?" he would ask. "It's a colonial view. I have no sentiment for the junk constructed by our ancestors by way of third-rate imitations of outdated European styles. Our greatest asset is the fact that we have no history. We're today's people. Our dimension is the future." And I must admit that there is a peculiar excitement in the skyscrapers he designs, with their steel and copper and reinforced concrete, their clean surfaces and sweeping functional lines, the accumulation of stories until they start boring the imagination with their inability to suggest anything beyond themselves. ("Why rely on suggestions? We're not Catholics, we have no mysticism. We're Calvinists, Puritans. We are interested in what exists tangibly and can be organized and structured.") It sounds convincing, but one should take it with a pinch of salt. It represents Theo's "official" facade. When he is not on the defense he is really much more limp and uncertain of himself. Like Dad.

He has an attractive if demure wife, and two children; and a house in the select suburb of Waterkloof. A balanced family man. He would never dream of having an extramarital affair or of staying away from church on Sundays. ("No, I don't regard myself as a very fervent believer. But that's not important. It's a matter of order and discipline in one's existence. A pattern. What's wrong with it? Without it one has nothing fixed to hold on to.")

I don't know what made me start this passage on Theo in the first place. He is of no importance to my narrative. None whatsoever.

✧ ✧ ✧ ✧

The service was concluded with organ music. Ma turned off the transistor.

"Morning, Sergeant," she said. "Right, now we can talk. Kristina, tea!"

"Sorry to bother you on a Sunday, Missus, but we must get a statement from you, you see. It won't take long."

The thin blond constable sat quietly at a far corner of the table, drumming his fingers on the wood while the redheaded sergeant opened his file and took down our short statements. When he'd finished, he read out the stiffly correct sentences, and pushed the file to us for our signatures. First Ma, then I.

"When can we have the woman back for the funeral?" asked Ma. "I've already sent a message to her people."

"The doctor will do his autopsy later today, Missus. You can have the body in the morning."

"Thanks. I hope Mandisi is behaving himself?"

"Yes, he isn't giving any trouble."

"Does this mean the death penalty?" I asked.

He laughed. "Oh no. If the judge hears it's a matter of tribal customs and stuff he'll be very lenient. Probably a year or eighteen months or thereabouts."

"I'll have to find another foreman," said Ma, sighing.

"*Ja*, these people really make it difficult for one." He rose, returning his cap smartly to his crew cut head, obviously relieved to have completed his business. "Well, time to go."

I accompanied them to the van. High on the hill there was a small cloud of dust: Louis coming back from town.

Just before they drove off, the constable got out again to collect something from the back. He came round the van with the grey blanket in which we'd wrapped the corpse.

"We brought this back," he said, embarrassed. "It's winter, you know, and we thought the children might need it in the night."

5

SOON AFTER THE POLICE had left visitors arrived: the Weidemans from a neighboring farm, Gert and Loekie, both youngish, in their thirties. He had the solid body and bandy legs of a lock-forward, his ears large and fleshy; there was an aggressiveness about his self-confidence which tended to irk me. Loekie, on the other hand, was timid and colorless, her body beginning to sag after three children in rapid succession, like a large soft fungus under her demure dress. I remembered her the way she'd been shortly after their marriage: a dynamic girl, bubbling with enthusiasm, ready to make a contribution to any conversation. Not much to look at, but with an attractive, provocative personality. She had a degree in modern languages, if I remembered correctly, and apparently she'd been quite a talented pianist. But all that had faded with the years and now she was placid and passive, and plain.

"Good day," said Gert, pumping my hand vigorously. "Thought we'd come over for a while. Sundays are so boring on the farm, you start missing people you don't even know."

"What about something to drink for the visitors?" I suggested to Ma.

"Don't suppose there's any beer?" said Gert, laughing.

"Coffee or tea?" said Ma, unamused.

"Whatever you have," said Loekie. "Please don't take any trouble."

"Make it coffee," ordered Gert, sitting down with his massive legs spread, his jeans stretched over the bulge between his thighs.

"Kristina!" Ma called.

"I heard you had such sports on the farm last night," Gert said jovially. "Isn't it just typical? I also had a close shave, you know, coming back from Queenstown. Went there for rugby and had a bit of a party afterwards." He grinned defiantly in Loekie's direction; she looked down. "It was past midnight when we came back in the fog. And coming round a bend there was a whole lot of kaffirs right in front of us. Strange creatures, aren't they, always walk right in the middle of the road. Jeez, I tell you that bus properly skidded sideways the way old Jopie had to stand on the brakes." He laughed, his dugs shaking loosely under the T-shirt he wore winter and summer. "But I can tell you one thing, when we got out of that bus we gave them a proper workout right there in the road, man. There wasn't one of them straight on his black feet when we drove off. I don't think they'll be a traffic hazard again after this."

From the distant past, an unpleasant memory: our university rugby teams returning to Stellenbosch on Saturday nights, singing uproariously and drunkenly. In those days I played wing for the seconds. Invariably a voice would ring out: "Right, boys, who's for beating up hottentots tonight?" The bus coming to a standstill every time a couple of Coloreds were spotted in the roads. The naked, savage pleasure in the sweaty bodies tumbling out to settle on the passersby like a great swarm of bees. I never took part. Of course, I couldn't stay high and dry in the bus to be jeered at: I jumped out with the rest of them, but then made sure I kept out of the throng. At that age one doesn't want to be "left out." But I never joined in the beatings: I must make that absolutely clear. And really, the blokes didn't mean to be cruel or anything. It was just a way of getting rid of excess energy; in later years, I'm sure, they all outgrew it. But in Gert it annoyed me. After all, he was by no means an adolescent any more.

Involuntarily I glanced at Louis, but he was holding a newspaper in front of his face, his knuckles showing white through the skin of his clenched hands.

Another car stopped outside. Stretching my neck, I looked through the window.

"Bet you it's old Lawrence," said Gert.

"Yes, it's the Lawrences all right."

"They probably also heard the story," he commented.

I opened the front door as the little mouse-woman was coming up the cement stairs to the stoop, followed by her husband, large and flabby in a shapeless green sweater and faded corduroy pants flapping loosely round his legs. Old Mr. Lawrence was an unusually hirsute man with a large mane, bushy eyebrows, and unkempt moustache and beard covering most of his face—looking for all the world like an armpit with a pipe stuck into it.

He removed the pipe. Through the hair on his face I could distinguish a glittering of eyes. "Hello, Martin. How are you, my boy?"

"So-so, Mr. Lawrence."

"Nasty business, hey?" he said. "One never knows with these people. And what's your Ma going to do now?"

"It won't be easy," I said neutrally, not wanting the neighbors to suspect anything yet. "I heard you've sold your farm?"

"*Ja* the old useless," commented Ma from inside. "And Gert too. The whole lot of them hands-upping just like that."

"Hey, steady, Auntie," said Gert. "It's got nothing to do with hands-upping."

"Oh really?" Behind her teasing tone was a solid layer of reproach, as hard as rock. "I could still expect it from Mr. Lawrence. But Afrikaners like you! Loekie, couldn't you have stopped your husband then?"

"*Ag*, Auntie, you know what men are like. And Gert knows best, I'm sure."

"You can't let a man have his way all the time," said Ma sternly. "In the old days it was the women who dug in their heels when their menfolk pulled in their tails between their legs."

"Louis," I said, trying to change the topic, "aren't you saying hello to the visitors? Where are your manners, man?"

Openly resentful, he put away his newspaper and rose to shake hands.

"Well, and how's the army?" asked Mrs. Lawrence.

"He's out of it now," I said quickly.

"Gave 'em hell, eh?" the old man insisted. "Good for you. In future they'll know to leave us well alone."

"You should have wiped the whole breed of vermin from the face of the land," said Gert.

"Why didn't you join us then?" asked Louis with a cool aggressiveness I hadn't expected. "Instead of staying behind on your farm?"

"We can't all go to the border, man," said Gert, off balance for a moment. "We've got to hold the fort over here too."

"I thought you sold out?" asked Louis. I didn't like the expression on his face.

"*Ja*, go on, tell him," chuckled Ma. "Withdrawing from all the frontiers, that's what they're doing."

"What's the use?" Louis demanded. "We're just exposing new vulnerable frontiers all the time. Angola, Rhodesia, Mozambique, South-West. And now you're starting right here too."

"Wait a minute," said Gert. "Don't underestimate our boys, lightie. We had a very good look before we made up our minds. Life here in the Eastern Cape just isn't worth one's while any more. You work yourself to death, until you haven't got any nails left to scratch your head. And before you can wipe out your eyes, the Blacks have got it all. What has three centuries of civilization done for them? They're just as savage as they were to start with. Look at what happened here on your own farm last night, man."

"So now you're running away to the city?" said Ma.

"No one's running away, Auntie. But you've got to use your common sense. If you want to get anywhere in the world today, you can only do it in the cities. Isn't that so, Martin?"

"I can't agree more."

"Gert is going to manage a big factory," offered Loekie, her pride shining through her self-consciousness. "Agricultural implements."

"Everybody is running after machinery," said Louis, sneering, with all the irritating confidence of his youthful romanticism. "In the end there won't be any place left for people."

"I thought you were going to be an engineer yourself?" I asked sternly.

"Didn't you know I gave that up long ago?"

"Back to the horse cart?" I said derisively.

In my childhood many farmers in our district had still driven their horse carts. On Sundays one would see at least ten or twelve of them fastened to the pepper trees surrounding the church; and even the farmers who'd come to town in their Buicks or Chevs or Mercuries, had regularly used their horse-carts to visit their neighbors.

Everything which had been so uncomfortable and primitive then acquired a wonderful romantic air after I'd gone overseas to pursue my studies. (Just as I tend to romanticize that sojourn nowadays? Or just as, writing in London today, I falsify that weekend in my mind? Is that what's been happening all the time I've been convinced of my absolute honesty in recalling it?)

My nostalgia, during those two years in England, was reinforced and nurtured by my friendship with Welcome Nyaluza. That night in Lambeth; the wild party. It was midwinter, and very cold. The first snow had fallen the week before and turned into slush in the soggy streets. I felt just like the slush. My funds were low after too extravagant spending trying to impress my first foreign girlfriend, only to lose her to a Kenyan sculptor in the end. Hell, and I'd thought that at least she'd been a girl with some taste. I tried to console myself by blaming it on English girls in general: all the culture in the bloody world, but when it came to men all they wanted was a big cock—and we all knew about Blacks, didn't we?

The prospect of a good party had persuaded me to leave my miserable digs and drown my sorrows. And there certainly was more than enough to drink that night. Bad and cheap, but enough. A congestion of bodies in the cramped flat. Like Aunt Rienie's birthday party so many years later. Bea. But that night it had been Welcome. A veritable United Nations of types and languages: English, Americans, French, Scandinavians, Germans, Greeks, Japanese, even a few Poles and Russians. How incredible that in that Babel I should have found Welcome Nyaluza. Or wasn't it so remarkable after all? Often, in the two years I spent in England, I would be struck by exactly the same phenomenon: the two people more or less predestined to drift together in the course of such a party, isolating themselves in a corner and excluding the rest of the world, would be an Afrikaner and an African. Strange.

The initial effect of the smoking and drinking on my depression was an even greater morbidity than before. I withdrew into a corner, half hidden by curtains. And then the voice said:

"You look lonesome."

Through a haze I saw a very small, very thin, very black man with prominent glasses—much like Charlie in later years, but several years younger.

"How'd you guess?" I asked.

"Because one lonesome man never fails to recognize another." He promptly sat down on the floor next to me. "Let's drink to it." Until that moment we'd been speaking English; but as he raised his glass he said: *"Vrystaat!"*

"Don't tell me you come from South Africa?" I said, staring at him unashamedly.

"Of course. You too?" He burst out laughing. "Oh brother!" And then we switched to Afrikaans.

"Wait till you've been here for as long as I have," he told me. "Then you'll really find out what it means to be lonesome, man."

"For how long have you been here then?"

"Ten years."

"What for?"

"Swotting. On an exit permit."

"Were you in politics at home?"

"ANC. But nothing special. You know how it is, don't you? The Boers just don't like learned kaffirs."

We refilled our glasses and returned to our secluded spot, talking nonstop. All the *d'you remembers* of compatriots in a foreign land. The pepper trees and the horse carts, the silence of Sundays, the din of stock fairs, the smell of woodsmoke in winter, the taste of green apricots and loquats, sweet *hanepoot* grapes and watermelons. Boys swimming naked in muddy pools. Bird-nesting, crawling along slack willow branches and dropping into the water. Cooking a tortoise in its shell. Fighting with clay sticks. Pumpkins on flat iron roofs. The scare of the *tokoloshe*. Sweet potatoes baked in their skins. Mud between your toes. Frost on the brittle white grass of winter. How irrational, the things one discovered one missed most. I told him about my earliest memory: how Ma would hand me over to the care of old Aia, our Black nanny, whenever I'd been unmanageable; to be tied with a blanket to her back, resting on the soft mass of her enormous posterior: my earliest and deepest experience of security. And how, as we'd grown up, Theo and I would join the servants for breakfast, squatting on our haunches round the three-legged iron pot, helping ourselves to tough *putu* porridge in our cupped hands.

Later in the evening, tearful with booze, I confided in him about Janet who'd dropped me for her Kenyan sculptor; and he told me about the Nozizwe he'd left behind although he'd paid the *lobola* in full before going away; they'd planned for her to follow him as soon as possible, but somehow it had never materialized. Oh no, we decided together, it wasn't good for a man to be alone and without a woman.

When he discovered how far gone I was, Welcome put an arm round me and escorted me outside where the icy wet air sent us reeling backwards. He hailed a cab to take us home, insisting on going with me all the way. Just as well, for as it turned out I couldn't remember my address in my stupor. The rest of the night is a very muddled memory. For how long we drove through the streets of London in search of a building with black front pillars, I don't know. In the end Welcome had to stop the taxi when the fare on the meter tallied with what he had left in his pocket: what had happened to mine, I still don't know—my wallet was missing. And then we had to walk back, from wherever in North London we'd left the cab to his digs in Stepney. The winter dawn was already beginning to light up drably when we reached his messy little room. How he'd managed to support me all the way with that thin body of his, God alone knows. As we crossed his doorstep I slumped to the floor. He must have put me to bed, for when I finally came round the dull grey afternoon sun was falling through the dirty window; and he was sitting at the foot of the crumpled bed with a cup of tea on his knees.

We became inseparable. Welcome, my friend. Now I'm waxing sentimental about *him* again: now it is his turn to be transformed by memory. But we were friends. We really were. At one stage, after I'd been kicked out of my digs, I shared his room for a few weeks until I managed to find something else. In a way he also acted as mentor to me, encouraging me to read stuff I would never have touched otherwise: not only economics and politics, but even novels and—true as God—poetry: the last time in my life I indulged myself in that way. Welcome himself had already obtained his Ph.D. in history, and he was lecturing at SOAS. What I'll always remember about him is the incredible variety of friends he had, ranging from professional vagabonds to nuclear physicists, from sculptors and painters to pale-ontologists, from bank clerks and street cleaners to drivers of Bentleys.

When he learned about Elise and discovered my anxiety about her and Bernard in my absence, he was adamant: "Not a damn. Then you must tell her to come to you. It's enough for one of us to have lost a woman that way."

In my turn I tried my best to prod him into applying for permission to return to South Africa. But, by a curious coincidence, on the same day I received Elise's cable to announce that she was coming over, Welcome was given his final No from South Africa House. And as it turned out, he never met her after all. He got an appointment at Stanford (for the hell of it he'd always posted applications for all sorts of posts all over the world) and a week before her arrival in England he left. The day of his departure was the second—and last—time I got hopelessly drunk during my stay abroad. Once again Welcome was with me. And it was so bad that he very nearly missed his plane.

We assured each other that he would come back to attend our wedding and that we would visit him in the States. But it came to nothing. Our correspondence dwindled and died. And something extraordinary happened: in all the months of our friendship I'd never even stopped to think of the fact that Welcome was black; it had been the only period in my life when it had truly not mattered. But from the day Elise arrived I became aware of an inhibition in me. Sometimes, having started a conversation about Welcome, I would allow it to end unresolved the moment she began to show interest. In a strange way I couldn't reconcile the two of them.

I remember his last letter, three months after our wedding. He reminded me of my promise to bring her to the States with me. It made me feel guilty: not about breaking the promise, but about the mere idea of introducing her to him. I never even told her about the letter; and I didn't reply to it either. It would have been useless anyway, for a few months later I happened to see the small report, somewhere in the middle pages of a newspaper, about a South African, one Welcome Nyaluza, who'd fallen to his death from a building in New York. Suicide was suspected. How can one hope ever to understand another person?

✧ ✧ ✧ ✧

Round me the conversation was going its confused way, relaxed, yet with submarine tensions. The women had formed their own little group, discussing servants and wages, pilfering, the cost of living. Loekie opened every statement with: "Gert always says—," or: "Gert thinks it's—," or: "I'll ask Gert about it, but—"

At some stage Mr. Lawrence pointed to Ma's little aloe painting which he'd never been able to stand: "So you've still got that masterpiece?" He chuckled. "Good thing, pictures. Cover up a wall nicely. You know, when I was young, I zigged and zagged my way through Europe. Instead of going to brothels I spent all my time museum-crawling. But now I've had enough. This art racket is grossly overrated if you ask me. Just draws one's attention away from the real issues. In a land like this there's no need for art."

"Look who's talking," said Ma. "Who's packing up and moving away, avoiding the 'real issues'?"

"Wait, Auntie," said Gert, returning stubbornly to the attack. "Moving away from the farm doesn't mean moving out of the country. We'll never leave the last trench."

"There were people in Angola who said the same thing," Louis remarked without looking at Gert. "We saw their farms. The endless ranches of the rich who'd invested in land. And then the war broke out."

"You can't compare us to a bladdy lot of Portuguese, man!"

Louis ignored him. "I remember one farm we came to," he went on. "Just a small plot really. Neatly painted blue cottage. One could see the fields had been well tended before the MPLA had passed that way. They'd plundered the lot. Followed by UNITA. Then us. Anyway, we broke a window at the side of the house to get in. Inside everything was still neat and clean. Not like some of the other houses we'd been in, broken and destroyed and covered in the mess and the shit of animals and people. This cottage was respectable. Not a wrinkle on the spreads covering the beds. Only a bit moldy, because it was raining nearly every day, and blotches of green were showing up through the wallpaper. There was a small niche in the dining room, with a plaster cast of the Virgin in it, a cheap little painted statue with a sweet, insipid face. And a row of photographs in front of it. A wedding photo of a young chap with a moustache and smooth hair, and a plain girl in an embroidered gown. And one of the man with two small children. Another of her with an elderly couple, probably her parents who'd come to visit them from Portugal. Everything abandoned just like that when they fled."

"Those people had no guts, man," said Gert.

Loekie got up quickly—as if she'd felt a shiver running down her spine—to make sure their three boisterous children were still playing on the white, patchy lawn outside.

"Everywhere we went we found refugees," said Louis. "Hundreds, thousands of them. Black and Brown and White, all the bloody colors of the rainbow. Some on foot, pushing wheelbarrows or carrying bundles on their backs. Others on rickety vegetable vans with wooden scaffolding on the back for all the chickens and pigs and beds and pots and pans and grandfathers and grandmothers. Rich, oily blokes in posh cars. Large pantechnicons. Baby prams. Some of the cars had broken down along the road or run out of petrol. They offered us all they had if only we'd help them. There was one woman, a smart lady with golden earrings, who started tearing the clothes off her body offering to sleep with the lot of us in exchange for a few liters of petrol. We saw them every bloody day, right from the border all the way up to Luanda, and back again. It felt like something dying inside one, seeing them like that. Because one knew: One day it will be our turn to take to the road just like that, with our little vans and our cardboard suitcases and our rolled blankets and our water bottles. And who will help us?"

"That'll be the bladdy day," said Gert. "I'll shoot to the last bullet, and then I'll get at them with my naked fists, man."

(Prof Pienaar: *I shall go on fighting until the blood rises to the bridles of our horses.*")

"Now, Louis, you're much too young to talk that way," said Ma, dissatisfied. "Don't tell me you became a coward in Angola."

"It's not a matter of cowardice, Gran," he said calmly. "It's just that I saw what was happening."

"Don't worry about what you saw over there," said Mr. Lawrence. "It can't possibly happen here. Don't be silly."

"You're already leaving the Eastern Frontier."

"But my goodness, we're not running away! We're free people in a free country, aren't we?"

"This is really too ghastly," complained Mrs. Lawrence. "How on earth did we get on this topic?"

"There was a murder last night," Louis reminded her flatly.

"Let them kill one another if they want to!" Gert blurted out. "They won't lay a finger on us."

"Quite," agreed Mr. Lawrence, filtering his voice through his beard stained by coffee and tobacco juice. "It's their tribal customs and things. Surely it's got nothing to do with us. One has to be very patient with them. After all, they're just like children."

"And for how long d'you think you're going to be safe in the cities?" Louis persisted. "Just a matter of time, then our frontiers will shrink as we draw our little laager more and more tightly. And what happens then?"

"Oh, nonsense!" said Mr. Lawrence, poking the long stem of his pipe back into the moist hole in the middle of his hairy face.

"You think you can keep everything nicely separated through apartheid," Louis went on, like a bloody fly on a windowpane. "White here, Black there. But this isn't chess. It's people."

"I can't see how we can solve our problems in any other way," I said firmly. "It was easy enough for England and France and those countries: they built up their colonial empires overseas and the moment things became too hot to handle they could drop them just like that. But we're living right here in the heart of ours. And unless we separate conflicting interests—"

"How can you do anything else but defend the system that has made you rich and powerful?" asked Louis with increasing insolence.

"You can add a bit of salt to your 'rich and powerful,'" I told him. "You have a terribly simplistic view of things, Louis. To you it's a matter of making or breaking here and now. I've seen rather more of life than you have. And I know what that sort of breaking can lead to."

"And I've seen what happens to people who refuse to change in time!"

"'We in our green youth,'" said Mr. Lawrence as if he were quoting, "'must settle eternal questions first of all.'"

"The point," said Gert, "is that we can best protect our interests in the cities. That's where we Whites belong. Here on the border we're exposed to the Blacks. If the crunch comes, the government will abandon us without batting an eyelid, that I can tell you. They're only feathering their own nests nowadays."

"They should have done more for the Blacks in time," suggested Mrs Lawrence timidly.

"They should have done more for *us*!" countered Gert.

"All I know," said Mr. Lawrence, puffing away, "is that none of this would have happened if old Jan Smuts had still been alive."

"I got a good price for my farm," said Gert. "Much more than it's worth in these times. I had to jump at the chance while it was there."

"*Ja*, Gert was saying that right from the beginning," confirmed Loekie, blushing.

"That's all that really matters, isn't it?" I said, deliberately avoiding Louis's eyes. "To conclude every transaction as favorably as possible."

✧ ✧ ✧ ✧

After the guests had left, Ma hurried into the kitchen to make sure dinner was served without any delay. She was irritable, as it was already half-past twelve and normally the Sunday dinner was announced promptly at noon.

"Well, Ma," I said as we sat down, "now you've heard what they're saying. So why don't you also make up your mind and have done with it?"

She looked at me attentively for some time. Then she said: "The important thing is not for me to make up my mind, sonny. The way I see it, I'm giving *you* time."

"For what?"

"To open your eyes and see what you're doing. Now please say grace for us."

6

B UT WHEN MA WITHDREW to her room after dinner "to lie
down for a while," something quite foreign to her nature, I
realized she must be more perturbed than I'd thought.

"Don't tell me your age is catching up with you after all?" I
intended it lightly, even sympathetically; but it sounded cruel.

"I didn't sleep too well last night," she said flatly. But on her
doorstep she stopped for a moment to look round at me. "Sometimes,
you know," she said, "sleep is like prayer. A way of appealing for help
to a place you can't reach otherwise." Before I could answer she
closed the door between us.

Louis was lying on his bed already, covered by the eiderdown,
reading the comics. I took off my shoes and my trousers and moved
in under the blankets. Rest invaded me like warmth. But beyond the
superficial satisfaction it stirred up older, familiar things. Turning my
eyes away from Louis, it was easy to imagine he was Theo (except
that I would have preferred not to think of Theo) and we were
children again.

In our childhood holidays there had been an oppressive feeling of
being caged in on Sundays which had made it different from any other
day of the week. Especially in the afternoon, those endless summer
afternoons with the sun burning over the valley, windless and hot.

Grandpa and Grandma had always taken a nap after dinner; Dad too, while Ma would retire somewhere with the Bible. And we boys would be instructed to stay in the stoop room until four, the curtains drawn to shut out the world outside. The slightest sound coming from our room before four o'clock would invariably result in a hiding for both of us, with the worn grey strap Ma had taken with her wherever she'd gone, even on holiday. Possibly that had been my earliest associations of good and evil: "sin" meant making a noise on Sunday afternoon; and being "good" consisted of lying motionless on your bed with the heavy heat pressing down on your body and itching in the perspiration in your armpits and between your legs.

As a special favor we'd been allowed, as we'd grown older, to take some reading matter to the room with us on those afternoons: religious journals Grandma had selected for us, or the brown volumes of Fanny Eden. Sanctity had been identical with boredom. Even in submitting to it—neither of us would have considered for a moment the possibility of resisting parental authority, unlike today's children!—there had been something about those Sundays disturbing me long before I could formulate it to myself: an awareness of the unnatural discrepancy between the two young boys imprisoned in that oppressive room, and the wild summer world outside, the dam and the stream, and moist earth and virgin forest and shady wild figs; the green smell of foliage and the shouting of piccanin voices down by the water; and all the extravagant ferocious heat of the sun. It wasn't the stuffiness of our little room in itself, even though that had been bad enough, but the shocking discovery of being separated from that luxuriant world you yearned for with an almost physical, almost sexual, fervor.

Sunday after Sunday we lay in that baking oven of a room, counting off the progress of the clock in the passage: one o'clock, quarter-past, half-past, quarter-to, two o'clock—and then three o'clock—and, incredibly, hallelujah!, the redemption of four decisive strokes, followed by Grandma's coffee and rusks and milk tart and green fig jam, and deliverance to the freedom of the farm. Only once in all those years had I dared to slip out on a Sunday afternoon, taking Theo with me, down to the piccanins cavorting in the dam. That had been the occasion on which I'd nearly drowned, to be saved by Pieletjie of the swinging prick. It had been God's way of punishing me. Followed, mercilessly, by Ma's grey strap.

Such had been the conditioning of the Sundays of my youth which had contributed to my dazed bewilderment, that afternoon on Bernard's farm, when Elise had taken off her clothes and dived naked into the dam. It had been an heraldic act, a ceremonial liberation from all the prescriptions of a Calvinist religion, a fleeting but unforgettable glimpse of a wholly free existence in a paradise beyond sin and Sundays and measured hours and the anger of God. She'd suggested something which, before that, had been no more than presentiment or hope. She would teach me to be free. She'd confirmed, in my absolutist adolescent mind, the possibility of innocence.

And it had all come to nothing. Those words on our wedding night—"Let's first ask the blessing of the Lord"—denied everything I'd hoped to find and achieve through her. Had it been no more than illusion then? Had I really misjudged her? Or had she herself been unaware of what, in that ephemeral magic moment, I'd recognized and fallen in love with in her? She had been the conclusion of my Early Romantic Period, my dreams of becoming a writer, my preposterous faith in happiness. And it was just possible that I'd never quite forgiven her for it.

I preferred not to read the papers that afternoon. I didn't want to see what they had to say about the riots at Westonaria; and I was even less inclined to read about Bernard's trial. So I turned past the news pages, glancing only briefly at the political comment. But in the business section something caught my eye: a photograph of myself in a column of the paper's *Businessman of the Week*. I scanned the report, mainly in search of errors, knowing one couldn't trust any journalist; but it was reasonably accurate. There had been numerous similar articles on my achievements in the newspapers before, mostly in connection with "Afrikaner leaders in business," etc.; occasionally more personal profiles of "the man behind the success formula." One learned to accept it as part of the routine; still, it remained reassuring, a barometer of achievement—like success with women.

Theo was also mentioned in a paragraph of the column, "Mynhardt's younger brother, an architect of considerable standing." In my interview with the reporter I'd made sure he took down the particulars about Theo, feeling that in a sense I'd owed it to him.

Perhaps I wasn't quite fair to Theo when I referred to him a little while ago. But I honestly believed at that stage that this narrative could do without him. Now I realize it's inevitable I bring him into it. Strange how compulsive this sort of writing can become.

I was amazed when he telephoned me that morning to find out whether he could come and see me at my office.

"Why don't you and Marie come over for dinner one evening?" I suggested. "Then we can relax and have a proper chat. It's a long time we haven't seen one another."

"Good idea," he said. "But there's something else I've got to discuss with you alone."

I consulted my desk diary. "What about Wednesday week? We'll be back from our visit to the farm by then."

"Actually I'd prefer to see you *before* you go. It's something—well, rather important—"

"When will you be in Johannesburg again?"

"I'm in town at the moment."

"Oh, well what about this afternoon then? I have an appointment for lunch but I can always cancel it."

"No, I'd rather not go to a restaurant. I prefer your office."

"You sound terribly secretive."

"It's not really as bad as that. It's just—oh well, I'll see you at three then."

It was in March, just after Dad's cancer had been positively diagnosed for the first time, fifteen months before his death; the time when, in spite of the discomfort and the actual suffering, he still found it possible to read and live with so much enthusiasm.

In the long-winded way reminiscent of Dad when he was embarrassed, Theo spent half an hour talking about irrelevancies without giving any indication of the real reason why he'd come. I had a lot of work to do and was planning to drive round to Bea's flat, too, in the evening, but I knew it would be futile to goad Theo.

Almost absently I sat studying him while he carried on with the small talk: taller and younger than myself, his hair thicker and fairer, his body in better shape and without my middle-aged spread, rather "too handsome for a man" as Ma had once said disapprovingly. The looks of a ladies' man: which I didn't think he was. I suddenly realized how little I really knew about him. Since high school we'd had almost no contact. Those had been the days I would make a habit of stealing his girlfriends, not in earnest really, more for the hell of it, to try and get some reaction out of him, which had never happened. Poor old Theo: without exception they really had been very attractive girls. Unfortunately his wife Marie tended to be bitchy. She didn't like me very much either. I had a pretty shrewd idea why, but there's no need to go into it now.

Theo went on talking: about some administrative building he'd just completed, with a group of statues in the foyer which had had to be removed after public protest about their nudity; a recent visit to Scandinavia with Marie and the kids; Dad's illness.

And then, without any warning, he asked: "Martin, do you regard yourself as a happy man?"

"What a question! Yes, I suppose I do. Why?"

"I just wanted to know. In your work, your everyday life. I mean—"

"Well, it's been a battle, but I've come out on top all right."

"I'm not talking about success. Are you *happy?*"

"To be honest, I'm so tired when I get home at night that there's no time for thinking about happiness or unhappiness."

"You haven't answered my question yet."

I reflected. I knew there had been a time when I would have replied in the affirmative without a moment's hesitation. The time just after our return from England, when I'd started as legal adviser to a finance company. It wasn't easy. I still had all my study debts to settle and I wasn't exactly earning a royal salary; and yet, undoubtedly, I was what Theo would have called a happy man. It couldn't last, of course. It didn't take me long to discover the limitations of any legal position. So I gave it some good, solid thinking. In a country developing at such a tempo, I decided, the most promising future lay in the economy, in industry. And right in the heart of our economic formula was mining. Once I'd sorted that out, the rest was, if not easy, at least predictable.

Experience on the Stock Exchange. I'd always been quick to learn. Then the transfer to Anglo-American. The advantage of the position lay in one's access to confidential information—often involving projects too trifling for such a giant company but an ideal starting point for a young entrepreneur. Provided one was willing to wait patiently for the right opening and then to pounce immediately. Sometimes a couple of hours could be decisive.

The moment I opened that particular file I knew my chance had come. Submissions and geological reports on a newly surveyed area in the Northern Transvaal. I didn't have nearly enough capital for such a project, but I knew it might be years before I would have another break like that. I simply had to get in before the file reached a Board meeting.

I didn't discuss it with Elise, knowing in advance what her reaction would be. Literally overnight I rounded up backers, personally risking every penny I possessed in the world, including everything I could borrow. And before Anglo-American had time to act, I'd acquired all the options myself.

There are people who have never forgiven me for it. And with Elise I had a series of bitter quarrels, the worst of our married life. But in my sort of work there isn't any room for sentiment. Kill or be killed. And if one is forced, from time to time, to step over corpses, well, then it is simply part of the game. One either has the instinct or lacks it; one either plays the game or stays right out of it. That is the first and, in effect, the only real choice involved. From that moment one only goes on. An experience no less exciting in its own way than big-game hunting. And the dividends are infinitely greater. Also the chances of failure: like the threat of death in the bush. Never a moment to relax or sit back. It is uphill, uphill all the time. Losing one's grip, even for an instant, may mean the end.

"Actually happiness is a sentimental notion, don't you agree?" I told Theo that afternoon. "But all right, to the extent in which it may be relevant, I'd say: Yes, I have nothing to complain about. Neither has Elise. Or my children. It won't be necessary for my son to go barefoot like I did."

He just sat looking at me, an expression of discontent on his face.

"But why do you ask?" I insisted. "Aren't *you* happy then?"

"No."

I hadn't expected such a frank reply.

"What's the matter then?"

"I've kept it to myself for years, Martin. One learns to live with it. But now that Dad has fallen ill—you know it's just a matter of time, don't you?"

"Yes, I know. But what has that got to do with your unhappiness?"

"When I was a kid, you know, I was quite content to follow you in everything you did." A wry smile. "I'm not blaming you, Martin. But at school it was hell to be told all the time, in every new standard I reached, that I had to follow my elder brother's good example. And you know how Dad and Ma always insisted that we had to do well in everything. So I decided I'd show you all. I'd show the whole world. I would become an architect and help to build a wholly new country. I'd force them to admit that I was *something* after all. Even if my heart wasn't in it."

"I still don't see what you're driving at."

"I want to be a farmer."

"A farmer?!"

"Don't laugh, please. I've always wanted to be one. But ever since we were kids everybody assumed you would inherit the family farm one day. And even though we could see you had no interest in farming we knew the place would be yours. That's normal, you're the eldest. But now that Dad has cancer..." He looked straight into my eyes; I made no attempt to avoid his stare. "Martin, you don't really want that farm, do you?"

I shrugged.

"I want you to discuss it with Dad. Ask him. Tell them. Perhaps it'll make him feel better. And it stands to reason I'll pay you every cent you want for it."

"Why don't you talk to them yourself?"

"You know very well they've never paid much attention to me, it's always been you. If you tell them, they'll listen to you."

"But if you're so keen on farming surely you can buy any farm you wish? You have enough money."

"I know. But it's more than just that. It's the family farm as such. I don't want to become a farmer just because I'm sick of the rat race. I want to go *there*. I want my children to walk barefoot and swim in the same dam I used to know when I was small."

I looked down at my hands.

"Will you do that for me, Martin? For heaven's sake don't get me wrong: I don't want to diddle you out of your inheritance. But I *know* you can't really care less about the farm."

"All right, I'll talk it over with them," I said, suddenly feeling grudging and threatened. I started paging through my files so he could see I was busy.

Naturally I didn't discuss it with anyone when we went down to the farm that weekend. I knew it would needlessly upset Dad. And what was the point of encouraging this new sentimental notion of Theo's? He'd always been a "man of the future": what was this sudden whim about returning to the past? My God, was he going soft in the head? Or had he just been hit by the blues which supposedly beset one in one's early forties? I had to protect him from himself.

After our return from the farm I telephoned him. To make it as easy as possible for him I said: "Listen, I discussed that idea of yours with Dad and Ma. But they won't hear of it. You know what Ma is like when she's made up her mind about something. And I honestly don't think it's wise to upset Dad too much in his present state."

"Of course." His voice was calm and drained of emotion. "I understand. Thanks anyway."

By way of recompense I saw to it that, soon afterwards, he got the contract to design a new business center in which I had a share. It would be one of the biggest projects he'd ever undertaken, a commission for which the best architects in the country had tendered. And it took some insistent diplomacy to persuade my colleagues, for I knew some of the other designs were really more promising than Theo's. But I wanted to help, him get over his sentimental delusion; and in the process he would be amply rewarded. No one could have expected me to do any more than that.

Why am I writing down more and more of what I would have preferred not to discuss? What is worse, it seems to become more and more of a "novel," dictated by a form of romanticism of which I've tried over many years to rid myself. And yet I have no choice but to take an unfaltering look not only at that weekend, but beyond it—the way one would peer through a windscreen smeared with gnats—at the entire landscape of my life. Perhaps that is the only remaining hell.

Strange that Charlie should also have spoken about "hell." As if one can never really escape from it.

We drove out of the city, towards the southwest. To Soweto. I'd never been there before (nor since). And what I remember of it is muddled—not just because of the accumulation of impressions, but because I was so furious with Charlie. And scared. I may as well admit it. It was, perhaps, the only experience in my adult life which truly scared me, while at the same time it was impossible to find any reason for it. For nothing happened. That was the worst. Nothing happened, but anything *might* happen at any moment. Suppose we were stopped by police? A man in my position. It would immediately be given a political angle. What was Martin Mynhardt doing in Soweto? They could break me for it if they wanted: in South Africa people had been broken for much less.

The houses. Not the shacks of iron and wood and junk I could vaguely recall from the Moroka one had driven past years ago, but identical oblong blocks with tiny doors and windows: tens, hundreds, thousands, tens of thousands of them. The mere uniformity was terrifying. My God, how would one ever escape from that maze once one was lost in it? Suppose Charlie dropped me and said: Now go home on your own? Smoke. It was still early afternoon, but the previous night's smoke still lay in a dark bank over the townships while a new layer was already beginning to form. Children playing and kicking up a row. Potholes and ditches in the dusty road. Rubbish dumps on every street corner. Ribbed dogs scavenging for food and slinking off whenever someone approached. Women in bedraggled little gardens behind wire fences: some wearing the long skirts and headscarves of rural areas, others in minis or the shrill colors of city fashions; slacks and platform heels. Some pregnant, with bulging bellies; others holding suckling infants to their breasts or carrying them on their backs; still others as thin as reeds, with sharply pointed bras. Boys gambling with cards or pebbles or coins in the middle of the street. Here and there an old man on a tomato box in the sun in front of his house. And then the open wastelands between townships. Rubble heaps, erosion ditches, the skeletons of old cars; children scuttling like cockroaches in the garbage of smoky mounds. Old thin women poking in the rubble like molting black fowls, or crows, or vultures. Teams of boys playing soccer in the dust, with soccer balls, tennis balls, bundles of rags, stuffed stockings. Netting-wire fences fluttering with windblown litter, like a parody of Christmas: papers, plastic bags, tufts of wool and hair, patches of multicolored rags. Churches, halls, schools with bare playing grounds surrounded by frayed trees. Jazzy shops. Petrol pumps. The face brick and barbed wire of police stations. And heaped up beside the dusty lanes serving as streets: all the refuse of a human existence—broken baths, tins, drums, cardboard boxes, torn-off car doors or shattered windscreens, bits of hose pipe and lengths of wire, tires, chamber pots, plastic buckets, three-legged pots, aluminum casseroles, the rags and remnants of discarded clothes, dead cats, turds, the tattered remains of carpets and curtains. At that time of the day there weren't many cars among the little houses and shanties, but what could be seen ranged from dilapidated old American models and patched-up Volkswagens to a few shiny Mercedes, Jags, and Citroëns.

"You could have come by bus too," said Charlie. "Did you know they organize coach tours through the townships, like through the game reserve? See the natives in their natural habitat. Please don't feed the animals."

"That's enough, Charlie. It's time to go home now. You wanted to show me, and now I've seen it. Let's go."

"How do you know what I want to show you? Give me a chance, man. We're first going round to my place. What makes you think I'm such a bad host?"

He paid no attention to my objections. Somewhere in the midst of all the identical little boxes he found his house and stopped. From all directions in the neighborhood swarms of small children converged on the Mercedes. If the car got damaged, I swore grimly, there would be hell to pay.

A thickset, neatly but plainly dressed woman opened the door.

"Meet my friend Mr. Mynhardt," Charlie said. (I still don't know who she was.)

In the small, tidy front room we sat down—Charlie on a straight-backed dining chair, I on the floral Chesterfield sofa. The cement floor was covered with a blue linoleum. Plastic flowers in a vase on the ball-and-claw table. A calendar on the wall.

"Charlie, are you sure it's not against the law for me to be here?"

"Of course it's against the law. But don't worry. Here's the tea." He rose to take the tray from the woman, offering it first to her, then to me.

"And how are you, Mr. Mynhardt?" she asked in a neutral voice.

What could I reply to that? I said something noncommittal. She smiled. And so the tone for the rest of our jolted conversation was set. I had the impression that Charlie, sitting back and watching me, was thoroughly enjoying himself, while all the time I was trying to concentrate, as unobtrusively as possible, on what I could see of the street behind the gingham curtains, in case a police van passed or stopped outside.

There was a constant backdrop of sound: radios or record players, playing mostly jazz, and just too far off to distinguish any tune (most of the stuff probably didn't have a tune anyway), leaving only a disquieting pulsation on the threshold of one's consciousness as accompaniment to our uncomfortable small talk. Children bursting out crying or shouting or screaming. The loud voices of women conversing in the street, undaunted by the three or four or five blocks separating them. Dogs barking; one howling interminably, accompanied by the rhythmic sickening smacks of the thong or rubber pipe with which he was being beaten.

It seemed like at least an hour before Charlie finally rose. I followed him in nearly indecent haste, almost neglecting to say goodbye to the enigmatic woman. Her hand cool and dry in mine. A secretive smile. "So nice to have met you, Mr. Mynhardt."

But that proved to be only the beginning. I don't think Charlie had planned it in advance; but he was a master of improvisation. I was still under the impression that we were on our way out of the labyrinth of child-block houses, threatening in their very passivity, when he suddenly stopped again.

"Something wrong?" I asked, startled.

"No, we're just dropping in on an old pal of mine."

"But Charlie—"

"Relax, man, be a sport. It's not every day I have the chance to treat you."

Did he want to treat me or to terrorize me? I'm still not sure. All I could tell with a measure of certainty after another hour had passed, was that he had no intention of taking me home before dark. And as the afternoon grew older, in our visits to one "old pal" after the other, the tone of the townships changed almost imperceptibly. One became aware of the piercing sirens of trains following each other in the distance in more and more rapid succession; of more cars appearing in the streets, sending clouds of dust up against the windows; of a low wave of sound approaching from far away, the dull thunder of the crowd—returning home—the thousands, the hundreds of thousands of workers vomited from Johannesburg, from *iGoli*. The din became more comprehensive, at the same time more general and more intimate. And with the coming of the dark the entire obscene spectacle of human life from cradle to grave was reduced to sound. In the hours we spent there I became conscious—not with the exact formulation of statistics, but with the warm biological shock of sudden discovery in my guts—of babies being born and old people dying in my immediate vicinity; of people being murdered and others raped; of men and women making love or assaulting one another; of fathers getting drunk and children beaten. All the events taking place all over the world every day, but here with an immediacy and an overwhelming obtrusiveness I'd never experienced so violently before.

Outside in the increasing dusk the noise of soccer-playing children went on until it was too dark to see; complemented by the deeper voices of men joining them after work. And gradually, as in a cross-fade in a film, the outdoor sound was transformed into indoor sound. More and more radios. People talking in loud voices. Great explosions of laughter. Terrifying quarrels, screams, shouts. Short staccato silences. And, because of the innumerable houses huddled so closely together, the staggering sensation of the *presentness* of everything became even more overpowering. And one reacted to it, not with one's ears, or nose, or mouth or whatever, but physiologically, with one's whole body.

More and more strangers drifted into the house of the friend where we were having drinks, lured like moths by an open flame. Not that there was all that much light, for none of the houses we visited had electricity. Outside, there were mesh-protected lamps on tall posts at street corners, each huddled selfishly over its own small pool of light. And in the distance, marking the course of the high barbed wire fences enclosing the townships, were blinding floodlights reminiscent of the photographs of concentration camps.

In the end there must have been twenty or more people crammed into the small front room. Women disappeared from time to time and reappeared with food—prepared in the kitchen and in the kitchens of neighboring houses, I presumed, judging from the seemingly endless number of plates and knives and forks passed from hand to hand until everybody had been served. We ate on our laps; what it was, I couldn't make out, and I didn't want to give offense by asking. All those bodies, the smell of perspiration, the powder and perfume of the women: in the unsteady light of candles and lamps there was an air of unreality about it all. I can't remember anything of the conversations—there were too many of them going on all around me at the same time. No one seemed to pay any particular attention to me anyway, I was just one of the many who'd happened to drop in, Charlie's pal, meet Mr. Mynhardt.

I felt a growing panic to get out. Oppressed by the heavy physical warmth of the room I made my way to the window to breathe in the cool, dusty night air. But after a few minutes I moved away again, not wanting to be spotted from the street by a roving police van.

At long last Charlie rose and announced: "Well, boys, see you. Got to go now."

I followed him hastily.

"Now listen, Charlie, this is enough."

"We're just beginning to loosen up, man."

"I'm not taking any more nonsense from you. I want to go home."

"We're going to a shebeen first."

"For God's sake!"

Laughing in his boisterous way, he turned the ignition key.

"Give me the keys," I ordered. "It's my car. I'll drive."

Much to my surprise he complied without any objection, leaving the car idling as he got out on his side so that we could change places. But of course: we hadn't been going for five minutes before I was hopelessly lost. Apparently unconcerned, he sat humming happily, drumming on the roof with his fingers to keep time.

"Now stop that, Charlie and tell me how to get out of here."

"O.K., man, don't get sore." He began to give me elaborate instructions, which I followed warily, not sure I could trust him. Suddenly he shouted: "Stop!"

I slammed on the brakes. "What's the matter?"

"We're here." He got out.

"Charlie, come back!"

"We're first looking in here."

"Go to hell! I'll drive home on my own."

"See you then."

I pulled away with screeching tires, but stopped within a few yards as soon as it hit me that without him I'd be in an even more hopeless position than with him. Not to speak of the very real danger of being attacked by a gang of tsotsis in the dark. And how would I be able to explain my presence if a police patrol were to stop me?

Furious and frustrated, I got out of the car and locked it.

I wasn't sure what to expect. But the shebeen turned out to be a house like any other, with a gathering of men and women inside, drinking in the front room, served by an unbelievably fat woman, Auntie Mame. After Charlie had introduced me, I was more or less ignored. And it was quite a shock when he ordered me a whisky as if it were the most natural thing in the world.

We went to other shebeens too, afterwards. At least one of them was a luxurious place by any standards, a double-storied house with soft carpets and modern furniture; here conversation was hushed, limited to small groups. Doctors, businessmen, journalists, according to Charlie's nonchalant introduction.

"But how can you bring me to a place like this?" I asked. "Suppose one of your journalists recognizes me—"

"Calm down. They're all off duty."

And then there was another place, a dingy little den, reverberating with sound, one dark whorl of bodies writhing and dancing to the rhythm of earsplitting music; one could hardly see for the smoke;

and mixed with it was the bittersweet smell of hash. By that time I had no defenses left and abandoned myself to whatever Charlie wanted us to do, too exhausted even to be angry. God alone knows what he gave me to drink. Probably *skokiaan*. Everything was pervaded with the sour, pungent smell of beer. *Mqombothi*, Charlie spelled it out for me, relishing every syllable.

It must have been nearly dawn when we stumbled out into the dangerous night, my eyes and temples throbbing with a headache worse than anything I'd ever experienced before. I couldn't see straight; unable to grasp what was happening I had to hold on to the car while Charlie unlocked the doors. Suddenly I began to vomit. Steadying me with his hands, he quietly went on talking and laughing, comforting me in the way Welcome Nyaluza had helped me once, many years before. It was the lowest I'd ever sunk in Charlie's presence, retching helplessly like that, my trousers and shoes covered in vomit, while he gently held on to me, unperturbed by it all.

Slumped in my seat I sat beside him, my head lolling against the half-opened window, barely conscious of what was going on around us. One thing did strike me, though: however dark it was, surely no later than four in the morning, the streets were already swarming with people, an endless throng of them on their way to the stations and to work. To *iGoli*.

"Well," Charlie laughed. "Not a bad party, hey?" His voice didn't even sound tired. I made no attempt to answer. All my anger and resentment and disapproval had been broken down; he'd shattered the last remains of my dignity and self-respect; the more miserable I'd become during the night the more it had seemed to stimulate him.

He stopped in front of my apartment block in Joubert Park. I didn't even know that he'd been aware of the existence of the place; I'd certainly never mentioned it to him before. But I was too tired to ask. With his arm around me he supported me, a few steps at a time, to the lift. In the apartment he ran a bath for me. He would probably have undressed me as well if I hadn't stopped him. Afterwards he helped me into my bed. He probably caught some sleep too; but when I stumbled, dazed, from my bedroom just after nine o'clock, he was already waiting on one of the deep chairs in the lounge, as fresh as any proverbial daisy.

It hadn't been the first time I'd stayed out for a night, so I knew Elise wouldn't be worried; but I phoned her from the office anyway. Women like these small attentions. In the course of the day Charlie saw to it that the suit I'd worn the night before was cleaned, so I could go home in the clothes I'd been wearing the previous day. Neither by word nor gesture did he ever refer to that night again. And I didn't either.

But I wish I could find an explanation for it. Did he really try to be hospitable and generous showing me "his place," or was it all part of a giant insult? Did he want to entertain me, or play cat and mouse with me? All I know is that it was entirely different from my friendship with Welcome in London. In many ways they were similar: I've said so before. But there was one major difference. Welcome and I had been friends. But with Charlie I always felt constrained to either defend or prove something. And it was the same with him. (For Bernard's sake?) So we could never go beyond a certain point. Except for that one inexplicable night.

Or can it all be reduced to the fact that I'd grown older since I'd known Welcome? Somewhere between the two of them something had happened to me: I'd lost something. Perhaps. Perhaps not. One should be careful not to dramatize it too much.

✧ ✧ ✧ ✧

Putting down the newspaper, I looked at Louis sleeping with his back to me. There was something terribly familiar about the situation: his bed against the opposite wall, mine here, the well-worn green carpet between us, the wash table, the gauze in front of the window. Bernard's room in the outbuilding. Our long nocturnal conversations. Seeing Louis's blonde crown above the blankets was like a blow in the solar plexus. Not because he reminded me of Bernard but because, in that fleeting instant, he *was* Bernard. A new Bernard. The inescapable Bernard.

Hurriedly I got up. As I put the paper on the small bed table, my wristwatch tinkled against the opaque glass shade of the lamp. The sound was so familiar it made me freeze for a moment, yet I had to search my thoughts before it came back to me. Of course: the sound of the flower-shaped shade on the wall the night I'd groped for the glass of water, during that illness in my childhood. By that time, the doctor had said, I had already survived the crisis.

7

ALTHOUGH IT WAS FIVE past four already, the house was still quiet. Only from the kitchen came subdued sounds. Ma's door was closed. For a moment I stopped in front of Dad's gun rack in the passage, stroking one of the polished butts with my palm. Perhaps I could try to find a duiker or a bushbuck in the veld.

But not without glasses! Thwarted, I left the house with empty hands, closing the gauze door gently behind me. Outside the winter sun was growing watery.

Without any aim or inclination I strolled through the yard and past the wild fig. High up on the slope I could still hear the steady rhythm of the picks, digging the grave.

"Goduka kwedini!"

I didn't feel like going up there again. Almost mechanically I sauntered past the dairy and Dad's study and the stone wall of the small graveyard towards the dry bed of the valley below. On either side of the footpath the fields lay scorched into the earth, blackened by the sun. The lower dam was quite empty, the mud cracked in an intricate web. The dam in which I'd nearly drowned.

Like a sleepwalker I went on, unable to choose or change direction or to stop myself; cursing, again, those expensive Italian shoes with their smooth soles which caused me to slip or stumble every few yards. I should have brought my old hunting boots with me. But of course, I hadn't really planned to go for any long walks over the weekend.

Hunting is the only relic of my Early Romantic Period which I still allow myself. Nowadays it is restricted to one trip a year, obviously in winter when the season is open; either in the Northern Transvaal Bushveld or in South-West Africa, where I can link it with a business trip to some of my mining concerns. Those few days every year, in the company of a small group of close friends, I can escape from the pressures of the world more completely than in any other way I know of. (Except for that week in Mozambique with Bea.) Nothing else is of importance on a hunt; the world is irrelevant and remote. All that matters is that daily excursion into the bush, three or four of us in our oldest clothes, with boots and khaki hats, each with his trusted .308. Crawling from the tent at the first sign of dawn when the frost lies white on the ground; scalding coffee on the fire kindled from last night's still-glowing coals; the gnashing of boots on the hard grass. Everything reduced to watchfulness, eyes and ears prepared for the slightest movement or sound in the bush. The sun rising. Beetles in the white grass. Cobwebs shimmering in the early light. Hornbills in the thorn trees. If you're unfortunate, a babbler following you from tree to tree, scaring off the game. Quails whirring up from right under your boots. By lunchtime, if all goes well, you already have your impala or kudu or oryx. Liver roasted on the coals: a somewhat overestimated dish, too savage and too rich to my taste, but part of the ritual.

The moment you see the buck jerking up his head. Taking aim. The final jump. Sometimes, as you come up to him, the death struggle is not yet completed, the surprisingly slender neck swaying and beating in the grass; the large black eyes clouding up under a bluish film; the thin trickle of blood from the nostrils.

On a few occasions I hunted bigger game; once a lion. Then the experience is even more intense because one's own death becomes a factor in the game. Danger; fear. In a situation without any hope of gain: risking your life in exchange for the possibility of killing an animal. No more. Perhaps it is the simplicity of the game which lends it its savage charm. Neither life nor death can be represented or superseded by anything else. One is driven back to the most elementary beginnings.

It isn't always neat or nice. Like the day I shot the oryx: I'd aimed dead on the shoulder; I'd heard the thud of the bullet—but all twenty or thirty antelopes in the herd thundered off through the yellow grass, behind red antheaps and dull green thorn trees. There wasn't even a blood spoor. And yet I knew I'd struck him, and we spent hours trying to find him in the grass; but when it became too dark I had to give up and go back to the camp amid the good-natured jeering of the others. Towards noon the next day we saw the vultures circling and we found him where he'd fallen, less than a hundred yards from where I'd shot him. Right in the heart. It often happens like that with a heart shot: the animal racing off at full speed and dropping, unnoticed, in its tracks. By that time the oryx had been torn to pieces, everything covered in blood and slime and dung. Only the graceful horns, more than a yard long, still testified to what he'd been. But it was senseless to hack them off. And I was left with a strange ambiguous feeling: satisfaction for having proved to my friends that I'd shot him after all; disgust about the loss. More than disgust. A peculiar aching sadness about something beautiful that had gone to waste so stupidly.

But even that is part of the game when you go hunting. You can never be sure of what you'll bring back with you, or whether you'll find anything at all. Death remains unpredictable. Everything lies exposed to its simplicity.

And then the nights in the camp, the meat strung up in the trees and the heavy leadwood logs burning as high as a house. Food and liquor and good male company. And later, the macabre laughter of the jackals or the chilling whoop of a hyena. There you're back in a primitive world reduced to your proper dimensions. Day and night death hovers in the air, and you learn to live with it. After a few days you can return home and resume your work, retaining what has happened to you: deep within you it lives on, beyond all dreams, bedded in your blood and bones. Africa is a basic and terrifying truth.

On the other side of the barren valley the bushes became more dense. Thorny shrubs, pale blue plumbago, euphorbias. It was the beginning of the stream running between the two rows of hills. Somewhere thereabouts Grandpa had hidden the illicit still in which he'd brewed his infernal white lightning. The stream itself was dry, but there must have been a subterranean course left, because after the outer layers of dried grey tanglewood the bushes became greener and more luxuriant, more massive. I was having problems with my shoes and without my glasses it was almost impossible to find my way. At the same time there was something exhilarating about this penetration of brushwood and bush, and the mere consciousness of subterranean water. Suddenly it became easier to understand the deeper passions of the old water diviner, his communication with those submerged forces which had caused the stick to twist and turn so violently in his fat hands.

As I progressed slowly into the narrow kloof, the bush grew steadily more dense. The trees were taller, with lithe vines suspended from the high branches. Bracken and wild fern. Even palms. It was the beginning of the virgin forest, with the musty smell of rotting vegetation, a resilient mass of decayed leaves and branches so thick I couldn't hear the sound of my own feet; only from time to time the sharp crackling of a breaking twig. There was an awareness of life all around me: rustlings in the grass, a whispering in the foliage, branches swaying suddenly without wind, small hooves pattering off.

Bushbuck, monkeys, lizards, louries. These were the very entrails of the farm. I could feel it and smell it and hear it, taste it on my tongue, while overhead the trees broke like a great green wave, a silence hissing in my ears.

Fighting my crisscross way through the strip of forest I finally reached the stream again. Here in the shade there were long shallow pools left, muddy and covered with green slime; dragonflies and large mosquitoes and other insects hovering above. A half-rotten log lay partly submerged in the thick water, like the carcass of a dead animal. Perhaps, if one stepped into this mud, it would get hold of one and start swallowing one like a big wet mouth, gulping one down into a slithery throat, down, down, through layers of loam and clay, to the rich fertile courses feeding the earth.

Clutching at monkey ropes and lianas I found it easier to make my way along the streambed, jumping from rock to rock. Once my slippery soles gave way, but a hairy vine saved me from falling. I stood still for a while, regaining my breath, uncertain of where to go next.

He was sitting so utterly still on his rock that, with my myopic eyes, I first thought it was a broken trunk. But then he moved. Thank God I hadn't brought the gun with me, otherwise I might have shot at him. Who would have expected to find a human being in that tangled wood?

It was an old Black man, I noticed as I drew nearer, so old that the wool on his head looked like grey fungus; wrinkled and humped like a monkey, with a long-stemmed pipe in his sunken mouth. He sat watching me in silence, unmoving on his haunches. But his small black eyes never left me for an instant.

"Molo," I said.

"Molo." He still didn't move.

"What are you doing here?"

He looked at me placidly.

Hesitant, I repeated my question in Xhosa.

Taking his time, he removed the pipe from his mouth. There was no single tooth inside, only bare pink gums.

"I came for the child that was sick," he said. "But now the mother has died."

"Who told you she was dead?"

"No one told me. I know it."

"You can't know it just like that."

"I know it."

"Where do you come from?"

"Far away." He made a wide, vague gesture with one of his stick-like arms. As his kaross swung open I could see his breasts, mere loose folds of skin, like the dugs of an old woman. "I go my way, here, there, like the wind."

"You must go away."

"Who are you?" he asked. There was nothing discourteous in his manner, just plain curiosity.

"I'm the *baas* of this farm."

"I've never seen you before."

"I don't live here. I only come from time to time."

"I see."

"Where do you live?" I asked.

"Nowhere."

Unable to think of anything more to say, I turned to walk on. He made no move to call me back. But just after I'd passed him, something made me turn round. He was still watching me, his toothless mouth wrinkled in a grin.

"What are you laughing at?"

"Nothing."

Having nothing better to do I returned to him and sat down on a rock on the opposite side of the dry streambed. In other circumstances I wouldn't have spoken to him, but in that forest, with nothing and no one nearby, I felt a strange urge to talk. Perhaps the same curiosity that had stirred in him.

"How come you don't have anywhere to live?" I asked.

"I'm following the Momlambo."

"I don't understand."

"Look here." From under his kaross he took a short stick. I went closer to have a look. It looked like a short walking stick, no more than a foot in length, finely carved on one end, and, as I bent over to have a better look, an amazing pattern of tiny inlaid shells.

"Where did you get it?"

"From the Momlambo."

"Who's the Momlambo?"

"Don't you know her then?"

"No."

He grinned. "If you put all the beauty of all women together, it makes the Momlambo."

"Where did you find her?"

"No one finds the Momlambo. She finds you." For a long while he sat puffing at his long pipe. When he started speaking again, he was looking right past me: "When you're young and you're walking all by yourself in the veld; or you're sleeping and you dream of woman and you wake up with a horn here"—pointing to his shriveled genitals—"then you know it's the Momlambo's work."

"And that stick?"

"It's Momlambo's stick."

"But you said—"

"When I was a young man," he said, interrupting me, "I lived in the Transkei. Other side of Umtata. My father was the headman in our village and I would have become headman after him. But then, one day, I went to Butterworth. On foot. Walking with this ache for a woman inside me. Now when one walks with that sort of ache, your head is like a pot of water on a woman's skull. Unless you cover it with leaves all the water spills out on the ground. And whatever gets spilled is drunk by the Momlambo. And when I looked up, she was coming towards me."

"How?" I asked. In spite of myself, spellbound by his tale, I became a child again, sitting among the huts, drinking in every word of the stories told by the old Black women.

"One moment all was quiet," said the old man. "Then a wind sprang up. A whirlwind, turning round me, round me. And in the wind I heard the laughter of a woman. Like water bubbling. The wind gathered more and more dust and leaves as it went on spinning until, all of a sudden, it died down. And there the Momlambo stood before me."

"What did she look like?"

"Beads, beads all round her head. And copper rings on her ankles and her wrists. And a small beaded *inciyo* in front here." He gestured again. "That was all. The most beautiful woman who had ever lived."

"Did she speak to you?"

"She just beckoned with her hand like this. But when I ran to her to catch her in my arms, she was gone. It was just the wind again, and the dust and leaves. And the sound of her laughter." Another long session of eager puffing at the pipe. "And when it was all over and everything was quiet again, I saw this stick lying there. I knew it was the Momlambo's sign. To say that she had taken a liking in me."

"Was that all?"

"That was all. And my head was so filled with her magic that I clean forgot what I wanted to go to Butterworth for. I turned back and went home. And my heart was jumping like a small buck inside me. But at the same time it was as heavy as a blanket in which a dead man is wrapped."

"Why?"

"Because I knew. The stick was her sign, you see. It meant she would come back to me if I wanted her. But she would only come if I did a terrible thing."

"What terrible thing?"

"If a man desires the Momlambo, if you want to sleep with her under one kaross and untie her *inciyo*, then you must kill your own father in your heart."

"Surely you didn't do that?"

"What else can you do when the Momlambo calls you? She is not a woman one can say no to."

"So you murdered him?"

"I went to see the witchdoctor, the *igqira*. And he spoke to the *izinyanya*, the spirits of the ancestors. And then my father died. It was I who killed him in my heart, because I couldn't do otherwise."

"And since that day you've been following the Momlambo?"

"All the time, all the way."

"And does she come when you call her?"

He nodded slowly, grinning.

"Why don't you call her now?" I asked on an impulse, deliberately taunting him. "Then I can see her too."

He looked at me in silence for a long time. "Every man has his own Momlambo," he said at last. "You must wait for your own whirlwind."

It was my turn not to answer. Screwing up my eyes to see better, I studied him in silence. Small and shriveled he sat opposite me, huddled in his stinking kaross of musk-cat skins. In spite of myself I remembered how, whenever we'd been naughty as children, we'd been scared by warnings about "the Kaffir." *Eat your food, else the Kaffir will catch you.—If you don't go to bed now, the Kaffir will come and get you.*

Here was the Kaffir, sitting a yard away from me, that hideous old monkey-man with his long-stemmed pipe and his exquisite little stick. And I wasn't scared. I smiled.

When I looked up again, he was gone. That was the most shocking moment of the whole encounter. There had been no sound to warn me, not a flickering of a movement. When I raised my head, he'd simply disappeared. Without a trace into that wilderness. As if he'd never been sitting there on his rock at all.

✧ ✧ ✧

Within a single moment the forest had become evil. The delightful luxury of a minute before—ferns and cycads, yellowwood, alder trees, stinkwood and brushwood—had become a menacing jungle. The dried bed with its string of green pools had become putrid; the tangle of thorns and branches and vines and growths a bewildering gloom. I had to get out. But in my panic I'd lost all sense of direction. Instead of following the streambed or looking for a game path, I thrust myself headlong into the densely matted bush. Within a few minutes I was lost. And behind me, somewhere close by but invisible, he was lurking like a shadow, the evil old man. The Kaffir. I knew he was watching me with his monkey eyes, from behind some trunk or thorny shrub; I knew he'd made up the whole fantastic story just to catch me. He wanted to ensnare me here and then kill me off like a trapped buck.

Furiously I jerked myself loose from the vines and branches clinging to me, feeling the thorns tearing and tugging at my clothes. Threads and small frayed tatters remained behind on the sharp twigs.

Inch by inch I fought my way through. It was dusky in the forest; the sun would probably be down soon. How would I survive the cold and terror of a winter night in these thickets?

Was I making any progress, or just penetrating deeper and deeper into the bush? Helpless, I stopped, wondering whether I should turn back. But in whatever direction I went on, I was bound to reach the edge of the wood sooner or later. The kloof wasn't all that wide. A matter of a few hundred yards, I tried to convince myself. I just had to keep on. Muddle through.

Slightly calmer than before I resumed my clawing and tearing. My hands scratched and cut, I forced a tunnel through the undergrowth, crawling on all fours on the crackling rotten humus for minutes on end. Whenever the tangle eased up, allowing me to proceed on foot again, my legs would get caught in vines or loose branches, causing me to stumble and fall every few yards. Every now and then I stopped, convinced that I'd seen him, here, there, behind me or to the left or right, bent double in soundless laughter, knowing he was going to get me sooner or later. The Kaffir.

My chest was burning. My breath came jerking through my raw throat. My God, if I were to have a heart attack here, no one would ever find me in time. Weeks or months later they might stumble on my skeleton. No one would know. Except for him. There was no time to rest, night was falling fast now. All I could do was to keep on and on.

The first time I stopped again was when I recognized something familiar on a thorny branch in front of me. A small patch of material. For a moment I refused to believe it: it had to be someone else's. But the rag belonged unmistakably to my expensive imported jacket. I could match it with a tear on my shoulder. How on earth had I started crawling in circles? If that was true I was really lost. Night would catch me here, and that would be the end. I wouldn't even see him coming in for the kill in the dark.

I had to keep cool. Good heavens, it wasn't the first time I'd been in the veld on my own. All those hunting expeditions. But it had never been quite as rough as this. One couldn't even see the sky, there were no landmarks. And the Kaffir knew it, of course.

There was only one way out: I had to climb a tree. For a few minutes I blundered on in search of one tall and strong enough, with accessible branches. I had to take off my shoes first. On tender bare feet I edged up against the rough trunk, cutting my soles on sharp ridges and thorns, until I managed to break through the network of smaller branches and look out across the kloof. Not that it was much use, shortsighted as I was; but at least it was possible to find my bearings again. That way. I had to hurry now. The sun was sinking fast, a mere hand's breadth above the hills.

Impatient, I put on my shoes again and struggled on. My whole body was aching. The sharp cuts and abrasions of thorns and nettles; the more dull and general pain of fatigue and overexertion. He followed me all the way. I knew it. I could smell his pipe and his filthy kaross. He must be a witchdoctor himself, communicating with evil spirits, with the *izinyanya*. But I grimly clenched my teeth. He wouldn't get me. I was *baas* on this farm.

Torn, and smeared with dirt, I crawled on, sometimes flat on my stomach where the branches reached down nearly to the ground. More slowly than before, for now I was trying to keep my wits and not to lose my direction again. If only I could make it before dark.

And at last, panting, exhausted, and ashamed, I broke through the last cluster of euphorbias to reach the fringe of the kloof. Peaceful and strange the dry landscape lay before me in the last light. Behind me the bush was dark, a green-black mass huddled over its terrible secrets. But I'd escaped. I was free.

You know, I think it's the people I'll remember long after I've forgotten all the rest. I still dream of them at night. Not our boys or UNITA or the FNLA or the MPLA or the Cubans. Not the Portuguese on the farms or in the towns and villages. Not even the refugees. But those people belonging to the land itself. The thin Blacks, like sticks planted in their fields, mostly women and children, because the men had gone off to the army. The people with their wooden ploughs and their pounding blocks and their homemade rakes. I'm sure, if we pass that way again a hundred years from now, we'll still find them there just like that. Living with the seasons, like plants and stuff. If it rains, they get wet. If the sun shines, it scorches them. It makes no

difference. They're right there, all the time. They didn't speak to us. They spoke to no one. They were just there. The armies came and went, like bloody swarms of locusts. They were robbed and beaten and plundered and murdered and raped and bombed and fucked around. But they remained. One might just as well try to get rid of stones. And that's why, every day, I asked all over again: What the bloody hell was I doing there?

✧ ✧ ✧

Limping, I went home slowly. My chest was aching so badly that only very shallow breathing was possible. I was covered in perspiration. The cold penetrated my clothes, burning my skin. But at least I was on my way home. From time to time I stopped to rest for a moment. Everything around me was vague and misty, as if the whole world had drawn away from me. There was nothing to hold on to; everything remained beyond my grasp.

Reaching the slope below the dairy, just after I'd passed the graveyard, I stepped into a fresh cake of dung. I looked down in helpless rage. My God, the final indignity. Wasn't I going to be spared anything at all? Scraping my shoe on the rough ground I tried to rid myself of the stinking mess, but a small wedge remained stuck in the corner between heel and sole. I picked up a twig to rake it out, but in my unsteady position, balancing myself on one leg, I smudged my hand. Nearly frantic with frustration I tried to wipe it clean on my trousers. But it wasn't so easy to get rid of it. It was as if part of the farm itself had rubbed off on me, a dirty smear.

8

IN THE LAST DARK RED dusk the woman arrived on the farm. Ma was feeding the chickens, and I had just come round the corner of the house in my torn and messy clothes, when she approached on the dust road down the slope, swinging her legs in long even strides. Seeing her, the dogs stormed towards her, barking madly. Unlike other Blacks, who invariably lost their heads immediately they saw those brutes, the woman stopped and waited, calm and dignified, until Ma had chased them off.

It was Thokozile's mother. I heard later that she'd walked more than thirty miles that day. A statuesque woman, more than six feet tall, brown as a rock, straight as an aloe, with the sort of aristocratic dignity one finds only among the poorest of peasants.

She addressed Ma in Xhosa. I stood on one side, listening to her, intrigued in spite of myself.

"My child is dead."

"Yes," Ma admitted. "Your child is dead."

"My daughter Thokozile."

"Your daughter."

"The *lobola* hasn't even been paid in full yet."

"We'll pay you from Mandisi's cattle."

She silently shook her head with the high black turban, as if it wasn't really important.

After a while she continued: "All her children are dead too."

"No," said Ma. "It's only Thokozile. The children were unharmed."

"But the children she hasn't had yet: they are all dead."

"Yes, they died with her."

"What about the other four?"

"They're up there. I've arranged for someone to look after them. I kept the baby with me last night."

"I must go to them."

Without waiting, she turned away from us to go up the hill behind the house, to the huts. She was just as straight as before, her strides just as long and steady. But now she was crying. More than crying: howling as I'd never heard man or beast howl before. Striding slowly and purposefully into the dusk, she raised her head to the sky and howled. The sound struck against the distant hills, and came back; and went on. It was no human voice. It was as if the dark red earth had itself become a voice, thrusting up through her feet and body, through bursting entrails and tearing lungs and breaking heart, howling against the bleeding night sky.

9

MA WENT TO BED EARLY. We'd spent a few minutes talking in the kitchen while we waited for boiling water to fill her bottle. In spite of having rested in the afternoon, she looked haggard and her square shoulders were drooping. I sat on a corner of the table while she went on poking the fire aimlessly, unnecessarily.

"And what happened to you this afternoon?" she asked after some time. "Did the jackals get hold of you?"

"I went down to the kloof, to the wood. Coming back I lost my way."

She gave a dry chuckle. "One can't get lost in that little strip of wood."

"I did."

She spent some time pushing about the pots on the stove.

"I found an odd creature there," I said after a moment's hesitation. "Old as the mountains, all shriveled up. Wears a kaross."

"Must be old Hlatikhulu. He sometimes comes here."

"Who's he?"

"I've heard he usually circumcises the boys when they're initiated. For the rest he just comes and goes. Now you see him, now you don't."

"He said he'd come to see the sick child."

"It's possible."

"But he also knew about Thokozile's death."

She shrugged. "They have a way of knowing such things."

"How?"

"It just happens. How must I know? I've seen strange things among them, I can tell you."

The water was boiling. She filled the bottle and held it sideways to turn in the screw top.

"What have you decided about the farm, Ma?" I prodded her gently.

"Tomorrow is another day."

"But we're going home tomorrow!"

"Time enough." She pushed the bottle under her arm. "Well, good night then, sonny. Don't stay up too late, there's a long day ahead of you. And it hasn't really been a holiday to you, this weekend."

After a while I went through to the lounge and sat down before the fire. Louis was lying on the mat, his back propped up against a chair. The newspapers lay in an untidy heap on one side. He was staring into the flames, not even looking up when I came in. I hoped his anger had settled by now: he'd had enough time to get it out of his system and calm down. I was tired and in no mood for further arguments.

"Where did you go this afternoon?" he asked, without looking up from the fire.

"Went for a walk."

"Why didn't you wake me to go with you?"

"I wanted to be alone." Just as well he hadn't been there to watch my ignominious flight. But then, if he'd been with me I would probably not have acted like a lunatic anyway. More indulgent, almost apologetic, I said: "I didn't think you'd want to go with me. You've been avoiding us so pointedly these last months."

"I can't help it." For a long time he stared silently into the grate. Small blue flames were flickering in the coals. Then he looked up: "It's just something—I don't know how to put it, Dad—something that's gone limp or lame inside me. Because of everything that's happening."

"What is happening?"

"Nothing in particular." He shifted impatiently. "All the ordinary stupidity, the inhumanity fossilized in a system, all the ritual cruelty, the bloody vulgarity and callousness. What can one *do* about it, Dad?"

"One's got to learn to live with it. What else?"

"Jesus!"

"We've already spoken about it today, haven't we?" I said quietly.

"But we didn't get anywhere. And then you just went off on your own. As always."

I didn't answer.

"You know, those few holidays I spent with Bernard in the Cape," he said pensively, staring at the coals. "I mean, before it all happened. We often went for long walks together. One weekend he took me to the Cedar Berg. With two old Colored guides and pack donkeys." A pause. Perhaps he didn't even realize he was talking to me. "Or else we explored the Cape. The Mountain. Along the beaches. All over."

"I suppose he would have made a better father for you than I," I said, unable to keep the edge out of my voice.

"Aren't you going to do anything, Dad?" he asked.

"About what?"

"To try and help him. A man with your influence—"

"He's already been sentenced."

"Even so."

"It's out of the question."

"You've been friends for so many years."

"He forfeited that friendship."

Leisurely picking up a fire iron he started poking the coals, sending a spray of sparks up into the chimney. He looked up at me again. "Didn't he ever try to get in touch with you while he was underground?"

I could feel the blood flowing from my face. "Of course not," I said hastily.

"Strange."

"What's so strange about it? Why should he have tried to contact me?"

"I just wondered."

A terrible suspicion stirred in me.

"Louis, did *you* see him during that time?"

"I was in the training camp. And then in Angola."

"But after you came back. He wasn't arrested before the end of February."

His back was stiff with silent resistance.

"I know he felt very close to you, Louis. It meant a lot to him to have you as his godson."

He didn't move. And in that instant I knew. And in a surge of bitterness and anger I thought: *This I won't forgive you Bernard. It's all right that you expected* me *to risk my life for you. But not that you tried to draw my son into it. Not that. He was mine.*

"I got a note from him," he said, restrained. "It wasn't signed, but from the things he wrote I had no doubt it was him. He asked me to meet him in town the following Monday morning. He gave me an address. A shop."

"And you went?"

"Yes. But he wasn't there. After waiting for nearly an hour I went away. Then an old woman stopped me. She'd been standing there distributing tracts. At first I didn't want to take one. Then she whispered without even looking at me: 'Love from Bernard.' And she pushed a pamphlet into my hand and walked off. There was a message written in the margin. In his handwriting. Giving me a new address for the afternoon."

"And when you got there the old woman was there again, I presume?"

He looked up quickly. "How do you know?"

Too late I realized I might have given myself away. But I tried to be nonchalant: "It was said in the papers and in court that he'd disguised himself as an old woman."

For a long time he sat scrutinizing me closely but in silence. Then he looked away again. "Of course," he said. Was there disappointment in his voice?

"And then he spoke to you?" I urged.

"He took me through a narrow passage next to the shop where I'd been asked to meet him. In Diagonal Street."

(Of course.)

"We went round to the back of the building. There was a car waiting."

"What did he have to say?" I demanded, conscious of breathing more rapidly.

"He just talked. Asked me about Angola and so on."

"He must have said more than that! I've got to know, Louis."

"I can't remember." His pretense of blunt ignorance was getting on my nerves. "All I could make out was that things were getting rather too hot for him. I tried to persuade him to go overseas, but he wouldn't hear of it. Then I told him to go to you. I was convinced you'd be able to help him." After a long pause he looked up at me again: "Are you sure he never contacted you?"

"Of course I'm sure."

"He was arrested before the end of the week."

It was obvious that I wouldn't get anything more out of him. And I *knew* there was more to it. They must have arranged something, planned something. A shiver ran down my spine: suppose they'd picked Louis up too! What a close shave. And what would have happened to me then?

"You've got to try something, Dad," he said again, even more passionately than before. "You know all the Ministers; there must be someone who can help him. To sit there for life—that's worse than a death sentence. Especially for a man like Bernard. The judge said he wanted to be merciful: but a life sentence was the worst they could have done to him. And they bloody well knew it."

"Now you want me to intervene," I said, restrained but angry. "All this time you've never even spoken to me. And ever since you started talking about Angola this morning you've been attacking me on every possible score. Now you expect me to help you!"

"It's not you I'm attacking, Dad." He was having difficulty in restraining his emotion. "Jesus, don't you understand? I'm trying to—just to reach you, to get through to you. I don't want to insult you or destroy anything. It's just that I can't go on like this any more. I'm looking for something. Can't you see I'm desperate? I'm looking for a father I can respect."

It was very quiet in the room. All the lamps were out; only the fire was burning, crouched low over the coals. Light flickered on his face. His eyes were in shadows.

I couldn't bear to look at him any more. The moment was too naked and too raw.

"All right," I said with a dry throat. "I'll try." Even as I said it I had no idea of how to set about it. All I knew was that I couldn't reject him again. I couldn't seal up this exposure, however unbearable it was. "I'll see what I can do."

"You promise?"

I was looking down at my hands. They were trembling.

"Yes, I promise. But I don't know what makes you think I can succeed."

"As long as you try." The shadows were jumping on the wall. "Sometimes one can do something, change something. But if you let it go by, you don't get another chance."

"What do you know of such things? You're so young."

"I'm not. I know all right." In the oppressive silence his voice came in a near whisper. "It happened in Angola. The Cubans were falling back. We were following hard on their heels. They tried to stop us by blowing up bridges and mining the road. In those swamps we were forced to stick to the main route. Sometimes we had to drive back sixty kilometers to fell trees for new bridges. At last our company managed to bypass the enemy on a side track, while the rest kept to the main road. It was hell, I can tell you. Days on end with mud up to your arse. Raining nonstop. At night we had to keep going in the pitch dark, because we couldn't risk being seen with lights. Until we got to where our commander wanted us: a small river ideal for an ambush. The withdrawing Cubans would walk right into it."

"Did it work out that way?" I asked when he fell silent.

He nodded. "Yes, in the end it did. But just before it happened, it seemed as if we'd had it."

"What happened?"

"We were lying in our trenches waiting for them. They weren't more than half an hour off. Then a boy came walking towards us in the road, a little cowherd or something, all on his own. Whistling. Unaware of anything."

"And then, Louis?" I had to draw every sentence from him now, it seemed.

"We knew that if he stepped on a mine, it would be all over. All those days trekking in the mud would have been in vain, for the Cubans would be warned."

"So you had to stop him?"

"*Ja.* Not only stop him. Silence him altogether."

I wasn't sure that I wanted to hear more. But after a long silence I asked: "What did you do?"

His black figure, outlined against the glowing coals, did not stir.

"Two chaps stalked him and jumped on him. And then drowned him in the river."

My jaws were taut. There was a bitter taste in my mouth.

"They said it was all we could do. It was either him or the lot of us."

I asked: "And you?"

"I did nothing to stop them. Perhaps it would have been useless even if I'd tried. I had no authority or anything. But perhaps. Perhaps if only one of us had protested they would have tried to think of another way. But no one did. Including myself."

❖ ❖ ❖ ❖

Later Louis, too, went to bed. I remained behind with the dying coals.

Perhaps, having written it all down, I understand it better now. In me, too, there is an abyss between the man I once was and the man I am. The transition cannot be traced to any single episode in one's life. Not even to the day I used the confidential information to obtain for myself the options intended for Anglo-American. It is, rather, a very slow process, imperceptible even to oneself. One day you simply look up to discover that the world has changed; that you yourself have changed; and all that remains is for you to acknowledge that change, since the choice has been taken out of your hands.

Perhaps there is a similar transition from a state of innocence to a state of guilt in historical processes. (Would Dad have agreed?) Somewhere in history there comes a day when, for the first time, a territory is annexed, not because land is necessary but because a nation has grown addicted to the idea of expansion as such. There comes a day when, for the first time, violence is used not because it is unavoidable but because it is easier. There comes a day when, for the first time, a leader is allowed to promote his own interests simply because he happens to be the leader. There comes a day when, for the first time, the weak one is exploited, not in ignorance but because he cannot offer resistance. There comes a day when, for the first time, a verdict in a court case is given, not on the basis of what is right but on the basis of what is expedient. And so on.

But this is, essentially, a romantic argument. I shouldn't allow the memory of my consternation, that afternoon, to impair my judgment. One must be rational and sensible. There is no point in praising innocence. Is innocence, as such, conceivable? Even as a child, on the farm, I was heir to an entire history of violence, revolt, and blood. In the historically extreme situation like ours there is only total complicity.

In physics, one is taught that heat is a positive phenomenon existing in its own right. The opposite, cold, does not exist as such: it implies merely the *absence* of heat, and cannot be defined except in terms of heat. I should like to propose that the same applies to innocence.

It is not a positive or real phenomenon, but simply the *denial* of the real phenomenon, guilt. It is part of our social foundation, part of our Christian tradition, that we are guilty by definition. Our dimension is that of guilt. The opposite, i.e. innocence, is an un-condition, an absence, a negative, a denial.

Bernard?

Perhaps that was what blinded me. The discovery that there do seem to be people in this world existing beyond moral considerations, in the way that fire or water is neither guilty nor innocent. My experience in the kloof that afternoon had nothing to do with good or evil, guilt or innocence: it was simply my subjective reaction to it which was different in the end from what it had been in the beginning. I must maintain my perspective at all costs. The world is neutral. And that is reassuring.

The wind came up again, in loose, irregular gusts, causing the chimney hood to grind and screech as it turned. I decided to go to bed. There was, as Ma had said, a long day ahead. And there was a long day behind me too. I had briefly lost my grip. Incomprehensible things had happened to me, and I had acted in ways inexplicable to myself. I was no longer sure of who I was. And so I could not exclude anything of what had happened or of what was still waiting to happen.

Monday

1

I T IS BECOMING IMPOSSIBLE. BEA. What can I really say about her now that, at last, I've come as far as this? Out of reach. Even on paper. But I've got to. Sucked into the vortex of myself. All the unnecessary, irrelevant things I've written down. Everything I would have preferred to leave unremembered. But what else is there left to do?

Deliberately didn't write a word all day. Resolved to stop. But I know it's impossible before I've gone back all the way, retracing it to the end. However dangerous it may be; and I now know it is.

Attempted to play the tourist. Not even that: just tried to return to whatever I'd known in London before, when I'd lived here. Bus to Lambeth (that, too, was deliberate, in search of a reality I'd known and lost; otherwise I would have gone by taxi). Looking for the house in which I'd met Welcome Nyaluza that night. The party. Couldn't find it; perhaps it no longer exists. It's twenty years.

The basement flat in Islington where Elise and I'd lived was still there. Dilapidated then; now chichi. I walked past without knocking. Didn't even stop to look properly. Feeling foolish, really, for the very act of going back had been unlike me. Just like this writing.

A couple of museums afterwards. The V & A, the British, the Tate. But they bored me. Bought a ticket for a nightclub tonight, but turned back at the door. Strolled through Soho for an hour, then returned

to my hotel, irritable and cold; withdrawing into this now familiar
room with blue-grey carpets and old-gold curtains and spreads.

Nothing of interest on TV. I phoned an agency and asked for a
masseuse to be sent round, hoping that would help me to relax
sufficiently to sleep; waiting for her, I had a bath and put on my
gown. Eurasian girl. Arriving breathless, nearly trapped by the security guards. After the formality of the straight massage I asked her to
undress for the rest, but when she returned from the bathroom and
kneeled naked on the bed beside me, I told her to go. Terribly flustered, poor girl. Thought I was dissatisfied with her. Smiled, though,
when she saw the notes I'd thrust into her hand. After she'd gone I
regretted it, of course. I simply don't understand myself any more.

But now I must pull myself together and get on with this.
Tomorrow afternoon my plane leaves for Tokyo. I can't care less,
really. But it means my existence in limbo is drawing to an end and I
must finish this. I've gone too far to stop.

Only, I'll have to be more careful. In the previous section I became
much too emotionally involved a couple of times. Watch out. In the
final analysis it's still up to me to decide what I want to write and how
to organize it. "When one loves," said Bea, "one forgets about oneself.
You no longer want to be yourself or know who you are." But self-
destruction is foreign to my nature. What matters is to survive, survive. To survive even the apocalypse.

2

"ALL RIGHT, THEN," MA SAID. "If there's really no alternative, then go ahead and sell. I won't stand in your way." "You must realize it's the best for all of us. For you too. And even more so after this murder business."

"I said it was all right, didn't I? Who are you trying to convince then?"

"But I can see your heart isn't in it."

"I never said it was. All I said was I wouldn't stand in your way."

"You'll enjoy staying with us, Ma. To relax a bit and stop going all-out all day long."

She sat drinking her morning coffee in silence. The lamp was burning. Outside the dawn was still sluggish and slow.

"It won't take long for you to make friends. You already know Aunt Rienie, don't you?—the old lady I stayed with in Stellenbosch. She's always looking for company. Lovely person."

"What about my dogs?" she asked, interrupting.

"Oh, we'll see." Avoiding her eyes I looked down, watching the light rippling on the surface of my coffee.

The wind was tugging irritably at the windows. A few times in the night it had died down, but now it was blowing again; the light was slow in coming, the weather inclement.

"I want you to know how grateful I am, Ma. I knew I could rely on you."

"You've known all your life you could rely on everyone else to let you have your way."

"Now you're being very unfair."

"I'm not blaming you, sonny. I suppose you can't help it, really. And perhaps it's a good thing for you."

"What do you mean?"

"I mean: perhaps it was necessary for our history to take the course it did to produce a man like you. Otherwise we might have gone under."

"I wish you would understand."

"Sometimes I think I understand you better than you understand yourself, sonny."

"You're just feeling morbid so early in the morning."

"Some more coffee?"

"Yes, thanks."

"Kristina!"

Shuffling on her thick bare soles the old Black woman entered.

"Some more coffee, Kristina."

"Yes, Madam."

After she'd gone, Ma sighed: "Poor old Kristina. What's going to become of her now?"

"They'll stay on the farm even if it's sold."

"Part of the livestock, you mean?"

"They'll be all right, Ma. And once the Ciskei becomes independent, they'll all be free in their own country."

"And we'll all die of freedom in our own country," she said morosely.

I decided it was better to leave her alone while she was in that mood.

"Just listen to that wind," I said deliberately.

"Weather's changing," she said. "There's something brewing."

❖ ❖ ❖ ❖

Something brewing: that had been the tone of the week in Ponta do Ouro, the most complete escape Bea and I had ever effected. A brief moment of paradise, remote from the world; and yet all the time there'd been a suggestion of ineffable threatening events all around us. Perhaps that was why I have always thought of that week as emblematic of our entire relationship; whenever I think of the two of us, that is the first memory to return.

I'd gone to what was then Lourenço Marques to negotiate a contract with a Mozambique mining concern. Afterwards, I was to accompany a group of Portuguese businessmen to Beira in connection with another deal I'd had lined up. But the leader of the group had fallen ill and the trip had to be cancelled. Instead of returning to South Africa I'd sent a cable to Bea, including money for an air ticket, asking her to join me the following day. Of course, I had taken a risk in sending the cable—but after the few months our relationship had been under way, I felt confident enough to take it. Even if I say so myself, I know I have a way with women; and I know that, deep down, they yearn for the sort of domination suggested by that cable which left her no choice.

Her work would provide no obstacle, I knew: she'd just reached the end of a rather unstable period of temporary jobs (secretary for a firm of attorneys; editorial assistant on a ladies' journal; helping out with evening classes at the Tech, etc.). She'd just been reappointed to the post of junior lecturer in Law which she'd had at Wits a few years earlier, before going overseas, but she was only due to start in a few weeks' time. At the moment she was free. In other words, available.

And the next day, at eleven in the morning, after the flight had been delayed for over an hour, she arrived.

I'd never been to Ponta do Ouro before. It had been suggested and arranged by an old business acquaintance of mine in Lourenço Marques, Pedro de Souza. Bea and I first had lunch with him and his wife that afternoon: an error of judgment, I confess, for the De Souzas thought Bea was my wife and addressed her as such; and, unwilling to offend their middle-class morality, I was content to leave it at that: but Bea was very agitated.

Although it was only early September, it was an excessively hot day and the house was filled with flies; the woman could only speak a few words of English and Pedro himself wasn't all that fluent; the heavy red wine gave us headache; and in their exaggerated hospitality the De Souzas refused to let us leave before three o'clock—by which time our nerves were rather strained.

So the atmosphere was tense when we finally drove off in my hired car. The first stretch of road was tarred and not too bad, although one had to be constantly on the lookout for swerving bicycles, playing children, lean black dogs and even, from time to time, chickens. But after we'd turned off to Bela Vista the road deteriorated into two sandy tracks with a dangerously high middle ridge. There wasn't much to see. Farmhouses and unkempt gardens at long intervals; bougainvillaea; pigs in the road. For the rest it was pretty desolate. After some time one started wondering whether it was the right road after all, for the only signposts we passed were either illegible or torn down. And to either side the land lay uncompromising and sullen, even hostile.

For a long time Bea made no move beside me, except to look at the map on her knees from time to time; but it was obvious that she was perturbed. Whenever I glanced in her direction she sat looking straight ahead, expressionless. But the moment I turned my head away again I was aware of her watching me. It didn't auger well.

"Why did you want me to come?" she asked unexpectedly, in her unnervingly direct way.

"Because the week suddenly fell open. I told you at the airport, didn't I? I don't know when we'll get another chance like this."

"And of course you never let a chance go by."

"What do you mean?"

She didn't answer my question. Returning to the attack again, she asked: "Why did you tell those people I was your wife?"

"I didn't. They just assumed it. But it makes no difference."

"Doesn't it? Not to you, perhaps. But have you thought about how I must feel?"

"Is it such a humiliation to be Mrs. Mynhardt?"

"No. But it is humiliating to have to pretend I'm not myself."

"It's really not important, Bea. Besides, it's over. And now we have a whole week to ourselves."

Her mouth moved. A small obstinate muscle tensed in her right cheek.

"Why did you want me to come with you, Martin?" she asked again.

"But I told you—"

"No, I want the real reason."

"I was missing you." I placed my hand on her knee. She didn't shake it off, but remained rigid.

"And if I hadn't come?"

"I would have been very disappointed indeed."

"Would you have sent a cable to someone else then?"

"To whom?"

"I don't know. But you must have other options."

"What makes you think so?"

"A man like you always plans ahead. 'For all eventualities.'"

"Bea, what's the matter with you today? Why should I feel any need to be with someone else?"

"Why should you have a need to be with me?"

"Because—"

"Whatever you say, don't say: 'Because you're you.' I may scream."

"Can't you understand that I need you?"

"No."

"You must believe me."

"You just don't want to be alone, that's what."

"Why do you say that?"

"I think you're terribly scared of being alone, Martin."

"Only people with something on their conscience are scared of being alone."

"And there's nothing on your conscience?"

"Of course not."

"If your wife should find out about this week?"

"She won't. That's the whole point."

"Why did you just send a cable?" she asked after a pause, the small muscle flickering in her cheek again. "Why didn't you phone me so we could discuss it?"

"I wanted to surprise you."

"Or were you afraid I might refuse?"

I smiled grudgingly. "All right, I admit I was afraid of that. And I was too eager to have you with me. So I didn't want to give you any loophole."

"I could have stayed away."

"But you didn't."

"Do you know that when they announced the flight had been delayed this morning, I turned round and walked out of the airport building? I almost felt relieved. It seemed as if it had happened specially to make me change my mind."

"But then you came back. That's all that matters."

"Do you really think so? Suppose I tell you I feel ashamed of having done it? Suppose I tell you I've never felt so humiliated in my life?"

I didn't answer. But after rocking and swaying across another hundred yards of deep sand I stopped the car.

"If you wish, I can take you back now."

I knew it would work. It always does.

"It won't solve anything, will it?" she said, restrained. "I'm here now. We may as well go through with it."

"What a wonderful way of starting a holiday!" I said bitterly.

"I'm sorry. I didn't mean to disturb you too. I hoped I'd be able to come to terms with it on my own. But all those hours we spent with those people: I suppose it gave one too much time for thinking. Now I feel—as if I need a bath."

"Surely it's not the first time in your life you've done this sort of thing!" I flared up, realizing that everything might be wrecked unless I became very firm, even aggressive.

Much to my surprise she agreed immediately. "I know," she said quietly. "And I don't suppose it'll be the last time either. One day, when all is over between you and me, someone else will—"

"For heaven's sake!" I said. "Why do you talk about everything being 'over'? We've hardly got to know each other."

"We're not going to grow old together, are we?"

"Bea." For a moment I felt helpless. "One can't think in terms of endings when it's only the beginning."

"You've got to, if you want to be honest with yourself."

"But while we're still together—"

"I can't bluff myself so easily, Martin. I wish I could, but I can't." She smoothed the map on her knees. "One day, I know, you'll drop me."

"I won't ever drop you, Bea."

She smiled. "You don't really want to get involved. Not with me. With no one. If ever I should really desperately need you, you'll drop me. Because then you'll get scared of me. Or of yourself."

"How can you say that?"

"All I want you to know is that I'm not asking anything. I don't *expect* anything."

"I've told you how much you mean to me, Bea. Ever since that first night. Now please—"

"No, don't try to soothe me with love talk. Please don't be scared that you'll hurt me or anything. Just tell me: what am I really to you?" And when I didn't answer immediately, she went on: "You see? We're just marking time, that's all. No use pretending it's different. Perhaps that's the most any person can expect of another—otherwise we start annexing and possessing and smothering one another."

In a moment of unreasonable anger I said: "Well, if it's all so senseless and wrong and sinful and God knows what else to you, why the hell did you come then?"

"My God," she said, so quietly I almost couldn't hear her, "because I'm lonely too. Don't you know that?"

I put my arm round her shoulders and pulled her closer, knowing I had to comfort her before she went too far. For a moment she resisted, then pressed her head against my shoulder. Another woman might have started crying, but not Bea. She almost never did. Only once I can think of. When she really felt desolate, as on that afternoon, one had the impression that tears were too facile for her, that her emotion came from so deep inside her that it belonged to an order different from that of crying. And I felt relieved, because I can't stand tears in a woman.

Holding her in my arms and caressing her gently, in the car beside the sandy road in that desolate landscape, I accidentally knocked off her dark glasses and we both burst out laughing. The distance between us was healed again. It was possible to go on. The matter hadn't been solved or cleared up in any way, but there appeared to be a silent agreement that, for the time being at least, we wouldn't refer to it again. Perhaps it helped us to be more careful in our consideration of each other; perhaps we drew a subtler form of compassion from it.

After Bela Vista, a small place with wide dusty streets and old colonial houses in overgrown gardens surrounding a tatty square, the bush grew denser on either side of the road. Our isolation from the familiar world became even more complete. And crossing a wide river on a ferry, it felt like severing a last remaining contact.

I was just beginning to feel nervous about the approaching dark—there is no twilight in Mozambique and the night comes down very suddenly—when the tall fence of the holiday camp appeared before us in the sunset, and a guard in military uniform stepped into the road.

After I'd filled in the forms in the superintendent's small office at the gate, the guard trotted off in front of the car to show us the way to our red bungalow in the farthest row, closest to the sea, separated from the beach by only a line of shady trees.

It was Friday, and a few cars were already parked in front of some of the other bungalows; there were children playing round the ablution block, and on the terrace of the restaurant a small group of people were drinking beer. The next day more cars arrived. But by Sunday afternoon all the strangers had left, for it was outside the holiday season and the only visitors were the weekenders. From the Monday we were all on our own in the camp. Except, of course, for the old pensioner in his office at the gate, and his guard, and some cleaners, and the couple running the restaurant—a man with a wooden leg, and a fat woman who spent her days knitting.

It was so deserted, in fact, that Bea sometimes walked about naked on the beach. I found her behavior slightly improper, but made no remark on it, realizing it would either irritate her or come as a complete and unpleasant surprise to her. She wasn't the sort of person to have any exhibitionist feelings about her body: if she did go without clothes from time to time it was simply that, quite unselfconscious, she couldn't care less. And in a way I suppose it was fitting in the circumstances: for, seen through romantic eyes, Ponta do Ouro was our little paradise, a territory in which we belonged exclusively to one another; a place of discovery and mutual exploration.

Apart from having our meals at the restaurant we were tied to no routine. Every second day a large green lorry brought vegetables and meat, but no newspapers. The news, broadcast loudly in

Portuguese by Radio LM whenever we sat down for a meal, was unintelligible to us; and the radio in our hired car proved incapable of receiving broadcasts in any civilized language. Which meant that for a week we literally knew nothing about what was happening in the world. At the same time, possibly because of the very unnaturalness of its absence, we were never allowed to forget about that world. Mainly because of the presence of the soldiers.

There was a company of them stationed on the other side of the camp, in the bushes beyond the fence. Early in the morning we would hear the jeeps and trucks starting up and driving off into the *bundu* seldom returning before late afternoon. Then the boys sometimes came down to play ball games on the beach or to have beer on the terrace, surrounded by scores of hornbills and metallic-blue starlings. That was all we knew of them. But they were there; even in their absence they were singularly present. Somewhere in those dense green bushes they were moving about on their secret maneuvers, often at night as well.

There was one special circumstance about the soldiers which ensured that we would never forget them; the small Black boy they had with them. In a long, fumbling conversation the fat woman of the restaurant once tried to explain to us, in her inimitable approximation of English, that the soldiers had picked him up a year or two before in a village they'd destroyed somewhere, and had kept him as their mascot ever since. He took part in all their games; when a ball was kicked too far away he ran to collect it. And when they returned to their tents one of the men usually carried him on his shoulder like a little monkey. He seemed to be well treated. But not once in the course of the week we spent there did we hear him laugh or even see the slightest sign of a grin on his ancient, wizened face.

During the second half of the week there were the planes too, even more unnerving than the comings and goings of the soldiers. Once a day without warning, they would come roaring overhead not more than a hundred yards above the beach, following the coastline from north to south; a whole squadron of them, at such speed that the impact of their flight sent one hurtling to the sand. The first time they caught us completely unawares; they were so close that the shock continued to throb in one for minutes afterwards. (It was the last time, too, that Bea went naked on the beach.)

Afterwards, they returned every day. Had a war broken out in our absence? Had there been a coup? Were there terrorists hiding in the bushes close to camp? There was no way of finding out; and with a curious reluctance we didn't want to ask the restaurant woman for information. There was an almost perverse satisfaction in the knowledge that the entire familiar world might have been destroyed in our absence. We felt like two shipwrecked survivors after a flood. Just the two of us in this small paradise: this minute enclave surrounded by soldiers lurking in the bush and surveilled by roaring planes. A dangerous idyll, wholly unreal, but cherished for that very reason.

From time to time she referred again to a distant future when all would be over between us: how we would then remember the past; what we would retain of it; what we should *like* to retain.

Usually I allowed her to have her way without interfering, for fear of turning it into another discussion like that one on the first day. But one day I couldn't restrain myself.

We were on the expanse of flat rocks on the southern end of the beach, just this side of the tall dune separating Ponta do Ouro from the South African border. At low tide the entire rock bed lay exposed, dotted with holes and pools and crevices, an incredible marine garden. She would spend hours there, squatting beside a pool and teasing the sea anemones with a stick, or collecting sea stars and shells, or catching small rockfishes. From behind, sitting like that, there was something childlike and girlish about her narrow, bare, brown back, something vulnerable about her shoulders. But watching her from the front, her grave, attentive face (even when she wore those large dark glasses) or the slight droop of her breasts with the elongated dark nipples only half concealed by the gaping cups of her bra, there was no doubt about her womanliness, a maturity which bore both the scars of pain and disillusionment and the vulnerability of suffering.

And when, in that late afternoon, she once again spoke of the inevitability of an end, I reacted. What she said was:

"Ends are the only things one can be certain of."

And then I demanded, as on the first afternoon: "Why do you insist on conditioning yourself for an end?"

"Isn't that one's only protection?"

"But by going on talking about it, you may be predestining an end which otherwise may not have happened at all."

"Do you still believe in immortality then?"

"No. But I believe in enjoying what one has while it's there. Without allowing the future to cancel the present."

"Sure, I agree. The difference is that you enjoy it pretending it will always remain with you, whereas I never allow myself not to see the end." She leaned over to catch a small fish in her cupped hand, but it escaped. Still bent over the pool waiting for it to show itself among the seaweed again, she said: "Every time I've loved a man, I knew it had to end sooner or later. The professor I told you about. The young Jewish student. The film producer in Perugia. Every time I knew it was quite impossible for it to last. Yet I refused to allow that knowledge to restrain me. One can't deny or refuse life, you can't close yourself to it." With the back of a glistening wet hand she pushed back her dark hair from her sunglasses. "Only once I thought it was really going to work out. Only once I allowed myself to believe in immortality. Afterwards one doesn't readily make the same mistake again."

"What happened?"

"It was just after I'd returned from overseas last year: the year in

Perugia and the few months in the States. I already told you about it, didn't I? Anyway, then I met Gary. He wasn't anyone special. My poor mother would have been terribly upset if she'd still been alive, she'd always wanted me to make a 'good' marriage, poor thing. Gary was a mechanic. He repaired my scooter for me. Actually he was just a boy still, ten years younger than me. I don't know what it was, but right from the beginning—there was something in him—it's difficult to explain—Bernard often reminds me of him. Oh I know it sounds ridiculous, one doesn't expect a woman of over thirty to talk like that, I suppose, but there was—well, something very clean about him. Even when he was covered in oil and grease. The first time he slept with me, there were oil marks all over my body. But his body was so very white inside the overalls. We were like two children loving for the first time. I mean: both of us had been with others before, and yet it was as if we were virgins. Everything was so marvelous, so teenage. We went to the movies. We went to the races at Kyalami. We danced in discos. But he also came to listen to records in my flat. He became fond of Mozart. I persuaded him to start reading books with me. He registered at the Tech for evening classes. If I think back now, I know it was just as impossible as the other times: that sort of frothy happiness can't last. It's really too much to endure. But we were content. For the first time in my life I didn't *want* to ask any questions, I didn't *want* to deprive myself of anything. I wanted to dissolve myself completely in him; I didn't want to be *me* any more. Oh I know it sounds exaggerated and ludicrous. But I think once in one's life one has got to love like that, else something inside you remains closed. I suppose it usually happens when one is very young, like Gary was. But I had waited for much longer. I'd always been so 'sensible.' Only this once I didn't care."

"And what happened then?" I asked, moved in spite of myself, but also affronted by it as it excluded me.

"We went for rides on his motorbike. I couldn't get enough of it.

Especially when it was raining and the streets were all wet and slippery and one knew it was dangerous, and yet you couldn't help yourself: you just wanted to go faster and faster all the time. Then we had a fall. One night in Hillbrow, just as the movies were coming out. There were thousands of people in the streets, in the rain. He swerved to miss a pedestrian, and then he lost his balance. I just slipped off and started rolling. But he was flung through the air, hitting a lamp post with his face. The crowd jostling and shouting. The cars. The lights in the rain. The blood. I got up and ran to him. I wanted to give him mouth-to-mouth. But he had no mouth left."

For a long time she was silent. With a ripple of its transparent body the small rockfish reappeared from behind the seaweed, but she made no attempt to catch it. The late afternoon sun lay warmly on her shoulders and her bare back.

"I was three months pregnant when it happened," she said. "But I lost his child. In the hospital I thought: It would have been better if I'd been killed instantly too. Apart from the baby, I'd escaped without any injuries. It was such a sudden, empty feeling. And once that has happened to one, you've got to start thinking in terms of endings again."

There was a spider in our hut one night, on the wall immediately above the wide bed we'd made on the floor after discarding the two stupid little camp beds in the bungalow. One of those horrible hairy baboon spiders. She was just pulling her dress over her head when I noticed the creature.

"Watch out!" I called.

"What?" She looked over the top of her dress, her hands still outstretched above her head.

"There's a spider behind you. Move over this way, I'll kill him."

But she looked round. And without any sign of fear she caught the hideous thing in a corner of her dress and went to the door to throw it out.

"Aren't you scared then?" I asked, amazed.

She gave a small nervous smile and shrugged her shoulders, before she resumed her undressing to prepare for bed.

"When I was small, I was terribly scared of all sorts of creepy-crawlies," she said, stepping out of her bikini panties. "I nearly had a fit if anything came near me. It was getting so bad that I had to do something about it. So I started catching them in matchboxes or bottles. I forced myself to handle them. And in that way I got over my fear. I was just as terrified of the dark, until I began deliberately to lock myself into a cupboard every day to cure me of it."

Lying on our floor bed, covered with a sheet, I gazed up at her standing over me with legs astride, leaning forward to look into the small mirror as she brushed her hair.

"Was that why you came to me when you got my cable?" I asked playfully. "Because you were trying to cure yourself of being scared of me?"

"Who knows?" The brush was moving evenly through her short dark curls. The white light of the gas lamp standing on the floor touched the bottom of her chin, the tips of her dark-nippled breasts, her small tangle of pubic hair forming a comic goatee below the pink protruding inner lips of her slightly distended sex.

"And now you're no longer afraid?"

"It's not a matter of losing one's fear," she said gravely. "One learns to control it and to live with it, that's all."

"Does it apply to me too?"

"I want to be *aware* of what's happening to me," she said, as if that answered my question. "I want to *know* about it, every moment." She sat down beside me. "It's all too easy to shut one's eyes and let go. But I can't."

"You're just making it difficult for yourself."

"I've got to *know*" she repeated. "Sometimes I envy other people. Girls who become Playmates, or who get addicted to sex, or who get married—just in order not to have to ask questions or to wonder about anything; to drug themselves into accepting that they're not really alive themselves, but living through others, vicariously. The men they're married to, the men they sleep with, the men leering at their pictures. But I can't switch off so easily. I need answers. Which means I've got to be prepared to live with all the answers I get, however painful it may be. It's just no use trying to pretend that things like cruelty or injustice or fear or violence don't exist."

"You're making it almost impossible for anyone else to live with you."

"Sometimes it's almost impossible to live with myself," she said lightly, laughing. "Do you really think I'm such a neurotic person?"

"You're demanding too much of yourself, that's all."

"I've got to know, I've got to know." Pulling up her knees she rested her chin on them. "When I flew to LM last Friday I despised myself. I'd sworn I would never allow myself to be ordered around by a man like that. And yet I *wanted* to come, I wanted to be with you. I hoped—oh it doesn't matter. In the process I discovered things in myself I'd never known of before. I felt like a stranger to myself and I wanted to get to know myself better."

"I know you."

"No, you don't. You don't even know yourself, Martin."

"That's one thing you can't accuse me of"

"That's the one thing I do accuse you of. You're on the run all the time. You don't want to know who you are. It's a congenital disease with you Afrikaners. At the same time you never stop talking about 'identity.' It's like whistling when you walk past a graveyard."

Far away in the night we could hear the cries of soldiers, vehicles starting up and driving away into the night. Had something happened? Was something going to happen?

Inside it was stuffy, as usual, in spite of the two small gauzed windows allowing a draft of warm air to drift lazily through the hut. And like many other nights we carried our bedding out to the beach. Swimming in the moonlight, trying, chafingly, to make love in the sea and failing; and resuming on the sand where she willingly submitted to my entry and my thrusts, but without coming herself. At my disposal—yet with something held back deep inside her, an invincible, unassailable independence, a secret center of pain into which she would never allow me to enter. Time and time again the same process was repeated, sometimes almost violently, assaults on that privacy within her: assaults all the more furious because I knew in advance I wouldn't succeed. Especially not in that way.

Our week came to an end. (As she'd predicted!) Innocent of time and space we'd been together, our movements determined by day and night and the rhythms of the sea; by wind and silences and sudden tropical storms. While all around us the soldiers had gone their way, moving through the bush; and overhead the squadrons thundered past. Suddenly it was all over and we had to leave. We took a solemn vow that one day we would return. But we knew we wouldn't. There are some places one can never return to. And anyway, soon afterwards the Portuguese withdrew from Mozambique and everything was changed irrevocably. Sometimes I wonder whether the small Black boy is still alive—and whether, in the end, he managed to bring anyone any luck.

3

FTER BREAKFAST LOUIS AND I took Ma's small van to go to town. I allowed him to drive—not an unambiguous confirmation on my part of all being well between us: basically I just didn't like to handle the jalopy. At the store I asked him to stop, and he sat waiting behind the wheel while I went in to Mrs. Lawrence.

"I've come for a coffin," I told her. "We're on our way to collect the body."

"*Ag*, it's such a business, isn't it?" she said with a small sigh. There was a transparent drop suspended from the tip of her nose. "I'll get a few boys to help you." In short, hurried steps she went to the back door to shout at a few helpers loitering against the wall in the sun. The coffins were stored with other unmanageable, bulky items in an outbuilding.

"I hope Louis wasn't upset by the conversation yesterday," she said apologetically when she returned to her high stool behind the counter. "It must have been a terrible thing to land in a war like that. He's only a kid really."

"He does seem to overreact from time to time," I said.

"And your mother was so upset too. About the rest of us selling our farms and stuff. But surely she understands—"

"It's all right, Mrs. Lawrence. We're also going to sell."

"What?" She gaped at me, the pink plastic of her dentures exposed. "You don't say?"

"Yes, that's why I came down for the weekend."

"Well, I never. I wonder what Mr. Lawrence will say when he hears that."

Outside there was a clanging from the van where the coffin was being loaded on the back.

"Well, Mrs. Lawrence, it's time to say goodbye."

"*Ag ja*, bless you," she said, taking a crumpled tissue from the sleeve of her sweater to blow her nose in sudden agitation. "Do keep in touch, Martin. Isn't it sad the way time just flies? Seems like yesterday when you were children."

I lingered for a moment, once again conscious of all the smells in the store, and of the dusky depths behind the shelves. Perhaps, when they cleared up the place one of these days, they would discover, among all the junk, a dusty and decayed little pair of girl's panties and wonder what on earth.

Louis blew the horn impatiently.

"Why did you stay so long ?" he asked when I got in beside him.

"Just said goodbye. I don't suppose we'll ever see them again." I laughed self-consciously and tried my best to sound comradely: "You know, in that little store your Dad had his first real clinch with a girl."

He glanced at me as if I'd said something improper; his eyes quizzical, uncomprehending. And I realized that even though the two of us might fleetingly recognize and acknowledge one another over a great distance, it didn't mean that we could either understand or forgive. For the rest of the dusty road we didn't speak. The bare drought-stricken veld swept past in a pastel blur. The naked knuckles of mountains, parched trees, bleak patches of red earth, aloes.

At the police station, from a cell in the yard at the back of the red brick building, two Black constables brought us the body, not even covered with a blanket, shockingly naked, with the long black cuts of the postmortem sewn up in rough stitches. Without ceremony they dumped it into the bare pinewood coffin; one of them went back for a screwdriver to fasten the lid.

The redheaded sergeant we'd met the day before came down the steps of the charge office to my side of the van.

"When would you like us to bring Mandisi?" he asked.

For a moment I didn't understand.

"For the funeral," he explained.

"About eleven," I said. "We'd like to get it over as soon as possible. I've got to be back in Johannesburg tonight."

"Hell, but you're in a hurry, hey?" said the sergeant.

"My work is waiting. I only came down for the weekend. On business."

"Well, see you later then."

On the way to the farm Louis drove more slowly, and from time to time I noticed him glancing in the rearview mirror to make sure the coffin was all right. Whenever we came to eroded patches or humps in the road he braked and drove with great care as if concerned about the comfort of the woman in the box on the back.

Dad's body had been brought out to the farm in the hearse, covered in flowers and wreaths. It was raining too. There was something outrageously morbid about the funeral in the rain. All those black umbrellas, the red muddy water at the bottom of the grave, the mud squelching under the artificial grass around the hole.

Something about Dad's death had remained unresolved, incomplete. The transitions had been too sudden. The long road back from Tzaneen. The night with Bea. And then the news, and the frantic arrangements, and the flight; Ma, the morgue, the funeral.

Bea had been waiting in my apartment when I returned late that Wednesday afternoon. She had her own key.

We'd spent very few nights in her own small flat in Berea: whenever we'd gone there it had usually been for a stolen hour or so in the afternoon, when the well-worn old building behind the jacarandas would be deserted. A friendly, cozy, messy little flat, lived-in and topsy-turvy and warm. Rather dark, as a result of the trees in front of the window; the kitchen small and uncomfortable and the bathroom pervaded by an old, sour smell; a leaking ball valve in the toilet. And yet a place in which one could relax completely. Unframed lithos and paintings by anonymous or unfamiliar artists on the walls, dried veld flowers and grass seeds in round clay pots on the floor, crammed bookshelves made of boards and bricks; sometimes coffee mugs or plates left on the carpet from a previous day; cushions; a couple of cozy armchairs. In the bedroom, scattered clothes on the three-quarter bed with its brass knobs (some missing) and patchwork quilt, on the two straight chairs and the Victorian chest of drawers, or draped over the wide-open doors of the wardrobe; a small medieval Spanish statue of the Madonna on the dressing table, now used for hanging scarves or bead necklaces; piles of books everywhere, some open and facedown. The whole place was pervaded with her. No wonder, for she'd lived there for so many years—ever since she'd started her LL.B. (after a double B.A. in modern languages). Even when she'd gone overseas she hadn't given up the flat but sublet it to a friend. It had been the longest she'd ever lived in one place in her life, she used to say. Her only image of constancy and security. It had to be judged against the background of her earlier years: Italy, and the States, and then Cape Town, and one temporary address after the other in Johannesburg. Now, at last, this flat was hers. And it would be difficult to understand Bea without it.

(Why do I so regularly get bogged down in these descriptions, these details? To define what I'm trying to say? To convince myself that I haven't lost touch with it? Or simply to try and put off what I know I must inevitably come to?)

But my own apartment was safer and more anonymous, better suited to the nature of our relationship. It was where everything had started on the night of Aunt Rienie's party. And that Wednesday night, too, we spent there.

She welcomed me at the door like a housewife, and ran me a bath while I relaxed in the lounge with a whisky. Afterwards, as I lay in the bath, she sat on the edge with her glass of white wine. A very mundane conversation. She inquired about my trip; I asked her about her work, listening without much interest to what she replied—there were always so many things she was involved in simultaneously. Not only her lecturing at Wits, but all the rest: the legal clinic she ran with a few members of staff and senior students, offering advice to Blacks unable to afford lawyers. Evening classes to help Black students who were having problems with their correspondence courses at the University of South Africa. In addition, she often drove to Soweto in her ramshackle old Volkswagen, on mornings when she wasn't occupied at the university, to help out in this school or that. She mostly taught Afrikaans, one of her majors—a choice I'd always found surprising in someone with her background. But as I'd come to know her better I realized it was, in a way, characteristic of her. A variation, perhaps, on the theme of collecting spiders.

A very mundane conversation, I said: yet there was an element of discomfort I couldn't explain. Not reticence, nothing definite. Just a hint of deliberateness about the polite way in which we questioned and answered one another. I didn't mention it to her, knowing well enough that she would bring it up herself if she regarded it as important.

When I got up to dry myself she went out to dish up the food: a roast chicken from a Kentucky Fry, salad, bread, cheese. Cooking had never been her line. Afterwards she went to the bathroom with her glass of wine, to have a bath too, while I put a record on the player, carefully sponging off dust and static, and lay down on the divan to listen to the music.

She returned much later, her white muslin blouse still unbuttoned; and as she bent over to refill her glass I could see her narrow breasts. Returning the bottle to the shelf she turned her head sideways, remarking almost noncommittally: "Incidentally, I met your wife."

I sat up, shocked. "How did that happen?"

"I went to your house." Was it intentional that she sat down in a chair out of my reach?

"But Bea, how the hell—"

A brief smile; the small muscle in her cheek. "Don't worry, it wasn't the sort of melodramatic confrontation you'd probably think of."

"But how did you do it? And why?"

"I was curious."

"Don't you realize—"

"It started quite by accident," she said flatly. "I was visiting Aunt Rienie when she referred to you and Elise. Quite on impulse I said I'd like to meet Elise one day and she promised to take me when she went to visit her again. So you see, there's no reason to be so upset at all."

"But you know Aunt Rienie is the world's worst gossip."

"What's there to gossip about? She doesn't know anything about you and me. She only knows I met you at her party, nothing more."

She rose to get a cigarette from the box on the table. The small flame darting up against her cheek; a hand cupped protectively around it, long nervous fingers. She sat down again. Her blouse was still open. I knew she wouldn't bother to do anything about it: probably she hadn't even noticed that she'd neglected to button it. But I did. And seeing her bare breasts while she sat there nonchalantly telling me about her visit to my wife, both unsettled and excited me unduly.

"Aunt Rienie phoned on Monday morning to ask whether I felt like going with her. She'd probably arranged it specially so I could take her in my car, you know what a lovable old sponger she can be."

"Then what happened?"

"You really have a lovely house. Lovely garden. Lovely everything. The perfect setting for a magnate."

"Bea, I asked you—"

"And Elise is a lovely woman." A short pause. "Or: was. For she doesn't seem to bother much about her appearance now." Looking at me over the rim of her glass, she asked: "Does she know about us?"

"What a question. Of course not."

"She isn't happy."

I got up. "Look, Bea, say what you want to say and get it over. What happened?"

"Nothing. What did you expect? She talked to Aunt Rienie most of the time. Inquired politely about my work and so on, but that was all. As far as she was concerned, I was just a friend of Aunt Rienie's who'd come along."

"I still don't see what you tried to achieve with such a foolish little adventure."

"I wanted to know. One gets curious. And you never wanted to tell me anything about her or your home."

"Obviously not. One tries to keep the different parts of one's life apart. What do you think would happen—"

"And for how long do you think your sort of apartheid is going to work?" she asked quietly.

I was vexed, but controlled it by first pouring myself another whisky and taking a sip. "It will last for as long as I have control over my own life," I said at last, sitting down again. "And now you've gone and—"

"I did nothing about it whatsoever. I only wanted to know, I told you."

"I never thought you could be so childish."

She didn't answer.

"Well, I hope your curiosity is satisfied now," I said after another silence. "And I hope it'll be the last time you—"

She leaned back, resting on her elbows. The loose blouse slipped off one of her shoulders but she made no effort to cover it up.

"You wanted to exclude me from the most important part of your life," she said flatly. "I had to go and see for myself. How often have I told you one's got to learn to live with everything one knows. It also means one must try to find out everything."

"And what are you going to do now that you know?" I asked, trying to control my breath.

"Oh I've accepted my role as mistress long ago," she said, staring deeply into her pale blonde glass. "Not a very honorable role, I admit, but I've resigned myself to the fact that I shouldn't expect much more than that from life. It's happened to me too often to be mere coincidence. One learns to accept responsibility. You can't be exploited unless you put yourself at someone's disposal." A bitter laugh. "Even being a mistress implies a measure of security. One learns to be satisfied with being only half a person. And for both of us it becomes easier just to carry on without asking too much."

"And now you've had enough?" I inhaled slowly, deeply.

"It's not that. But now I've seen the rest of your life at last. Or at least part of it. Before, you were the man who came and went, sharing stolen hours with me. It wasn't easy, but one learns to be thankful for small mercies. For any form of compassion. But now I've also seen you as someone else's husband. You think you can keep us apart. But when you come to me, you bring part of her with you. And when you leave, you take part of me home. If we try to deny that, we're denying part of ourselves. We can't go on like this. It's not—worthy. For either of us."

"What do you want to do?" I asked.

"It's up to you to make up your mind. You're the man in the middle."

I looked down. And up again, but only after a long pause.

"Button your blouse."

Almost in surprise she looked down at her breasts, and halfheartedly drew the two lapels of the blouse closer, a small cynical smile on her face.

"Button it up, I said!"

"Don't be silly, Martin."

All of a sudden I was blind with rage. I jumped up and pulled her from her chair by the arm. Her wineglass fell on the floor and rolled along the soft carpet. When I grabbed her open blouse to close it with force, it tore. And then I became wild, with a violence I'd never suspected in myself. Grabbing the thin muslin blouse again, I went on tugging and tearing until I'd ripped it completely off her; and then, throwing her to the ground, I took her forcibly, raping her. Only after some time it slowly dawned on me that she hadn't put up any resistance, that she'd yielded quite passively to whatever I wanted to do to her. For a moment the discovery made me even more furious than before. Suddenly, as I climaxed, she began to cry. The only time she'd ever cried in my presence. Not loudly: deep, smothered sobs shuddering through her while she lay biting on the second joint of her forefinger trying to control it.

Withdrawing from her I turned away to readjust my clothes. I went to the bathroom. From the door I looked back. She was lying motionless on the carpet, her knees still drawn up and wide open. Like, once before, Bernard's wife Reinette.

In the bathroom I scrubbed myself as if to rid me of every sign and stigma of her. But I knew it was useless. I was addicted to her more totally than to any other woman in my life: with the exception of Elise in those early days of our love, before our marriage.

Later I went back to her, and took her to the bedroom. Until deep in the night we lay together, talking, in a close embrace without any sexual overtones. The storm had subsided. In the deep desolation following it we were able to discuss everything down to the very bone.

It was the critical moment of our relationship. She made it very clear, but without any bitterness or insistence; with weary compassion only. I had to choose. I had to go back to Elise the next morning and talk it out with her. And then I would have to either get divorced or leave Bea. In the defenseless, small hours of the night it all appeared so clear, so simple, so obvious. I would make a decisive move. And then we would start anew, together.

But when I came home the next morning, Elise awaited me with the news that Dad was dying. In a strange way that suspended everything. When I came back after the funeral, each of us seemed to be waiting for the other to refer to the matter again. But neither of us did. The one moment when it had been possible, had passed. Now we allowed it to go on as before. Perhaps each of us secretly blamed the other for it. At the same time we were grateful for the reprieve. One cannot live with high drama day after day.

If I think back now, remembering the disconcerting old man in the wood on the farm that weekend, I find it easier to understand his fantastic story: how he'd followed the Momlambo and received the decorated stick from her. And her message. *If you really want the Momlambo to come to you, and if you want her to sleep with you under one kaross and remove her* inciyo *for you, you must first kill your father in your own heart.*

That night I'd spent with Bea: and Dad died.

Every man has his own Momlambo. You must wait for your own whirlwind.

Shortly after eleven the police van stopped in the farmyard in a cloud of dust. The Black constable went round to let Mandisi out; then returned to the front where he sat waiting beside the White driver. Unmanacled, Mandisi went up the hill to the small enclosure of aloes. Ma and Louis and I followed at a distance. She was walking as erect and as fast as always, but when we reached the top she was too breathless to speak; and I'd never seen her look so old.

From the huts two rows of people approached, men and women

separately. There were no children. (Nor virgins, Ma explained, since death was still taboo to their eyes.) They were singing as they came, those men and women in their separate rows, deep and clear voices like earth and water. And all the time the wind was blowing, more violently than before.

Inside the aloe hedge Mandisi was waiting on a rock close to the raw dry mound of the newly dug hole, his back turned to the others who crowded together on the far side of the grave. We stood farther back, in the entrance to the kraal, as we didn't really have any part in what was happening.

All the time the ceremony lasted, Mandisi remained sitting with his back to his people, looking far away to the hills where the clouds were beginning to gather; apparently unconcerned with whatever was taking place behind him. And while the hole was being filled up, he walked off alone, first to the huts to take leave of his children; then down to the yard and the waiting van. By the time we came back the van had already left with him. The line of dust was still visible up the side of the hill, beyond the flamboyants; soon scattered by the wind.

4

LUNCH WAS SERVED EARLY. As usual, the table was overloaded. "It's impossible to eat so much, Ma!" I protested as she handed round the heaped plates.

"There's a long road ahead, sonny. And one never knows when we'll all be sitting down to a meal together again."

As it turned out, it was the last meal we ever had together on the farm. (A month later, when Ma had to be fetched, I was in the middle of an important transaction and couldn't leave, so Elise had to go to the farm to help Ma with the final arrangements and the packing and to bring her home.) Inevitably, there was a sense of ritual about it, although I deliberately tried not to weigh the atmosphere down with references either to past or future. For the matter was concluded and we owed it to ourselves to make as little fuss as possible over it.

But dishing up the dumplings (Ma always knew exactly what to prepare for me) she said: "If I knew a month ago what I know now, it would have knocked me out on the spot."

"In the final analysis it's for the good of the country, Ma," I tried to mollify her. "We must be prepared to make sacrifices."

"You're fortunate," said Ma quietly, a malicious glint in her blue eyes. "You get other people to make your sacrifices for you."

"Is that what you think?"

The plates were removed; coffee was served.

"And when do you want me to pack up my caboodle?" she asked.

"I'll let you know. There's no great hurry." I tested the coffee with my lips; it was scalding. "But of course one can't postpone it indefinitely either."

Louis pushed away his chair. "I'll go and load the car while you finish your coffee."

Ma and I remained at the table. Only banalities remained to be said. But behind our banter and our irrelevancies lay the weight of lives and generations, fear, bewilderment and silence. Everything we would never be able to pack up and cart away.

When Louis returned from outside at last, loitering very obviously on the doorstep, I also got up.

"My goodness," said Ma. "We haven't even said grace."

"*Ag,* it doesn't matter."

From the bedroom I collected my few odds and ends. Wallet, keys, the pistol. On an impulse I stopped in the passage and took the key to Dad's study from the hook. Leaving through the front door so Ma wouldn't see, I went down to the small outbuilding behind the dairy. While I was struggling to maneuver the heavy hand-carved chair through the door, Louis said outside:

"Let me help you."

"I'll manage." With a final effort I heaved the chair through the opening.

He took it nevertheless. Annoyed, I pulled it away, knocking it against the wall beside the door. One of the arm rests came loose.

"Now look what you've done!" I cried.

"I only tried to help you, Dad." He examined the chair. "It's not serious. We can easily fix it again at home. Now let me carry it for you."

"I told you I can manage!"

"You're not supposed to handle such heavy objects."

"For God's sake, man, I'm not an invalid!"

I picked up the chair. He took the other side. For a few moments we stood glaring at one another. I felt a furious urge to wrench it away from him; but the humiliating thought occurred to me that he might be stronger than I. And the chair might be damaged further. Breathing deeply, and avoiding his eyes, I began to follow him as he led the way across the uneven, stony slope to the yard where the Mercedes was waiting.

Ma watched in deadly silence as we loaded it on the back seat, not without considerable effort. She appeared even more erect than usual, tall and gaunt and grey.

Louis had already opened the driver's door when I took him by the arm. He was taking too much for granted.

"I'll drive," I said.

"But how can you see without your glasses?"

"I've been going without them for two days. One's eyes get used to it."

"But suppose something happens, sonny?" asked Ma, dissatisfied.

"I know the Mercedes and I know the road."

"You know I can drive, Dad. Right through the war in Angola—"

"Now say goodbye to Grandma and get in on your side."

Her long, thin, strong arms; her old dry mouth pressed against mine. An impression of bones. Even our greeting became an affirmation of death. All the many dead in the dried earth, the fresh grave, the inescapable deaths of the future. More finally than anything I'd experienced over the weekend, I was aware of an end in our goodbye kiss: the end of everything capable of ending. I was aware, too, of the silence.

In the yard nothing moved. The ducks and chickens were silent. Even the birds were silent in the wild fig tree. The dogs had stopped their frantic barking and were standing by the water tank, waving their tails, their large open mouths slavering. No sound came from the dairy, or from the huts on the hill, or anywhere else. Even the wind had died down momentarily. Deep down in the hollow of the valley, where the two rows of hills met, the dark thicket of the wood lay in utter silence.

❖ ❖ ❖

Nothing determines an end so fatally as a beginning. But I don't think that is why I have not written about the beginning of my relationship with Bea yet. I had hoped it would prove to be irrelevant; I'd hoped to be able to say enough about her without having to return to that first night; to that first morning. But I realize now that I have no choice. It no longer depends exclusively on myself. It simply has to be written down, with everything related to it. Even if it means a return to Bernard.

Arriving at Aunt Rienie's flat that evening, in one of the charming old-fashioned buildings in Parktown, high above the snarling traffic of Jan Smuts Avenue, it was already overflowing with people. From my experience of her previous birthday parties I'd expected it: that crowd of strangers drawn together from all over the country and all strata of society. God knows how and where she'd met them all.

In her youth Aunt Rienie must have been a beauty; and, in addition to the three husbands she'd buried one after the other, she'd often hinted slyly at a staggering succession of lovers in her life, even now that she was in her late seventies. I know that once, when she was seriously ill, she summoned Bernard to her bedside (for among all her friends and acolytes he'd always been her favorite) and made him promise that, in the event of her death, he would remove the hatbox filled with old letters, hidden behind the bottles of Roodeberg in her wardrobe; he was given permission to read them if he so wished, but afterwards they had to be burnt before any of her five children could lay hands on them.

The lounge, the balcony, the bedroom, the minuscule kitchen, even the bathroom was crammed with guests; the front door stood open, allowing people to spill from the flat into the interior of the impressive old building, down the staircase and even into the driveway. To the roar of the crowd was added loud music—not the sort of music one would expect at a party, but Vivaldi, Telemann, Scarlatti, Haydn. Incredibly, Aunt Rienie immediately located me in the throng.

"Martin! I couldn't wait for you to come."

Kissing one of her highly rouged cheeks I offered her the present I'd chosen for her, a Victorian brooch with nine small rubies, which she promptly pinned to her blue dress.

"And where's Bernard?"

"He very badly wanted to come, Aunt Rienie. He kept it open until the last minute. But this trial is keeping him busy full time and he had to do some urgent preparation for tomorrow."

"Oh what a pity." Her disappointment was as immediate and as fleeting as all her quicksilver moods. "I specially invited a girl for him."

"She won't have any problem finding another partner in this crowd."

"But that's not the point, Martin. I chose her with the greatest of care. All right, I know I'm trying every year, don't pull such a face. But this time I knew immediately: she's just *made* for Bernard, it's written in the stars. And she's in the legal profession too."

"Sounds formidable."

"Wait till you meet her." And while I found it almost impossible to move a finger in that crowd, she nonchalantly ducked under the raised elbows of a group of men and disappeared, returning within a minute with her treasure: "Well, Martin, what do you say? This is Beatrice Fiorini." She pronounced it in very correct Italian. "You may call her Bea."

We were an island in the crowd, pushed and jostled from all sides, yet isolated at the same time. Her hand was cool and firm. A small mocking smile, perhaps to hide her nervousness. The tiny muscle in her cheek. The mystery of eyes obscured behind dark glasses—even though it was night. She was wearing a knitted mauve coat reaching down to her calves, and a denim dress; a small silk scarf tied round her neck.

"Martin will keep you company," Aunt Rienie assured her. "Such a pity Bernard couldn't come. But I'll see to it that—oh, excuse me, there are some new guests at the door." And she disappeared.

"I'm quite relieved this Bernard bloke didn't turn up," Bea confided with a smile. "I was beginning to feel like a cow brought to auction."

"I don't think you would have regretted it. Would you like something to drink?"

"I had a glass somewhere, but God alone knows what's happened to it."

Her Afrikaans pronunciation was faultless; but with something sing-song in her intonation, an unusual roundness in the vowels, a slight hesitation on double consonants.

"Are you really Italian?" I asked over my shoulder, forcing a way for us through the crowd; she followed in my wake.

"Oh I'm a potpourri of everything."

When we later reached a small open space on the balcony, I asked: "And how did you meet Aunt Rienie?"

"Pure coincidence," she said. "A few of us have clubbed together to give legal advice to people in trouble. Mostly Blacks. The man working in the gardens of this building had a pass problem, and in the course of our inquiries I came to see Aunt Rienie." The hint of a smile. "So she swallowed the fly."

"That's just her way." I raised my glass. "Well, shall we drink to a pleasant evening?"

"It's not really my sort of scene," she said, hesitant. "If she hadn't insisted so much—have you known her for a long time?"

"Since I was a student. I boarded with her."

We started talking, the meaningless sort of conversation typical of such parties. And yet, even in those early hours there was an undercurrent—or is it wishful thinking, in retrospect?—of closeness, a form of recognition. Perhaps we were both relieved to have found someone to talk to in that mass of strangers.

In the slowly moving whirlpool of people—as some forced their way inward to find food or liquor, pushing out others in the process— we lost one another. Recognizing some other acquaintances I began to drift in their direction; and when I looked round, she'd gone.

The party reeled on into the night, in its boisterous way. Small groups of men tightly huddled together and bursting out in sudden gusts of laughter. The shrill voices of excited women. Glasses passed on overhead from hand to hand. Arguments. Mild flirtations. Smoke. Snatches of conversation:

"He didn't have a choice, he just *had* to kick."

"I'm no critic, but any fool can see—"

"What else can you expect of the bladdy government?"

"It's a lovely party, isn't it?"

"You haven't seen her when she's in the mood yet—"

"Her father was a sculptor. He either died or failed, I can't remember which."

Once I suddenly saw her again in the distance, on the opposite side of the room, her white face and large dark glasses in a whorl of smoke; I waved at her and she waved back—not a greeting but a signal of distress.

I tried to jostle my way through the crowd towards her, but when I reached the place where I'd seen her, she was no longer there. With a strange feeling of loss I leaned back against the wall. Later it happened again, in exactly the same way. Something about her stark white face and large black eyes was beginning to haunt me. I felt a need to get back to her, to offer her some protection, standing in for Bernard for whose sake she'd been invited. But I couldn't find her.

Deep in the night Aunt Rienie made her appearance in the center of the crowded floor, clutching a thin volume bound in dark-red leather in her tiny hand. A small space opened up around her, from the center of which she began to read to us. There was so much noise that no one more than a yard away from her could hear a word, but she was undeterred. After a while, pushing through to her immediate vicinity, I managed to catch a few phrases. It was Blake, the *Songs of Innocence*, read with exaggerated feeling:

> *"Till the little ones, weary,*
> *No more can be merry;*
> *The sun does descend,*
> *And our sports have an end."*

It was just then that the commotion broke out close to me. What the immediate cause had been, I still don't know; all I heard was the redhaired English lady shouting in a sudden outburst of quite uncontrolled hate:

"You bloody Boers, just a lot of hairy backs, that's what you are!"

The next moment a hunk of a man with the physique of a lock forward grabbed her dress in front of her flat chest, shaking her and asking in a broad accent: "Listen, you got a husband?"

"Let me go, you bloody brute!"

"I say, you got a husband?"

"Of course I have a husband," she said, on the verge of hysterics. "There he is." Pointing to a man on the far side of the room.

Giving one look in that direction, the lock forward bulldozed his way towards a man seated on a chair, his back turned to his wife, quite oblivious of what had happened. The first he noticed of anything amiss was when the lock forward picked him up bodily with his left hand, hooking him with the right and sending him sprawling into the crowd. The next moment everything was in uproar. Chairs breaking, bottles splintering, women screaming; and the whole room began to spin and mill around in confusion.

It is my principle to keep out of such frays. And when I was halfway to the front door, I suddenly discovered her beside me again: the strange pale girl in the dark glasses. Bea.

"I've had enough!" I shouted in her ear—the only way of communicating in the hubbub. "I'm going."

"Please take me with you," she said, clutching my arm in near-panic.

From the front door I looked back across my shoulder. Over the heads of the jostling, trampling crowd I could still see Aunt Rienie in the middle of the floor: a delicate porcelain figure with her book clasped to her breast and silent tears rolling down her cheeks.

Suddenly, shockingly, we were outside in the night, the warm autumn air on our faces.

"Good God," Bea said after a few moments. "What a mess. Poor Aunt Rienie."

"Oh she's used to everything. There's some sort of drama every year."

We walked on through the quiet night lanes, passing under street lamps from time to time, aimlessly, just to get away from the noise.

"Thanks for taking me with you," she said once. "I couldn't stand it much longer."

"I've been trying all evening to find you again," I said impulsively. "But every time I missed you in the crowd."

"And I tried to reach you. It was like a nightmare in which one tries to move but can't."

We stopped under a lamp post. I raised my hands and lay my open palms on her pale cheeks. I could feel her lips trembling. She was looking up at me.

"Do you always wear those sunglasses?" I asked.

She nodded.

Moving my hands on her face I took off the glasses. For a moment she tensed, then relaxed.

"Why do you do it?" she asked.

"Because you needn't be afraid of me." I put the glasses in my top coat pocket.

"I'm not afraid."

We walked on again.

I have no idea of where we wandered that night. At some stage we reached the Zoo Lake. Vaguely in the back of my head I knew it was supposed to be dangerous in the dark, but I made no move to steer her away from it. We explored the entire geography of the night, over gravel and grass, through patches of light and long stretches of darkness, past trees and shrubs; sometimes we sat down for a while, on benches or on the grass. When the air became cooler I took off my coat and placed it over her shoulders, keeping my arm round her. And all the time, for hours on end, we went on talking. It was quite different from my experience with other women: even with my arm round her there was something comradely between us, rather than desire.

I'd often picked up girls at parties before. It's so easy. And the sequence of events is so predictable, give and take a few minor variations or surprises. But not with Bea. We were interested in talking, not cuddling.

She told me the whole intricate history of her life: her mother's affair with the German soldier in the war, and the subsequent move to the United States; later, after her mother's death, the emigration to the Cape, in the company of her Hungarian stepfather. His garage business in Mowbray. The smell of oil, a detail which had haunted her like an obsession all her life. Some nights, after the Hungarian had already gone to bed, she would steal into the bathroom and pick up his greasy overalls and press her face into them. The shock, in her fifteenth year, when late one afternoon in the dark, locked garage he'd pressed her against the wall and started fondling her passionately. Nothing had "happened." It was only the shock. The smudges of oil

453

and grease on her dress and legs and breasts. The man falling to his knees and bursting into tears, begging her forgiveness.

The inheritance money which had reached her unexpectedly from one of her Italian-American uncles in the States. University, where she'd fared brilliantly. Languages; then law studies. The compulsion in her to go on studying. In search of something impossible to find because it couldn't even be defined.

"Two years ago I decided to go overseas. Something had happened, you see. One of my professors—but I don't want to bore you."

"Of course you won't bore me. Please tell me."

"I was still a student when we fell in love. He was much older than I, he could have been my father. It was he who found the post for me. Junior lecturer in the Faculty of Law."

"Why didn't you stay with him?"

"He was married." A pause. She picked a stalk of grass and began to chew on it. Much later she went on: "His wife was an invalid. I never meant to—anyway, it happened. And I was too stupid or too weak to move out. Then his wife died. And all of a sudden—it's difficult to explain—the spell was broken or something. It was all over. He wanted to marry me. But it was as if the death of his wife had made me realize for the first time how petty and sordid our love had been. I couldn't forget her. You know, she'd often thanked me for helping her husband so much." Another pause. "So one day I just decided to go overseas."

"To escape?"

"Yes. But it was more than just running away. There was also something I wanted to go *to*"

"What?"

"Well, you see, all my life I'd been unsettled. I'd known my mother for a few years only, and my father not at all. I still had some vague, confused memories of Italy, of our town, and of bombs and shooting and buildings being blown up." She fell silent. Feeling her trembling lightly against me I tightened my arm around her. "And then the States, a foreign country I couldn't adapt to at all. And another foreign country, South Africa. And Stepan, my Hungarian stepfather. Strange languages, and people, and lands, and cities. All the time. Somewhere in the midst of it all I think I'd just, somehow, lost myself. Can you understand that? And then the prof. For a year, for eighteen months there seemed to be a new stability in my life. Then I discovered it had just been another drifting island. So I thought, you know, perhaps if I went back to where it had all started, it might clear things up. I wanted to return to Perugia to try and find myself again."

"Did you succeed?"

She shook her head. Repeating it after a minute. And then said: "Perhaps I was mistaken from the beginning. I thought one needed to define oneself in terms of a geography, and a language, and other people. I thought there *must* be people and places where one belonged automatically. But if there really is such a place I still haven't found it. Perugia was beautiful, it's the most beautiful country I know of. All those little spires, and the fields with white oxen plowing, and the red poppies in the grass, and Fra Angelico and everything. But I remained a stranger. Here and there I still found someone who could vaguely remember my mother or my grandparents. But what use was it to me? It made no difference to *me.*"

"And then you came back?"

"Not directly. I stayed there for a year to finish my course. I was there on a grant, you see. And then I went to the States. I thought maybe I'd find some trace of myself there." A short harsh laugh. "I couldn't last there for more than just a few months. I was welcomed with open arms by my mother's relatives and all the friends of the family. They had an incredibly strong clan feeling. But it was no use. I could never become one of them. I always remained *me*. And when I came back, I found that Stepan had also died. Poor Stepan, I really think he loved me. But it was all in vain."

Insects were whirring and chirping in the grass. In the trees a nightjar shrieked.

"In a strange way it also made me feel free," she went on. "Completely liberated. And now I'm responsible only to myself." A pause. "But it isn't easy to bear. Sometimes one thinks: If only I could come to rest for a short time, give myself to some cause, lose myself in something, it will be easier to carry on. But of course it can never happen."

When she remained silent again, I asked: "What are you thinking about?"

She gave a short laugh: "A game."

"What sort of game?"

"A party game. You probably know it. One is taken into a room and shown everything: all over the floor objects have been arranged—suitcases, bottles, chairs, plates, whatever they could lay hands on. Then you're blindfolded and spun round, and left to find your way through all the obstacles on your own. In the beginning you're terrified of bumping into something. Later you become almost panic-stricken in your wish to touch something, so you can find your bearings. But you're lost. And when they finally remove the cloth from your eyes you discover the room is empty: they quietly removed everything while you were blindfolded. They all kill themselves laughing while you stand there feeling ridiculous. That's the way it is for me. Trying to pick my way, blindfolded, through an empty room, feeling for obstacles which don't exist."

"I'll hold on to you," I said, touched by the terror in her words.

"It's no use."

"How do you know? You've only tried your prof. And he was an exception."

"No, he wasn't."

"What do you mean, Bea?"

"He wasn't the only one I loved." She appeared reluctant to reveal any more, but changed her mind after a while. "When I first went to university there was a young Jewish student in my class. Benjamin. He was the first boy I ever went to bed with. But after he'd taken me to his parents—he'd never wanted to, I had to insist—I realized it had been an illusion. They were very orthodox, they would never allow him to marry a *shikse.*"

"And so you ended it?"

"What else could I do? He couldn't understand what had got into me. Men are scared of facing the truth even though they know it's there, don't you think so? I tried to make it as easy as possible for him"—a shrug—"but that was that."

"Was he the only other one?"

"Why do you keep on asking?"

"Because you came with me tonight."

"We're going back just now. One can't go on walking for ever. Don't forget: sooner or later your blindfold is taken off."

"But we're here now. And I want to hear whatever you're prepared to tell me." (Women have always found me a good listener: it's more than half the answer. Still, I really meant it that night, I'm sure.)

She laughed again: "What will Aunt Rienie say if she knew?" Before I could reply she went on: "You know, that's what really got me at the party. I recently read Ardrey; what he says about baboons. How the females, when they're on heat, make sure their inflamed red backsides are turned towards the males all the time. I always thought a baboon male must be bloody perverse to fall for it, but they do. And whenever I get to parties nowadays and watch the women carrying on, I can't resist the thought: " Jesus, so that's what they're really doing!" She turned her head to me, watching me with her wide, naked eyes. "Is that why you brought me away with you?"

"I felt just as cornered as you were."

She pressed my hands. "Thanks, Sir Galahad."

"Why do you mock me?"

"I'm not. There really is something old-worldly about you. You're so polite. I almost feel safe with you."

It was too dark to make out how much of it was cynical.

"Like a father confessor?" I asked.

"Why do you say that?" she asked quickly.

"I didn't mean anything. Except that you're free to confide in me whatever you want to."

Her mood changed, and became lighter. "I once went to confession with a rather deaf old priest," she said, chuckling. "It was awful. It was just before Easter and everybody was queuing to get their bit done in time. But he was terribly hard of hearing. And every time I told him something he would ask in a loud voice reverberating right through the church: "You did *what*?" Followed by a ripple of giggling all down the queue."

"Are you Catholic?"

"No."

"Why did you go to the priest then?"

"I *was* Catholic."

"Why did you drop it?"

"The first twenty years of my life—in spite of all that happened, all the people passing me on from hand to hand and from country to country—that was the one constant factor of my life. The Church. It was quite neurotic, the way I clung to it. At Mass I often went into a near-trance, taking an almost incestuous delight in devouring the flesh and blood of Jesus." She turned her head to me again, but I couldn't read her expression in the dark. "Then, after Benjamin and I had broken up, I realized the Church was just a dope. It made it even more impossible to be honest with myself. And so I had to break away from it." She was silent for a minute. I could hear her breathing gently. "In a sense it was almost more painful than to break away from a man I'd loved. Because I knew that once I was out of that, there would be nothing left. It was the very last of the obstacles they took away from my blind room."

"Why did you go through with it?"

"I had to. What else?"

"And now?"

"Now I'm trying to go it alone. One has got to stand on one's own feet. I don't need any crutches. And I want to look the world squarely in the face."

"I'll help you."

"No one can help me."

"I shall. Just give me a chance."

We kissed for the first time. In that brief touch—for it was very light and almost fleeting, as if both of us were scared of what might happen—I knew it would be worthwhile.

We went back to Aunt Rienie's building. The noise had subsided somewhat in our absence and a number of guests had left, but the party, I knew, would continue until dawn. Unlocking the car, I opened the door for Bea to get in.

"Wait for me. I'll be back in a moment."

From Aunt Rienie's flat I telephoned my apartment (there were so many people around, no one paid attention to me). Bernard answered.

"Have you gone to bed already?" I asked.

"Of course not. I told you I'd wait for you to come back."

I was silent for a moment.

"Listen, Bernard, we can find some other time. Tomorrow, any time that suits you."

"Oh." I couldn't hear the disappointment in his voice. "Aren't you coming back then?"

"Yes, I am. But I'm bringing someone with me. Do you mind moving into the spare room?"

He said something I couldn't hear; then he rang off.

Avoiding Aunt Rienie's crowded, smoky lounge I hurried outside again, down to my car.

The hands of the clock on the dashboard gleamed on a quarter to three.

As we turned into Joubert Park, she said:

"My flat is in Berea."

"Stay with me." I looked straight ahead. "Will you?"

She uttered a small sigh, but said nothing.

There was a parking place a block away from my building. In the ghostly neon light of the foyer we stood waiting for the lift. On the way up neither said a word.

Only the reading lamp was burning in the front room.

"Would you like to have a bath?" I said. "I'll make us some coffee."

"All right."

I put a Mozart on the record player, the sound turned down low so as not to disturb Bernard. It struck me as very strange that he should be there, behind the closed door of the spare room. After all, if he'd gone to Aunt Rienie's with me, he would have been the one introduced to Bea. It would have been they who escaped into the night. To him she would have told everything she'd now confided to me. She'd been "meant" for him. In a sense I was only standing in for him, his surrogate. We'd changed places. Now he was asleep next door.

Half an hour later she came from the bathroom wearing my dressing gown, barefoot, her hair damp. We drank our hot coffee in silence, listening to Mozart. From time to time, at very long intervals, a car passed outside. In a low, almost inaudible drone the innumerable lives of the city hummed on. Through the open window the night breeze came in, an almost unnoticeable stirring in the curtains.

When I came from the bathroom, later, she was already in bed.

"Put off the light," she said as I lifted the sheet.

I moved in beside her and began to stroke her. Once again I heard her sigh.

"What's the matter?" I said. "Don't you want to?"

She didn't answer. She only took my hand and placed it between her legs. There was something wry about the gesture, a compassion which moved me. As if, in doing so, she wanted to say: *What else have we got to share? It may as well happen.*

All the time we were making love I was conscious of Bernard next door, hearing her gasps and moans, and her wild cries as she lost all control in a wildness which both amazed and excited me.

Outside, the leaves of the plane trees began to stir, rustling. I fell asleep. When I woke up—the sun wasn't out yet—the bed beside me was empty. For a moment I groped for her in a daze. Then I sat up. She was standing at the door, already dressed, looking round in bewilderment as she heard me.

"Where are you going?" I asked.

"Nowhere. I—" She looked like a cornered animal. "I didn't realize you were awake already."

"Stay here, please."

She shook her head. "I've got to go. The buses are running already."

"I can take you home any time. Why are you in such a hurry?"

"I didn't want to wake you up." She had a helpless, hopeless look on her face.

"But why did you want to go away?"

"It's all over, isn't it? It can't go on."

"You know it isn't over, Bea. It has only started."

"Oh no. Please. Not again."

"Don't be so scared. Nothing will happen. After last night—"

"No!" she interrupted me vehemently. "Please forget about it. There's nothing that binds us. Don't let's start with anything now. It's over."

In the other room a door clicked. Then came a sound of running water.

Startled, she looked at me: "Who's next door?"

"A friend. He's using my apartment." I looked into her eyes. "The Bernard Aunt Rienie wanted to introduce you to."

"I don't want to meet him."

"You'll like him."

"I don't *want* to meet him. Not now."

5

M Y MYOPIA WAS AS BAD as a swarm of gnats on the
windscreen. Worse, actually, because in the smudge of the
gnats there had at least been clearer patches: now
everything was uniformly dull. I could see enough of the road to know
where I was going, but all particulars were blunted. My reactions were
determined by memory and intuition, not by what was really
happening from moment to moment. And as we went on, a headache
began to press on me more and more heavily.

Cathcart, Queenstown, Jamestown.

On the way down it had been dark on this stretch; now the sun
was shining, sporadically obscured by masses of drifting clouds; but
it didn't make any difference to my vision. And in submitting myself
to our progress I gradually became conscious of a curious impression
of driving in against myself, against my own past. If only I could see
more clearly, I felt, I would be able to see myself coming on ahead on
my way down to the farm. From time to time I caught myself leaning
forward and screwing up my eyes, as if I actually expected to see myself
emerge from the obscurity ahead.

Monday was moving in against Friday. Nothing was isolated or
concluded. All that was required was a fractional shift in dimensions:
then I would be back in that crowd in the street below the building
where the man had been sitting on the ledge, and I would hear them

shouting ecstatically: "Jump! Jump!" And he would come tumbling down like a bundle of old clothes. And Louis would come up from behind to touch my arm again, looking at me with the darkness of knowledge in his eyes, as on that other, more innocuous, day beside a swimming pool rippling with barely nubile nymphets. A small shift, and a little girl would once again be skipping on a pavement, her dress flying up, revealing everything. One saw without looking. Everything I had begun to see anew, in spite of a dull desire to remain in ignorance.

I seemed to be on my way back to everything I'd momentarily discarded: Charlie pulling off his clothes to prance naked, like a savage, at the head of the angry mob, and shattering my windscreen with a brick. Stag parties with stripped and shaven writhing girls. Smart soirees, Prof Pienaar and his collected poems; the meticulous aesthetics of his wife's menu, the oracles of Koos Cunt. Rev. Cloete on the brown bench in the charge office. A disturbance in the backyard, a man hurled into a police van: *But Baas, it's my husband:* behind her the open servant's room, the iron bed supported on bricks, high enough for the *tokoloshe* to pass under.

And, inevitably, Bernard. His blonde hair and brown back in the canoe ahead of me, sweeping dizzily past rocks and boulders, and spinning past the lethal vortex of the pool. (And Elise losing her baby a week later. Nothing wrong organically, assured the doctor, mainly nervous tension. Next time, Mr. Mynhardt, you really should try to stay with her during the first few months. It upset her terribly to be alone—but my God, you can't blame me for it! It was Bernard who'd insisted.)

Bernard on the farm. Behind the dam, that Sunday afternoon. Her knees touching my chest, her mouth filled with pomegranate seeds. And years later, late one night in a half-dark room, a woman with her hand outstretched to receive a glass: two faces in profile, an eternally incomplete moment. My body still bruised by the girl Marlene; deep inside me the awareness of distances confirmed for ever. Between her and me: between him and me. Everything just as absurd as a body with a blue circle painted round its navel.

The courtroom with its paneling and dusty curtains, and the fan swinging crookedly from its stiff rod. *Were I to ask forgiveness today I would betray my cause and my convictions, for I believe that what I did was right.* The people rising to sing *Nkosi sikelel' iAfrika.* His pale, tense face. So totally different from the seedy old woman who'd entered my car that drizzly night and suddenly addressed me in his voice.

It was on her birthday in September that she took me to Diagonal Street. What made her do it? So often I found her motivation incomprehensible. (Why did Charlie take me to Soweto?)

A bewildering little street, with the fruit vendors' carts heaped with bananas and tomatoes and late oranges and early strawberries. The small Black boys shouting their heads off to advertise their wares. The dingy little stores. Secondhand junk shops, exotic wares, items from a lost world (yokes and harnesses for ox-wagon teams, whips of rhino or hippo hide, quaintly plaited sjamboks).

"Why did you bring me here?" I asked her. "I've often driven past here."

"But you don't know it. You never notice anything when you whiz past like that. I want to show you something of your own city. My birthday present to *you*. We may never have another chance: one of these days they're sending in the bulldozers."

"High time."

"Come on," she said, putting her arm through mine to lead me to her "witchdoctor place." The incredible, dark, stinking little shop specializing in herbs and *muti*, anything from *dolosse* to musk-cat fur, dried ostrich heads and monkey tails, the skins of porcupines and snakes and iguanas, shriveled beaks and nails and claws and unrecognizable inner organs, under the morbid surveillance of a large shapeless Indian in a cloud of incense behind the counter. It was a visit to a world just as extraordinary, and just as preposterous, as that of the old man in the wood, months later. Only more disconcerting, since it occurred in the heart of the city I thought I knew so thoroughly.

Bea had a hearty greeting for the sulky old Indian, as if they knew each other well. And towards her he did warm up for a moment: but in front of me he maintained his surly, frowning, suspicious silence.

"What are we looking for?" I asked, overcome by the stench of the place.

"Shall I buy some *muti* to put in your coffee?" she suggested blithely.

"Do you want to get rid of me for good?"

"No, it may make you fall in love with me."

"Don't you think I'm in love with you already?"

"I doubt it." On our way out she turned to wave to the morose shopkeeper. "I don't think you really know what 'love' means."

In the dazzling street light, amid the web of sound woven by pennywhistles on the pavement, I stopped to look at her. "What do you mean, Bea?"

In the same light, bantering tone she went on: "You think 'to love' means 'to have.' Isn't that so?"

"I'm very sorry if you really think so."

"Martin, Martin, you're incorrigible." She restored the dark glasses to her nose: quite surprisingly she'd taken them off in the shop.

"I don't understand you," I said gruffly.

"It's not me you don't understand, it's yourself."

"I know myself perfectly well, thank you."

"Grumpy." Putting her arm through mine she started whistling a tune the pennywhistles had been playing.

Earlier that morning, when I'd given her my present, she'd reacted just as unpredictably. It had been a small golden locket—very simple and old and expensive—which she'd admired in a jeweler's shop before. I'd expected her to be enraptured. Not that she'd been disappointed or ungrateful: her reaction had just been strange, that's all.

"You shouldn't have given it to me," she'd said.

"But the other day you said it was beautiful."

"It was beautiful without having it. Don't you understand?"

"Now it's yours."

I must have looked crestfallen, for she'd put her arms round my neck and kissed me. And it was then she'd said: "Come, I want to give you something too," and had taken me to Diagonal Street.

"Do you know the shopkeeper in that witchdoctor place?" I asked her, back in the familiar streets of the city center.

"Not very well."

"He looks like a bloody criminal to me."

"Possibly. He has a very kind heart. I once helped him with a case. They planted stolen stuff on him."

"And you believed his story?"

"I helped him."

"You sound more like Bernard everyday."

"Bernard also rather liked him," she said flatly.

"How did he meet him?"

"I once went to show him the street."

"Bea." Once again I stopped on the pavement. "Do you see Bernard often?"

"Only from time to time when he's up here." She made no attempt to avoid my stare.

A moment of fear and suspicion. (Reinette.) But I pulled myself together angrily. My God, I knew Bernard well enough; I knew Bea. Neither of them would ever—the mere thought was absurd and unworthy. I trusted him. I trusted her. Without that conviction everything would become intolerable.

"What's the matter, Martin?"

"I was just wondering."

"You know I like Bernard very much. I see him seldom enough. Surely you don't think—"

"I'm not thinking anything."

Something gloomy had settled on the spring morning. But on our way to her flat, driving in against the Saturday morning traffic, the old trust between us was restored. She knew well how to handle my occasional moods. And back in the chaos of her flat, while she was bustling about in the small kitchen, humming to herself, I soon relaxed.

"D'you realize I'm a Virgin?" she asked playfully as she brought in a tray and I rose to take it.

"How do you manage that?"

"I was referring to the sign of the zodiac."

"You don't believe in such nonsense, do you? I thought you were an academic and an agnostic."

"Right. But it still doesn't make a computer out of me."

"How silly can you be?"

"I'm no ordinary Virgo either. I was born on exactly the ninth day of the ninth month, do you realize?"

"And what does that make you?" I asked patiently, the way I would treat Ilse in similar circumstances.

"According to the old Mysteries it makes me a hermit."

"Not far wrong," I conceded.

"And a prophet."

"That sounds a bit exaggerated, don't you think?"

"Yes, I agree. But one never knows." In the confusion on her shelves she immediately found the book she wanted. Obviously I didn't try to memorize what she read out to me. But, paraphrased, the gibberish boiled down to the fact that nine was the number of prophet-hermits, generally despised if not actively persecuted, and making their appearance "on the eve of great disasters." That phrase

I do remember. *On the eve of great disasters.* She looked almost smug when she pushed the book into the shelf.

"What do you think of that?"

"Suppose it's harmless enough as long as it remains a game."

"It's not harmless. It's extremely dangerous."

"Why don't you stop it then?"

"For the same reason which makes me love Diagonal Street. Do you know one is in danger of one's life if one goes there after dark? You can be zapped in the back any moment. It's dangerous even by car."

"I hope *you* never go there after dark!"

"Not really. You needn't be afraid."

Exactly the same words she'd said that morning after she'd first met Bernard. *You needn't be afraid.*

When he came from the bathroom with just a towel wrapped round his waist, we were having tea. He stopped for a moment. His face looked tired and tense, as if he hadn't had much sleep. But when he saw her, he smiled spontaneously:

"Miss Livingstone, I presume?"

She also smiled, in spite of herself, and said lightly: "You should be grateful to Martin. He's saved you from a fate worse than death. According to Aunt Rienie I was meant for you, not him. Destined, if I understood her correctly, since the beginning of the world."

"Hm." With an amused frown he looked from her to me, and back again. "Oh well," he said, with exaggerated feeling. "Trains passing in the night and all that. Too late, forever." His boyish grin. "Anyway, glad to meet you."

"I'm sure you would like to get dressed," I said coolly, noticing Bea's eyes on him.

He immediately withdrew to his room, joining us again a few minutes later—but not for long, as he was in a hurry to confer with his attorneys before the day's proceedings.

"Perhaps I'll look in at the court one morning," Bea said when he left.

"Just warn me in time so I can put on my full act."

There was a long pause between us after he'd gone.

"You see?" I remarked at last. "I told you you would like Bernard."

"'Like' is a rather neutral sort of word."

"What do you mean?"

"I'm sure he must have many violent enemies. And very loyal friends. He doesn't seem to be the sort of person one can feel lukewarm about."

"Yes, you're right."

"He must have many women too," she said, looking at her hands.

"Oh yes, all the years I've known him."

"Is that a long time?"

"Nearly twenty years."

"Strange how one builds up one's own impression of someone. I've often read about him in the papers, you know. But he's different from what I expected."

"How different?"

"I don't know what it is, but when he looks at one it's as if your stomach contracts and your legs go all watery. I don't generally react in such an adolescent way."

"You see, it would have been better if you'd met him last night." I tried to sound neutral, but couldn't prevent a touch of sharpness.

"Why do you say that?" she asked, offended. "You don't think I would have—"

"Most women seem to regard it as a privilege."

"You think because I came back here with you—my God, what *do* you think of me?"

With a shock I recalled how she—this woman sitting so correctly opposite me, with the scarf round her neck, and her mauve knitted coat over her denim dress, and her protective dark glasses on her straight, small nose—how last night, only a few hours ago in fact, she'd taken my hand in hers and placed it between her legs. In the stern light of the new day it appeared preposterous.

"Do you regret what's happened then, Bea?" I asked, very tense.

"No. I never regret anything. What's the use of it?"

"Would you have preferred it different?"

"Oh stop all this questioning!" she said. "Is it necessary to have a postmortem?"

Realizing that the conversation was becoming fraught with danger, I put my hand on hers. "It's important for me to know. Because if we later—"

"I told you it's over, Martin. And if we can't accept it like that here and now—"

"I don't want it to be over."

Shrugging her shoulders, she pushed back her cup. "Will you take me home now, please?"

On our way through the heavy morning traffic she said: "Why can't one always be together as on a first night? Why must it always be complicated afterwards? Why does one try to force the future?"

Sitting beside her I knew—a shaming thought, perhaps, but nevertheless—that if she hadn't reacted to Bernard the way she had, I might have accepted it as a one-night stand. It wouldn't have been the first in my life; nor the last. But now he was there, somewhere, invisible, threatening. Last night I'd stood in for him. And what other usurpations were waiting ahead?

"When may I see you again?" I asked when we stopped at her block.

"Please, Martin!"

"Or would you rather see Bernard?" I asked impetuously, even though I realized the childishness of my attitude.

She removed her sunglasses to clean the lenses with the hem of her skirt. With wide dark eyes she looked straight at me. "Bernard will be an abyss to me," she said. "You needn't be afraid."

A strange thing to have said, wasn't it?—*You needn't be afraid.*

"Will you prove it to me?"

"I'm not promising anything." With a small strained smile she put on her glasses again, and bent over to kiss me lightly on the lips. "Thank you, Martin," she said. And before I could get out to open the door for her she was on her way to the front entrance.

It was no use going on grimly like that: one had to acknowledge one's limitations. The constant concentration on the road had made my headache unbearable. And when we stopped at Aliwal North for petrol, I laconically told Louis:

"You may take over now if you want to."

He looked surprised, elated. I handed him the keys and took some Disprin from the cubbyhole. *Take the keys,* I thought, looking right past him. *But I shall have the last word after all. Don't expect me to intercede for Bernard any more. Both you and he have forfeited that chance.* Anyway, the very idea had been sentimental.

6

THERE WAS A FEELING of something coming to a head: of ends being approached. Leaning my head against the headrest I half-closed my eyes, listening to Ingrid Haebler. After Bloemfontein I took out the round biscuit tin in which Ma had packed our food for the road. As always, there was too much of everything. Bluish hard-boiled eggs, slices of lamb, chicken drumsticks, sandwiches, cheese, a Thermos with sweet black coffee. Louis pecked listlessly at a sandwich, with no more appetite than I. After we'd finished I cleaned out the tin and threw the remaining food and papers through the window. Louis glanced swiftly, sharply in my direction *(Keep your country clean)*, but didn't say a word. I didn't pay any attention to his silent disapproval. I felt relieved, as if we'd shed ballast. One was growing lighter all the way.

There was so much behind us now. Dad's excruciating illness and his death (General Wim Mynhardt buried at last): Dad with his political monthlies and his bookshelves and the hidden frayed cane. Oom Hennie of my childhood, who could turn his saw and chisel into musical instruments, working with old Freddie. And the undertaker I'd had to fetch from his coffins and his vulgar pinups so that he could trim my hair with his blunt cutters. A boy praying passionately for fire from heaven, and an altar washed away by the flood. Mpilo in the muddy dam. The morbid old diviner and his invisible water courses, the white stick blistering his hands. And the old black wizard in the wood, with the exquisite little stick of the Momlambo. The torture of Sunday afternoons. Ma milking with her strong, swift hands, the pail held between her knees, the foam bulging over the edges. Ma comforting the Black baby in her bed, or working among the sick in her little clinic. Thokozile's mother arriving in the dusk and howling up the hill. Mrs. Lawrence in her store; Cathy squirming under my hands in the sweet-smelling dark. Cow dung on my shoe. But everything grew odorless in time and fell from one. Marlene's odor, Cathy's odor, Greta's, Elise's, long ago. And one day Bea's too? Together with the sea smell of Ponta do Ouro and the humus under the shady trees. Everything sterilized by memory; pliable, manageable. *And have not love* in the early dawn. I'm sorry, Grandpa. I can't remember anything, not a single word. And going back in history: nothing.

Nearly two months passed before we spent another night together. Had Bea been any other woman, I would have left her long ago: if one cannot reach one's goal with a woman within a reasonable time, the relationship becomes uneconomical, the investment too large for the eventual return. But I couldn't abandon Bea—and not only because of Bernard, but for herself. I can't stand "intellectual" women. But in Bea intellect itself was a form of passion and a challenge. Often our discussions became fierce arguments: not repelling one another, but, on the contrary, almost fatally drawing us closer together—I suppose that was the most remarkable aspect of it.

We went out for a meal from time to time, taking a very formal leave at her front door ("No, I'm not inviting you in. I know you don't want coffee, you want to make love to me"—"Well, why shouldn't I?"—"I don't think I know you well enough"—"You didn't object that first night"—"No, because it was the first night"). Once, more than a week passed without any sign of her: when I telephoned her flat there would be no answer; and when finally I went round there personally, the door was locked. I was just beginning to feel worried, when she had herself announced by my secretary one afternoon.

The moment after she'd closed the door again I went up to her. "Bea, what's happened to you?"

"I've been working, that's all."

"But I could never find you at your flat."

"Didn't you read about the floods?"

"What about them?" Through a haze of statistics and prognoses I tried to remember what the newspapers had said: a cloudburst to the south of the city, houses submerged, people left roofless, the usual disaster stories.

"I went to help them."

"What did you do?"

"Everything was in such a mess in the beginning, they needed people just to organize things. Arranging for tents and blankets, distributing food and medicine and so on. I spent most of my nights there."

"But isn't it dangerous?"

"Not more dangerous than any apartment in Joubert Park."

"Bea, this is no time for joking."

"No, it isn't. It's damn serious. There's a danger of epidemics breaking out and they need more help."

"I can give you a check."

She looked at me without saying a word.

"Well, what's wrong now?"

"I wish I could tell you to stuff your check," she said. "But I suppose I'd better be grateful."

"Where shall I send it?"

475

"You can give it to me right now. Unless you want to arrange for a photographer and a couple of reporters first?"

I nearly lost my temper with her. But, collecting myself, I pressed the intercom and spoke to the accountant. When I looked up again she was standing by the window, her shoulders sagging slightly.

"Bea, you look exhausted. Shall I order you some tea?"

"If you wish. I haven't slept for three nights."

"But why didn't you get in touch with me?"

"I was afraid you might give me a check."

I went to her, stopping behind her. "You really can't stand me, can you?" I said bitterly. "You despise everything I represent."

"Yes," she said, unflinching. "But that doesn't mean I despise *you.*"

"You think I can still be redeemed?"

"There's a small possibility." There was a brief flickering behind her dark lenses. "Have you always been like this, Martin?"

"Like what?"

"You know what I mean."

"Your problem is that you are an incurable romantic," I said.

"And you're a fanatic materialist."

The tea was brought in. She gulped down her first cup and immediately poured another.

"I'm not a fanatic materialist," I said tersely. "You know I collect paintings, I love to listen to music, I give away thousands every year to art museums and literary prizes and God knows what else."

We were interrupted by the accountant, bringing in the check.

"Thank you," I said. "I'll sign it later."

"Are you joking about all your donations or are you really serious?" Bea asked after he'd left.

I looked at her in surprise. "What makes you think I'm not serious?"

"Do you really think you can save the world in that way?" she asked.

"I have no aspirations to save the world. I leave that to you."

Pouring her third cup, she said quietly: "I have no illusions about myself, Martin. I'm a nobody. I can help distribute blankets and comfort children and arrange for housing. But in your position—my God, Martin, you can do almost anything."

"Don't you think I'm doing enough? Not as spectacularly as you might like it, I concede. But through better wages, better working conditions—that's what people really need, you know. Improving their standard of living. It has nothing to do with politics."

"And how long will it be before you've improved the world enough in your way? Do you really think there's still *time* for it?"

"Everybody is always going on about time, time," I said. "As a matter of fact we have all the time we are prepared to allow ourselves. Only changes introduced gradually and naturally have any hope of surviving. The moment you go too fast, you stimulate a revolutionary situation—and then all is lost."

She got up and went to take the check from the desk. After a moment, the slip of paper still in her hand, she looked round:

"Do you know what shook me most of all in these floods, Martin? Not the dead or the injured or the sick or the broken shanties. That was bad enough. But there was something else. A young man smiling from ear to ear, one of the few in that crowd of soaked, miserable people who seemed happy. And when I asked him the reason, he said: 'Madam, because I was just in time to grab my *dombook* before the water took it away.'"

"I suppose he was suffering from shock. Then one often acts strangely."

"He was very serious, Martin. If that passbook had been washed away, he would have been nothing. Don't you see? Everything he is, is in there. His name, his number, his address, his whole life. Without it he can't go anywhere. What do you think of a society in which a man's *dombook* is his highest priority?"

"You're reacting emotionally again."

"Every time you have no answer you blame me for being 'emotional.' You're just another male chauvinist, you know."

"That's the easiest swearword of our time."

"No. You're an Afrikaner, so you must be a male chauvinist."

"I fail to see what the two can have in common."

"Everything." She sat down opposite me again, on the edge of the chair, her knees primly together. "Because this is a man's land, don't you see? Big game, rugby, industries, power politics, racism. You Afrikaners have no room for women. The only place you assign to us is flat on our backs with our legs open for the Big Boss to in-and-out as he pleases."

"Is that what you think of me?"

She rose and kissed me gently on the forehead. "You, my darling Boer," she said, "are free to convince me of the contrary. And don't forget to sign your check. We'll send you a receipt."

✧ ✧ ✧

So many of our conversations during those few months developed along the same lines, as if all the time we were trying to provoke or test or challenge one another, moving closer and closer to what had probably been inevitable from the start. Yet the turning point, when it came, was very sudden.

She made a formal appointment to come to my office again soon after the end of the terrorism trial, when Bernard had already returned to the Cape. This time she wanted me to arrange jobs for two young matriculated Blacks she'd met at one of her evening classes.

"But we have no vacancies for that type of person, Bea."

"You can create posts, can't you? Or else you surely know other people who can help."

"Now if they'd been looking for jobs on the mines—"

"They have their matric, Martin. I'm looking for decent work. They're not bloody little teaboys."

"I'll see what I can do."

"You're going to offer me something concrete before I leave your office. I *promised* them."

"That was taking rather much for granted, don't you think?"

"I thought you were an influential man." She was teasing again. "Or do you only use your influence to lure women to bed?"

I matched the lightness of her tone: "I'm afraid I've lost my touch with women lately."

"Poor man. Have you been to a doctor?"

"Yes. He said there was only one remedy. To make love to a half Hungarian-American girl of Italian-German descent. But it's rather difficult to find one. You don't know of one you can recommend?"

"I'll make inquiries," she said. "Now what about those two young-sters?"

"You know," I said, suddenly reproachful and not without bitterness, "whenever you have a chance you accuse me of being a bloody Boer or a racist or a chauvinist pig. But the moment I can do something for you, you don't hesitate to make use of me."

"Oh, I'm not using you at all," she said, still teasing. "I'm offering you a chance of becoming a better man."

"Thank you very much. In exchange, I'll make sure I find some-thing for your needy wards."

"I knew you would. Thanks, Martin." She rose to go.

"Don't go so soon," I said.

"Why not? Do you first want to seduce me on your couch?"

"What about the desk? Then I needn't stop working. I can read over your shoulder. Listen, Bea: I have something much more impor-tant than two young tsotsis to discuss with you."

"What?"

"I have a job for you."

"What sort of job?"

"I'm considering appointing a legal adviser and he'll need an assistant. It's a very responsible position."

She studied me for quite a while before she asked: "Why me?"

"I know you're desperate for a job. And I'm sure you'll be excellent."

"You think you'll stand a better chance once you're my boss?"

"That has nothing to do with it."

"Don't fool yourself. For heaven's sake stop trying to annex me. You Afrikaners are all imperialists by nature. Always want to be the boss, even in love."

(Charlie once expressed it more brutally: "Deep down you have a very simple philosophy, Martin: 'What I can't buy or screw, I either tear down or fuck up.'" Typical of his way of thinking.)

"Can't you see I sincerely want to help you, Bea?"

"I'll accept the post on one condition," she said unexpectedly.

"What's that?"

"That from that moment we'll communicate strictly on a business basis."

"But you—"

"I learned a lot from my prof." Coming closer to me she touched my cheek with her hand. "Sorry, Martin. Surely you know I can't accept it."

I'd planned it as a last maneuver. Now, defenseless, I stood looking at her, depressed and ashamed. She went to the door. As she touched the knob she looked over her shoulder to say goodbye.

"How about dinner tonight?" I asked wretchedly.

"No."

Nothing surprised me any more. I turned back to my desk.

"I have another suggestion," she said behind me.

"What?" I remained with my back to her.

"Are you going to your apartment after work?"

"No, I didn't plan to." I turned round. "Why?"

"It just occurred to me that if you were there I might come and spend the night with you." And before I could open my mouth to say a word she'd closed the door quietly behind her.

◇ ◇ ◇ ◇

Nearing the fork in the national road, Louis decreased his speed.

"Shall we go back via Winburg?" he asked.

It was the route I normally followed; the route I would have come if I hadn't accidentally taken the road to Westonaria on Friday. But this time there was no doubt in my mind.

"No, we're going back the same way we came," I said laconically.

It was a trifling matter; yet it felt like a momentous decision. Was I yielding to the same hidden powers acknowledged by Bea in her addiction to astrology? Ludicrous. But dusk was falling and Brandfort lay ahead, where we'd stopped at the garage to have the gnats washed from the windscreen, and where the little girl had been skipping on the dusty pavement: and somewhere ahead, invisible but inescapable, we were approaching ourselves. The point of encounter couldn't be very far away. And what would happen then? A moment of illumination, or the apocalypse? Neither. I wasn't really so naive. And yet I refused to consider the alternative route for one moment. I wanted to go straight on, upstream against whatever was awaiting me, denying nothing, refusing nothing, avoiding nothing.

(Was I really thinking all this on my way back, or am I projecting it on that journey from my isolation in this London winter? I'm not sure that I thought *anything* on that journey. So it has really become a novel after all, nothing more. History reduced to story. It is no longer accurate. And yet in a way it seems more true to me now than it has been before. All I can do, is go on; all I can do, is to finish.)

✧ ✧ ✧ ✧

"I met one of your employees yesterday," she remarked casually. "Charlie Mofokeng. Remarkable man."

"What's so remarkable about him?"

"To have come all this way, starting as a farm boy. Studying abroad and all that."

"I've come the same way."

"You've had everything on your side. Charlie is Black."

"He had Bernard on his side."

"He'll be a great help to me in Soweto," she said, ignoring my remark. "He's like a fish in water in the townships. You must come with us one day."

"No thanks. I have no desire whatsoever to see the place." (I didn't know yet what was in store for me.)

"Charlie spoke a lot about you."

"I can well imagine. We argue all the time."

"I had the impression he was feeling quite paternal towards you."

"Paternal?" I couldn't help laughing. "Towards *me?*"

"Yes. He thinks you still have a lot to learn. I tend to agree with him, you know."

"How did you run into him?" I asked.

"I run into lots of people all the time."

I found it disturbing, the mere fact that she knew him. Perhaps Bernard had had something to do with it. But she refused to answer my question directly. And Charlie was just as evasive when I confronted him with it a few days later. I came close to losing my temper.

"Let me warn you, Charlie: you're trying to influence Bea. And I don't think you realize what you're doing."

"Bea is more than capable of making up her own mind."

"But she tends to get emotionally involved, and then she overreacts."

"Thank God for people still capable of reacting in *some* way!" he burst out. "Look at the bloody mess the land's in already—just because nobody seems to care."

"You can't hold me responsible for everything happening in the country."

"Of course I hold you responsible. You and every White in the country."

"Now you're being unreasonable, Charlie. I inherited this situation exactly as you did. Neither of us can be blamed for what our forefathers did."

"That's not what I'm blaming you for. What gets me is that history didn't teach you anything at all."

"My history provided me with the means to survive in this land!"

"That's what you think. All your history taught you was to mistrust others." Etcetera.

"It's a matter of survival, Charlie. I'm not trying to defend the methods of history. But what else could my people have done to survive?"

"Do you expect me to approve of survival achieved at the expense of others?"

"You're just generalizing as usual, Charlie."

"Jesus, Martin: your people started as pioneers. I respect them for it. But that you still haven't shaken off the frontier mentality—there's the rub."

"What do you so glibly call a 'frontier mentality'?"

"Protecting your identity so frantically. My God, the very phrase gives me a cramp in the arse. Because the only way you've managed to maintain your identity was by fucking around my people."

"Things are improving every day. Look at yourself: ten years ago you wouldn't have been able to get a job like the one you have at the moment."

"So what?" He glared at me through his thick glasses. "You know, when I came to work this morning, down there in Sauer Street, the van stopped beside me. 'Kaffir, where's your pass?' I gave it to him, but I said nothing. I don't speak to people who can't even read properly—let alone the writing on the wall. He looked at my book and threw it down on the pavement. 'Pick it up!' he said, laughing." Charlie involuntarily put his hand into his breast pocket again as if to retrieve his passbook. "What the hell's the use of this job of mine you're bragging about? Is this what I swotted for, here and in London? Is it this I've come back for? Sorry, man, I told you before and I'm telling you again: in my book Sisyphus isn't metaphysical, he's straightforward social. And on the brink of my abyss it's not suicide that awaits me, but murder. It's as simple as that."

It had been Bernard who'd introduced her to Charlie, as I'd suspected. It was on the Day of the Covenant she admitted it. The memory is absurd. But she insisted on going to Pretoria for the day to attend the annual panegyric in commemoration of the victory over the Zulus. The Voortrekker Monument, and all those women in their long Voortrekker dresses, and the men in their corduroy jackets and checkered scarves. We stayed to the very end of the solemn festivities, through the long-winded opening speeches and the historical tableaux and the choral singing and the interminable prayers and the Ministerial speech: "In these troubled times we as a nation rediscover the presence of Blood River in our midst. On our borders, once again the forces of darkness are gathering as in the time of our fathers when the full might of the Zulus was massed against them. Once again our future is at stake. But as on that great day when the Lord delivered the enemy into the hands of our fathers, He will once again provide salvation."

She insisted just as firmly that, afterwards, we visit the Monument itself and explore it from floor to roof: the marble friezes and the tapestries and the granite sarcophagus—*We for you, South Africa!*—and up the endless steps, into the hollow depths of that vast, heartless edifice. "I don't want to be spared any iota of it," she said, with that grim little smile on her lips, that peculiar stubborn tension of her jaw. "For this is the heart of your Afrikanerdom, isn't it? Perhaps it'll help me to understand you better." And when we emerged at last, she added quietly: "You know, this is my idea of hell: exactly on the scale of this Monument and this festival."

"And Beatrice, of course, doesn't belong in hell," I said facetiously. "Well, are we going home now?"

"No, take me to the zoo first. The other one. The real one."

She enjoyed it with the abandon of a small child, walking from cage to cage, dawdling in front of every one, eating ice cream; even popcorn, so help me God! Teasing the crows and feeding the monkeys, pulling faces at the chimpanzees, with the same exhilaration she'd shown in Diagonal Street.

"I'd love to live close by," she said impulsively when we finally left. "To hear the lions at night, and the hyenas and things. Just to remind one that this is still Africa."

"You have a nineteenth-century idea of Africa. Don't forget about the skyscrapers of Nairobi or Lusaka or Lagos."

"I'm not forgetting them. But I won't forget the lions either." And, getting into the car: "It's as real as Soweto. I was there again yesterday."

"Why did you go?"

"There was a journalist Charlie wanted me to meet."

"I don't like this sudden closeness with Charlie, Bea!"

"Bernard doesn't easily misjudge people."

I looked at her: "So it *was* Bernard who introduced you to him?"

"Of course."

"You didn't want to tell me when I asked you before."

"Didn't I? I really can't remember. In any case, what does it matter?"

Her words acquired a new nuance when the telephone rang that night and Charlie informed me that Bernard had been arrested by the Security Police.

❖ ❖ ❖ ❖

Sitting beside Louis on our way back to Johannesburg, I realized it was time I took another hard look at Charlie. It had been on Bernard's recommendation that I'd originally employed him. Of course, I'd also been prompted by the fact that he'd reminded me so strongly of Welcome Nyaluza; and I'd kept him on because he'd proved to be a brilliant worker, and because, in spite of our many arguments, I couldn't help feeling fond of him. But I could no longer take Charlie for granted. I had to know why Bernard had really brought him to me to start with. Only to find a job for the playmate of his youth? Or had there been more subtle and more sinister reasons? Was it coincidence that Charlie had been the first to know about Bernard's arrest? All right, he'd explained that: a journalist had told him, he'd said; and I knew he had all sorts of friends. But after what had happened to Bernard he was becoming a risk to me. Bernard's stigma was now attached to everyone who'd been associated with him.

I might have been prepared to give Charlie another chance— in spite of his questionable role in the Westonaria affair—but with Bea in the picture too, the implications were growing too serious to ignore. All those years I'd based my survival on the efficacy with which I'd succeeded in separating all the components of my life. Charlie; Bernard; Bea; Elise; my parents; my work; even Louis. Now it was becoming more and more obvious that there were subtle undeniable links between them, threatening me. I had a group of companies to attend to; I had a family; through many years of meticulous planning and hard work I'd attained a certain status in my society. I couldn't afford to risk the loss of all that.

I'm sorry, Charlie, I thought. *I'm really deeply sorry. But when I get back to my office tomorrow morning I'll have to call you in and sack you. You needn't worry: you will receive adequate compensation. As long as you realize that I really have no choice. You yourself have made it impossible for me to decide otherwise.*

7

A LIGHT DRIZZLE WAS COVERING the windshield with a brilliant, trembling smear. The clouds which, all day, had been drifting through the sky in large restless masses, were accumulating in a solid bank overhead, darkening the bleak landscape. It was oppressive, threatening. And the wipers were still out of order! What would happen if the rain grew worse?

Louis had already switched on the lights. And suddenly, while I was still thinking about possible remedies, he put out his hand to turn on the wipers as well. To my amazement they responded immediately, swishing to and fro in mechanical precision.

Louis looked at me. With a smile of satisfaction he said: "I fixed them on Saturday when I washed the car. Just a loose connection."

It was a sensation both of relief and singular humiliation. As if he had finally and independently taken control himself. Much more decisively than when I'd handed over the car to him. More damning. I knew I had to act before his threat to my authority could go much further. I would put an ultimatum to him. As soon as we were back home. Tomorrow. He would have to stop his idleness forthwith and start doing something constructive—otherwise he'd have to move out of the house. I was still in charge; it was up to me to do what I regarded as necessary. Whatever the price. (I anticipated Elise's reaction.) One had to be prepared to make sacrifices.

The rain was coming down with greater urgency, but Louis's wipers kept the windshield clear. There was something brewing, more than just an ordinary shower. The dry grass, barely visible in the deep dusk, was flattened by the increasing wind. Still, the big Mercedes was solid, fast, heavy, invincible. Not entirely infallible since Friday. But at the moment our progress was perfect and controlled.

It was much worse than the drizzle on the night when I'd picked up Bernard in Diagonal Street. The sturdy old woman in the dark alley beside Bea's witchdoctor place. And then the deserted mine road, the hissing wipers, the impossible conversation.

And it had been Bea who'd called me that night. She'd known about Bernard: they must have arranged the meeting between them. Only one day after he'd met Louis in town.

She hadn't attended the trial. ("There's nothing one can do for him there. And simply to go there to watch him would be like spectators staring at an accident. I can't take it.")

How had he got in touch with her during his spell underground? Why had he gone to her of all people, and what had prompted him to endanger her life so blatantly? My God, didn't he know what he was doing?

I'd asked her about it immediately after his arrest. Three days after our meeting in the drizzly night. But she'd been in a state of shock and refused to discuss it.

"What difference can it make, Martin? All that matters is that they caught him. Why didn't you help him?"

"It was out of the question. There's no need even to discuss it. Use your common sense."

"There's no point in recriminations, Martin."

"But I can't understand why in God's name he should have gone to you. Suppose he was followed? How could he have exposed you to such danger? One simply doesn't do it to one's friends."

"What makes you think I was drawn into it against my will? Don't you think I could have chosen freely not to see him?"

"He must have known how easy it is to make use of you."

"That's not much of a compliment, is it?"

"You can't deny it."

"I've never entered blindly into anything in my life."

"Not even with your prof at the time?" I asked brutally.

"No." Behind her dark glasses her eyes were invisible. "Don't you think even then I knew what I was doing?"

"Bea, really—"

Irritable, she interrupted: "The only thing that matters at the moment is that Bernard has been caught. We've got to decide whether there's anything we can do for him."

It was the pattern of most of our conversations in that period. There were times I felt like resorting to physical violence to force the truth out of her. But I knew only too well she would refuse to discuss what she regarded as either irrelevant or too private. And perhaps I was afraid too. In the same way as, after Dad's death, I'd never dared to discuss her ultimatum about a divorce again, I now chose not to press the matter too far. Sooner or later it would have to come into the open anyway. Preferably later. For I knew that such a conversation might be our last; and I couldn't bring myself to face up to it yet.

Moreover, there was a business trip pending, to the U.S. and Brazil; and even in a temporary, provisional goodbye like that I found unnerving undertones of finality. So I preferred not to deliberately disturb anything in the precarious balance of our relationship.

The day after my return from abroad I telephoned her. She was occupied full time, lecturing at Wits and filling in with Afrikaans classes in Soweto; even her evenings, she said, were full until after midnight. I felt hurt that she wasn't prepared to give up even one evening for my sake, but I knew that Bea would never allow anything, not even love, to come between her and her responsibilities. And so we had to wait until Friday when she had the whole afternoon and evening free. We agreed to meet at "our" place, Dullabh's Corner.

I wasn't feeling very well that morning. Some bug I'd picked up in Brazil, I thought. A dull feeling of nausea; a pressure on my chest. If it hadn't been for the long time I'd been away from her, I would have phoned to cancel the date. But I felt a curiously intense anxiety to be with her again. In New York I'd had a brief affair with the American secretary of our conference; in fact, she'd even accompanied me to Rio afterwards. But she'd been a pastime, entertaining and exhausting at the same time—something of a nympho—and her presence had increased my longing for Bea.

I'd brought her a special present, jewelry from one of Rio's most exclusive boutiques in a small street behind Ipanema: the kind of place that employed an armed guard to let down the steel shutters after you'd entered and before the wares were displayed.

We met at the hole where the building had been. And to allow her dismay to subside I drove to a restaurant out of town, near Kyalami. She wasn't very excited about the gift; as on other occasions I had the impression that she was almost depressed by having to accept it; strange. Still, I tried my best—even though I was still feeling rather off-color—to cheer her up by telling her about Rio and New York. The latter proved to be a less fortunate choice, as it brought back disturbing memories of her childhood in the States and her disastrous return there, after her year's study in Perugia (and another unhappy love affair with a French movie producer).

On our way back to town we were both feeling depressed.

"Would you rather go back to your own flat?" I asked as we turned off the M1.

She quickly looked at me, almost in despair. "Oh no, please don't. I want to be with you."

Back in the security and the peaceful luxury of my own apartment, I took her in my arms to ask: "Are you sure it was only that demolished old building that upset you?"

She shook her head, but offered no explanation.

Like so many other times I removed the dark glasses from her eyes and put them away.

"Good. Now I can see you."

"What is there to see?"

"I wish I could look right into you."

"You won't find any secrets there."

"Are you quite sure?"

"I think so." With a restless, anxious gesture she disengaged herself from my embrace and went to the bathroom; then she withdrew into the bedroom where she started brushing her hair in front of the large mirror, something she regularly did when she wanted to regain a grip on herself.

I followed her.

"It felt like an eternity without you," I said.

"I wish you didn't have to go away right then."

I lay down on the bed. She went on brushing her shining, dark, short hair, rhythmically, slowly, deliberately, her head held at an angle.

"I missed you," she said. "I needed you."

"Why?"

"Bernard."

"Is there any more news?"

"Mere speculation. Protests and things. The Minister warned them he'd make them eat their words."

"And now?"

"We can only wait, that's all." She stopped brushing, but still held the brush in her hand. I could see her face in the mirror. "Everything is being broken down. Something new every day."

"Dullabh's Corner, you mean?"

"Yes. And much more besides. It's as if people have lost all reason. A passion for destruction. And no one really knows why. Whom the gods want to destroy—"

"Don't be so morbid."

"But how can it go on like this? Soon there'll be nothing left. Just one vast hole."

"They don't demolish without putting up new buildings."

"Camouflage for the holes, that's all."

With two angry, jerking movements she drew the curtains, as if the light pained her. She was still deeply perturbed. Without looking at me, she undid the zip behind her back and peeled the dress over her head. The ageless gracefulness of the motion with which a woman strips off pantyhose, toes pointed, knee bent. Kicking the small black briefs from her ankle in a single nervous gesture. She was breathing deeply, more from tension than desire; but the two are related so subtly. Once again I was moved by the vulnerability of her body, the white pendulous breasts, the exposure of the dark nipples.

"I wish you would hurt me," she said unexpectedly, lying in my arms. "Just to help me forget about everything for a while. Even pain would be preferable to this."

I was conscious of the slowly increasing pressure in my chest. In a way I almost wished we could do without sex: I just wanted to hold her. Stroking her, I went on talking, trying to comfort her, aware of the unnatural tension in her body pressed against mine.

"Have you been very lonely?" I asked.

"Yes. I don't know what it is, but for the first time in my life I sometimes feel I've lost all control. I don't know where I'm going."

"Is it because of Bernard?"

"Don't talk about him now."

"So it *is* because of him?" The old, aggressive lust was throbbing back into me; my caresses became more insistent.

"You were just as shaken by it."

"Did you see much of him, Bea?" I asked in her ear. "I mean, before he went underground."

"We were friends. You know it."

"And while he was in hiding?"

"Oh Martin, don't."

"Bea, did you and Bernard ever—" My voice became unsteady, and I stopped.

"Suppose I said: 'No,' you wouldn't believe me, would you?"

"I've got to know."

She moved her head against mine. Her breath was warm on my cheek. "You were the one who always said one had to keep the people in one's life apart. Do you remember? When I spoke to you about Elise. Why don't you allow it to me too?"

"You're trying to hide it from me."

"For God's sake don't go on asking. Don't break down everything we have."

"You're in love with Bernard. You've been in love with him since the first day you met him. Isn't that so?"

"I love *you*, Martin. I do. Really. Please come inside me now."

In a sort of frenzy she grabbed me and forced me into her, heaving and moaning and uttering animal cries. Something was quickened inside me too. I wanted to thrust myself violently into her, lose myself in her, and never come back to myself again. Perhaps it wasn't even Bea I was trying to reach or crush, but something impossibly deep within her, behind her, beyond her. Bernard? Myself? I was desperately groping for something which had eluded me all my life, but it remained beyond my grasp. It was the same inexplicable panic which, later, beset me in the wood after the encounter with the old man. Equally unreasonable, equally wild. And when my orgasm started, I began to shake uncontrollably. It was as if something was smashed inside me. I doubled up in spasms of quite unbearable pain, gasping for breath. Then I lost consciousness. I thought I was dying.

✧ ✧ ✧ ✧

I don't know how she managed to roll me off her. I don't know how she went about arranging for an ambulance to take me to hospital, or how she kept her wits to contact Charlie so that he could get in touch with Elise. I don't know how or when she collected her car from the demolition site at Dullabh's Corner. All I heard afterwards was that I'd been close to death and that I'd been in a coma all day.

Once I was allowed visitors again, she came to the hospital occasionally, staying very briefly, something restrained and remote about her. It was six weeks before I could return to my office. Then, obviously, we started meeting more regularly again. But I found it impossible to discuss that day with her, or anything connected with it. It was a strange experience, like seeing one another from afar and waving in despair, as on that first night in Aunt Rienie's flat. It was too delicate to try and force anything. We would have to be very gentle with one another. And perhaps one day….

Then came the trial. And the mine riots at Westonaria. Our attempt to arrange a weekend together: at last, just the two of us, like that distant week in Ponta do Ouro. But the trip to the farm made it necessary to cancel our arrangements and postpone our weekend. Only temporarily, of course:

"I'm terribly sorry, Bea. You know how much I've been looking forward to this weekend. But we can always do it later. Next week. Any time. We're not bound to anything."

"Of course."

"Please, Bea, you must believe me."

"I told you it didn't matter."

"But I can hear you're upset. Tell me what's the matter."

495

The brief silence before she said: "There's something I must discuss with you. But not on the telephone."

"I'll see you on Tuesday."

"I know. It's just—it seemed rather urgent, but I suppose it can wait. Anything can wait."

"Look after yourself. It's only a few days."

Her sudden surge of passion: "Martin, is it really quite impossible to postpone this farm business just for one week? I *must* see you."

"But I told you."

"Oh well, if it's out of the question." And then the smothered, final exclamation: "Oh, God," before she rang off.

8

SOON AFTER WE'D CROSSED the Vaal River, just after leaving Orkney on the pitch-black road to Potchefstroom, I turned on the radio for the nine o'clock news. The weekend was over. Within an hour or so we'd drive past Westonaria again. It was time I caught up with whatever had been happening in the world in my absence. But nothing had prepared me for the contents of that fatal broadcast.

"Violence broke out on an unprecedented scale in Soweto and other Black townships in the vicinity of Johannesburg today. There is still considerable confusion about the causes of the riots, but according to reports received by the SABC large crowds of Black pupils marched out of their schools this morning and started rioting in different parts of the townships simultaneously. Different reasons have been advanced for their action, including the fact that they have allegedly been forced to take some of their school subjects through the medium of Afrikaans. The situation soon got out of hand and police reinforcements were rushed to the scene from other parts of the Rand and Pretoria. Many vehicles were stoned and numerous cases of arson have been reported. The police were forced to open fire to control the rioting children and make an end to the violence. The casualty figure is not known yet, but it has been reported that an undisclosed number of bodies, mainly of children, have been taken to mortuaries in the city, and according to our information the Baragwanath Hospital is overflowing with wounded and injured Blacks...."

Dazed with shock I sat listening to the commentator. Glancing towards Louis, I saw him staring fiercely ahead of him into the night. The wipers were whirring evenly, almost useless against the now blinding sheets of rain. It took a long time before the words on the radio started making sense again:

"...police undertook raids in all major cities. It is not yet known how many people are being detained in terms of the security laws. Among the names for which the SABC has been able to obtain confirmation, are the following. In Johannesburg: Isaac Joseph Katzen, a student at the University of the Witwatersrand; Henry Dudley Johnstone, a press photographer employed by the *Star*; Beatrice Fiorini, a junior lecturer in the Faculty of Law at Wits; Buster Nkosana, a—"

I didn't link it with her immediately: the announcer had pronounced her name "Bitriss," something she'd never been able to stomach, probably because it reflected on the only bit of security left to her. Not that it really mattered any longer.

From the beginning I'd believed that she needed me, that I could help her, that I could offer her protection. But she'd insisted on being independent and alone. What she'd really needed, Bernard had given her: that was the only conclusion I could come to. They wouldn't have arrested her without good reason: and she was now finding herself in the ripples of water caused by his own irresponsible actions.

Louis was sitting beside me. I had no assurances about him. I could only wonder, and suspect, and fear. (*For everyone like Bernard who's silenced there are ten others to take his place.*)

But as far as Bea was concerned, it was concluded and clear. She had chosen. And whatever the price, I had to respect that choice. I could neither influence it nor help her any longer. I had no right to. (Ponta do Ouro: *If ever I really desperately needed you.* No, no, it wasn't that. It wasn't that at all.) If it should become known that I'd been involved with her in any way, my own position would be in jeopardy. It should be clear to anyone that I couldn't possibly interfere. It was the end for us. Something like a life sentence.

If only I could find out what it was she'd so urgently wanted to discuss with me when we had that final conversation on the telephone. But we were doomed to incompleteness.

9

WHEN THE OLD-GOLD CURTAINS in the hotel room are drawn, one isn't even conscious of the rain outside. But whenever I leave off writing to go to the window, the whole city lies before me in its dull grey wetness, a blur, a smudge, as if I were shortsighted. Inside, one feels isolated from the world, protected from it; but it is an illusion. I have no defense against anything. Everything I've recalled through my writing surrounds me and threatens me. It wasn't an "intellectual exercise" after all, nor "a form of mental massage." All frontiers, all lines of demarcation, have been destroyed.

I have finished writing. Or nearly. But I am not yet free.

Incomplete and incompletable, like a gesture in a half-dark room, a man and a woman reaching out to touch, and missing by a hair's breadth. Incompletable, because I have entered the situation.

The evil-minded might say: So many lives destroyed. A land destroyed. Preposterous.

In our time the notion of an apocalypse need no longer imply actual or active destruction. It is much more subtle. We have our Soweto, we have our Voortrekker Monument, we have thickets among hills on farms: but we no longer have hell.

I'll go on. I'll survive. But I have lost everything who might have redeemed me. Ma and Dad and Theo. And Elise. Louis, who left our house after the ultimatum and never came back: leaving us only with the possibility, the certainty, of an inevitable telephone call one day; one night. Charlie. Bea. And the common denominator in our lives, Bernard.

I have tried with so much care to keep all the elements of my life apart and intact. But now they merge and run into each other like streams of rain forming rivers and pools and dams. Pools covered by monstrous water lilies that never stop growing. Dams in which one can sink and drown: with no hand, black or white, to offer help. Does one inevitably become the victim of one's own paradoxes in the end? I've tried so hard, I've acted with the best of intentions. I've tried to remain loyal to the simple fact of my being here and the need to survive. Isn't that enough?

That night, on our way home, it was raining just like now. And it became harder every moment. What would happen if a small mechanical fault were to occur and the lights went off or the engine stopped? It was all quite unpredictable.

Like a flood it washed over us, every yard of the way, with no end and no beginning, ahead for as far as one could see, behind for as far as we came from. All the rumors of months and years suddenly come true.

Ceaselessly, irresistibly, it came down from the dark skies. In a blunted stupor I resigned myself to the thought that it would never stop again. I didn't care any more. Let it go on, I thought, let it increase and grow worse and worse, a flood to soak the earth and uproot trees and split rocks; causing the red earth to run down the hills, streaming, streaming endlessly, red water as if the earth itself was crying, as if the earth was crying blood. *Nkosi sikelel' iAfrika.*

Thrice nominated for the Nobel Prize for Literature and twice shortlisted for the Booker Prize, André Brink is one of South Africa's eminent novelists. He is the author of more than twenty works of fiction, many of them written during the years when apartheid dominated his country. His first openly political novel, *Kennis van die Aand* (1973), became a cause celebre; it was banned a year after its publication under new censorship laws applied for the first time to an Afrikaans writer. Brink later translated the work into English under the title *Looking on Darkness* (1974). A prolific literary critic and dramatist, Brink has also translated works such as *Mary Poppins* and the Shakespearean plays into Afrikaans. As an academic, he has inspired and challenged social reformists for more than forty years. André Brink, now 72, is an outspoken recorder of South Africa's turbulent history, from the days of apartheid to the present.